MOTIVE FOR MURDER

"Now, Johnny," the deputy said quietly, "let's make some sense of this. You say that Strickler had a spell on you."

"Yeah, and I had to get a copy of the pow-wow book, or a lock of his hair, to break the spell. Well, he wouldn't give me the book. First he said he would, then he didn't. We had a fight about it, kind of. And when he was tied up, I cut some hair off like the old witch told me. She told me to get the book, or a lock of hair, and bury it under our crabapple tree and the spell would be broken. And I did."

Painter drew a deep breath. "What happened then? What did you do with Strickler after you cut off the hair?"

"Nothing," Johnny answered defiantly. "And if Charlie says I did, he's a liar. He knows I needed the hair if he wouldn't give me the book. He knows that!"

The deputy looked at him for a long moment before speaking again. "Charlie Strickler doesn't know anything of the kind."

"Sure he does!" Johnny insisted.

"He can't know it, Johnny," Painter said without dramatics, "because Charlie Strickler is dead."

THE WITCHING

CHET HAGAN

LEISURE BOOKS   NEW YORK CITY

A LEISURE BOOK

Published by

Dorchester Publishing Co., Inc.
6 East 39th Street
New York, NY 10016

Copyright © MCMLXXXII by Chet Hagan

All rights reserved. No part of this book may be reproduced or transmitted in any form or by any electronic or mechanical means, including photocopying, recording, or by any information storage and retrieval system, without the written permission of the Publisher, except where permitted by law.

Printed in the United States of America.

1 THURS., NOV. 27, 1969 (THANKSGIVING DAY)

Something was wrong. David Mitzel was sure of that.

The farmer hurried along County Road 203, covering the three hundred yards between his barn and Charlie Strickler's farm house at a brisk walk. The sounds of the distressed lowing of Strickler's cows grew louder as he neared his neighbor's property.

Damned strange, Mitzel thought. *Strickler's an odd sort, but he's a good farmer. He should have had his cows milked by this time of day. Maybe the old fool got himself drunk. That wouldn't be anything new.* But Mitzel couldn't remember any time in the twenty-five years he had known Strickler that, drunk or sober, Charlie had neglected his livestock.

Mitzel, impelled by his misgivings, half ran into the barnyard. "Charlie!" The only answer came from the suffering animals. Again: "Charlie Strickler?" Still no human answer. He knew he wouldn't get a reply from anyone else, because Strickler lived alone. Charlie's wife lived on a farm nearby, also alone. It was a strange relationship, so strange that David Mitzel didn't like to think about it. *Evil,* that's what it was.

He turned toward the simple, two-story frame house. "Charlie!" At the door he pounded hard. No response. "Charlie!" Mitzel thought that he might have to break down the door, but when he turned the knob the door swung open.

An odor assailed him. Something had been burned, that was clear, but the odor was an alien one. He stepped into the kitchen. Light streamed through the uncurtained window over an old, slate-topped sink. Strickler was not one for modern conveniences; a small hand pump still was used to draw water into the house. A few dishes lay on the slate top. A heavy, cherry-wood table filled the center of the room, with three chairs of the same wood pushed close to it. In the corner, a large wooden cupboard held what utensils Charlie Strickler needed for his simple existence.

It took Mitzel only a few seconds to survey the kitchen, find it in order, and move into the dining room. It was dark there, with stiff green window shades pulled down to the sills. The room was nearly empty. A threadbare rug covered most of the floor and one wooden chair (from the kitchen, Mitzel reflected) was the only piece of furniture. The strange odor was stronger now and the farmer moved hesitantly.

In the living room he saw it. There was a brief moment when he thought he was going to be sick. "Good Christ," he said aloud, "Charlie!"

The body was lying on the carpeted floor, face down. Strickler was a big man, a couple of inches over six feet and weighing perhaps 250 pounds. His heavy legs were tied together with rope, bound around the ankles. His arms were pinioned behind his back, bound at the wrists.

It was as dark in the living room as it had been in the dining room, and Mitzel moved to the windows to raise one of the shades. Added light only served to reveal the total horror of the scene. Again, Mitzel had the feeling that he was going to be ill. He fought against the nausea. Charlie's body had been partially burned; there was excelsior strewn over it. By the body was a coal-oil lamp, without its glass chimney, and pieces of broken wood were scattered about. It appeared that a chair had been smashed.

Mitzel forced himself to look more closely. *The head, my God, the head!* It had been bashed in, blood caking the ugly depression. Strickler's open, staring eyes looked up at him in anger. The legs were bent almost ninety degrees at the knees, as though a planned kick had been arrested by the moment of death. And the burns! The back, the thighs and the lower legs were charred black.

The farmer had seen enough. David Mitzel turned and ran.

Thanksgiving Day 1969 began as a happy one for John

Mosser. He'd been feeling poorly for a long time, but now he felt better. Not many of the days in his thirty-three years could be classified as happy. But without question, this one had a good feeling about it.

For one thing, he was home. Ordinarily, this would have depressed him. But as he lay under the covers in his bed, stretching contentedly, he was glad he was home. Also, he had seen Amos Maier on the street the day before and the owner of the cigar factory had told him he could come to work again next Monday. That thought buoyed his spirits even more.

Mosser got out of bed and dressed quickly. He had worn his underwear to bed and even that seemed to be a fortunate thing for him; it would cut down on his dressing time. His blue work shirt and his trousers lay crumpled in a heap on the floor. Johnny had no concern for his personal appearance; no one else cared, either. He looked around for his shoes, then remembered he had kicked them off in the kitchen the night before.

His room on the second floor of the crumbling old frame farm house was sparsely furnished. There was an ancient mahogany bed, with a high headboard. A tall, mahogany chest of drawers stood against one wall, two of the drawers pulled halfway open. Both were empty. There was one chair with spindly legs and a broken cane seat. That was all the furniture in the room. The floor was bare; there were no pictures on the wall. Sunlight streamed through a single, uncurtained window, filtered by a patina of dirt untouched for years.

John Mosser was not a handsome man. His straw-colored hair was already thinning on top; it had never had the attention of a professional barber. He was broad across the shoulders, but his body appeared poorly constructed. His chest didn't have the depth to match the breadth of the shoulders; he was heavy around the hips, had a small pot belly, and his legs were heavy—massive even—and seemingly the same circumference from knees to ankles. He was only five feet, eight inches tall, but he must have weighed 220 pounds. His face portrayed a lack of strength not necessarily akin to physical weakness. His limited mental capacity was written there for all to see.

Johnny padded out into the hallway. Two other rooms, almost identical to the one he had just left, had doors off that hallway. Those doors were closed. No one had used the rooms since his brothers and sisters had left home. At one time, seven children had lived in this modest home.

One of his sisters, he remembered (had she been younger or older than he?) had died here. But the memory was a vague one. And the others? What had happened to them? Even the names didn't come easily. His oldest brother, Harry, had gotten into some kind of trouble in Georgia. Was it Georgia? Well, somewhere down South—and Harry had been sent to the penitentiary. Harry always was a bad apple, John thought, but he didn't want to remember those things today. He felt too good to be concerned with sad recollections of the past.

He made his way down the closed, unlighted staircase, remembering to step over the booby-trap of boxes his mother had stored on the steps. The door to the stairway opened into the kitchen and before he reached the door he could hear his mother at the cast-iron stove. She had just placed something on the stove. The coffee pot, he hoped.

His mother was startled when he opened the door. "Ach, Chonny," she said. "I didn't know you vas home."

"Yeah. Came in last night, late. You were asleep."

His mother slept in the kitchen, on an old army cot covered with soft, hand-made quilts. After the children had left home she saw no point in climbing the stairs each night just to go to bed. His father slept (and he was snoring now) in the living room, having moved a bed in there with the dusty, overstuffed furniture. It didn't bother him that mice had built a nest in the sofa.

The kitchen was circa 1900. A monstrous, black cast-iron stove dominated it. There was a large, heavy wooden table pushed against one wall, covered with oilcloth that had been tacked fast along the edges. Five chairs were at the table, not any of them a match. His father had built open shelves along another wall, and all the dishes, pots and pans, and food staples were on those shelves. There was no sink, no cupboard, no icebox. A pail of fresh water sat on the floor in the corner next to the coal scuttle that had not known coal for many years. Now it was used to hold the wood and paper scraps that fed the stove.

In the manner of those old, utilitarian farm houses, no fewer than five doors led out of the big kitchen. One opened to the outside, another went to the upstairs, yet another to the living room. There was a door to the pantry, long unused for that purpose, and the fifth led into a bare room that once was called a dining room. It had been several years earlier that the elder Mosser had taken the few sticks of furniture out of that room and had sold them. He had mentioned to his wife several times that he could also sell the bed and chest of drawers upstairs, but she had insisted that they stay in the house for the only child they ever saw any more.

The Mossers had fourteen acres around the dilapidated house, most of them grown over with weeds. Occasionally, if the spring weather was congenial, Mrs. Mosser would start a small garden, but it seldom prospered. In the front yard was a good well, perhaps the only thing of real value on the property. And near the back of the house there was an outhouse, with the door sagging so badly on its hinges that it could not be fully closed.

For five years, ever since Johnny's father had done his last work as a basket-maker, the Mossers had lived on county welfare. It brought them only fifty-six dollars a month but that seemed adequate. Several times Johnny had been called to task for his failure to help in the support of his parents, but he worked only fitfully, primarily because he frequently was not well.

He had not been in this house for almost a month. He had gone to the western end of the county to do some odd jobs on a farm, and had lived in a barn there. Four nights had been spent in the Young County jail, after he had been picked up as a vagrant—a drunken vagrant. He had been released when he volunteered to work on the Salvation Army collection truck. Now he was home again, feeling well and anxious to help his parents.

"On Monday, Mom, I start work again." He sat down on a kitchen chair to draw on his shoes.

"A good job?"

"Goin' back to Maier's, cigar-makin' again."

"That's nice for ya." There was no enthusiasm in the mother's comment. Enthusiasm was not something the Mossers could afford. For the very poor, emotions are a luxury, and there were no luxuries here. It was Thanksgiving Day, a fact that was totally ignored. There had been very few things in their grim lives that would have caused the Mossers to give thanks.

Mrs. Mosser got two cups from one of the shelves, lifted the battered coffee pot from the stove, and shuffled to the table. She wore a washed-out print dress that seemed three sizes too large for her. On her feet were felt slippers with holes that permitted several toes to stick out. Her face was deeply wrinkled. She seemed a small woman, barely five feet tall, but that may have been because she was so stooped. And she was very thin.

Johnny thought how old she looked. But what was so strange about that? She was old. *Gosh, Mom must be 75, maybe even 80!* Young County welfare records showed that Clara Mosser (nee Biehl) was just 61.

She poured steaming coffee into the two cups, placed the pot in the middle of the table, and sat down with her son. As she sipped her coffee she looked at him with care. He always had been her favorite and she worried about his health.

"How do you feel, Chonny?"

"Fine! Never felt better!"

She smiled and reached over to pat his hand. She wanted to be reassured. "Are you sure you feel good, Chonny?"

"Yeah, yeah, fine. And you know something, Mom? I'm gonna stay good. I took care of that last night."

"Last night?" Her face became worried again.

"Yeah. Last night I went to see Charlie Strickler and now everything is okay."

She frowned now, the wrinkles cutting deep creases across her face. "He's a bad man, Chonny!"

Her son laughed. "Well, maybe, Mom. But last night fixed it

and I feel real good today."

Mrs. Mosser sighed deeply, knowing it was futile to question Johnny about the details of the previous evening. Somehow, she didn't want to know. As she rose from the table and reached across for the coffee pot, he grabbed her hand.

"Honest, Mom, everything is good now. So don't worry no more."

"Yah, yah."

Phil Stauffer turned off the ignition and got out of the car. The sheriff of Young County, Pennsylvania, didn't look the part; at least, he didn't project the image most people associate with a sheriff. Motion pictures and television programs had established the stereotypes: a big, rugged man for a Western sheriff, fast with his gun; a big, fat, somewhat ugly man for a Southern sheriff, fast with his prejudices. Was there a stereotype for an Eastern sheriff—a Pennsylvania sheriff? Not likely. But even if there had been, Stauffer would not have fit it; the title and the man simply didn't go together.

He was small in stature, only five feet seven inches tall. He was handsome. His square-cut face was without a flaw; good teeth smiled out of that face. His dark hair, with only a flattering graying at the temples, was full and neatly barbered. His well-tailored dark gray suit covered a finely-proportioned body. His light blue eyes were clear, yet without any coldness in them.

Phil Stauffer was basically a gentle individual and people who did not know him well were always misreading him. Some might have looked at him and imagined *ladies' man.* But that didn't fit him. He had been married, since just after graduation from high school, to the girl who had been his sweetheart for four years. He was the father of three children, all of them exemplary young citizens. Some people misinterpreted his gentleness; if they were lucky, they missed seeing him when the toughness surfaced. Phil had been an M.P. in World War II, serving with Patton in North Africa, Sicily and Italy. He had not been a hero, but he had been a fine military policeman, and had earned a battlefield promotion from buck sergeant to second lieutenant. In the service, he found he liked police work, and he pursued that career when he returned home to Nancy, his high-school sweetheart.

Those who didn't like Stauffer—and every man has his detractors—were always looking for the flaw and not finding it. It was the mark of Phil Stauffer that he knew his own shortcomings better than anyone else. He constantly battled against them, but the battle was private.

He was genuinely modest. He didn't wear a badge; that stayed in his pocket. He never carried a hand-weapon. He didn't own a uniform. The car he had just left displayed no lettering and no whirly-bird red light. Only the long, whip antennae indicated that it might be a police car. Phil was an individualist, although he would have resented the appellation. *Individualist* to Stauffer would have meant a *strange character*.

The sheriff, as he walked from the car to the porch of Sarah Strickler's dingy frame house, looked fully fifteen years younger than his fifty years. That look of youth was another thing that infuriated his critics, especially his periodic political opponents. He could have been mistaken, on this late morning, for a prosperous young business executive, probably in insurance.

But Mrs. Strickler, who waited for him on the porch, knew Phil Stauffer as the sheriff; their paths had crossed numerous times. She was a middle-aged woman, perhaps in her middle sixties. She was plainly attired in an off-the-rack Sears house dress; her hair, streaked with gray, was pulled straight back into a bun on her neck; she wore no make-up. The face was tired—it had the look of a face that had always been tired. Yet there were hints that she had once been a very attractive woman.

"Good morning, Sarah." The voice was soft, gentle. "I have some bad news." He walked up onto the porch and, when Sarah didn't invite him to enter the house, he just planted his feet comfortably. "Sarah, Charlie is dead."

There was no emotional reaction. The woman looked at him for a long moment, dropped her gaze to the porch floor, and sighed. Finally, some words: "Yes, well . . ."

"I'm sorry, Sarah."

Her eyes came up again. "How?"

"Pretty bad, Sarah. Someone beat him to death. Last night, we believe."

She just nodded. The lack of emotion didn't surprise Stauffer. He knew, as well as anyone, of the strange, unloving relationship between Charlie and Sarah Strickler. He had arrested Charlie any number of times for wife-beating, only to have Sarah refuse to press charges.

"Sarah, I'm sorry, but I have to ask you some questions."

"Sure."

"When did you see Charlie last?"

"Two, maybe three weeks ago. Oh, I saw him working in the fields a couple of times, but he was here . . . oh, three weeks ago, I guess."

Phil nodded. "Did he say anything unusual?"

"Unusual?"

"Yeah. Did he mention any arguments, any fights with anyone?"

"No."

"Nothing out of the ordinary, then?"

"Not a damned thing." A note of anger crept into her voice. "He just came over here one night, climbed into bed, and when he got what he came for, he left."

The sheriff found himself embarrassed by the directness of the answer. He looked away for a moment and fingered the knot of his tie. "Have you seen any strangers around here lately?"

"Strangers? No, no strangers."

"Anyone familiar, then?"

Sarah thought for a moment. "What's today?"

"Thursday. Thanksgiving Day."

"Then it was Tuesday, I guess." Another pause for thought. "Yeah, Tuesday. Johnny Mosser was here. You know Johnny, the nutty one?"

"I do."

"Well, he was here," the woman continued, "looking for Charlie. I told him he wasn't here, and they left."

"*They?* Someone was with Johnny?"

"Some young kid. Never saw him before. Johnny didn't say who he was and I really didn't care. They were only here a minute or two."

"What did the kid look like?"

"Kind of funny looking. He was skinny and had kind of a pinched-up face . . . ah, like a weasel."

"Tall? Short? Blond? Dark hair?"

Sarah Strickler's hand went to the bun of hair on her neck as she pondered an answer. "Oh, I don't know. I didn't pay much attention to him. He had blond hair, I guess."

"And how old would you say?"

"Just a kid. Young. Maybe eighteen. Yeah, about that age."

"Did they say anything when they left?"

"Sure," she said. "Johnny said they were going to go to see Charlie. The kid didn't say nothing."

"What time was that?" Stauffer was being more insistent now.

"Oh, it was dark already. But not dark very long."

"Were they driving a car, or walking, or what?"

"I didn't see no car," she answered quickly. "But they could have had a car up on the road and I wouldn't have seen it. There's so much brush growing up around here that I can't see what's on the road any more."

"Now, Sarah, this is important." Phil paused to let the gravity of his next question register with the woman. "Are you *sure* it was Tuesday night?"

She put her hand to her bun again. "Yeah, Tuesday."

"It wasn't Monday?"

"No, no. Monday I went to late market." She was quite firm about that.

"Tuesday, huh?"

"Yeah."

"Not Wednesday—not last night?"

She was annoyed. "No, it was Tuesday for sure. Don't you believe me, sheriff?"

Phil was as gentle as he could be. "Of course I believe you, Sarah. I just wanted you to be sure." The sheriff shrugged. "Well, Sarah, that's about it, I guess."

"Sheriff?"

"Yeah."

"You didn't ask me if I did it."

"No need to, Sarah. I know you wouldn't do anything like that."

She was pleased with the reply. People didn't usually say kind things to her. "Thanks, sheriff."

"Okay." He smiled. "Got to go now."

As he left the porch, Sarah spoke again. "Sheriff, do you know who killed him?"

"Not yet." Again he started to walk away. This time he was nearly to his car before she shouted to him.

"Sheriff!" Phil turned to the woman. "It don't surprise me none! Charlie Strickler was a hateful old witch!"

"This has been a hell of a way to spend Thanksgiving Day!"

Dr. Edward W. Myers, the coroner of Young County, was unmistakably an unhappy man. He had stalked into the sheriff's office, and had slammed his autopsy report down on the desk. Then, in disgust, he dropped his lanky frame into a chair and slumped down.

"At least," said Sheriff Stauffer, "you're a bachelor and don't have a wife and three kids waiting for you at home, wondering when in the devil they're going to eat the turkey."

"That's damned small consolation. It may come as a shock to you, Phil, but bachelors *do* have social lives."

The sheriff smiled. "So I've heard. Anything unusual in this autopsy?"

"That depends on what you call unusual." Dr. Myers sat up straight in the chair. "Strickler died of brain damage caused by a blow to the head. Multiple blows, actually. He was really clobbered, apparently with the leg of a chair. The state police lab will have to confirm the weapon used. But the blows didn't kill him instantaneously. He was still alive when he was set afire."

Phil grimaced. "Pleasant thought. Have you been able to fix the time of death?"

"Within a two-hour period only. Sometime between ten p.m. and midnight last night."

"Well, that ought to be close enough. Anything else?"

"Yeah, but it's just a theory. Maybe it can't even be classified as a bona fide theory," the coroner admitted, "but it *is* interesting. Want to hear it?"

"Hell, yes!" Phil was emphatic. "Right now I have damned little to go on."

The doctor reached over and retrieved the autopsy report folder from the sheriff's desk. Quickly, he riffled through a series of photographs, selected one of them and pushed it in front of Stauffer. It was a gruesome closeup of the battered head of Charlie Strickler. "This is the first one I want you to look at, Phil."

"Pretty. What am I supposed to see here?"

Dr. Myers leaned over and, with his pencil, pointed to an area of the head away from the depression caused by the blows. "Now, right here is something I didn't notice at first, primarily because the blood had matted the hair together. But when I released the body to the undertaker after the autopsy, and he started to clean it up, it became apparent that someone had cut off a big clump of hair, and probably had done it hurriedly."

He selected another photograph and continued. "This picture, then, was taken at the funeral home. It shows very clearly that some hair has been cut off. The old man had a good head of hair for his age."

"Do you have any idea why?"

"*Zounds!*" The doctor's voice reflected his enthusiasm and a smile lighted his bony face. "The gentleman has asked the key question! Yes, sir, I *do* have an idea why." He rose to his feet and began to pace. "Now, someone had just bashed in our victim's head with a sturdy piece of wood—the chair leg found at the scene, most likely. And, before that someone left the scene, he reached down, grabbed a shock of hair, and hacked it off. I'll speculate that it was done with a pocket knife. Or a hunting knife, something like that. Evidently, whoever did it took the hair with him, out of the Strickler house."

"How do you figure that?"

"Well, I checked with your deputy, and he swears he went over the room carefully and didn't find anything remotely resembling a bunch of hair."

"Okay, let's assume you're correct—what does it mean?"

Dr. Myers stopped his pacing, placed his hands flat on the sheriff's desk and leaned close to Phil. His words were deliberately spaced, like the ties of a railroad track. "It means that this might have been a hex killing!" The doctor dropped into his chair.

Stauffer looked at the young coroner steadily, determined that he was deadly serious, and nodded solemnly. "Ed, I have great respect for your ability and your judgment. But, damn it, this is 1969, not 1769! Hex killing! That seems like utter nonsense!"

"It's crazy, I'll admit. But take a look at Charlie Strickler's background."

"A real bastard! Wife-beater and all that."

"Right. But remember back about five or six years ago when Dr. Oberdick had him hauled in for practicing medicine without a license?"

"I'd forgotten that. But Josh couldn't make it stick, could he?"

"That's true. He moved too fast, and then couldn't get any of the so-called patients to testify against Strickler. But it established Strickler as a pow-wow practitioner, even though he couldn't be convicted as the charlatan he was."

"So?"

"So," the coroner went on, "when I remembered that episode, and when the undertaker called my attention to the hair being cut off, I thought of some things I had read one time about *hexerei* here in the Pennsylvania Dutch area—that hair plays a big part in this stuff."

He fished some notes out of his coat pocket, searching through them as he talked. "For example, there's a cure for the whooping cough that says: *Cut three small bunches of hair from the crown of the head of a child that has never seen its father; sew this hair up in an unbleached rag and hang it around the neck of the child having the whooping. The thread with which the rag is sewed must also be unbleached.*"

"Splendid!" The sheriff smiled broadly. "But, unless the

murderer had the whooping cough, it doesn't tie in with the Strickler killing."

"No, damn it," the doctor said stubbornly, "I'm trying to make a point, by weight of evidence, about hair and this witchcraft stuff. Now do you want to hear this, or do I leave?"

"Sorry, Ed, but this stuff is so incredible."

"I know it seems that way." Dr. Myers glanced at his notes again. "Now, here's another one: *How to make cattle return to the same place. Pull three bunches of hair, one between the horns, one from the middle of the back, and one near the tail, and make your cattle eat it in their feed.*" He looked up from his notes. Phil remained silent and the coroner started to read again. "*If you have a gun that is bewitched, load that gun with a bullet of hair.*"

Stauffer chuckled. "A *bullet* of hair?"

"Yep, that's what the man said—a bullet of hair. Here's another: *When a person is prevented from passing water, take a good handful of hare's hair*—hey, that's hard to say—*burn it till it becomes a powder, wrap it in a handkerchief, add three handfuls of watercress and a half quart of wine, boil the powder and herbs therein. Drink it warm.*"

There was a moment of silence as Dr. Myers turned the pages of his notes. "Don't wait for me," the sheriff interjected. "I hate watercress." They both laughed.

The doctor continued, "I kept digging on this hair thing and found considerable preoccupation with it. *To cause the hair to grow wherever you wish—Take milk of a slut and saturate therewith the spot wherever the hair is desired to grow.*"

Phil broke in, "No, sir, I'm not going to comment on that one!" Laughter again.

"As I continued to research these so-called cures," said the coroner, "I came across two things that seemed germane to the missing hair on Charlie Strickler. Example: *If a horse is injured by pressure, swellings or tumors which have to be cut—After cutting the horse, approach to the front of the horse, tear some hairs from under its mane, and pronounce: In the name of the Father, the Son and the Holy Spirit. Then walk around the horse and also take a few hairs from under the throat and speak as before. Walk again around the horse and take some hair from the tail and pronounce the same blessing, then walk around the horse and stand still just as you received the horse. Pray the Lord's Prayer three times, three Ave Marias, and the Creed once. Now, take the hair all together, bore a hole into a pear tree, put the hair therein, or draw the bark, and put the hair between."*

Sheriff Stauffer leaned forward, shaking his head in disbelief. "You know, I think I'm beginning to see what you're getting at, Ed—and I also think I'm nuts!"

Dr. Myers grinned. "Join the crowd. This is going to be a nutty case, believe me. But what really sold me on the hair theory was this jolly one: *For a youth contracting hernia or rupture—Cut three bunches of hair from the crown of the head, tie it in a clean cloth, carry it noiselessly into another county, and bury it under a young willow tree so that it may grow together therewith. It is a sure remedy.* Now, none of these things really fitted the Strickler situation exactly, so I called Josh Oberdick to get a reading on this stuff. And he confirmed what I suspected—that down through the years the pow-wow doctors have done considerable ad libbing with the old remedies and cures. And he said it was possible that the cutting of the hair from the head and burying it under a tree, might be used to break a spell—any kind of spell."

"Good Lord! It's too fantastic to believe!"

The coroner nodded his head in agreement. "It *is* fantastic, but it does lead to the final theory I've cooked up. Would you like to hear it?"

Stauffer waved his hand. "Go ahead. We've come this far."

Dr. Myers cleared his throat. "Well, we know that Strickler was a pow-wow doctor. It's not beyond the realm of possibility that someone thought Old Charlie had a spell on them, that they went to his house, clobbered him on the head, cut some hair off . . ."

The sheriff interrupted. ". . . and then they just went ahead and set the body on fire."

"Why not? I think you're looking for logic, Phil, and perhaps there's no logic to it. Anyone who's foolish enough to do the first part of this act is foolish enough—and unbalanced enough—to try and burn the body." He took a deep breath. "Anyway, to complete the theory, this someone cut some hair off Charlie, took it out of the house and buried it somewhere, probably at the base of a tree, thereby breaking a spell."

Stauffer shook his head. "It still sounds insane to me."

Dr. Myers pointed his finger at the photograph showing where some hair had been hacked from the head of the dead man. "Insane?" He left a momentary pause. "Exactly, sheriff, exactly."

Ernest Wheel uncoiled his slim frame from the Jaguar XKE and glanced up at the sign on the two-story brick building: *The Missionville Star.* "Shit!" No one heard him utter the word; he was alone on the sidewalk in front of the newspaper office. He didn't want to be there. He had just driven three hours from New York City, on assignment from the Continental News Service, because his editor had a friend in this hick town who thought he had uncovered a story that merited wire service handling.

Jim Edgett was a good editor, but he had a blind spot. Stories about the Pennsylvania Dutch captivated him. Wheel had heard all kinds of Pennsylvania tales from Edgett. Hell, he even had a brightly-colored, round hex sign on the wall of his office at C.N.S. And he bored all the new staffers at the wire service with his explanations of how the hex signs were used to ward off evil spirits, or how they protected crops and/or livestock, or how they were used to protect a barn from lightning, especially if they appeared in the magic number of seven. It was really strange, because Edgett came from New Hampshire. Now, because of his boss's preoccupation with the Pennsylvania Dutch, Ernie Wheel was on this damned wild goose chase.

Wheel looked around him at the deserted streets, stretching to relieve the muscles cramped by three hours in the Jag. *It's funny how these small towns close up on a holiday.* He always seemed taller than his actual six feet two inches because he was so thin. But with the slimness came a rugged handsomeness; his face was well made and was without the bony edges so often associated with a thin man. He always dressed in the current fashion and was a confirmed ("confirmed" was the adjective he used) bachelor. At 32, he was considered one of the best writers at the Continental News Service.

The New Yorker entered the newspaper building and followed the signs to the editorial room. He found it nearly deserted. In one corner, a typewriter clicked nervously. He followed the sound and said to the round-faced man at the keyboard, "Hiya! You Nick Willson?"

The typing stopped and the man came quickly to his feet. "Yes, I am. You must be Spin Wheel."

Wheel cringed. He hated the nickname. But Jim Edgett used it continually and he had apparently passed it on to Willson. "Well, I'm Ernest Wheel. Ernie, if you prefer." He tried for a smile. "The 'Spin' nickname is strictly an invention of my boss."

Willson stuck out his hand. "Okay, Ernie. It's nice to have you here in Missionville. I think you're going to find that your trip will be worthwhile."

Wheel grasped Willson's hand and shook it warmly. "I hope so. Edgett seemed pretty enthusiastic about the story."

"Jim Edgett and I are old friends." Willson smiled broadly.

"So I've heard."

"We went to journalism school together. Penn State."

"I've heard that, too."

Willson laughed. "I'll bet you have. Well, I imagine you want to get started. Let me fill you in." Nick motioned Wheel to a chair by his desk. He was almost the exact physical opposite of Ernie Wheel—short, stubby, running to fat. There was a studied sloppiness about him, suggesting that he was more interested in his work than in his appearance. "As I told your boss," Willson began, "there's nothing certain about my theory—not yet. But it's very possible that we have a murder here with the overtones of witches and hex."

"Go on."

"Charles Strickler—that's the victim—was a known pow-wow practitioner. A hex doctor, some folks would call him.

Some years back I did a series of articles on this home-grown witchcraft, and old Strickler was one of my contacts. He talked freely about it at that time and seemed to have quite a thing going for him."

Wheel nodded. "When was that?"

"In 1964."

"Got anything I can bone up on?"

"Sure do." Willson conveyed enthusiasm for the subject. "I've pulled the file on those articles from the morgue and I've fished out what I need for tomorrow's lead. Be my guest." He handed the folder of clippings to Wheel. "After you get through those, I'll give you my carbon of tomorrow's story."

"Thanks. I'll try to bring myself into the 16th century."

Nick grinned. "Don't scoff too soon. At least, not until you've read those articles. Take that desk over there."

Wheel really didn't know what he expected to find in the clippings. This was a new field to him. Only through his editor's boring stories did he know that such things existed and, in all of his travels for C.N.S., he had never come face to face with it before.

Willson had done a good job with the articles—six on the weekdays and a substantial wrap-up in the Sunday edition. He had interviewed many of the pow-wow doctors in the area and many more of their patients. Wheel was impressed with the number of testimonials on the effectiveness of the pow-wow doctors.

I talked yesterday, Nick had written in one article, *to Benjamin Stoudt, 43, of Hanover, who had been unable to work as a carpenter because of the crippling effects of what seemed to be arthritis. A number of medical doctors had diagnosed it as arthritis, but their treatments gave him little relief. Stoudt admitted it was desperation that brought him to a pow-wow doctor here in Missionville, on the advice of a neighbor.*

The pow-wow doctor had a different diagnosis. Stoudt, he said, had been hexed, bewitched. He was uncertain as to the source of the hexerei, but he was certain he could help. He then got out an old book and, very solemnly, he read from it. Stoudt didn't remember it all, but he knew it had to do with the Trinity. "It sounded like it was out of the Bible," Stoudt told me.

That was all there was to it. Stoudt's neighbor had told him to leave a "donation" and the carpenter placed a five-dollar bill on the kitchen table at which they sat. He says he doesn't remember any mention of money. What Stoudt is sure about is that the next morning his affliction was gone. Not just relieved. It was gone. It has not returned. Benjamin Stoudt made his visit to the Missionville pow-wow doctor four years ago.

Willson went on in the article to suggest that the book used was a volume called *The Long Lost Friend,* written in the early 1800's by an itinerant preacher-doctor named John George Hohman. And he found in the book a passage that, when read again to Stoudt, seemed to be exactly the same incantation used by the pow-wow doctor.

Nick had included the entire passage in his article: *"Three false tongues have bound thee, three holy tongues have spoken for thee. The first is God the Father, the second is God the Son, the third is God the Holy Ghost. They will give you blood and flesh, peace and comfort. Flesh and blood are grown upon thee, born on thee. If any man trample on these with his horse, God will bless thee, and the holy Ciprain; has any woman trampled on thee, God and the body of Mary shall bless thee; if any servant has given thee trouble, I bless thee through God and the laws of heaven; if any servant-maid or woman has led you astray, God and the heavenly constellations shall bless thee. Heaven is above thee, and earth is beneath thee, and thou art between. I bless thee against all tramplings by horses. Our dear Lord Jesus Christ walked about in his bitter afflictions and death; and all the Jews that had spoken and promised, trembled in their falsehoods and mockery. Look, now trembleth the Son of God, as if he had the itch, said the Jews. And then spake Jesus: I have not the itch and no one shall have it. Whoever will assist me to carry the cross, him will I free from the itch, in the name of God the Father, the Son, and the Holy Ghost. Amen."*

Ernie Wheel shook his head skeptically. Nevertheless, he

was impressed with Willson's documentation of the many claims of cures, both from the pow-wow doctors and from their patients.

Item—A man in Reading, afraid to go through an operation for a cataract on his eye, went, instead, to a pow-wow doctor. The cataract disappeared.

Item—A woman in Spring Grove had a persistent cough; a physician's diagnosis was tuberculosis. He recommended hospitalization. A pow-wow doctor "cured" her.

Iterm—A young boy in rural Berks County was badly burned while tending a fire intended to clear brush from a patch of land. He never got to a medical doctor, because his parents took him immediately to a pow-wow practitioner. In a single visit the burns were "healed," without medication.

Item—A young woman in Lebanon County scalded herself with boiling coffee when the handle of the pot broke as she was removing it from the stove. An uncle, who was a pow-wow doctor, was present when the accident occurred. He "banished" the burning. The arm did not get sore and was healed completely the next day.

All of those cases, and more, Nick Willson had detailed in his seven articles. It was almost six o'clock when Wheel had finished reading them. What fascinated Ernie most was what Willson had left out of the articles. They cried out for some expert comment from medical authorities.

Wheel put the clippings back into the folder, reviewed his own notes briefly, and then called to Willson, "Hey, Nick, I'm curious about the position of the Young County Medical Society on these so-called pow-wow doctors. Who might be my best contact on that?"

Nick looked up from his typewriter. "A good many of the leads for stories in those articles came from a Dr. Joshua Oberdick—O-B-E-R-D-I-C-K. He's retired now, but he used to be the president of the medical society and he's a real authority on the subject."

"I didn't see his name in the articles."

Nick smiled. "That's right, you didn't. I had a deal with him at that time. Lots of information, but no direct quotes."

"Why no attribution?"

"Well, at the time, Oberdick was trying to nail one of those bastards on a charge of practicing medicine without a license, and he thought it best to keep himself out of the newspapers."

Wheel nodded. "Did he get his man?"

"Not quite. The guy's name was Charlie Strickler!"

On his way to Dr. Joshua Oberdick's home, Ernie Wheel tried to visualize what he'd find there. On the telephone, the doctor's voice was soft with age, but he really didn't seem to be an old man. There was a sparkle in the manner in which he spoke. There was an enthusiasm, Ernie thought, even in the delivery of the courteous, but trite, phrase, "Mr. Wheel, I'm looking forward to meeting you."

Certainly, the address didn't indicate an old man. He was living in the Yountz Apartments, a new building that had been given over to single tenants only, preferably young ones. New York and Washington and San Francisco had such accommodations for young adults, but an apartment complex for "swingers" was still a bit scandalous in a conservative small town like Missionville.

Dr. Oberdick lived on the top floor, in what could only be classified as a luxury pad. He greeted Wheel at the door and ushered the reporter into a large living room, modern in decor, with floor-to-ceiling glass across one entire wall. It was still mild, on this Thanksgiving Day evening, and the doctor had one of the sliding doors open to a large terrace-balcony.

The doctor himself was an impressive figure—six feet tall, slim and erect. His hair was white, as was his carefully trimmed mustache. He was dressed in light blue slacks, a pale yellow sport shirt and spotless white tennis shoes. His handshake was strong.

"Thank you for seeing me, Doctor," Ernie said. "And may I ask a question meant only to reflect a reporter's personal curiosity?"

"Certainly."

"How old are you, sir?"

The physician laughed heartily. "Eighty. But, who counts?"

"Good Lord!"

"Mr. Wheel, my apparent good health comes from clean living. Which means clean food, clean Scotch, and clean women."

"You're a hell of a good testimonial for that kind of cleanliness."

"Please sit down, Mr. Wheel. May I get you a drink?"

"Some clean Scotch would be fine." Ernie sank into a Saarinan chair. "By the way, it seems only right that we should not persist in this formality. The name is Ernie."

"Right, Ernie, just call me Doctor Oberdick." He laughed out loud at his little joke. "Josh is better, really . . ." he paced the line with comedic professionalism ". . . Josh for Joshua, like the fellow who fit the battle of."

He had gone to an ultra-modern bar in the corner of the room during the banter and had poured two stiff Scotches into wide-mouthed glasses. No ice, no soda. As he placed them on a small glass-topped table next to Ernie's chair he said, "Drink it neat. Better for you that way." The reporter, who liked his Scotch with soda and ice, didn't think it was appropriate to disagree with the doctor.

"As I told you on the phone," Wheel said, "I'm interested in the subject of pow-wow, or hex, doctors. Have you heard about the murder of a man named Charles Strickler?"

"Yes, the coroner spoke to me about it."

"Then you must know that there's one theory that pow-wowing might have something to do with it."

"It's possible." Oberdick's tone was flat. "I knew Charlie Strickler quite well. We had a couple of run-ins when I was president of the medical society here. He was a shrewd old bastard. Reprehensible, actually. Do you know about his wife?"

"No."

"She didn't live with Charlie. I'm not even sure they were legally married. But anyway, she lives alone on a farm next door to his and she was scared to death of him. He caught her in the barn one time with a hired hand . . . oh, that must have been more than twenty years ago . . . and he put a spell on her—said she'd never have any children. And he banished her to live alone. Even bought another farm for her."

"You're kidding!"

"Oh, no I'm not." Josh was insistent. "At the time all this started, Sarah Strickler was still a handsome woman and she really didn't believe in Charlie's curse. She defied him, told him she'd have as many children as she damned pleased, and set out to prove it. She moved into Missionville and set herself up in an apartment. Took on every stud in town, trying to become pregnant. She never did, though. And periodically, Charlie would come into town and beat the hell out of her. If he caught her with another man, he'd get a beating, too."

Ernie shook his head. "Sounds jolly."

"Well, anyway, the police picked up Charlie at least a half dozen times, but each time Sarah refused to press charges. Finally, she came to accept the banishment and moved to the farm he had bought for her. It really hasn't been a working farm; she has a small vegetable patch there and some chickens. It became her own particular hell." Dr. Oberdick paused to sip the Scotch. "I gather that, over the years, whenever the spirit moved old Charlie, he'd hike over to the other farm and go to bed with Sarah."

"Would it be crude to say that he wanted his pound of flesh?"

"Crude as hell!" Josh laughed heartily.

"But good Lord," said Ernie, "it seems that Sarah's plight became something akin to slavery."

The doctor nodded agreement. "Not in the legal sense, of course. She was free to go anytime she wanted to go. And she really didn't have to work too hard; Charlie provided for her. What happened was that she came to believe that Charlie's *hexerei* kept her there, and that belief was as powerful as chains."

Wheel wanted to proceed with the conversation. "You said that you had a couple of run-ins with Strickler in your capacity as head of the medical society?"

"Right. You see, most of these pow-wow people deal entirely in mumbo-jumbo and the laying-on of hands. Lots of incantations. They know that giving any kind of medicine gets them into trouble with the authorities, so they stay away from it." Oberdick rose, took the two empty glasses, and moved to the bar. "But Charlie liked the medicine bit. He often came up with bottles of root juices and herbs and like that. His favorite item, however, was powdered chicken dung."

"Huh?"

"Oh, yeah, he was great with that." Josh returned to Wheel, the glasses replenished with Scotch. "If we could have learned that Charlie was dispensing that kind of thing, under the guise of being a medicine, we'd have brought him in. Never could prove it, though. I thought I had him about five years ago, but the patient got cold feet, and that was that. No case. It still pisses me off!"

"Ever try to use a decoy to catch him?"

"Several times, but he spotted them every time. Charlie Strickler, as I said, was a shrewd old bastard."

Wheel drew a deep breath. "Doctor, I'd like to try to get some line on what is behind all this. When did it start? What is the real power of it? Just what *is* a pow-wow doctor?"

"Well, first, let's get the terminology correct. The word *hexe* is German for witch; the word *hexerei* means witchcraft. And who knows how far back we go with witches and witchcraft?" Oberdick paused, apparently expecting some comment from Wheel. When none was forthcoming, the doctor continued. "Witchcraft probably goes back to the beginning of human life. In this area—in the geographical area of Eastern Pennsylvania where the Pennsylvania Dutch settled—witchcraft is practiced by pow-wow doctors, or hex doctors. Some will tell you that pow-wow doctors practice only for good and hex doctors only for evil, but the terms are really interchangeable. I'm not sure any such distinction ever existed. I doubt it."

Ernie was making careful notes in his stenographer's notebook. "But what was the start of it in this area?"

"Again, way back. The touchstone of it all seems to be a fellow named John George Hohman. You've probably already heard of him."

"I came across a mention of him in Nick Willson's articles."

"Right." Josh picked up a book from the coffee table. "I got this out to show to you. It's a comparatively recent issue of a book originally printed in German in 1819." He flipped it open. "In the preface, Hohman says that part of the book is derived from a gypsy, part from secret writings, and collected with what John George calls 'much pain and trouble.'"

Ernie grinned. "I'll bet."

"Let me read to you an apologia to end all apologias." Dr. Oberdick read slowly, almost in a monotone. *"I did not wish to publish it; my wife also was opposed to its publication; but my compassion for my suffering fellowmen was too strong, for I had seen many a one lose his entire sight by a wheal, or his life or limb by mortification. And how dreadfully has many a woman suffered from mother-fits? And I therefore ask thee again, oh friend, male or female, is it not to my everlasting praise, that I have had such books printed? Do I not deserve the rewards of God for it? Where else is the physician that could cure these diseases? Besides I am a poor man in needy circumstances, and it is a help to me if I can make a little money with the sale of my books."*

"*Did* he make money with the books?"

"Oh, I guess he did," the old doctor replied. "But it's safe to say that 20th century printers have made a hell of a lot more from reprints of *Long Lost Friend* than Hohman did. He thought of himself as a physician, and in the early 1800's people took their doctors where they could find them. In the rural areas, doctoring was more or less a personal thing. But Hohman had something else going for him."

"My gosh, did he need something more?"

"He apparently thought he did. He was a peculiar mixture of physician and clergyman. He wrote what he called a 'note' in his first edition. I read again: *'There are many in America who believe neither in a hell nor in a heaven; but in Germany there are not so many of these persons found. I, Hohman, ask; Who can immediately banish the wheal, or mortification? I reply, and I, Hohman, say: All this is done by the Lord. Therefore, a hell and a heaven must exist; and I think very little of any one who dares deny it.'* So Hohman filled two voids in the rural areas of Pennsylvania—physician and preacher. Many of the farm communities had neither, and Hohman, in his travels, brought them healing and spiritual solace." Dr. Oberdick paused reflectively. "You know, it's strange, but no one knows what happened to John George Hohman. We know that when he first published *Long Lost Friend* he lived at Rosenthal, which was near Reading in Berks County. But his final resting place is unknown. It doesn't seem right, somehow, that Hohman should lie in an unmarked grave. He wasn't the charlatan a lot of people imagined him to be."

Wheel was startled. "You sound as though you agree with a lot of this stuff."

"I do."

"I'm certain you'd like to qualify that."

Josh smiled and his voice was very light when he spoke again. "You know, we human beings in the last third of the 20th century are pretty damned smug. We can put a man on the moon, to leave his footprints for future generations; we can transplant one man's heart into another; we can fly faster than the speed of sound; we can blow the whole damned human race off the face of the earth; perhaps we have the power to destroy the globe itself—but what do we really know?"

Ernie made notes swiftly.

"We know, for example," the doctor went on, "that Charlie Strickler was a reprehensible character. But he was able to keep a woman in psychological slavery. And, when you think about it, that's no mean trick. We profess to understand every nuance of the human mind. Yet we cannot explain—at least, not to our logical satisfaction—why an ill person cannot be helped by a highly-trained and licensed physician, but *is* helped by some ignorant lout who practices some mumbo-jumbo out of a book 150 years old!"

"Have ill persons *actually* been cured by pow-wow doctors?"

"Of course!" Josh was speaking with more determination now. "Some people who are sick are not *physically* sick, yet they have some exact symptoms of a physical illness. Right?"

Wheel nodded agreement.

"Fellows like Hohman—and he wasn't the first—figured

that out a long time before Freud. Perhaps Hohman knew of the work of Friedrich Mesmer; they were contemporaries."

Ernie interrupted. "Mesmer as in Mesmerism, like in hypnotism?"

"Sure. Mesmer believed that some occult force resided in him by which he could influence others—cure others. Well, in a sense, so did Hohman. And what they practiced was a crude form of psychiatry. Oh, psychiatry with some meaningless incantations, and in Mesmer's case, the use of magnets and all, but a type of psychiatry, nevertheless. And they cured some people who were really ill."

"I can understand that," Ernie said.

"Good." The doctor smiled briefly and then set his face into a serious mask again. "Now, let's move a step farther along. We know today that psychiatry is not the answer for every illness. But Hohman and his ilk were not sophisticated enough to know that, and they tried the mumbo-jumbo on everyone. Some people who were really ill with physical ailments were not cured by pow-wow doctors—could not have been cured by them, period. They died, probably, but the pow-wow doctor wasn't blamed. After all, do we keep score on the licensed medical doctors? Some of their patients die, too, and a seemingly valid explanation of why they died is forthcoming. Well, when the pow-wow doctors fail they have an excuse, too; a ready explanation. The patient did not *believe*. The Bible says it perfectly: *Oh, ye of little faith.*"

"Faith healers?"

"Absolutely! Could psychiatry succeed, for example, if a patient did not believe in it? Faith healers have been with us since the beginning of time. Every area of the United States has them. It happens that the Pennsylvania Dutch pow-wow doctor is a bit more colorful, that reprints of Hohman's *Long Lost Friend* make fascinating reading, and that the Pennsylvania Dutch talk funny. And so, one can be left with the impression that the last vestiges of the superstitions of the Middle Ages lie here in the Pennsylvania Dutch area. That's nonsense! The same superstitions, if that's what they are, persist everywhere."

Wheel turned a page in his notebook. "Could you give me

some examples?"

"Certainly. A simple one first. A four-leaf clover is supposed to be lucky. Right?"

"Right."

"Would you say that it's a universal superstition?"

"Sure."

"Well, there's an old Pennsylvania Dutch expression," Dr. Oberdick continued, "that says: *Wann en mann en firbletterich gleblat nedrakt kann en naimand ferhexe.* Wear a four-leaf clover and nobody can bewitch you. Now, that's so old no one can even imagine where it started. And the fact that it exists in an old Dutch phrase doesn't mean that the Pennsylvania Dutch started it, or are alone in perpetuating it. For all I know, it could have had its origins in Egypt, if Egypt has four-leaf clovers."

The doctor rose and went to the bar to refill the glasses again. "Or try this phrase: *Wann en hex in haus is soll mer mit der linke hand enhandfoll grop salz insfeiar schmeisse.* If there is a witch in the house, throw a handful of coarse salt into the fire with the left hand."

Wheel looked up from his note-taking. "The spilling of the salt at the Last Supper?"

"It's allied. Spilling of salt is equated with bad luck. There are superstitions dealing with salt that are older than Christianity. Are they now the exclusive property of the Pennsylvania Dutch? Of course not! But these superstitions have been perpetuated here, as has the bastardized German lingo." Josh put the glasses down on the table. "The Pennsylvania Dutch are proud of their heritage. They cling to it. *I* cling to it, even though I don't relish all of this pow-wow crap. And because there is this clinging to a heritage, pow-wow doctors are with us still, even in the enlightened year of 1969."

"I gather," said Ernie, "that there are pow-wow doctors and then there are pow-wow doctors."

"Indeed." Dr. Oberdick paused to take a large swallow of Scotch. "I put these guys into three categories. One is the pow-wow doctor who really believes he has the power to heal. Blind faith is everything with him. He, or she, can be dangerous because there is no recognition of real physical illness. Indeed, they believe all illnesses are inspired by the spiritual. You're ill because of something evil you've done; or you're ill because of what some evil person has done to you — the spell. The patients of this type of pow-wow doctor may die because they fail to receive treatment in time for a treatable disease. Tuberculosis is an example. Cancer, too. Charlie Strickler was one of those."

The doctor took a deep breath. "Number two is the pow-wow doctor who isn't really sure of his ground. He is aware that, in some cases, his pow-wow is ineffective, and he worries about his limitations. When something shows up that he's not sure of, he refuses to deal with it. When I was practicing, more than a few of my patients were sent to me by pow-wow doctors."

Ernie smiled. "Now, there's an angle."

Oberdick went on: "So, we come to number three — the real bastard of the bunch. The outright charlatan. The cynic. The man who's in it for the buck, or what he can get out of it, one way or another. This is the guy who doesn't believe in anything, but who has taken Hohman's *Long Lost Friend,* has memorized it and can spout chapter and verse. Frequently, this type advertises in the personal columns on the newspaper's classified pages. This is one who . . . who . . . well, hell, who is a real lousy character!"

"How about an example of that?"

Josh was silent for a moment. He closed his eyes. "Right. An example." The eyes came open. "I sent one of those sonofabitches to jail once. Thirty or more years ago. Let's see . . . it was 1934."

"And you recall the details?" Wheel flipped another page in his notebook.

"Perfectly," answered the old man firmly. "I was the county health officer at the time. It was in the middle of the Depression, you know, and we had a handful of visiting nurses touring the county, trying to help the poorest of the poor. I guess everyone was poor in a way then. In any event, in one of the remote rural areas one of my nurses came across a family with a very pretty daughter, about fifteen she was, and that girl was damned sick."

The doctor rubbed his hand over his eyes. The recollection seemed to pain him. "The nurse recognized right away that the girl had acute appendicitis. The merest touch of the abdomen brought excruciating pain. She asked the parents whether they had tried to get a doctor. They had, they assured her, taken the girl to a doctor; a fellow named Marvin Kramer—a pow-wow doctor. They saw nothing wrong when he prescribed sexual intercourse with the girl as a form of treatment. Not once, but twice!"

Ernie Wheel leaned forward. He could read the anguish on the doctor's face.

"The nurse," Oberdick continued, "got the girl into her car and drove as fast as she could to the hospital here in Missionville—35 or 40 miles on bad rural roads. By the time I got her on the operating table, the appendix had burst. The whole thing was complicated by the fact that she was two months pregnant! She died in just a few minutes."

"Horrible," said Wheel, almost in a whisper.

"But I got the bastard!" Josh's emotions were on the surface. "Had him arrested for statutory rape. Had to force the parents to sign the complaint and testify against him. Hell, they had actually been *present* during the rapes! They simply couldn't see that Kramer was to blame. But I got him!"

Ernie broke in. "Statutory rape didn't keep him in jail too long, though, did it?"

The words of the reply were rock hard. "Long enough! A fellow prisoner stuck a knife into him. Police thought the murder might be the work of an uncle of the girl, who was in jail on a robbery conviction. Never could prove it, though. No one in the jail admitted seeing anything."

"That's pretty grim stuff."

"Yeah, a lot of it is," said the old man. He sighed deeply. Then he smiled, slowly. "But there's an occasional laugh, too."

"A laugh?"

"Oh, sure." Oberdick was trying to get his emotions under control, and Wheel waited. "I remember this one case where an old man, over eighty he was, had an infected penis.

He went to a woman pow-wow doctor whose gimmick was the laying-on of hands. The old man wasn't cured, but he sure had a hell of a good time with the treatments!"

They both laughed uproariously. Wheel glanced at his watch. It was nearly 9 p.m., and he rose to his feet. "Josh, I appreciate all the time you've given me, and the interesting information. I've got to go now, because I have a morning deadline facing me."

The elderly doctor shook his hand warmly and led the reporter to the door.

"Oh, by the way, doctor," Ernie said as an afterthought, "Nick Willson's articles mentioned some cures of things that can't be classified as psychosomatic in origin. Burns, for instance. What about those?"

Dr. Oberdick laid a hand on the younger man's shoulder. "My friend, there are many things in this world that we cannot explain. And I, for one, am not arrogant enough to try."

It was just a few minutes past nine o'clock when the sheriff put the key in the lock of his front door. But before he could turn it, the door swung open. His wife, Nancy, concern written on her face, put a warning finger to her lips. She whispered, "Phil, I tried to reach you at the office, but you had already gone."

"What's wrong?" He followed her cue, also whispering.

"Dottie Kissinger's in the living room, with her son. She arrived just a few minutes ago."

"The waitress at the Central Diner?"

Nancy nodded.

"What does she want?"

"I don't know. She says she has to talk to you. It's very important, she claims."

"Damn!" He kissed his wife lightly on the cheek. "Well, let's get this over with and eat that turkey."

Nancy grasped his arm lightly. "Phil, I'm sorry, but the kids and I have already eaten. It was just getting too late and I didn't want everything to spoil."

"That's okay." He tried to hide his disappointment. "I'll get some cold turkey after I talk to Mrs. Kissinger."

As Phil walked into the living room, the woman sprang to her feet. She was blonde. Her once good figure had fleshed out a bit, but she was still a very attractive woman. Beautiful, even. She was agitated. "Sheriff, I'm so sorry to bother you at your home. But I'm so worried!" She seemed genuinely apologetic.

"That's all right, Mrs. Kissinger." Phil's voice was soft. "Won't you sit down and tell me what's wrong?"

She returned to the sofa and sat beside her son. The boy, thin-faced and blond, was sullen. His head was bent, the eyes apparently studying a pattern on the rug. Phil knew the boy as a chronic truant. A few months earlier, he had run away from home in an attempt to join the Marines, even though he was only 14. He looked older than that. *Let's see, now,* thought Stauffer, *the kid's name is Saylor. He's the son of Dottie's first husband, who deserted her. That's right—the kid's name is Larry Saylor.* Mrs. Kissinger reached over to pat her son's hand, but there was no response from the boy.

Phil spoke. "Go ahead, please, Mrs. Kissinger."

"Sheriff," she said slowly, "I'm frightened to death. And so is Larry." Again she patted the boy's hand. "It's so terrible!" She began to cry. For the first time her son looked up at her.

Crying women annoyed Phil and he found it difficult to hide his annoyance. "Please proceed."

She tried to control her sobbing. "Sheriff, Larry had something to do with that Strickler thing we heard about on the radio."

One piece fell quickly into place for the sheriff. *The blond kid who had been at Sarah Strickler's place with Johnny Mosser!* Phil prodded the woman. "Go on."

"Well, Larry went to Strickler's place the other night. . . ." She paused and looked at the boy. "Maybe he ought to tell you what happened."

"Perhaps he should," Phil agreed. "Larry?"

When the boy spoke he kept his eyes averted, but the words came quickly. "Johnny Mosser asked me to go along with him and Clay Burkholder to Charlie Strickler's. . . ."

The sheriff stopped him. "Wait a minute! Clay Burkholder?"

"Yeah, the kid whose old man owns the lumber yard."

"Of course. Go on."

"Well, Johnny asked Clay and me to go along with him, because Johnny wanted to get something from Strickler and he thought he might need some help, and we went there and Johnny had a fight with old man Strickler and we tied him up." The youngster paused, raised his eyes, and spat out the next words. "But we didn't kill him! We didn't, we didn't, we *didn't!*" He was crying now, sobbing deeply. Dottie Kissinger reached over to take the distressed boy in her arms, but he pushed her away. "We didn't kill him!"

Stauffer tried to return some calm to the emotional scene. "That's all right, Larry, nobody's accusing you of killing anyone. Calm down now, and let's take it one step at a time."

Larry's gaze dropped to the floor again. He muttered sullenly, "We didn't kill him."

"Mrs. Kissinger," the sheriff said quietly, "perhaps we ought not go into details now. This is a serious matter and I must tell you that you ought to have Larry represented by a lawyer." She nodded. "But," Phil continued, having planted his warning, "I would like to clear up a few points right now, if you don't mind."

The woman gave her consent.

"Now, Larry, when did you go to Strickler's house?"

"Wednesday night." His sobbing had ended.

"What about Tuesday night?"

"Oh, yeah, well . . . we only went there to talk to him Tuesday night, and nothing happened."

"Did you go to Mrs. Strickler's house on Tuesday night?"

"Yeah, we went there first because Johnny thought the old man might be there instead of his own house."

"Was he?"

"Huh?"

"Was he at Mrs. Strickler's house?"

"Nah," he answered, now totally in control of his emotions. "So we went over to Charlie's house, and he was there. We went in and Charlie got out some beer and pretzels. And Johnny and him talked some and then we left."

"What did they talk about?"

"Well, Johnny wanted Charlie to give him some kind of book and Charlie said Johnny didn't need it and Johnny said he did and Charlie said 'Okay, come back tomorrow for it' and Johnny said he would and we left. That's all."

"What book was it that Johnny wanted?"

"Oh, I don't know . . ." Larry showed annoyance at the question. ". . . some dumb thing about hex and all. Old man Strickler was a pow-wow doctor, you know."

Phil nodded his head affirmatively. "So the three of you went to see Strickler on Tuesday and again on Wednesday?"

"That's right. When we got there on Wednesday, Johnny and Strickler right away got into an argument about that damned book." Larry was enjoying his role as story-teller. "Charlie said he didn't have the book and Johnny was getting madder and madder. Then, all at once, he just kind of jumped on Charlie and knocked him over on the floor. . . ."

The sheriff held up his hand. "One moment. Was Strickler standing or sitting when Mosser jumped on him?"

"He was sitting, and when Johnny jumped him the chair broke into pieces."

"All right, continue."

"Well, they were kind of wrestling around on the floor and Johnny hollered for us to help him and me and Clay grabbed Strickler and held him down. Then, Johnny tied him up with a rope."

"Where'd he get the rope?"

The question surprised the boy. "Hell, I don't know. All of a sudden, there it was."

"Okay, then what?"

"Johnny and Charlie were swearing at each other." A smile crossed the young man's face. "Boy, could that Charlie swear! Johnny kept hollering, 'Where's the damned book?' And Charlie kept saying he didn't have no book. So Johnny started to look around the place for it, pulling down drawers and stuff. Then me and Clay started to help him look for the book."

"Did you find it?"

"Nah. But out in the kitchen we found an old coffee can with some money in it, only about five bucks, and Clay said he was gonna keep it because he was the one that found it and I thought, what the hell, and I stopped looking."

Stauffer kept pushing. "And then what happened?"

"Well, Johnny went back into the living room and swore at Charlie some more and then took out a pocket knife." Larry's eyes opened wide at the recollection. "I got scared! I thought he was gonna stab him!"

"But, he didn't stab him?"

"Nah, he just grabbed Charlie by the hair," the boy raced on, "and tried to cut some off, but Charlie kept moving his head around so much that Johnny couldn't do it. So he yelled to me to hold the old man's head and I did and Johnny cut some hair off and stuck it in his pocket." Larry paused.

"And then?"

The boy shrugged. "And then we just left."

"Did Johnny hit Strickler with anything?"

"No." The answer was firm.

"Did Clay Burkholder strike Strickler?"

"No."

"Did *you* hit Charlie Strickler?"

"No!"

"With a broken chair leg, perhaps?"

"No, no!" Panic was rising in Larry Saylor's voice. "We didn't kill him!"

Sheriff Stauffer studied the boy's face for a few moments, as Dottie Kissinger tried to comfort her son. "Okay," Phil said finally, "I believe you, Larry. Just a couple of more questions, now. When you left the house, Strickler was tied up, but wasn't hurt. Is that correct?"

"Yeah, that's right," insisted the boy. "Johnny said he wasn't tied up too tight and could get loose easy."

"And when you left the house, what time was it?"

Larry pondered the question. "Oh, maybe a few minutes after eight. About that time, I guess."

Phil spoke deliberately. "Could it have been after *ten* o'clock?"

"Nah," Larry said with complete assurance. "When we got back to Missionville it wasn't even nine o'clock yet."

"How can you be so sure of that?"

"I looked at the clock on the courthouse when we got back."

The sheriff paused. He thought perhaps he ought to end the interrogation at that point. Or, at the very least, he ought to advise Mrs. Kissinger again about getting a lawyer for her son. He dismissed both thoughts; he had an opportunity to break the Strickler case right now. Phil turned to the boy. "How was it that you came to go to Strickler's house in the first place?"

"Oh, I was just hanging around the bowling alley on Tuesday and Johnny hangs around there sometimes, too, and he told me that Clay was gonna get his old man's car and they were gonna take a ride out to Strickler's and did I want to go along."

"Just like that?"

"Yeah, that's the way it happened."

"So, then Clay came with his father's car. . . ."

"No, the first night he had the lumber company's pick-up. On *Wednesday* he had the car."

"But it was Clay Burkholder who drove you to Strickler's both nights?"

"Sure. Me and Johnny didn't have no way to get out there unless we walked, and I sure as hell wasn't gonna walk."

Phil took a deep breath and exhaled slowly. He looked into the distraught face of the mother. "Mrs. Kissinger, I guess there's not much more we can do tonight. If you will assure me that you'll bring Larry into the courthouse tomorrow morning, I think you ought to go home now and. . . ."

Suddenly, Larry screamed, "He'll kill me! He'll kill me!" Phil jumped to his feet and Nancy rushed into the room.

"Phil, what on earth. . . ." his wife started. She fell silent when the sheriff raised his hand to her.

Larry was now sobbing hysterically, cradled in his mother's arms. Stauffer dropped to his knees in front of the boy and gently took his hands. "Larry." A tear-stained faced turned toward the sheriff. "Larry, are you frightened of me?"

"No." The sobbing continued.

"Of Johnny Mosser?"

"No."

"Who, then?" The only answer was more sobbing. "Larry,"

Phil continued, "we only want to help you. We're not going to let anything harm you. But we have to know who you think is going to kill you."

Dottie Kissinger pushed back her son's hair from his wet eyes. "Tell him, Larry."

In the midst of a choking sob he blurted out one word: "Clay!"

"Clay Burkholder?"

"Yes! Yes!" The boy was screaming again. "He said he'd kill me if I ever said anything about going to Charlie Strickler's!" He buried his head in his mother's breast. The weeping seemed uncontrollable.

Phil got to his feet and said quietly to Nancy, "Call the office, please, and ask them to send a squad car over here." Then to Mrs. Kissinger: "I think we'd better keep him in a cell for the night. I'd just like to be a little cautious until we can sort out all of this."

The mother agreed as he comforted her distressed son.

Nancy came back into the room. "The squad car's on the way."

"Thanks, hon." Phil's voice was tired. "Would you stay with them for a couple of minutes?" He gestured toward Dottie and Larry. "I think I ought to call Barringer."

Stauffer moved to the telephone in the den, dreading the call to the district attorney. He dialed Fred Barringer's home number. An answering tape told him that Mr. Barringer was out for the evening, but could be reached at 929-4546.

The sheriff swore silently to himself. He had forgotten about the Thanksgiving Day cocktail party at the Burkholders'. He and Nancy had been invited, but he had neglected to tell his wife. Anyway, that's where Barringer was now and Phil dialed the number. An unfamiliar voice answered, probably the butler, and Phil asked for the district attorney. A few moments went by.

"Barringer here."

"Fred, this is Stauffer. I'm sorry to bother you at the party, but we have a problem."

"The Strickler case?"

"Yep. We have a witness—a participant, you might say—

who has implicated Clay Burkholder."

"Oh, for Christ's sake!"

As succinctly as possible, the sheriff outlined what young Larry Saylor had confessed to him. Barringer was uncharacteristically silent during the entire recital.

"Do you have any doubts about the kid's story?"

"No, not really. I can't believe that he could fabricate anything that elaborate."

Barringer sighed. "Well, I think you'd better get over here. This is something I don't think we ought to keep until morning."

Phil Stauffer grasped the ornate cast-iron knocker on the white door of the Burkholder home. His duty as sheriff didn't take him to the impressive house very often. It annoyed him now that he was ill at ease. He was fully aware of the influence of the Burkholder family in the community of Missionville — wealthy and politically active. They had been the principal backers of Fred Barringer's campaign for district attorney; they had also contributed to all of the sheriff's bids for office. Phil liked his job and he wanted to keep it.

The Burkholders were, as the newspaper always liked to point out, among the first families of Missionville and Young County. They owned the largest lumber yard in the area, the base company for numerous enterprises: home building, real estate development, even a profitable franchise in one of the top national fast-food chains. It was a source of family pride that there had been a Burkholder on the Missionville School Board for more than seventy-five years. Virtually every civic club and community project had a Burkholder involved. All those thoughts raced through Phil's mind as he raised the knocker and dropped it against the heavy wooden panel. He waited a few moments and, just when he had decided to knock again, the door opened.

Mrs. Burkholder stood there, smiling. To find her answering the door surprised Stauffer. He stammered, "Good evening, Mrs. Burkholder." Apparently, Barringer had not said anything to the Burkholders about the nature of his mission.

"Sheriff, it's so good to see you." She extended her hand warmly. "Fred said that you might drop in for a drink and we're so pleased to have you." She motioned Phil inside the house and took his arm, leading him toward the den. "This terrible murder must have ruined your Thanksgiving Day."

"It has."

"Fred's in here," she said, opening the door to the den. "Just as soon as you get finished with your business, now, you must come out and join the others for a drink." She turned to leave and then had another thought. "You know, Phil, we really don't see enough of you, although I do see quite a bit of your pretty wife at the hospital auxiliary meetings. I was hoping she'd be here tonight."

The sheriff tried to keep a tone of light banter in his voice. "That's kind of you. Nancy speaks of you often."

"Isn't she sweet?" The matronly Mrs. Burkholder squeezed his arm, then left to rejoin her guests.

Stauffer eased through the half-open door into the book-lined room heavy with the memorabilia of an affluent family. The district attorney stood by the fireplace, a glass in his hand. Otis Burkholder, tall and distinguished as befitted his station in life, rose from a deep leather chair, extending his hand.

"We thought it best not to say anything to Mrs. Burkholder," he told the sheriff, "until we've had a chance to discuss this. I'm sure there's some kind of error."

"I hope there is, sir," Phil said with studied formality. "Has Fred filled you in on the details?"

"Yes, he has." Burkholder motioned to a chair. "Please sit down. But what Fred has told me sounds so ridiculous. . . ." The sentence went unfinished.

"I know that it must sound improbable," the sheriff agreed, "but I'm bound to follow up on all our leads. It's only because of our esteem for you that we—Fred and I—decided to approach you directly with this matter before we proceed."

Barringer gave Phil a faint smile, nodding his head in agreement with the sentiment.

"I appreciate that," Burkholder said smoothly. "Now, how

might we help you?"

Phil almost stammered again; he was irritated by his lack of confidence in Burkholder's presence. "Well, sir, I really think it's necessary to talk to Clay . . . ah, to ask him some questions."

"Certainly," said Burkholder, rising from his chair. "Just let me get him for you. I don't want to alarm his mother." He left the room.

"He's pretty cool about all this," Phil commented when the den door closed.

"What a God-damned mess," the district attorney moaned. "What a God-damned mess!" There was a moment of silence. "Boy, I sure hope you're wrong about this!"

Again silence. Then, the den door opened again.

"You know both of these gentlemen," Burkholder said to young Clay.

"Yes, sir," he said politely, shaking the hands of Stauffer and Barringer. He was tall, trim and blond. He had the self-assurance of a Burkholder.

Phil spoke first. "Did your father tell you why I wanted to talk to you?"

"No, sir."

"Well, Clay," the sheriff said, carefully picking his words, "I have reason to believe that you might have some information that will help us in the Strickler murder case. You know of that case?"

"Oh, sure," the young man said lightly. "I heard about it on the radio earlier this evening."

"Well, now, I'd like to know whether you know a man named Johnny Mosser."

"No, sir, I don't."

Stauffer was startled by the flat denial. He looked over to Barringer, whose face was a noncommittal mask. "Do you know a boy named Larry Saylor?"

Clay thought for a moment. "No, I don't believe I do."

Either he's a cool customer, thought Phil, *or a damned confident liar.* The sheriff's next question seemed irrelevant. "How old are you, Clay?"

"Seventeen, sir, almost eighteen."

"A senior at Missionville High School?"

"Yes, sir."

Phil leaned forward, his words coming slowly. "You know, then, the meaning of perjury?"

"Yes, sir. It's a lie told under oath."

"Right. Now, you're not under oath here, but I'd like you to imagine that you are." The boy nodded. "Do you know John Mosser?"

"No."

"Do you know Larry Saylor?"

"No."

"Have you ever been to the home of Charles Strickler?"

"No, sir."

There was a pause. The sheriff looked steadily at the elder Burkholder. "Otis, this is difficult for me, but please understand that I have a job to do. I believe your son is lying."

Fred Barringer gasped, but did not speak. Otis looked long and hard at the police officer before turning to his son.

"Clay, you've heard the sheriff. Are you lying?"

"No, sir," he said calmly, "I am not."

"To my knowledge," Otis told Stauffer, "my son has never lied to me. I would be the worst kind of father if I picked this moment to disbelieve him."

Phil decided, as he listened to Otis, to change his approach. His voice hardened. "I understand your position, Otis, but I have good reason to believe that Clay went to the Strickler home on two separate occasions. That he drove there in the company of John Mosser and Larry Saylor. That, on the second visit on Wednesday—just last night—they wrestled Strickler to the floor and bound him with ropes. I have reason to believe that Clay helped to ransack the Strickler house, finding and removing some money."

"That's outrageous!" Otis began.

"And that perhaps," Phil pressed on, "Clay joined Mosser and Saylor in beating Strickler so badly that he died of his injuries!"

The D.A. was on his feet. "Just a moment, Phil, you said nothing about. . . ." He stopped when the sheriff waved his hand.

Otis Burkholder, deep anger written in his face, asked, "Are you prepared to arrest my son for murder?"

"No," said Phil, "I only came here to find the truth."

"I submit," Burkholder snapped, "that you *have* gotten the truth." He was trying to control his anger.

"Excuse me, sheriff," young Clay interjected, almost apologetically, "did I understand you to say that I drove Mosser and Saylor to Mr. Strickler's home?"

"That's right," the sheriff answered. "On the first visit, on Tuesday night, you went in the lumber company pick-up truck. The second time, last night, you drove your father's car."

Otis laughed out loud. His son's face was wreathed in a smile.

"What's so funny?"

"Phil, this *has* to be some kind of horrible error," Otis said in a manner that indicated he was back in command of the situation. "Clay doesn't have a driver's license. He's prohibited from driving, as a matter of fact, because he's an epileptic!"

Stauffer was stunned. He tried not to show it on his face. *What kind of a mess have I gotten myself into now?*

For the first time, District Attorney Barringer took over. "Otis," he said pleadingly, ". . . and Clay, of course . . . I can't tell you how sorry we are about this. Obviously, Phil had some information he felt was correct. We know now that it isn't, and I appreciate your understanding."

Phil said nothing. He'd been shot down, and Barringer had preempted his apology. *Now, wait a minute,* he wanted to say, just because the kid isn't supposed to drive doesn't mean that he didn't drive! And, he wanted to say, *I have a lot of questions still to be asked.* But the moment for additional questions had passed.

"Look, Phil," Otis said, "you were doing your duty and we appreciate that. We also appreciate the manner in which you handled this."

"Yeah. . . . " The sheriff rose and headed for the door of the den. To Barringer: "We'll get back on this in the morning. It's very late now, and. . . ."

"Sheriff Stauffer," Clay said pleasantly, "you have a very difficult job."

Phil stopped, looking at the boy quizzically. *Is he putting me on? No, he's just being a damned Burkholder!* The sheriff forced a wan smile. "Oh, I don't know, young man, the job does have its moments."

2 FRI., NOV. 28, 1969

Johnny Mosser sat on the unpainted wooden steps of the porch of his home. He stared out over the weed-infested fields and idly flipped pebbles at the opening of the well about fifteen feet away. Occasionally, one of the pebbles would drop into the water and he smiled broadly at that.

Behind him on the porch his father sat in a wicker chair he had made himself while he still worked as a basketmaker. He appeared to be dozing in the bright sunshine of the late November morning, but every minute or so he would speak to his son.

"How much money vill ya be gettin' at that job?"

"Don't know, Pop. It's piece-work. Depends on how many cigars I roll."

"Umhum." Several minutes went by before the elder Mosser spoke again. "Somebody's comin', Chonny."

"Yeah, I hear it." Johnny turned his head to look down the dirt road leading to the Mosser farmhouse. Far in the distance he could see the dust cloud being raised by a car moving along the road. Father and son watched silently as the car drew close enough to recognize.

"It's the sheriff," Johnny said finally. The old man didn't answer; neither of the Mossers appeared surprised that the sheriff would be coming to see them. It was Deputy Sheriff Barry Painter who got out when the car had stopped at the broken wooden gate. Barry yawned. It was just a few minutes past 8 a.m., and yesterday, Thanksgiving Day, had been a long one for him. Today, too, promised to be busy, starting with the apprehension of Johnny Mosser.

Painter was almost an exact opposite of his superior. He

was a big man and extroverted. The uniform he wore, patterned after the uniform of the Pennsylvania State Police, had been specially tailored. His holstered gun was carried lower on the leg than necessary. At one time he had wanted to tie it down to his leg in the manner of a Western gunfighter, but Sheriff Stauffer wouldn't permit it.

The deputy was blond and his hair had thinned considerably. It was typical of him that he had a ready explanation for his growing baldness: "*Too many showers when I was playing football.*" Barry had been a star fullback at Missionville High School, had gotten his varsity letter at Penn State, and had made honorable mention on the Associated Press All-Eastern team. He had wanted to play professional football. As a senior at State, he had sent a resume to every team in the National Football League. The NFL's college draft had passed him by, but the Philadelphia Eagles did invite him to their try-out camp at Hershey. He was cut loose after three days.

The coaches' report on him said: *Has the talent, but lacks necessary mental attitude. Runs well with ball. Blocking desultory. Showboat.* When he returned to Missionville from Hershey he told everyone that he had "popped the knee," and he limped around town for weeks.

Painter had been married, to a girl he met in college, but the marriage would have merited the same evaluation given to his pro football try-out: *Has the talent, but lacks necessary mental attitude.* The marriage lasted less than two years. Some days it took a conscious mental effort by him to remember her name.

But Barry was a good deputy for Phil Stauffer. He worked hard and was thorough. Since the position gave him a necessary feeling of importance, he did nothing that would jeopardize it. Painter swaggered as he walked toward the Mosser house.

"Hiya, Barry," Johnny called out as the deputy neared the porch.

"Hiya, Johnny," Barry answered in a friendly manner. He turned to the old man. "Good morning, Emanuel."

" 'Lo, sheriff."

There was a strange silence then, a calm period of waiting heightened by the Mossers' apparent lethargy. They seemed not the slightest bit interested in knowing why the deputy sheriff of Young County had come their way.

Barry broke the silence. "Johnny, I'd like to come in and ask a few questions."

"Okay," said Johnny, holding the door open for the police officer. He followed Barry. His father, after a moment's hesitation, went through the door also. Inside, Mrs. Mosser stood by the stove, doing nothing. Barry nodded to her, but she didn't speak.

"Bet this is about Charlie Strickler, ain't it?" Johnny's sudden question, delivered in an airy tone, surprised Painter.

"What makes you think that?"

"Oh, I was out there the other night and I guess Charlie is sore about the way we handled him. He gets real mad sometimes." There was a matter-of-fact nonchalance in his words.

"Yes, he does," Barry agreed. "Now, tell me, when was this, and what happened?"

"Wednesday night. Me and Charlie had an argument and we had to tie him up a little because he got so mad at me."

"We?"

"Yeah, that Saylor kid—you know, the one whose old lady works at the diner—and Clay Burkholder. They went along."

"Wait a minute. Are you sure about Clay Burkholder?"

"Sure. We went in his old man's car."

"Okay," said Barry, not wishing the press the point. "So the three of you went to Strickler's, Charlie got mad at you, and Saylor and Burkholder helped you tie him up?"

"That's it," Johnny agreed. Then, proudly, "But I did the tying up, Barry. They just helped hold him down. Boy, Charlie was mad!"

"Because you tied him up?"

Johnny laughed heartily. "Nah, hell, Barry, he was mad because I found out that he put a spell on me. And, when he couldn't give me his copy of the *Long Lost Friend,* I had to cut some hair off him, and he didn't like that. But it's all okay now. We really didn't hurt him or anything. Just tied him up, but not too tight so's he could get loose."

"Now, Johnny," the deputy said quietly, "let's make some sense of this. You say that Strickler had a spell on you."

"Yeah, and I had to get a copy of the pow-wow book, or a lock of his hair, to break the spell. Well, he wouldn't give me the book. First he said he would, then he didn't. We had a fight about it, kind of. And when he was tied up, I cut some hair off like Lizzie told me."

"Lizzie?"

"Lizzie Zearfoss, over by Miller's Grove. She told me to get the book, or a lock of hair, and bury it under our crabapple tree and the spell would be broken. And I did."

"A lock of hair from Charlie Strickler?"

"Yeah, because Charlie was the one who had the spell on me, you see. And you know what?"

"What?"

"That old witch was right!" Johnny was elated. "When I buried the hair I didn't feel bad no more. I'm good now!"

Painter drew a deep breath. "What happened after you cut the hair off Strickler?"

"I told you," Mosser insisted. "I buried it under the crabapple tree like Lizzie told me."

"No, no. What did you do with Strickler after you tied him up?"

"Nothing," Johnny answered defiantly. "And if Charlie says I did, he's a liar!"

"But you *did* cut the hair off?"

"Sure, but what the hell's he getting so excited about? He knows he put a spell on me, and he knows that I needed the hair. Hell, Barry, he's a pow-wow man. He knows that stuff!"

Painter began to show exasperation. "Now, listen to me, Johnny. After you tied up Charlie, and after you cut off some of his hair, *then* what did you do to him?"

"Nothing! We just went home."

"Did Clay Burkholder do anything to Strickler?"

"Nope."

"How about Larry Saylor?"

"Nope. We just went home." Mosser laughed again. "I just can't see why old Charlie is getting his ass up in the air about this. If he gave me the book, everything would have been okay. But he had to fart around, and he knows I needed the hair if he wouldn't give me the book. He knows that!"

The deputy looked at him for a long moment before speaking again. "Charlie Strickler doesn't know anything of the kind."

"Sure he does!" Johnny insisted.

"He can't show it, Johnny," Barry said without dramatics, "because Charlie Strickler is dead."

Johnny's mother screamed. But from the two Mosser men there was almost no reaction.

"Christ, Barry," Johnny said, "I didn't hurt him. I just tied him up."

"And cut off some hair?"

"Yeah, and that's all, damn it!"

Painter knew that he had reached the end of the line in his interrogation. He shrugged his shoulders. "Well, Johnny, I want you to come in to talk to Sheriff Stauffer about this."

"Sure."

The old lady rushed to her son and, sobbing deeply, she threw her arms around him, holding tight. He struggled free. "Mom, everything is okay. I didn't hurt Strickler, and when I go in and tell the sheriff it'll be okay. Won't it, Barry?"

"Yeah," the deputy lied, "sure it will."

He turned toward the door and Johnny followed him. As they left, Barry could still hear his weeping mother in the kitchen. But the old man, he didn't seem to give a damn! It was procedure, in the apprehension of a suspect in a crime, to use handcuffs, but this time Barry couldn't see the need for it. As they arrived at the car, the deputy said, "You can sit up front, Johnny."

"Are you gonna use the siren?" the prisoner asked hopefully.

"Not today, Johnny, not today." Then Barry added, "We only use that when we're bringing in dangerous criminals."

Johnny beamed.

As they drove down the dusty, unpaved road away from the Mosser farmhouse, the deputy sheriff asked, "Where'd you bury the hair, Johnny?"

"Under the crabapple tree."

"Show me."

"No!"

"Why not?"

"If I tell you," Johnny said excitedly, "you'll dig it up and then the spell will come back!"

"Okay, Johnny," said Painter, "we'll let the sheriff decide about that."

Several miles went by in silence.

"Barry," Johnny said suddenly, "I ain't gonna dig it up for the sheriff, neither!"

There was only one customer in Kolb's hardware store when Sheriff Stauffer entered. He stood quietly while clerk Frank Bupp waited on him.

"Hello, sheriff," Bupp said as the customer departed. "Official or unofficial visit?"

"Official, Frank." Stauffer removed a length of rope from a large manila envelope. "Do you sell this kind of rope here?"

Bupp took it from Phil and looked at it closely. "Burned a little."

The sheriff just nodded.

"Yeah," Bupp said, "we sell this kind. It's common enough. Cotton, you know. We sell a lot for clothes lines."

Stauffer nodded again.

"Come on over here," the clerk said as he led the way to a corner of the store where various sizes and types of rope were wound on large metal spools. "It's just like this," Bupp said, pointing to one of the spools.

The sheriff retrieved the scorched piece of rope from the clerk and held it next to the rope on the spool. "Looks the same."

"It *is* the same. Of course, I can't say it came off that roll. Lots of stores sell this kind of rope. Used for clothes lines, you know."

Phil ignored the redundancy. "Cut me off about a foot from that roll, will you, Frank? That ought to be enough for a lab comparison."

As the clerk went for a knife to grant the sheriff's request, the questioning continued. "Could you remember, Frank, who you sold some of this rope to recently?"

"Well, this morning. . . ."

"No, earlier in the week."

"Gosh, sheriff, I sell a lot of this rope."

"Try anyway."

"Well . . ." Bupp thought for a moment, slicing off the foot of rope the sheriff wanted. ". . . let's see. Yeah, your wife was in on Monday for light bulbs. And when she passed the rope there she remembered she needed some for a new clothes line."

Stauffer smiled. "Try again, Frank."

"Yeah," chuckled the clerk, "I guess you're not checking up on your wife, eh, sheriff? Well . . ." Another pause. "Gosh, I guess I don't sell as much of it as I thought."

"You're not here all the time, are you, Frank?" Phil asked. "Maybe Mr. Kolb sold some of it."

"Not this week, he didn't." Bupp was firm. "Says he's been feeling poorly and he hasn't been here all week. Kind of makes it tough on me, though. Have to send out to the diner for lunch."

The sheriff tried to be sympathetic. "I'm sure it's not easy, Frank. Now, let's see. On Monday you sold some of this rope to my wife. Any other sales Monday?"

"Nope. Don't think so." The door opened and a customer entered. Phil signaled to the clerk to wait on the new arrival. He put the two pieces of rope in the manila envelope and stood silently, watching Frank sell a pair of lawn shears.

"That's two thirty-five, Mr. Schneck," Bupp said. "You know those shears normally sell for three dollars, but we don't get many calls for them in November, so they're sale priced."

"That's a good break for me," said the man. As he paid his bill, he handed the clerk a cigar. "Have a cigar, Frank. Guess I can afford it now that I've saved sixty-five cents." They both laughed and the customer departed.

"That's funny," Bupp said to Stauffer. "That's funny him giving me this cigar, because that reminded me of somebody else who bought some rope. On Wednesday it was."

"Who was that?"

"It's funny how this cigar should remind me. Do you know Johnny Mosser?"

"I do," replied the sheriff.

"Well, he's a cigarmaker, you know?"

"Yeah."

"He was in here Wednesday and bought some rope. Only ten feet. He didn't give me a cigar or anything, you understand, but getting that cigar from Mr. Schneck just now reminded me. Yep, Johnny Mosser it was."

"You're certain about it being Wednesday?"

"Oh, I'm certain," Bupp assured him. "I remember how we talked about Thanksgiving Day coming up, and how it was lucky he came in for the rope then because we were gonna be closed the next day. It was Wednesday, all right."

"Was he alone?"

"No. Will Burkholder came in with him. Otis Burkholder's boy. One of them, anyway."

"*Will* Burkholder? Not Clay?"

"No, it was Will."

"Could you describe him?"

"Oh, sure, I know him real well. Tall kid, well-built, dark hair."

"How old, would you say?"

"Seventeen or eighteen. He graduates from high school next June."

"And blond," Stauffer said.

"No, Phil, not blond. I said he had dark hair."

"So you did. Sorry." The sheriff continued, "Now, what time of the day did Johnny buy his rope?"

"In the morning," the clerk said quickly, "only about fifteen minutes after I opened up, and we open at eight."

"Anyone else buy any rope this week, Frank?"

"Not that I can recollect. Funny how that cigar reminded me about Johnny."

"Most fortunate."

"Is Johnny in some kind of trouble again, sheriff?"

"Not that I'm certain of. Thanks for your help, Frank. Oh, say, tell me one other thing."

"What's that?"

"You didn't sell my wife a short piece of rope, did you?"

"Oh, gosh no, sheriff!" He was genuinely concerned. "She asked for twenty-five feet, and I cut off twenty-five feet, right to the exact inch."

Phil laughed and, when the clerk realized that the sheriff was joking, he laughed, too.

Outside, Stauffer was still grinning, but not about his little witticism. How about that? It was Will Burkholder, not Clay! I never thought of the brother!

"No, I will *not* permit you to get a warrant for Will Burkholder's arrest!" District Attorney Fred Barringer pounded on the sheriff's desk. "First, we had that embarrassing confrontation with the Burkholders last night and now this . . . this . . . We're going to be up to our asses in trouble if we're not careful!"

Phil grunted derisively. "Look, Fred, don't you see what has happened? Larry Saylor *thought* the fellow who drove them to Strickler's was Clay Burkholder. So did John Mosser. Or so he's told my deputy. But it was really Will, posing as Clay."

"Damn it, Phil," the D.A. complained, "you're going to drive me into an early grave!"

"You know Frank Bupp. Would he lie about something like this? What would be his motive for a lie?"

Barringer was upset. "I don't know . . . I don't know! But how in the hell are we going to go back to the Burkholders with this?"

"We go back," Phil said firmly, "because we have a new ball game. Okay, I was mistaken last night, but I'm not now! Don't you see that the pieces are falling into place?"

The D.A. shook his head sadly. When he spoke again the

voice was subdued. "Yes, Phil, they're falling into place, and right on our heads."

It was 2 p.m. before Stauffer and Barringer had prepared themselves for the second foray against the fortress Burkholder. Both Mosser and Saylor, in requestioning, said the young man who accompanied them called himself Clay Burkholder. But they admitted that they had no way of knowing whether it was Clay or Will. The Burkholder family was not in their normal social contacts. Now a warrant had been issued to effect the arrest of Will Burkholder on a robbery charge.

The district attorney had called in lawyer Paul Reisinger, the Burkholders' family attorney, and he had agreed to cooperate with the authorities in an effort to clarify the Burkholder situation. It was Reisinger who had argued against the issuance of a writ charging assault and battery, as the sheriff had wanted. Barringer, trying in every way possible to prevent a repetition of the previous evening's debacle, agreed with Reisinger. It was agreed, too, that Reisinger would meet the sheriff and the D.A. at the Burkholder home at 2:15. And, finally, Larry Saylor was to be taken along for the purpose of a positive identification of the young man who had been at the Strickler home.

There was almost no conversation as Barringer and Stauffer drove to the Burkholder home, with young Saylor slumped in the back seat.

"Now, Larry," Phil said as they turned into the Burkholder driveway, "I want you to stay out of sight until I call for you. Just stay low in the back seat. Do you understand that?"

"Yeah."

"There's Reisinger," Barringer said, pointing his finger, "just getting out of his car." The sheriff stopped behind the attorney's car, and he and the D.A. got out quickly.

"Paul, I appreciate this," Fred said.

"It makes sense to me to proceed this way," the attorney answered, "although, frankly, I hope you're wrong about this, too."

Phil was firm. "Not much chance."

The trio approached the door and Reisinger dropped the knocker. The door opened immediately.

"I saw you arriving," said Otis Burkholder. "What kind of nonsense is going on now?" His restrained attitude of the evening past was no longer evident.

"We'd like to talk to you for a few minutes," his lawyer explained, "because there's a new development."

"Another false charge against Clay?"

"May we come in?" Reisinger asked, ignoring the question from his client. "It's rather important."

The elder Burkholder opened the door wider to permit entry. He quickly led the way to the den, motioning the visitors to chairs. Then he positioned himself in a dominant position in front of the big stone fireplace, and remained standing. "Well, what is it?" Otis was not happy.

"Otis, there has been a new development," Reisinger started, "which likely will clear Clay completely."

"Of course! I thought we had disposed of that last night!"

"Which likely will clear Clay completely," the attorney repeated, "but threatens to implicate his brother."

"Willard? What kind of insanity is this?"

"Otis, please be calm," Reisinger pleaded. "This is very serious, and the district attorney is being as cooperative as he can in this matter. Fred, would you tell Otis what you know?"

"It's this way, Otis," Barringer explained. "The identification of Clay by John Mosser and Larry Saylor came about because the young man who drove them to the Strickler house, first in your pick-up and then in your car, *told* them he was Clay Burkholder. They accepted that, because they aren't familiar with the members of the Burkholder family. But now, we have every reason to believe that it was *Will* who was at the Strickler house, posing as Clay."

Otis stared at the D.A. "I see what you're trying to do! You're trying to muddy up the waters so much that I won't press any charges over last night's fiasco!" His voice got louder with each phrase. "And you, Paul—I'm shocked that you'd go along with this charade! But all you damned lawyers stick together!"

"Otis, please," his attorney said, "shouting is not going to help the situation. We're trying to clarify this thing, and Phil and Fred need to talk to Will."

"No, damn it, *no!*" Burkholder had moved to the center of the room. "Get the hell out of here!"

Reisinger went to Otis, trying to reason with him, but was pushed away. District Attorney Barringer slumped in his chair, the picture of dejection. Sheriff Stauffer rose and extended a paper document to Burkholder.

"Sir," Phil said with deliberate formality, "I'm here as the sheriff of Young County, and I don't have time for these games. This is a warrant for the arrest of one Willard Burkholder for robbery. I intend to do what this warrant gives me the right to do, whether you like it or not!"

The sheriff's outburst put a rein on Burkholder's rage. Otis dropped into a chair, staring dumbly at the arrest warrant. Finally, he looked up at his attorney. "Is this all legal?"

"All legal," Reisinger assured him.

No more was said until Burkholder left the room and returned with his youngest son. The two Burkholders sat stiffly on a large leather-covered sofa.

"Now, Will," Reisinger said, "the sheriff has some questions. I want you to answer them, unless I advise against an answer." He looked at the father. "We have every intention of protecting your rights."

The boy said nothing.

Stauffer began the questioning. "Will, how old are you?"

"Sixteen, almost seventeen."

"A year younger than your brother?"

"Yes."

"And a year behind him in school?"

"No, sheriff, we're both in the same class. I was moved ahead in the sixth grade. We both graduate in June."

"Okay," said Phil, satisfied that he had established the interrogation on a calm note. "Now, do you know John Mosser?"

"Sure."

"How well do you know him?"

"Oh, I've seen him around town." The slim, dark-haired boy seemed perfectly at ease. "He's kind of a town character, you know."

"When was the last time you saw John Mosser?"

"Last Wednesday."

"When and where?"

"In the morning. At Kolb's hardware. We talked about cigars. He's a cigarmaker, you know, and I asked him about what were good cigars, because I wanted to get some for my Dad's Christmas present." He looked at his father, seeking approval. The elder Burkholder's face was stony.

"Was that outside or inside the hardware store?"

"Both," the boy answered. "I bumped into him on the street, and then walked into the store with him. He wanted to buy something."

"What did he buy?"

"A piece of rope. For a clothes line, I guess."

"And when," the sheriff went on, "did you see him again?"

"I haven't seen him since that time."

"Didn't you drive him that evening—Wednesday evening—to the home of Charlie Strickler?"

"No."

"Didn't you go with him to the Strickler home on last Tuesday evening?"

"No."

Sheriff Stauffer leaned back in his chair, just looking at the young man for a hard moment. "Do you know Larry Saylor?"

"Yes."

"And how do you know him?"

"He hangs around the bowling alley. I go there sometimes."

"Did you go to the Strickler home with Saylor last Wednesday night?"

"No."

"Tuesday night?"

"No." Will leaned forward. "Look, why don't we save a lot of time? I don't know anything about this Strickler business. Nothing. Period." The voice was calm, carefully modulated.

Then he smiled. "I thought that was Clay's bag."

"Will!" Otis Burkholder was shocked by his son's flippancy.

"Look, Dad," Will tried to explain, "I don't know anything about this. Those two nuts said *Clay* was the guy with them, didn't they? Well, if the sheriff can't make that stand up, then why should he try to make me the patsy?"

"Okay," Stauffer said quietly. Without explanation, he got to his feet and left the room. He could feel the tense silence he had left behind. Phil moved rapidly to the front door, opened it, waved to Larry Saylor in the squad car, and the boy ran to join him. The sheriff whispered something to Larry just before they went into the den.

"Do you know this fellow?" the sheriff asked Will. Phil had his arm around Larry's shoulders; he could feel the trembling. There was no immediate answer from the younger Burkholder. Phil's question was sterner now. "I asked you, Willard, whether you know this fellow?"

"Yeah." Doubt began to show on the confident face of the Burkholder boy. "That's Larry Saylor."

"And, Larry," the sheriff said, "would you tell me who that is?" He pointed to Will.

"Sure," said Larry, "that's Clay Burkholder!"

"I'm glad I'm not a cop."

Ernie Wheel made the statement to Nick Willson as they drove along County Road 695 looking for the turn-off to Miller's Grove.

"Okay," said Nick, "I'll be the straight man. Why are you glad you're not a cop?"

"For one thing, when you're a cop you can't really play with this Strickler case the way a writer can. We can talk about hex and witches and all kinds of strange things, but we really don't have to prove it. We can speculate. Phil Stauffer, on the other hand, has to prove that witchcraft had something to do with the Strickler murder, or he has to prove that it did not. All we have to do is write about it and, primarily, only about the interesting parts at that."

Nick laughed. "Do I detect a note of the conscience-stricken journalist concerned about the worth of his trade?"

"Not at all," Ernie said quickly. "All I said was that I'm glad I'm not a cop. I like being a reporter. It is, to state it simply, fun. Most of the time, anyway."

"Well, certainly this little jaunt ought to prove interesting."

They were on their way to Miller's Grove, on the morning after Thanksgiving Day, to see Lizzie Zearfoss, a pow-wow practitioner in the area, whose name had been dropped by Deputy Sheriff Painter. Ernie and Nick had been at the courthouse when Johnny Mosser was brought in. They pressed the sheriff for details.

Phil was brusque. "I am not at liberty to tell you anything at the moment. Mr. Mosser here may be able to shed some light on the Charles Strickler affair, but I cannot determine that until our interrogation is complete."

"Was Mosser at the Strickler home?" the sheriff had been asked.

"Yes."

"Why?"

"I am not at liberty to divulge that at this time."

"Is Mosser under arrest?"

"He has been asked to come in for questioning. He did so without the issuance of a warrant."

"Did the fact that Strickler was a pow-wow doctor have anything to do with Mosser's visit to him?"

"No comment." The sheriff turned away from the newsmen and led Mosser into his inner office. As he moved away, the questioning turned to Deputy Painter.

"Did pow-wow have anything to do with it, Barry?"

Painter, aware that he was now center-stage, could not resist the opportunity for the spotlight. "We believe that it may have," he began pompously. "You see, Mr. Mosser had been to see Lizzie Zearfoss, at Miller's Grove, and she had informed him. . . ."

That was as far as Painter got in his statement. The sheriff shut him off. Nick Willson's subsequent call to Dr. Josh Oberdick had confirmed that Lizzie was a pow-wow doctor.

The reporters were following up on that lead.

Up ahead of the car a road sign, with an arrow pointing to the right, indicated that it was two miles to Miller's Grove. Nick made the turn and the road became a lane-and-a-half dirt strip. It was rough. It had been a long time since it had been repaired in any way. Large ruts, the work of months of erosion, slowed the going to fifteen miles an hour.

Dr. Oberdick had told them that Lizzie lived in the third house on the left after making the turn onto the road to Miller's Grove. They drove for nearly three-quarters of a mile before they spotted a long-abandoned farm house, a huge hole in the roof.

"That must be number one," said Nick.

Six hundred yards farther on they saw another house. It, too, was in a poor state of repair, but smoke could be seen rising from the chimney.

"Number two," Ernie said, "and not exactly in the high rent district."

The condition of the road grew worse. Nick shifted into second, then into first, reducing his speed even more. The muffler hit bottom several times. Just when it seemed that they might have missed seeing the third house, Nick spotted it half buried in brush on a small hill just off the road. "There!" he said, pointing.

"Cripes," Ernie exclaimed, "I didn't see it. Looks like a fine place to film a Hitchcock thriller."

There was no road up to the house, only an almost concealed footpath. Nick pulled the car as close to the edge of the dirt road as he could. Even before they got out of the car they could see a woman moving down the path toward them.

"Who are ya?" The voice was old, high-pitched. *Witch-like*, Ernie thought. "Vot do ya vunt here?"

As she approached the car the reporters made her out as tiny—perhaps less than five feet tall—and skinny, even emaciated in appearance. "Who are ya?" she demanded again.

Ernie, being closest to her, asked, "Lizzie Zearfoss?"

"Yah, yah!" She was agitated about having these strangers at her home. "Vot do ya vunt here?"

"Miss Zearfoss . . ."

"*Mrs.* Zearfoss!"

"*Mrs.* Zearfoss," Wheel started again, "my name is Ernest Wheel, of the Continental News Service. And this is Nick Willson, of the Missionville Star."

"Get out! Get out!" she screeched. "I don't vunt no reporters! Get out! *Raus!*"

Nick volunteered, " . . . friends of Johnny Mosser."

The anger began to vanish. "Ach, Chonny Mosser."

"That's right," Nick went on. "Johnny told us how you helped him with his problem."

"Yah." A slight smile came to the wrinkled face, but there was still some suspicion.

Ernie permitted Nick to carry the verbal ball. "We'd like to find out just exactly what it was you did for Johnny," Nick said, "so that our stories about you are accurate, correct."

I hope this works, thought Wheel, *because I haven't the slightest idea what the hell it is she was supposed to have done for Mosser.*

The old lady looked at them intently, squinting through ancient and watery eyes, measuring the two young men. She ran a bony hand over her mouth and chin, deep in thought. The hand appeared to be only bone and blood vessels, encased in transparent skin. Then, surprisingly, "Come in," she said. She turned and led the way up the narrow, weedy path.

The house, as they approached it, was surrealistic; it conjured up a fantastic juxtaposition of shapes and angles. Ernie thought he had never seen anything like it outside of a horror movie—but one with a big budget. It was a shack, really, unpainted for decades. It had not been built as a single project; it was the work of numerous builders, in several eras. Windows were nonexistent, having been boarded up years earlier. The door stood open, sagging dangerously on rusted hinges. Would its next opening be its last? Two rotting steps led up to the broken door sill.

Mrs. Zearfoss led the way into a darkened room (it was impossible to tell what room it was), and when the two men entered they were almost felled by the odor. Wheel gagged momentarily. As their eyes became accustomed to the dingy interior, they could see cats everywhere. Too many to be counted.

"You like cats," Ernie said, more as a comment than a question.

"Yah," she said. "I don't neffer chase none avay. They haff to go some place. They iss Gott's creatures. And the cats like me."

"I can see that," said Ernie. "How many do you have?"

The question surprised her. "How many? Oh, Gott, lots! I don't count. They chust stay here mit me. They iss goot company for an old lady."

"How do you feed them all?"

"I don't. In the country, they make for themselves."

"Well," said Wheel with a grin, "I'll bet you don't have any problems with mice."

Lizzie glared at him. Nick, waving his hand in a slight movement to tell Ernie to restrain his sense of humor, took over the questioning. "Mrs. Zearfoss, I have a personal question first. Just how old are you?"

It was strange, but Ernie thought he saw the old lady blush. Certainly she giggled. Are all women coy about age, even old hags?

"Old enuff," she chuckled. "I'm so *fergesslich.*"

"Oh, come now," Nick laughed, "you're not that forgetful. A lady ought to be proud of her age."

"Vell, I vas born in Chanuary in the same year of the Chicago Fire."

Nick gasped. "But that was a hundred years ago!"

"Nah," she said, still giggling. "It vas in 1871."

"You're 98?"

"Yah, 98." She said it proudly.

"Gosh," Ernie interjected, "you don't look a day over 80." He knew, even before he finished the remark, that it was a mistake. The coy giggles stopped and the old woman's face turned hard.

"Vell, it's 98, chust the same," she snapped.

Nick laughed, trying to cover Ernie's blunder. "My friend," he said to Lizzie, "likes to joke with the ladies. I think it's marvelous, Mrs. Zearfoss, how you live here alone and take care of all these animals. And you certainly don't show your age."

She smiled at Nick, a toothless grin. Ernie told himself to keep his mouth shut and let Nick deal with the strange old harpy.

"Mrs. Zearfoss," Nick said, "we're interested in knowing exactly what you told Johnny Mosser when he came to see you."

"Chonny didn't tell ya?"

"Sure," Nick lied, "but you know Johnny. He gets a little mixed up now and then. We wanted to get all the details from you."

"Ach, I chust helped him a little." A wave of her hand seemed to dismiss the subject.

This is going to be tough, thought Nick. But he continued to probe. "Well, Johnny thought you helped him quite a lot. He told us that without you he wouldn't have been able to solve his problems."

Lizzie simply nodded, not volunteering any comment.

"And it was Johnny," the reporter pressed on, "who suggested that we come out here. He told us how to find you, and asked us to talk to you personally, because he couldn't remember exactly how it went." Nick had reached the end of his fabrications. If the old woman didn't open up now, their visit would be fruitless.

"Vell, I don't rightly know . . ." she said slowly. "Chonny vas sick, ya know."

Both men nodded, perhaps too enthusiastically.

"Und ven he came here," Lizzie went on, "he didn't know vot vas the matter. He vas alvays feelin' bad, *dormlich* and all."

"Dormlich?" Nick tried to pronounce the unfamiliar word correctly.

"Yah, yah, dormlich . . . ya know, gitty . . . dizzy. Ennyvay, sometimes he vas so bad that he vas veek and didn't sink he could vork." She paused.

Willson urged her on. "Did *you* know what was wrong?"

"Ach, yah," she said confidently. "He vas *ferhext*. Chonny vas a strong man, but he vas under a spell. I asked him who had a spell on him, but he didn't know. So ve hadt to findt out who it vas."

"How'd you do that?"

"Vell, we took a dollar bill. . . ."

Nick interrupted. "Could you show us?" He quickly reached into his pocket and pulled out a bill.

She took the money. "Hold out your hand."

Nick stretched out his right hand. The old woman smoothed out the bill in his palm, with the picture of George Washington face up.

"Now, I told Chonny he shud stare at Vashington. Then, ven I took the bill avay he vould see the face of the vun who *ferhext* him in his palm."

"And did he?"

"Oh, yah. He said it vas Charlie Strickler."

Wheel could not resist joining in on the interrogation. "Johnny actually saw Charlie Strickler's face in his palm after the dollar bill was removed?"

"Yah, und it vas for schure Charlie who had a spell on Chonny!" The tone of her voice left no room for doubt.

Ernie continued, "Did *you* see Charlie Strickler's face in his palm?"

"Nein, only Chonny couldt see it, because he vas the vun *ferhext*."

"You didn't suggest to him that Strickler was the one?"

Her face went hard again. "If ya don't believe me, vhy dit ya come here onct?"

Ernie didn't answer, looking to Nick for help.

"Of course, we believe you," said Willson. "It's just that we're trying not to make any mistakes. Now, after Johnny saw Strickler's face in his palm, what did you tell him to do?"

"I told him," Lizzie said, directing her answer to Nick, "that he could break the spell by gettin' Charlie's *Lange Verborgene Freund* . . ."

"What's that?"

"The pow-wow book . . . the Long Lost Frendt. Or, I told him, he could chust get a lock of Charlie's hair. Und ven he got it, to bury it under the roots of a crabapple tree on his farm."

"What did Johnny do then?"

"Vhy, he said he'd do it. Und ve said some vords together, und he vent avay."

"Words?"

"Yah, against ewil spirits . . . the hex."

"Can you remember them?"

Lizzie Zearfoss closed her eyes meditatively, intoning the words in a slow monotone. It seemed she was trying to fight against her natural, heavy Pennsylvania Dutch accent. "The cross of Christ be vit me; the cross of Christ owercomes all vater und ev'ry fire; the cross of Christ owercomes all veapons; the cross of Christ iss a perfect sign und blessing to my soul. May Christ be vit me und my body during all my life at day und at night. Now I pray Gott the Father for the soul's sake, und I pray Gott the Son for the Father's sake, und I pray Gott the Holy Ghost for the Father's und the Son's sake, und I pray the holy corpse of Gott may bless me against all ewil things, vords and vorks. The cross of Christ open unto me future bliss; the cross of Christ be vit me, above me, before me, behind me, beneath me, aside of me und ewerywhere, und before all my enemies, wisible und unwisible; these all flee from me as soon as dey but know or hear. Enoch and Elias, the two prophets, ver neffer imprisoned, nor bound, not beaten und came neffer out of their power; thus, no one of my enemies must be able to inchure or attack me in my body or my life. In the name of Gott the Father, the Son, und the Holy Ghost. Amen."

There was a deep silence as Lizzie finished her incantation. Her eyes opened and she looked first at Ernie and then at Nick. Nick broke the silence. "Do you know what Johnny did then?"

"Yah. He vent to see Charlie und he got a lock of hair. Und he buried it, like I said, under the crabapple tree."

"Did Johnny tell you that?" Nick asked.

"No, he ain't come back here since he seen Charlie's face."

"Then how do you know what Johnny did?"

"I know."

"Who told you?"

"Nobody told me!" Anger was creeping into her voice. "Nobody got to tell me, because I know. I haff that power!"

Ernie spoke. "Do you have the power to know what has happened to Charlie Strickler?"

"He's dedt." Her statement was flat, without emotion, matter-of-fact.

"Who told you that?"

"Nobody. I chust know."

"And do you know who killed him?"

"The divel."

"Not Johnny Mosser?"

Emotion returned to her face, now, and to her voice. "No, no, not Chonny! The divel killed Charlie Strickler!"

"Does this devil," Wheel asked sarcastically, "have a name?"

Lizzie looked at him coldly, muttering one word: "Aesel."

"Thank you, Mrs. Zearfoss," Nick said softly. "We appreciate your help." He turned to leave and Ernie followed him.

At the car, Ernie said, "Jesus Christ, that was weird!"

"Yeah," said Nick, starting to laugh, "and the weirdest thing of all was that line: 'You don't look a day over 80.'"

Wheel joined in the laughter. "I'm sorry, buddy, but sometimes I just can't resist . . ."

"Never mind. The old lady had the last word anyway—aesel."

"Yeah, just what the hell does that mean?"

A grin lighted Nick's broad face. "It's simple. It means 'jackass.'"

"Ouch! But, Nick, do you believe her?"

"About the jackass part?"

"I had that coming," Ernie laughed. "No, the whole

damned story, especially the part about knowing what Johnny did after he left here."

"Yes, I believe every word of it!"

"You're kidding."

"Nope," said Nick seriously. "Think about it for a moment. How'd she learn that Strickler is dead? She's way out here in the sticks, no radio, no newspaper, alone. Who told her?"

"Someone must have."

"But who *could* have?"

Wheel shrugged. He had no ready answer. They got into the car and, as they started back down the rutted, dirt road, Nick Willson announced, "Next stop—the Mosser farm. To look for a lock of hair under a crabapple tree!"

Wheel and Willson drove along the rural road toward the Mosser homestead. Nick looked at his watch. "Gawd! It's after six. I'm famished. Let's grab something to eat after we check at the farm."

"Umm." Ernie was trying to make notes on their encounter with Lizzie Zearfoss. It flashed through his mind that the story he would write would get good play in newspapers across the country. "I hope we're not going off the deep end on this pow-wow stuff."

"Again, the doubts?"

"Yes and no. I'm certain that pow-wow is at least a peripheral part of the story. I'm just not certain whether or not we're being led down the primrose path. That close-to-the-vest sheriff impresses me as being a pretty smart bastard."

"He is."

"Maybe he's happy to see us making asses of ourselves about pow-wow, when the real story is somewhere else."

"Maybe so," admitted Nick, "but right now our story is strung up on the pow-wow line. But do you know what will clinch it for us?

"What?"

"Finding that lock of hair under a lovely crabapple tree."

Wheel groaned. "Every ounce of logic and intelligence in me tells me not to believe that crap. And if we *do* happen to find a lock of hair, I'm just not sure what it's going to do to my precious logic and my so-called intelligence."

The car approached the Mosser farm in the semi-darkness of early evening. As Nick slowed the auto near the gate, the two reporters could see the blinking of a flashlight somewhere near the ramshackle house. As they stepped from the car they could make out a figure with a shovel, digging.

"Someone else seems to have the same idea," Ernie said.

"The sheriff's department, I'll bet," added Nick. "That's probably Barry Painter."

They walked toward the light. As they got closer, the working silhouette did indeed turn into Deputy Painter. He was digging in the ground near the base of a tree. Emanuel Mosser was holding the flashlight. Barry stopped and looked up as the newsmen approached.

He challenged them. "Who told you I'd be here?"

"A pow-wow doctor," answered Ernie.

"Very funny!"

"Well, not so funny," Nick said. "We had a talk with Lizzie Zearfoss, and put two and two together. Seems that our arithmetic wasn't fast enough, however. Find anything?"

Barry returned to his digging without comment.

"You're not going to hold out on us," said Ernie, "now that we're here?"

The deputy didn't reply.

Nick continued to prod. "Stauffer give you hell for talking to us?"

"Damned right he did," Barry admitted, not stopping his digging. "He said to keep my mouth shut around reporters. And I intend to follow orders!"

"You might," Nick suggested coyly, "find the lock of hair a last faster if you had help."

Barry looked up sullenly. "And *you* might get the hell out of here!"

Ernie watched him digging for a few minutes. "Is this a crabapple tree?"

"Of course it's a crabapple," Painter snapped, continuing his work. "Do you think I'm stupid?"

The reporter raised his hand apologetically. "I had no such thought, deputy."

Barry continued moving small shovelsful of dirt out of the hole, very carefully examining the earth as he moved it. Ernie and Nick watched intently. So did Emanuel, who said not a word. Suddenly, the deputy lowered the shovel, dropping to his knees. He moved his body around, trying to shield the hole from the reporters. He was not successful. "Bring the light closer." The old man obeyed.

With his hands, Painter moved small bits of earth. There it was—a bunch of hair! Ernie, who had been thinking about a *lock* of hair, was surprised that there was so much of it. The deputy tried to pick it up as a clump, shaking dirt from it. Quickly, he reached into his pocket, extracted an envelope, and slipped the hair into it. He stood up.

"Thanks for the help, Emanuel," he said.

The elder Mosser acknowledged the thanks with a slight nod of his head. Barry picked up the shovel, retrieved the flashlight, and moved toward his squad car.

"Is that the place," Ernie asked, "where Mosser told you you'd find the hair?"

Painter started the motor, shifted, and was away, throwing up dust and small stones with his spinning tires.

Ernie shouted after him. "Do you believe that it's Charlie Strickler's hair?"

Without looking back, the deputy put out his left hand, with the middle finger extended stiffly into the air.

Wheel laughed and looked at his watch. On his note pad he wrote the time: 7:06 p.m.

Sheriff Stauffer spread out the dossier on John Mosser on his desk. He was aware of the type of thing he would find and it depressed him. But he had to refresh himself on the details. Perhaps there was something in the records that would further suggest that Johnny Mosser had something to do with Charlie Strickler's murder. He found himself hoping that he would not.

Phil began to read, slowly. He didn't want to miss anything

of significance.

John (no middle name) Mosser. Caucasian. Date of birth: January 9, 1935 or 1936. The sheriff hadn't remembered that descrepancy in the records. The poor guy didn't even know when he was born. He was either 33 or 34. It didn't matter much.

Height: 5 feet, 8 inches. Weight: 220 pounds. Hair: Light brown. Eyes: Brown. Complexion: Ruddy. General Physical Health: Good, apparent. Now that, thought Phil, doesn't mean a damned thing. What is "good health, apparent"? *Distinguishing Physical Marks: Long, diagonal scar; outside right forearm.* The sheriff remembered the circumstances of how the scar happened to be. Mosser had been in a fight at the Bright Star Café, and had been slashed with a knife. That went back as far as 1957.

Occupation: Cigarmaker, farm worker. Marital Status: Divorced. The former wife's name was not included. *Mother: Clara, nee Biehl; housewife. Father: Emanuel, basketmaker. Brothers and Sisters: Harry, born 1928.* Stauffer remembered Harry; he had been convicted of manslaughter after killing a man in a fight somewhere in Georgia. *Clara, born 1930, deceased. William, born 1932. Walter, born 1934. Martha, born 1934.* Twins certainly, thought Phil. It annoyed him now that the notation had not been made and he wrote in the word "twins." *Hettie, born 1938.*

Peculiar, the sheriff mused, Harry's the only one I remember. Wonder what happened to the others?

The record began detailing Johnny Mosser's troubles with the police in 1950, when he was 15. (Or was he 16?) He had been picked up as a chronic truant and the court-appointed social services investigator, a woman named Ida Schmehl, had been brief, but precise.

John Mosser, age 15, one of six surviving children of Emanuel and Clara Mosser, Clair Township, Young County. Neither parent literate. Showed marked unconcern when informed of son's truancy. Home conditions deplorable. Common sanitary facilities totally lacking. Boy dirty and unkempt. Question whether Mosser boy gets ade-

quate nutrition. Teachers interviewed say he "daydreams," is almost always inattentive, becomes defiant when disciplined. Several examples in school records of being punished because of fighting with other children. School principal reports punishment seems ineffective. IQ tests well below normal. Simple tests given to subject by investigator indicate he is barely literate, or unwilling to cooperate. Difficult to make clear determination on that point without more detailed study. Complained of frequent illness. Physical examination revealed general health is good (physician's report attached). Recommendations: Institutional care because of appalling home conditions; psychiatric examination.

A Children's Court judge declared Johnny a ward of the court and sent him to the children's wing of the County Home. The sheriff glanced through the long psychiatric report, looking for the conclusion of it. *Damn, don't those guys ever write these things in English?* Finally, he came to the key paragraph:

Patient is suffering from a neurosis determined to be obsessional psychasthenia: a persistent feeling, from which the patient cannot escape, of mental weakness and exhaustion. It accounts for his apparent unwillingness to learn. Indeed, in the full grip of this neurosis, he cannot learn. Extended psychiatric treatment is recommended. Prognosis: Good, in light of growing documentation of successful treatment of obsessional neuroses.

John Mosser stayed at the County Home for two years. The sheriff's records did not show how well Johnny had responded to treatment, nor the extent or quality of the treatment he received. In any event, at 17 (or 18?) he was released from the County Home; no comment on the release was in the files. It was no longer necessary for Johnny to attend public school, because he was old enough to drop out of school if his parents approved. Whether that approval was ever given or, indeed, whether anyone had even made another effort to get him back into school, also was not a matter of record.

The first criminal arrest came in 1957, when Mosser was 22. Sheriff Stauffer had answered the call himself. It was just two days before Christmas, and a telephone call told of a fight in the Bright Star Café on the north side of town. When Phil arrived on the scene, Johnny was sitting on the curb in front of the cafe, cradling his bleeding arm. The sheriff called for an ambulance on his car radio, then tried to learn what had happened. It all came back to him as he reread his own report:

Mosser was uncommunicative. Refused to speak a word. Witness inside café said that Mosser had started argument with short-order cook and came behind counter to strike cook. Cook claims he defended himself with knife, cutting Mosser on right arm. Says argument started when Mosser accused him of putting something in tomato soup to make him ill. Cook denied allegation; struck by Mosser. Charge against Mosser: Aggravated assault. Satisfied cook only defending self.

Johnny pleaded guilty and was sentenced to nine months in the county jail. The records showed that he had been paroled after seven months. Stauffer recalled that he had been a good prisoner; a hard worker in the prison laundry. The warden had told him, Phil remembered, that Johnny rarely spoke to anyone.

There was a gap of nearly five years in the records during which time Mosser stayed clear of the law. It had been in the Spring of 1960 when the sheriff's office had received a complaint from a woman who identified herself as Mrs. John Mosser. Sheriff Stauffer had gone to the hospital to talk to her. She had been brought in by a neighbor of the Mosser family who found the woman—she was only a teen-ager, really—stumbling along a dirt road, bleeding and incoherent. At the hospital she was found to have severe contusions of the head and upper torso. It was obvious she had been beaten; blood had come from several facial cuts.

Her maiden name had been Martha Lotz, the youngest of four children in the family of Ira and Hanna Lotz. They lived only a few miles from the Mosser property, and the marriage to Johnny had been "arranged" by the two sets of parents. Martha was the only daughter in the Lotz family; she had learned to explicitly obey her parents.

She told Stauffer that her husband of six months had accused her of putting "something bad" in his food and, when she denied it, he flew into a rage that led to her beating. She fled the Mosser home to look for help. A medical report in the file indicated that she had been pregnant, but, because of the beating, she had aborted.

Mosser was arrested. He was calm, almost too calm, and was uncommunicative. The sheriff's dossier had a copy of the transcript of his interrogation of Mosser.

Question: *Did you beat your wife?*
Answer: *Yes.*
Question: *Why did you do that?*
Answer: *(Prisoner shook head. No verbal answer.)*
Question: *Were you angry because she put something into your food?*
Answer: *(No reply.)*
Question: *Were you angry because she was pregnant?*
Answer: *She ain't pregnant.*
Question: *But she was, Johnny, and your beating has caused her to lose the baby. Is that why you beat her, because she was pregnant?*
Answer: *She ain't pregnant.*
Question: *Didn't she tell you about her pregnancy?*
Answer: *How can she tell me? She ain't pregnant.*
Question: *Well, then, were you angry because she put something in your food?*
Answer: *(No reply.)*
Question: *Martha says you were angry because you thought she put something in your food.*
Answer: *(No reply.)*
Question: *What did she put in your food, Johnny?*
Answer: *(Inaudible.)*
Question: *What was that?*
Answer: *Hex.*
Question: *I couldn't hear you too well, Johnny. Did you*

say hex? Did she put a hex on you?
Answer: *(No reply.)*
Question: *How did you know that she put a hex on you?*
Answer: *(No reply.)*
Question: *Aren't you sorry for what you've done?*
Answer: *(No reply.)*

Mosser remained mute. The District Attorney's office had recommended a psychiatric test, based on Johnny's past history. The court had agreed. A summary of the findings was clear: *John Mosser is suffering from paranoia, a chronic form of insanity characterized by systematic delusions. Prognosis: Poor. Recommendation: Institutionalization.*

He was admitted to the State Mental Hospital in Wernersville. That was on March 28, 1960. On May 9 he escaped after only 43 days of confinement. The records showed that the sheriff had gotten a bulletin on Mosser's escape and that his office had tried to find him in Young County, without success. They had also looked for Martha Lotz Mosser, fearing for her safety, but her parents claimed they did not know of her whereabouts; she had left home almost immediately after being discharged from the hospital.

John Mosser's file was blank, then, until Christmas Day of 1963. Deputy Sheriff Painter had spotted Mosser coming out of a diner on Liberty Street and had brought him in. Painter wrote a report: *Apprehended prisoner 1:35 p.m. No resistence. Said he has been working as a migrant farm worker. Currently working on farm of Charles Strickler, Young County. Claims he did not escape from State Hospital, Wernersville, but was released. Holding in custody pending check with hospital authorities.*

Stauffer, himself, had called the State Hospital the next day. It took them some time, he remembered now, to find the Mosser file. When they did find it, the patient had been listed as "discharged." That was standard operating procedure, the hospital superintendent said, for those patients who walked away and were not apprehended and returned to the institution within one year. As far as hospital authorities were concerned, that ended it. "Of course," the superintendent told the sheriff, "if he's in trouble again. . . ."

Mosser was not in trouble again—not then. Since that time there had been only two minor incidents to be listed in the police files. On January 1, 1967, he was arrested for public drunkenness and released after he sobered up. In 1969, just a few weeks earlier, a rural constable had arrested him as a vagrant. He had been released after several days when he volunteered to work on the Salvation Army collection truck.

Sheriff Stauffer was certain he did not have the total story of Johnny Mosser in his files. Certainly the man's unhappy life was more complex than the records indicated. The whole thing depressed the sheriff: poverty, mental illness, ignorance. *Not exactly the Four Horseman of the Apocalypse,* reflected Phil, *but scary anyway. Isn't there a better way for society to deal with a Johnny Mosser?*

The sheriff realized that his reexamination of the Mosser dossier had opened no new avenues in the current investigation. That was depressing, too. His note pad contained only one scrawled entry: "Martha Lotz Mosser. Where is she?" But even that unanswered question didn't appear to suggest a fruitful investigative lead. *Put it aside,* he told himself. *It has nothing to do with the Strickler case.*

As he started to put the varied items back into the file folder, the telephone rang. He glanced at the clock as he picked up the receiver. It was just a few minutes after 7 p.m.

"Sheriff," an excited voice said, "this is Harry Meltzer at the lock-up. That new prisoner, Mosser, is sick! He's raising hell and I think it's serious!"

"Is the coroner still in the building?"

"I don't know."

"Well, see if you can find him. I'll be right there." Stauffer sprinted out of the office and halfway down the corridor to the stairs leading to the basement, where the cells were located, taking two steps at a time. As he neared the cellblock, he could hear someone screaming.

Meltzer, the turnkey, was in one of the cells bending over Mosser. The prisoner was writhing on the floor, desperately clutching his abdomen. His screams were piercing and unending. He was bathed in sweat; his hair was matted to his head.

"What the hell happened?" the sheriff demanded.

Harry stood up. "Christ, I don't know, sheriff! I was just starting my regular seven o'clock check when he just kind of fell off his cot and started screaming, like he's doing now! And he started to roll around like that. Christ, I don't know what's wrong with him!"

"Were you able to reach Dr. Myers?"

"Yeah, he was just leaving and he'll be here in a minute."

"Has Mosser said anything?"

"Well, once he hollered: 'He's killing me! He's killing me!' But, that's all. Otherwise, he's just been screaming."

Ed Myers came on the scene. "Any idea what set this off?"

"No," said Phil, "it apparently came on suddenly."

Mosser looked up at them with wild eyes. "Help me! Help me!" he screamed. "He's killing me!" As he rolled around his wet body left marks on the cement floor.

Dr. Myers opened a medical bag he carried, quickly removed a syringe, filled it with a drug, and knelt down by the stricken man. Mosser continued to writhe and scream. "Give me a hand," the doctor shouted, and the sheriff and the turnkey got a firm hold on Mosser. The injection took only a second. A few seconds more and the prisoner was silenced.

"That stuff works fast," Meltzer commented.

Dr. Myers nodded, reaching for Mosser's pulse. "God, it's racing! I can't do anything here. Better call an ambulance, Harry."

Sheriff Stauffer let his breath exhale slowly. "What a day!" he said wearily. "Do you have any ideas at all, doc?" He pointed to the sedated prisoner.

"You saw what I saw," said the coroner.

3 SAT., NOV. 29, 1969

Only one word was needed to describe District Attorney Frederick Hamilton Barringer—distinguished. He was of only medium height, but he had a good, well-balanced frame. He was darkly handsome, although there was a little gray at his temples, just enough for the proper image. In spite of his age, which was in the mid-thirties, he was more the picture of a judge than a D.A. Indeed, several generations of Barringers (and a couple of Hamiltons) had held judgeships in Young County. It was assumed by all that Fred would, when he left the district attorney's office, vie for a position on the bench.

It was Barringer's obvious political ambition that made him so uncomfortable now. A son of his chief political patron was seated in his office, and he wasn't involved in a mere teenage peccadillo. This was a murder case!

Fred's small office was crowded. There was Mollie Sameth, his stenographer; Dr. Ed Myers, the county coroner; Sheriff Stauffer, attorney Paul Reisinger, young Will Burkholder, and Barringer himself. Only six people, but every available chair was filled. The D.A.'s spartan accommodations mirrored the conservative nature of the Pennsylvania county.

"Please have the record show," Barringer began, "that the date is Saturday, November 29, 1969, at 9 a.m., Eastern Standard Time, and that this is a formal interrogation of one Willard Burkholder, a minor. And, Mollie, please indicate on the record all those present and their correct titles."

Miss Sameth nodded as her fingers sped over the quiet keys of the stenographic machine.

"Now, Willard," Fred continued, turning to the youth, "I want you to understand what this is all about. You will be questioned about whatever knowledge you may have of the events surrounding the death of Charles Strickler on the evening of Wednesday, November 26, of this year. Your attorney, Mr. Reisinger, is present and available for consultation and advice. But—and this is *most* important—when this interrogation is concluded, it will be typed. You and your lawyer will have an opportunity to read it, and you will be asked, under oath, whether or not that transcript is correct and truthful. Then you will be asked to so swear and to sign the transcript. If you are not truthful, you will have perjured yourself. Do you understand what that means?"

"Yes, sir." The boy's reply was barely audible.

"You are going to have to speak up so that Miss Sameth can keep the record correctly."

"Yes, sir." This time the voice was firm.

"Good. Now, I'll ask Sheriff Stauffer to preside over the interrogation." Barringer waved his hand at the police officer.

"Will," Stauffer asked immediately, "do you know a man named John Mosser?"

"Yes."

"How long have you known him?"

"Oh, a couple of years, I guess," Will said lightly. "He just hangs around the bowling alley."

"And do you know a young man named Lawrence Saylor?"

"Yes."

"What is your relationship with him?"

"I don't know him too well. I've seen him every once in a while at the bowling alley. And that's about it."

The sheriff shifted his weight in his chair. "Now, Will, tell us what you and John Mosser and Lawrence Saylor did on the evening of Tuesday, November 25. That was last Tuesday."

It was plain that Will Burkholder was well prepared for the question. He launched into a recital of the Tuesday evening that was in agreement with what the sheriff already knew from Saylor and Mosser: Will drove the lumber company pick-up truck, first to Mrs. Strickler's home and then to Charlie Strickler's farmhouse; all three went into the house briefly; Strickler and Mosser argued about a book Mosser wanted; they left the Strickler home within a short time after Charlie agreed to have the book for Mosser the next evening.

"Do you know what the book was about?" Stauffer asked.

"The title?"

"If you know it."

"I don't, not really," the boy said confidently, "but I gathered it was about hex and that kind of stuff."

"Now, Will," the sheriff went on, shifting again in his chair, "after that Tuesday evening visit to Strickler's home, did you agree to return again the next night?"

"No, it wasn't that way," young Burkholder insisted. "The next day . . ."

Phil interrupted him. "Wednesday, November 26?"

"Yeah . . . well, the next day I met Johnny on the street and he asked me whether I could take him to Strickler's again. I said I would if I could get my father's car."

"Did you go anywhere with Mosser that day?"

"Go anywhere?" Will seemed puzzled. "Oh, yeah," the boy remembered. "When I met him on the street he was in front of Kolb's hardware store and, while we talked, I just sort of went inside with him. He wanted to buy something."

"Did he buy something?"

"Some rope."

"For what purpose?"

"I don't know. It was just a hunk of clothesline, I guess."

"And when you left Mosser you agreed to meet him again that evening?"

"Yeah, at about six-thirty at the bowling alley."

"Did you meet him?"

"Sure. You know I did!"

Stauffer smiled. "I know some of this may seem needlessly detailed, Will, but we have to get it all on the record. Now, had you also made arrangements to take Larry Saylor with you?"

"Not really," the boy explained. "He was just hanging around again and so we took him along."

"Why?"

"Just because he had been along the night before. There was no special reason."

"Didn't you take Saylor along because you thought you might need his . . . ah, muscle?"

"No!" There was emotion displayed for the first time.

"Okay," Phil said. "Now, on this trip, however, you went directly to Charlie Strickler's house."

"Yes." Will took a deep breath. "We went inside and almost right away Johnny and Charlie got into an argument. Johnny wanted the book and Charlie said he didn't need it. Johnny said he *did* need it because Charlie had a spell on him. And Charlie said he didn't. They swore at each other. Charlie called Johnny some kind of name and walked out of the kitchen and went into the living room." Young Burkholder paused.

"Go on," the sheriff urged him, "you're doing fine."

"Well, we all went into the living room and they kept swearing at each other. All of a sudden Johnny jumped on Charlie and knocked him down. . . ."

Stauffer cut in. "Just a moment, Will. When Johnny jumped on him was Strickler standing?"

"No, he was sitting on one of those old straight-back chairs, kind of leaning back on two legs, and when Johnny jumped him the chair was smashed to pieces."

"What happened then?"

"They were kind of wrestling on the floor," Will said, warming to the story, "and Johnny hollered for us to help him. So Larry and I jumped on him, too, and we held him down. He was strong, too. While we held him down, Johnny tied him up."

"With the rope he had purchased at Kolb's store?"

The question surprised the young man. "I guess it was."

"Are you certain it was that rope?"

"No . . ." The boy was flustered. "I . . . ah . . . I don't know where it came from. All of a sudden there it was and Johnny was tying him up."

"Did you help him with the rope?"

"No, we just kind of held him down on the floor and Johnny tied him up."

"Then what went on?"

"Well, Charlie was kicking and screaming, and swearing like crazy. Johnny asked him where the book was, and Charlie said he didn't have the damned book. They kept hollering and screaming at each other. Johnny finally got real mad and started to go through drawers and things, looking for the book."

"Did you help him look for the book?"

"Yeah, but we didn't find it."

"What did you find?"

"Hardly anything," Will insisted. "There wasn't much in the place."

"You didn't find any money?"

"Oh, Larry found a couple of bucks and he kept them."

"But you didn't find any money and keep it?"

"No, sir!" The boy looked straight at the sheriff, his face defiant.

"All right, then what?"

"Johnny was really upset about not finding the book. He went back to Charlie and took out a pocketknife and grabbed a hunk of Charlie's hair and tried to cut it off. But Charlie was hollering and moving his head so much that Johnny couldn't do it. Then he picked up a leg of that busted chair and he hit Charlie over the head with it. Charlie was real quiet and Johnny cut off some hair and put it in his pocket."

Stauffer looked intently at the young man. "Did Mosser strike Strickler more than once?"

"No, only once that I saw."

"That you saw?"

"When Johnny hit him and cut his hair off," the boy said, "I got scared. And so did Larry. We ran out of there."

"So if Mosser hit him more than once, you weren't there to see it."

"That's right."

"How long was it before Johnny came out of the house after you and Larry left?"

"Oh, a while."

"How long is that? One minute, five minutes, ten minutes?"

"Maybe five."

"Let me put it another way," said the sheriff. "Was Johnny alone in the house long enough to hit Mosser several more times and then, perhaps, set the body on fire?"

Will shrugged his shoulders. "He could have been."

"Was Charlie Strickler alive when you left the house?"

"I don't know."

"Did you think he was dead?"

"I don't know."

"Were you *afraid* that he was dead?" Stauffer stretched out every word in his delivery.

"Yes!"

"Is that why you threatened to kill Larry Saylor if he ever mentioned anything about this incident?"

"No! No!" Tears started from the boy's eyes. Phil had the uncomfortable feeling that young Burkholder was acting.

Attorney Reisinger was on his feet. "No more, Phil. I'm going to recommend that Willard answer no more questions. Frankly, I think you're getting pretty far afield."

"Far afield?" Stauffer was annoyed. "Good Lord, Paul, this is a murder investigation!"

District Attorney Barringer sighed. "I think we have gone as far as we can." His voice was tired. "You may return Will to his cell."

"Just one other point I'd like to clear up," Phil insisted, glancing from the D.A. to the Burkholder lawyer. "It will take just another moment." They nodded agreement. "I'd like to know, Will—just how well did you know John Mosser and Lawrence Saylor before this incident?"

Will made a show of brushing the tears from his eyes. "Not well. I used to see them every so often at the bowling alley."

"They weren't what you'd call friends, then?"

"No."

"How well did they know *you*?"

"Huh?"

"Did Mosser and Saylor know who you were before last Tuesday night?"

"Sure."

"Did they know that your name was Willard Burkholder?"

The boy was silent. Stauffer looked at Reisinger and raised his eyebrows.

"Answer him, Will," the lawyer ordered.

"Well," Will mumbled, "I guess not."

"And you told them you were *Clay* Burkholder?"

"Yeah." His eyes were fixed on the floor.

"Why?"

"Oh, just because." Those in the room had to strain to hear him.

"That's not an answer," the sheriff said firmly.

Will raised his head and looked directly at the sheriff, as though studying his face. He turned and stared at his attorney. Neither man spoke. Finally the young man said, "I don't want to answer that."

Stauffer looked away. "There's no point in pursuing it now," he said to no one in particular.

Barringer agreed. "Mollie, that will conclude the interrogation. I'd like a transcript as soon as possible."

Turnkey Harry Meltzer was called in to take Will back to his cell. Mollie Sameth followed, carrying her stenographic machine. She closed the door behind her.

"I thought, Fred," the sheriff explained, "that the sibling thing was not important at the moment. It may be something we'll have to get into later. But, now, well . . ." His voice trailed off.

"It's not a pretty story," Barringer commented.

"No, it's not," Stauffer said, shaking his head. "It's not pretty at all, especially since the kid's lying!"

Attorney Reisinger sputtered. "Lying? I thought he was right down the line with his answers."

"Counselor," said Phil, exhaling loud and long, "I don't believe that Mosser struck the victim with that chair leg. Oh, someone did—but not Mosser. I believe young Burkholder was telling us what he thought we wanted to hear. Also, there was a little cover-your-ass stuff there."

"Phil, really!" Reisinger was disgusted.

"Keep in mind," the sheriff said quietly, "that both Mosser and Saylor have told essentially identical stories. Will, now, has come up with a revised version. And the most important part of that revision is that Johnny hit Strickler with the chair leg."

"Mosser and Saylor probably cooked up their stories together," Reisinger suggested.

"It doesn't figure," said Phil. "Together those two don't have enough intelligence to find their way to the bathroom. No, I think Will lied about seeing Johnny hit Strickler, because he felt he had to make enough smoke to thoroughly minimize his role in the whole thing. That role, I believe, is considerable." He paused, expecting another protest from Reisinger. It didn't come. "And, honestly, Paul, I think the kid's more frightened about how his old man will react than about what we—the law—might be able to do to him."

Reisinger permitted a weak smile. "Well, old man Burkholder can be formidable."

"Amen," added the D.A.

"By the way," the sheriff went on, "the kid also lied about the money. He found some money in Strickler's house after they tied him up. And, gentlemen, he kept it! I'm afraid we're never going to be able to prove that, but I'm certain that he did."

Reisinger ran a shaking hand through his hair. He turned to the district attorney. "I hope, Fred, that you'll see your way clear to release my client into my custody. He's a minor, and I really don't think you have enough evidence—in spite of the sheriff's characterization of Will's statement—to hold him."

"Oh, I think we do," Barringer said. His strong position surprised the sheriff. "There's assault, for one. The boy admits to that. And there's the robbery thing. And perjury? Of course, he hasn't sworn to the statement yet, but. . . ."

Reisinger was stunned. "I'm left with no alternative, then, but to ask the court for a writ of habeas corpus."

"That's your prerogative," said Barringer coldly. "This is Saturday, however, and you might have trouble finding a judge to hear your petition."

The Burkholder attorney slumped in his chair. "Phil," he pleaded, "talk to this man." He pointed to the D.A.

"I wish I could, Paul," Stauffer said earnestly. "But there's one thing that stops me."

"What's that?"

"No one outside of the investigation knows that the chair leg is the possible murder weapon. We have carefully withheld that fact from the press. Yet here we have Will

Burkholder stating flatly that the chair leg *was* used to crack Strickler over the skull. If I'm right in saying that Mosser didn't strike Strickler—and I really believe that I am—then how in the hell did the kid now that the chair leg was used?"

The D.A. whistled through his teeth. Reisinger just stared at the sheriff.

"What I'm saying, gentlemen," Phil continued, "is that this case is a devil of a lot more sinister than we thought. I'm going to recommend to the district attorney, and I do it right now, that we hold young Mr. Burkholder in protective custody. If he knows about the murder weapon, then he knows who used it, and I think he might need our protection. I hope you'll go along with us, Paul."

Reisinger grimaced. "All right, I'll go along for now. But what the hell am I going to tell Otis Burkholder?"

"Anything you want," the sheriff said, grinning broadly. "Just don't mention the damned chair leg. I want to keep that knowledge close to the chest for the moment."

"You're a big help," groaned Reisinger.

"Well, at least one thing held up in this interrogation," Coroner Myers interjected, speaking for the first time.

"What's that?" asked the district attorney.

"The hair theory."

"Good Christ!" Barringer said disgustedly.

"It sure did, doc," Phil said, patting the young coroner lightly on the back. "Got any other good theories?"

At the same hour, Deputy Barry Painter arrived at the home of Willis Greiner, the principal of the Missionville High School. As he walked to the front door of the small, neat brick house, Painter recalled his own days at the high school, when Greiner was the vice principal and the tough-minded disciplinarian of the school. The kids then called him "Willie Grinder." It was an appropriate nickname. No one wanted to be called before Greiner for a serious infraction of the rules; it usually meant a heavy-handed application of Greiner's old college fraternity paddle. Barry remembered two such encounters with the vice principal and, even today, he could conjure up the sting of that heavy piece of wood. But, times had changed. Corporal punishment was no longer allowed in the schools, Greiner had been promoted to a position that required more propriety, and age had mellowed him—a bit. The deputy wondered, as he rang the doorbell, whether the changes were really improvements.

Greiner's appearance had altered little since Barry's high school days. He was still ramrod straight, with a commanding presence that was dominated by steely blue eyes. His hair had grayed, there was a slight suggestion of a paunch, but he still carried the aura of "Willie Grinder." He was a bachelor; everyone said he could never find a woman who could match up to his demanding requirements for a wife. He greeted the deputy warmly; it was plain he was pleased to see his former pupil. Greiner motioned his visitor to a chair in the austerely furnished living room. Barry remembered to sit erectly.

"Mr. Greiner," he started, "as I told you on the phone, we are anxious to get some background on Willard Burkholder. This is part of an investigation, but whatever you tell me will be in strictest confidence. I'd appreciate it if you would be frank."

The principal grimaced. "Ah, yes, Will Burkholder. A tragic waste of talent."

"How's that?" Barry flipped open his notebook.

"Willard Burkholder is a very intelligent boy. He could be an 'A' student. Instead, he is barely passing. Indeed, if I had my way in this matter, I would . . . well, I'd handle it differently."

"If you had your way?"

There was a crooked grin. "One learns over the years, Barry, that not everything can be handled as firmly as one might wish. You asked me to be frank, and I shall be. The Burkholders, as you are aware, are most prominent people in this community. Their influence—I rather like the word 'clout' in this context; it's more expressive—their clout is substantial. Will, unfortunately, takes advantage of that. He uses it to cut corners, to bully teachers, to just get by in his school work. He subverts the good family name."

"Could you be more specific?"

"Well, there have been numerous times since he has been in high school when the most appropriate treatment should have come from 'Willie Grinder.'" He laughed lightly. "Oh, I know what the students used to call me. In any event, Will has been outrageously offensive to several teachers in the last few years, at least twice using what can only be described as gutter language in the classroom. There have been numerous incidents of bullying other students. Not the name-calling, or prank-playing, of your days, Barry, but vicious acts—beating someone, destroying personal property . . . why, earlier in this session he grabbed an essay paper from a girl in his English class and burned it."

Barry halted his note taking. "Does Otis Burkholder know of this?"

"Of course," Greiner said firmly. "I am a frequent visitor to the Burkholder home." There was a pause, and another grimace. "One does not summon a Burkholder to the principal's office. *You* go to *them.*"

"And what was Otis's reaction?"

"Always shock. Our good friend Mr. Burkholder can register parental shock better than anyone I have ever met. Actually, he is rather firm with his two sons, restricting their social activities, limiting the money they have to spend. Even, at times, as I understand it, administering some physical punishment. All of this fails with Willard."

"I gather," Barry commented, "that you don't care very much for Will Burkholder."

There was a protracted pause. "I never thought I'd say this, Barry, because I've always been able to see the hidden good in people, especially in young people still being molded. But I dislike Willard Burkholder intensely! There is something inherently evil about him, and I cannot like evil."

"Does he lie?"

"What's the phrase—like a trooper?"

Barry laughed. "That's the phrase, sir."

"He lies constantly. You get a lie from Willard even when the truth would be more advantageous to him." Another pause. "Let me give you an example: last year, after a basketball game, a girl came to me with a complaint that Will had molested her—had made sexual overtures to her under the gymnasium bleachers. It was not difficult for me to believe that he might have. Indeed, when I confronted him with the accusation, he admitted it. Yet, after I investigated further, I found that the girl (for whatever reason) had trumped up the story to get him into trouble. Her charges were totally false. Still, he had said they were true. He lied, perhaps getting some perverse satisfaction from the lie."

"Was Otis informed of that?"

"Oh, yes. I recommended to Mr. Burkholder that Willard receive some psychiatric care. The recommendation was dismissed out of hand. Willard was, I am led to believe, the recipient of some stern parental discipline at that time. But it apparently had no effect on him. The girl who had falsely accused him in the first place was, several days later, actually sexually molested by young Mr. Burkholder. By this time, she was too frightened to come forward again."

"How'd *you* hear of it?"

The principal shrugged. "There are more informants in a high school than can be counted. You must know that."

"Yes, sir, I do."

"There's almost nothing that goes on at Missionville High School that I don't know about." A slight grin. "Sometimes I learn things I'd rather not hear about."

Barry laughed. "Maybe it's true that sometimes ignorance can be bliss."

Greiner surprised the deputy by joining in the laughter. "I'd say that there is a monumental truth in that cliché."

"Well ... to get back to our subject—what is Will Burkholder's relationship with his brother Clay?"

"A relationship of underlying hate," the principal said strongly. "Clay is an exemplary boy. He is not as natively intelligent as his younger brother and, as you may know, he has a continuing physical problem. But he's a hard worker, has an outgoing and positive personality, and is admired by all. Willard cannot abide Clay's popularity." Greiner changed the tone of his voice to a confidential near-whisper. "In truth, Barry, I worry at times for Clay's safety."

"You mean that Will would harm his brother?"

"He's certainly capable of it. In a quick summary, Willard is capable of almost anything. You see, when you called me and told me you were investigating him, I was not at all surprised. Such a call was inevitable."

Barry studied his notes for a brief time. "If you'll pardon the question, Mr. Greiner, is there any chance that you could be wrong about Will?"

"If you asked me a question like that about any other subject," the principal said stubbornly, "I would have modestly acknowledged that I could be wrong. But about Willard Burkholder? No, I'm not wrong, deputy. He's a dangerous young man. Of that, I am certain."

"You paint a very black picture." Barry closed the notebook.

"Black? Yes. It's the soul that's black, Barry, the soul!"

"I can't really tell you anything substantial," said Coroner Ed Myers. He was standing in the lobby of the Missionville Hospital talking to reporters Wheel and Willson. "John Mosser's condition is fairly stable, compared with the way he was when he was brought in last night. But he's still critically ill."

"With what?" asked Wheel.

"We just don't know," admitted the doctor. "He has severe abdominal pains, but we don't know what's causing them. Tests are underway now."

"Any idea when you'll have the results of the tests?" Willson wanted to know.

"Nope. Soon, I hope."

Wheel looked directly at the coroner. "Does any of this have a *hexerei* context?"

"What?"

"Witchcraft. Are you considering the possibility that this may have anything to do with the hair cut from Charlie Strickler's head?"

"Oh, hell," Dr. Myers said disgustedly, "you guys are reaching."

"We understand," Wheel persisted, "that it was *you* who came up with the theory that pow-wow was involved in Strickler's murder, based on the missing lock of hair."

"Yes, and that was based on physical evidence—the hard

physical evidence that hair *was* cut from Strickler's head. Tying that in with Strickler's known pow-wow background led to the theory. But there's no such hard physical evidence to tie to Mosser's sudden illness."

"Maybe there is. What time was it that Mosser became ill last night?"

"A few minutes after seven."

"According to my notes, the Strickler lock of hair was dug up by Deputy Painter at exactly 7:06 p.m. That's probably the identical time that Mosser became ill."

"Utter nonsense!" said Dr. Myers, waving away the speculation with his hand. "What the hell, Ernie, Strickler is dead! Are you trying to tell me that some force came forth from the grave and struck down Johnny Mosser with a mysterious illness?"

"I don't know," Wheel admitted with a smile. "I'm just fishing. But isn't that a marvelous coincidence?"

"And that's *all* it is," insisted the coroner, "a coincidence."

Nick joined the conversation. "Are you going to consult Josh Oberdick on this matter?"

"Why should I?"

"Because he's a doctor *and* an authority on pow-wow."

"Look," said Dr. Myers, "there will be a perfectly logical explanation for Mosser's illness once the medical tests are completed. There are plenty of competent doctors here on staff. We don't need an authority on pow-wow and hex and all that folderol."

"You didn't think it was folderol when you found that hair was missing from Charlie Strickler's head." Wheel was challenging him.

The coroner smiled. "If you guys want to keep this pow-wow angle alive, why in the devil don't *you* ask Dr. Oberdick? But for my money, most of that stuff is crap. I'm sorry—" the tone was genuinely apologetic—"but I've got a lot of work to do. It's been fun chatting with you." As he walked away he called back over his shoulder, "Yeah, go see old Josh. He's always good for a story."

Dr. Oberdick, lounging on his terrace in the warming sun

of a November afternoon, was smiling. "From what you've told me," he said to Ernie and Nick, "the Charlie Strickler case is turning into a real circus. It's just like that bastard Strickler. He was trouble when he was alive and he's driving everyone crazy now that he's dead."

"That's about the size of it," said Wheel. "When I first came to see you, Josh, we had a long conversation...."

"I remember it well. A very pleasant experience."

"... and you said something about transference of power, but we never developed it. It popped into my head again when I realized that the digging up of Strickler's hair and the sudden illness of Mosser coincide exactly in time."

"Transference of power is, I'll admit, a term that I've coined myself. It has to do with the interaction of events, not unlike the digging up of Strickler's hair and Mosser's sudden illness."

"Then it *is* possible," said Nick, "that the two events were related in some way?"

"Oh, I don't want to be that dogmatic," Josh said, showing a wry smile. "But perhaps some examples of stories I've heard over the years might give you a better idea of what I had in mind when I called it transference of power. Up in Clinton County, there was this farm lady who had a bewitched cow — a cow that couldn't let down its milk even though the udder was filled. On the advice of a pow-wow doctor, the poor animal was killed and what they called the *inwards* were burned. The next day a medical doctor nearby was called by the family of a very ill woman, who was dying. On a post mortem examination, it was found that her intestines were burned. She, then, was the person who had bewitched the cow."

"Sounds brutal," said Wheel. "Do you believe it?"

"I was never able to verify it, but I found it a fascinating story. I recall another tale of this type, also unverified. This was supposed to have happened on a farm somewhere along the Schuylkill River in Berks County. There was a farmer who was bothered every night by a cat yowling in a tree outside his bedroom window. He tried everything he could think of to get rid of the cat, including shooting at it. But, nothing seemed to work. He went to a pow-wow doctor, finally, who told him that the cat was a witch, sent by another witch to torment him. The only way to end the torment, he was advised, was to shoot the cat with a silver bullet. So the farmer melted down two silver buttons, fashioned a bullet, and that night he knocked off the cat. The next morning a neighboring farmer was found dead, shot with a silver bullet. The offending witch, no doubt."

Everyone laughed. "And I always thought," said Willson, "that silver bullets were the exclusive property of the Lone Ranger!"

"More like the lone pow-wow doctor," added Wheel. Again, laughter.

Josh became sober-faced. "To get to the matter at hand, however. Was there a connection between the hair being dug up and Johnny's sudden illness? I don't really know. But I don't believe that you can flatly say that it did *not* have a connection. And if it did, wouldn't that make an interesting story?"

"Our sentiments exactly," said Wheel, grinning broadly.

"We have a damned mess!"

Phil Stauffer was slumped in a chair in the office of District Attorney Barringer, reviewing the developments in the Strickler case. "We know this much: Mosser, Saylor and Will Burkholder went to Strickler's home last Wednesday night, binding him hand and foot after a struggle. Mosser and Saylor say it was mostly a wrestling match, and that Charlie was not struck with anything. The Burkholder boy says Mosser hit Strickler — only once that he saw — with the leg of a broken chair."

"Right," said the D.A.

"We know, from all parties involved," the sheriff continued, "that Mosser cut some hair from Strickler's head, using a pocketknife. We know, by Mosser's admission, that he took the hair and buried it on his property at the roots of a tree — a crabapple, as we know now. This was done, says Mosser, to break a spell he believed Strickler had on him. By the way, Barry has sent the hair to the state police lab to make certain it matches the hair we took from Strickler's corpse."

"Okay," said Barringer, "I'm with you up to that point."

"Now, aside from the who-struck-Charlie discrepancy, we have a couple of others. First, both Mosser and Saylor say that Strickler was alive and kicking, literally, when they left the house. Will Burkholder says that he's not sure, because he left the house some minutes before Mosser did. But he has said that Mosser had enough time alone with Strickler to hit him again, and time even to set the body on fire. The other two deny knowing anything about the fire. So none of the three really knows anything about the fire first-hand, if we are to believe them."

The district attorney shook his head. "Go on."

"We know, too, that Saylor said that young Burkholder took some money from the house, as little as five dollars. Will says it was Saylor who took the money. Basically, I guess, it's a small point, except that someone is not telling the truth. If we take into consideration Willis Greiner's evaluation of Will, then we must brand him as a consummate liar, and assume that it's Saylor who's telling the truth on that point."

Stauffer got to his feet and began to pace. "As to the medical evidence, Dr. Myers says death was caused by a blow, or blows, to the head. Powerful blows. He *was* struck more than once. The body was set afire *before* Strickler died from the injuries caused by the blows."

The D.A. interrupted. "There's one thing about the fire I've been meaning to ask. What prevented the whole damned place from burning down after the fire was set?"

"It appears to me," answered the sheriff, "that there had been only a few drops of coal-oil in the lamp found beside the body, and that there simply wasn't enough fuel in the lamp to get a good fire going. Also, the haphazard way in which the excelsior packing from an old sofa was strewn over the body would indicate that the act was done hurriedly."

"So hurriedly that it might have been done by Mosser during the few minutes he could have been alone with Strickler?"

"That's certainly possible," admitted Stauffer.

"So, where do we stand?"

Phil paused for a moment. "Where we stand is that we have

another major discrepancy. The coroner tells us that death came between 10 p.m. and 12 midnight. Yet everything we know about the doings of Mosser, Saylor and Burkholder indicates that they were well away from the Strickler house long before ten o'clock. As a matter of fact, Saylor says it wasn't even nine o'clock when they returned to Missionville. And his authority for that is the venerable courthouse clock."

"Of course," said Barringer, "death might have occurred *after* ten o'clock as a result of an injury Strickler sustained *before* eight o'clock. The time element doesn't necessarily eliminate Mosser as our murderer."

"True. For the moment, then, we have this situation: if we believe Will Burkholder, we have, at the very least, a charge of attempted murder against John Mosser. The kids, then, might be charged as accessories. Against all three, it seems to me, we have valid assault charges. And either Saylor or Burkholder might be charged with robbery, depending on who you believe."

"What are you recommending?"

"I'd like to see the district attorney's office," the sheriff said strongly, "do everything possible to keep those three under our thumbs for right now. Having them roaming around free just might muddy up the waters. So, Fred, in addition to the assault and robbery charges, I'm asking that you file first degree murder charges against all three!"

"Isn't that a bit much?" Barringer's face was creased with concern. "Otis Burkholder is going to. . . ."

There was a knock on the office door.

"Come in," called the D.A.

Deputy Painter entered. "I have the lab reports, Phil."

"Let's have them."

Barry looked at the clipboard he was carrying. "First, all the fingerprints found on the scene have been identified. The four sets we sent to the lab match the fingerprints of Strickler, Mosser, the Saylor kid and Will Burkholder."

"Okay, what else?"

"Second, the rope used to bind Strickler came off that reel at Kolb's Hardware."

"So that item falls into place," commented Stauffer.

"Anything more?"

"Yeah," answered Barry, "there are *no* fingerprints on the chair leg. The blood on it matches Strickler's blood. It was a medium rare type—O-RH negative. But, there are no prints on it. None!"

"What the hell does that mean?" Barringer asked.

"It means, at the risk of oversimplifying it," Phil explained, "that Johnny Mosser did *not* kill Charlie Strickler. It means, too, that Will Burkholder lied when he said that Mosser struck Strickler with the chair leg. It would have made no sense at all for Mosser to clean his prints off the chair leg and leave them everywhere else in the house. So Johnny did not handle the murder weapon." Stauffer took a deep, weary breath. "It means, Mr. D.A., that a person or persons unknown probably killed old Charlie *after* our infamous trio left the premises. It means, also, that we're going to have trouble keeping our pigeons behind bars very much longer. And, finally, it means that we're moving back to square one—or maybe just back to square two."

The district attorney groaned. "Je-sus Christ!" He forced a grin. "It guess it means, too, that all that stuff about a pow-wow killing is just so much bullshit!"

"Maybe," sighed Phil, "only maybe."

"The diagnosis," Dr. Ed Myers was saying to the sheriff, "is internal bleeding—severe internal bleeding."

"Like bleeding ulcers?" asked Stauffer.

"No, nothing like that. This is a lot more massive. There's widespread hemorrhaging in the intestinal tract. We don't know what's causing it and we haven't been able to arrest it satisfactorily."

"And the prognosis?"

"Guarded, to use the cop-out phrase. Mosser has had continual transfusions, but if we can't stop the bleeding somehow, well. . . ." Myers shrugged his shoulders.

The two men were standing in the corner of Johnny Mosser's hospital room. In the bed, Johnny looked like a hulking rag-doll, limp and lifeless. His usual ruddy color had disappeared. His eyes were closed. His breathing was shallow.

"May I talk to him?" the sheriff asked.

"Only briefly, Phil."

Stauffer went to the bed and bent over the ill man. "Johnny, can you hear me?"

"Yeah." The voice was very weak.

"The doctors tell me they're going to fix you up." Phil tried for a cheerful tone.

Mosser opened his eyes and looked up at the police officer. "Did you dig it up?" he asked softly.

"What?"

"Did you dig up Charlie's hair?" Both men at the bedside had to strain to hear him.

Stauffer looked to the coroner for guidance and Dr. Myers nodded. "Yes, Johnny, we did," said the sheriff. "We had to verify your story."

Mosser's eyes opened wide in fright. "Put it back!" He was trying to shout, but his weakness prevented it. "Put it back," he repeated, "or Charlie will kill me!" The eyes closed again and the only sound was his sporadic breathing.

Phil straightened up. "What do you make of that?"

Dr. Myers signaled him to leave the room and the two men went out into the corridor.

"I know you're going to think that I've lost my senses," said the coroner, "but could you bury the hair again?"

"Ed, do you *believe* that shit?"

"It's not important whether I believe it or not. But what harm is it going to cause by putting it back where you found it?"

"I can't. The hair is still at the lab in Harrisburg," the sheriff explained, "being matched with the sample we took off his head." Then, defensively, "We had to verify the match, you know."

"I know," said Dr. Myers, "and I feel as stupid as you do about this. But we can't seem to stop the hemorrhaging. If we don't stop it soon, Mosser is going to die."

He took Stauffer by the arm. "What harm, Phil, what harm?"

Anger—gut-wrenching and uncompromising anger—was

not an alien emotion with the sheriff. But he had long since learned to control it under most circumstances. Now, however, he was angry. It wasn't because of the actions of other persons, but because of a circumstance that, to him, violated all common sense. Stauffer had driven the fifty-seven miles from Missionville to Harrisburg to regain possession of a clump of human hair. Crime lab technicians had completed their comparison tests by the time he had arrived there and told him that the hair dug out of the ground from beneath roots of the crabapple tree had, indeed, come from the head of the late Charles Strickler.

"I drove up here," Phil lamely told the lab personnel, "because I need the material (he meant "hair," but could not bring himself to say it) in my investigation. There's been a new development."

The lie, weak as it was, began the anger. At first, the idea of re-burying the hair had only embarrassed him; that was the reason Deputy Painter was not assigned to make the trip to Harrisburg. But now, heading back from the state capitol, the anger grew. He found himself driving too fast and too erratically as he headed for the Mosser farm. *What the hell am I doing, allowing myself to be used this way? That fucking coroner and his goddamned theories!*

Stauffer tried to force his mind to concentrate on the mechanics of driving. He watched carefully the patterns his headlights made on the two-lane blacktop country road, and he was extraordinarily conscious of lowering his high beams when another car approached him. But when he encountered a slower moving vehicle in front of him, he suddenly flicked on the siren switch, as though trying to blow the other car away. "You bastard, move it!" he said aloud, and then swept by the car in front of him, still sounding the siren. He couldn't remember when he had ever done that before. His anger was very real.

By the time the sheriff had reached the turn-off onto the dirt road leading to the Mosser property, he had conjured up another reason for anger. It had occurred to him that he didn't know the location of the crabapple tree where the hair had been buried. *Stupid! Why not just tell Mosser that the hair has been reburied? The whole damned thing is just something in his simple mind anyway!* But Phil kept driving and, within a few minutes, he was at the Mosser home.

There was no moon and the old farm house was totally dark. There was nothing to indicate that anyone was there. Taking a flashlight from the glove compartment, the sheriff made his way to the door of the house and banged on it hard. Echoes were set up by the pounding and, from inside the house, a voice called, "Who the hell's there?"

"The sheriff," Phil called.

Within a few seconds the door was opened. In the beam of light stood Emanuel Mosser, dressed only in a set of dirty long underwear.

"I need your help, Emanuel," Stauffer said, trying to be calm and reasoned, "and I really regret having wakened you."

The old man ran a bony hand over his eyes and mumbled, "Okay."

"Do you remember where the tree is where Deputy Painter was digging the other night?"

"Ower there." Emanuel pointed into the darkness.

"Would you mind showing me?"

Unperturbed by his bare feet and his lack of outer clothing, the elder Mosser stepped out on to the porch and led the way across the weed-choked front yard to a smallish tree almost leaning on the fence. Or was the rickety fence leaning on the tree? "Right here."

Stauffer swung his flashlight beam to the ground. He could see where the earth had been freshly dug. "Hold this, please," he said to the old man, handing him the flashlight. Dropping to his knees, he dug into the earth with his hands. Almost surreptitiously, he slipped the envelope containing Strickler's hair into the depression he had made. He scooped loose earth over the envelope and stood up, brushing his hands together to remove the dirt.

"Thanks a lot," the sheriff said to Emanuel. "And I apologize again for waking you up."

"Okay." He returned the flashlight to Stauffer, turned and moved toward the house. He asked no questions about the strange actions and Phil was grateful for that. But he couldn't understand the old man's apparent lack of interest in the episode. Stauffer let the beam of light guide the father of Johnny Mosser to the door. He watched as Emanuel opened the door and went inside. Sad old man, he thought. The sheriff slipped into the driver's seat of the squad car and headed back toward Missionville.

Once on the blacktop county road again, Stauffer started to look for a lighted phone booth along the road. Within a few minutes he saw one, wheeled the car to a quick stop beside it, and dialed the hospital number. "Dr. Edward Myers, please," he said when the operator answered. There was only a short wait.

"Dr. Myers," a voice said.

"Ed, this is Phil. I've done it."

"I know."

"What the hell do you mean?" Stauffer demanded, his anger rising again.

"I mean, I know," the doctor said firmly. "You buried the hair about ten minutes ago, right?"

"Yeah, that's right." Phil was perplexed. "But, how did. . . ."

"That was when we finally got Johnny's hemorrhaging under control!"

4 SUN., NOV. 30, 1969

*Lead, kindly Light, amid th' encircling gloom,
Lead Thou me on, lead Thou me on!
The night is dark, and I am far from home,
Lead Thou me on, lead Thou me on!*

The congregation of the Missionville Evangelical United Brethren Church sang the old hymn with fervor. Young County Sheriff Philip Stauffer was among them. Phil would have made light of any suggestion that he was a Bible-thumping Christian, yet every Sunday morning—whenever his duty allowed—he led his family to the historic old church. It was more than just a family ritual, more than something he did to project a good image in the community. Stauffer found that the church filled a need for him after a week of dealing constantly with the cruel realities of the world.

On this Sunday morning after Thanksgiving, the need seemed almost desperate. He had done something the night before that had made him ashamed. The Strickler hair-burying episode had shaken him; the suggestion that Johnny Mosser's recovery was somehow tied in with that clump of hair appalled him. He had slept poorly during the night, running over in his mind the strange details of the Strickler case, and always ending by seeing himself on his knees, scooping dirt over an envelope filled with human hair.

His wife Nancy had not been told of the incident. It was something he could not share with her. Phil had sworn Coroner Myers to secrecy on the matter and indeed, the doctor himself didn't want to admit that perhaps the hair and John Mosser's illness were related.

Now Stauffer stood with Nancy and his three teenage

children in church and sang the hymn:

> *I lov'd to choose and see my path,*
> *But now, but now, lead Thou me on.*

Phil looked over at Nancy and smiled. *What a woman!* He glanced at Debra, 16 years old and the image of her beautiful mother. Next to her was Kimberly, 15 and a marvelously independent soul. And Phil Jr., only 13, but already firmly convinced that he could solve the ills of the world in a political career. *I'm a lucky man,* he thought, and sang:

> *Thy pow'r hath blest me,*
> *Sure it still will lead me on*
> *O'er moor and fen, o'er crag and torrent,*
> *Till the night, the night is gone.*

Stauffer, reassured by the words of the hymn, felt his spiritual strength returning in these familiar and safe surroundings. The hymn ended and the congregation was seated. Phil smiled as he watched the Reverend Nelson Fenstermacher, pastor of the church for the past 41 years, take his place in the pulpit. Fenstermacher's presence also seemed reassuring to the sheriff. The minister carefully arranged several pages of notes in front of him, raised his head, and looked out across the worshippers.

"Those of you who know me well," he began, "know that I might be considered something of a fanatic in the preparation of my Sunday sermons. They know that my Thursday afternoons and evenings are given over entirely to that purpose. I have always believed that those who come here on a Sunday should have the best of me and, with the Lord's help, I strive to make my messages meaningful and worthwhile. This past Thursday, although it was Thanksgiving Day, was no different. After a lovely dinner with my family, I again retreated with my Lord to prepare for this morning. And prepare I did. But what I prepared then, I have now discarded. You will accept my apologies, I hope, for what I am about to say to you has the benefit of preparation time extending only from my breakfast this morning."

Reverend Fenstermacher paused. Again his eyes swept the congregation.

"It was at breakfast," the pastor continued, "that I read an article in this morning's edition of the *Missionville Star*. Reading the newspaper at meal time is not a habit of which my dear wife approves . . ."

A titter ran through the audience.

". . . but, sometimes, it has its merits. This article—and some of you may have read it—carried the by-line of one Ernest Wheel, and reported on an interview with Young County resident Mrs. Lizzie Zearfoss, a woman of 98 years. Mrs. Zearfoss is described as being a pow-wow doctor, a practice that one would hope would not have survived into 1969, nearly two thousand years after the birth of Jesus Christ. But apparently, it *has* survived. And because it has, and commands our attention again in the public press, I have elected to speak about it this morning."

Phil groaned lightly. Nancy Stauffer, sensing her husband's discomfort, reached over and squeezed his hand.

"I have heard it said," the minister went on, "that pow-wowing is part of the Pennsylvania Dutch heritage in this area. But to me, heritage implies something worth keeping; something to cherish and preserve. If you read the article you will find that Mrs. Zearfoss . . . and, apparently, other pow-wow practitioners, as well . . . invoke the Trinity in their ritual incantations." He looked hard at his congregation. "Perhaps I should say: In their *evil* incantations. Because that's what they are!"

The sheriff shifted uncomfortably in the pew.

"I have lived all of my life in this beautiful area, and the fact that there is something called *hexerei* is not new to me. Indeed, I have run into supposedly intelligent scholars who have argued that *hexerei* (and that word means "witchcraft," you know) is merely a lay extension of what I, as an ordained minister, do day in and day out. Pow-wowing, they would have us believe, is an art of healing by the recital of a portion of the Holy Scriptures. And somehow, they see in pow-wowing an alliance of the so-called pow-wow doctor and the minister. After all, they say, doesn't the minister use the Scriptures in prayng for the sick, the troubled, and the needy?"

Fenstermacher shifted his notes on the lectern. "These learned men—and thank God they are not in a position of leadership in our church—try, in their convoluted thinking, to equate the holy miracles performed by Christ in his brief lifetime with the work of the pow-wow practitioners. That kind of argument, even though wrapped in a scholarly mantle, is a subversion of Christ's glorious life. A subversion, I tell you!" There was anger in his words.

The pastor held the front page of the newspaper above his head. "In reading this article you will find that Mrs. Zearfoss's use of seemingly Biblical incantations in advising a poor, deluded man had an almost immediate result. And that result, my friends, was MURDER!" He let the newspaper drop to the floor, discarding it as something unclean.

"If we truly love God, and honor Him," Reverend Fenstermacher continued, moderating his tone, "we cannot, at the same time, believe in the satanic mumbo-jumbo that accompanies pow-wowing. Love of God and belief in pow-wow, my friends, are as different as the day is from the night. One is bright and clean; the other is dark and foreboding. One speaks of life and happiness; the other tells of death and despair."

Phil dropped his head into his hands; sweat came to his brow.

"Are you ill?" Nancy whispered.

"Yes."

"One cannot be a Christian . . ." the minister said slowly. He repeated, raising his voice for emphasis, "One cannot be a Christian and also profess to believe in what these charlatans. . . ."

The words seemed to be roaring at Phil through a giant echo chamber as the sheriff suddenly rose from his seat and walked hurriedly down the aisle. Nancy, shocked, followed him. The three Stauffer children stayed in their seats, unsure of what to do.

Outside the church, Phil stopped on the steps and drew deep breaths. Nancy, coming to his side, was nearly in tears. "Phil, what is it?"

"Nothing, nothing. I just don't feel well." He shook his head. "It was pretty hot in there."

"Phil, you know it wasn't hot in the church." She pleaded, "Tell me what it is!"

He looked into her face and took her gently by the arms. "Nance," he said, trying to reassure her, "I'm just overtired, I guess. It's been a tough week." He forced a smile. "Listen, I think I'll feel better if I take a walk in the fresh air. You wait for the kids and drive them home."

Without waiting for a protest from his wife, the sheriff went down the steps of the church and started off down the street, walking briskly.

As he walked, he could still hear the echo of the pastor's words: *"One cannot be a Christian . . ."*

"I absolutely will not wake him to come to the phone!" Nancy was speaking quietly, but there was determination in her voice.

"But, Mrs. Stauffer," Deputy Painter said, "this is serious. Sometime late this morning, there was a fire out at Miller's Grove. Lizzie Zearfoss was burned to death!"

Barry's news made Nancy even more determined to shield her husband. "Deputy," she said firmly, "the sheriff is ill; he became ill in church today. Just about fifteen minutes ago he finally fell asleep. I'm not going to wake him now."

"Gosh, Mrs. Stauffer, it's Lizzie Zearfoss . . ."

"What do you expect Phil to do," the wife snapped, "bring her back to life?"

Her outburst silenced the deputy on the other end of the line.

Nancy's tone turned apologetic. "I'm sorry, Barry, but Phil is really ill and I'm worried about him. I'm sure you can handle the preliminaries and just as soon as he wakes up, I'll tell him about it. You understand, don't you?"

"Oh, sure, I understand. I'll handle things here."

"That's marvelous," Nancy said sweetly. "And Barry?"

"Yeah."

"Thank you very much."

As Painter hung up the phone, Coroner Ed Myers came into the room. "Phil in?"

"Nope, he's sick." Barry came to his feet. "I'm in charge right now."

"Sick? Anything serious?"

"I don't think so. He got sick in church this morning. He's asleep right now and Nancy . . . ah, Mrs. Stauffer . . . doesn't want to disturb him." He repeated, "I'm in charge."

"Okay," the coroner acknowledged, dropping into a chair. "I have just had the dubious pleasure of examining the badly burned body of a human female. What do you want to know?"

Deputy Painter sat down at his desk, got out a note pad, and rather ceremoniously picked up a ball-point pen. "Can we be absolutely sure that the body is that of Lizzie Zearfoss?"

"Absolutely is tough," answered Dr. Myers. "The fire consumed a good deal of the body. Certainly no one would be able to make a visual identification. I do know this. The body was found in Lizzie's house, it's female, and there is advanced age."

"Any chance of a dental identification?"

"None. There was not a tooth in the head."

"Any idea of the cause of death?"

"Without question," the coroner said, "death was caused by asphyxiation. She was dead before the flames got to her. Death was pretty quick, I would imagine. As near as I can determine she was suffering from an advanced case of emphysema, which simply made it easier for her to be quickly asphyxiated."

"She couldn't have died any other way?"

"You mean hit on the head, shot, strangled, and like that?"

The deputy sheriff nodded.

"No chance. This was an easy one, albeit a bit messy in examination. Asphyxiation."

"Anything else?"

"Nope, that's it."

Barry sighed. "Ed, you know about this stuff. Do you think that this had anything to do with pow-wow?"

"Hell no!"

"Just like that?"

"Just like that!" The coroner got to his feet and left the office.

The deputy stared after him. Now, what the devil was all that about?

Ernie Wheel walked into the coffee shop at the Missionville Inn and joined Nick Willson at the counter.

Nick grinned at him. "Do you realize that you've become famous in this here town?"

"You talking about the Fenstermacher sermon?"

"Yeah, how'd you hear about that?"

"I've got contacts, too," said Ernie. "As a matter of fact, I received three different calls from people in the congregation after the service. I talked to the pastor—a very nice old gentleman. And my friend, it's all a part of the a.m.'s lead I just filed on the Lizzie Zearfoss death."

"I received a call, too, this morning about the Zearfoss article," said Willson. "From Josh Oberdick."

"Really? What'd he want?

"Allegedly—and please notice that word—*allegedly* he was calling to give his congratulations on the story. He said he tried to reach you here at the Inn, without success, so he called me instead."

"Allegedly? You have doubts about his sincerity?"

"I'm not sure," Nick admitted. "He was properly complimentary about the article, but I had the feeling I was being pumped."

"What makes you think that?"

"Well, he asked me, in numerous ways, about how much old Lizzie told us. At first, I put it down as Oberdick's natural interest in the subject. But since the old lady's sudden death, I don't know."

"You know what?"

"What?"

"This case," said Wheel, "is beginning to get to us. I really think we're reaching too hard to tie everything into this pow-wow stuff. You saw that old run-down house of Lizzie's—one spark from her cook stove would have set it off."

Nick smiled. "Maybe you're right."

"Then again, maybe I'm not."

"Huh?"

"Did you hear about the sheriff's performance at Fenstermacher's church this morning?"

"No."

"One of my informants," Ernie said, "told me that Phil Stauffer got up and left the church right in the middle of the sermon. Right in the middle of the old pastor's tirade against pow-wowing."

"What does that mean?"

"I don't know." Ernie laughed. "I suspect it's about as significant as your information about Josh Oberdick."

Willson joined in the laughter. "We are reaching, aren't we?"

"Yep, and I, for one, am going to stop for the day. Got any plans for dinner?"

"None. But I have an idea. The dining room here at the Inn isn't bad and, on the weekends, there's this Pennsylvania Dutch comic, calls himself Doctor Fuszganger, who's pretty funny."

"Fuszganger?"

"Yeah. It's a Pennsylvania Dutch word that translates into something like walker, or hiker, or explorer."

"Well, let's do it," Ernie said enthusiastically. "I could use some laughs."

"Vell, goot ewening, ladies undt people. I'm happy to see so many pretty girls here tonight. I hadt a lot of girls in my time. I vent onct vith a school teacher. She hadt a lot of class, but no principle."

Laughter rolled across the Missionville Inn dining room. Doctor Fuszganger represented one of the last vestiges of the old burlesque comics—baggy pants, ill-fitting multicolored coat, a derby hat, and a goatee. His forte was stories in the broad Pennsylvania Dutch accent, and he was a pro.

"Is he for real?" Wheel whispered to Willson.

"Oh, yeah. He's an honest-to-God Pennsylvania Dutchman, and he used to work the Orpheum circuit. If you like rural corn. . . ."

"I *love* it."

"Lookin' at me," Doctor Fuszganger continued, "you'd neffer sink dat I vas married already three times. But I vas. Tvice in Allentown, undt onct legitimately. N' I'll neffer forget ven ve got married the first time. Together ve looked like a brandt new house—she vas painted, and I vas plastered. . . . At the ceremony, I asked the preacher how much I owed him. N' he saidt, 'Ach, chust pay me vot ya sink she's vorth.' So, I gave him a quarter. . . . But, ya know, he vas a nice fella. After she lifted her weil, he gave me fifteen cents change. N' ven ya get married, ya know, you get a mother-in-law. Now, lots of fellas haf trupple viss mothers-in-law. But not me. My mother-in-law likes me werry much. I remember ven I got drafted, n' vent off to var, my mother-in-law vas the last vun to see me off. I can still see her, standin' on the dock, lookin' up at me. 'Hiram,' she saidt—that's my name, Hiram—'Hiram,' she saidt, 'I bought a gold star, so don't disappoint me!' "

Ernie and Nick joined in the laughter.

"He's marvelous," said Wheel. "They don't make comics like that any more."

"No, they don't." Nick grinned.

"What's this Fuszganger's real name?" asked Wheel.

"Earle Gensemer. He has a little radio show on one of the local stations—a 250-watter. But this kind of date is his biggest gig now."

"He's a very funny guy," said Ernie. "I'd like to meet him."

"Okay, we'll have him over to the table when he's finished."

Doctor Fuszganger was rolling now, picking up his pace. "Speakin' of marriage, my neighbor, oldt Ben Greisemer—he's 82 now—chust the other day decided to gedt married. He hadt a young lady chust about 20 years oldt. N' he godt his license n' ewerysing. He vas ready to go off viss the whole shootin' match. Undt then the preacher took him aside n' saidt, 'Ben, I'd like to talk to ya first. I vant ya to figure this thing oudt right. Now, you're 82 years oldt, n' this young lady is only 20. You gott to sink of the mortality rate here, 'n how it's gonna vork oudt.' Oldt Ben scratched his hedt avhile n' saidt, 'Vell, reverend, I guess you're right. I chust haff to take my chances—if she dies, she dies!'"

After he had finished his routine, Doctor Fuszganger took his bows, to much laughter and applause. The comic saw Nick Willson gesturing to him, and walked toward the two reporters.

"Earle, I'd like you to meet a reporter friend of mine," Nick said. "Ernest Wheel. Ernie, this is Earle Gensemer."

Wheel warmly pumped the comic's hand. "Fine job," he said. "I really enjoyed the routine."

Gensemer smiled broadly. "Vell, idt's oldt, but idt still vorks. I saw Nick here wavin' undt, since I'm a choiner, I came on ower onct."

Ernie was puzzled. "A joiner?"

"Yah, ewery time somebody looks like they're gonna buy a drink, I choin 'em."

As the three men sat down, Nick volunteered that Ernie was in town to cover the Charlie Strickler murder case.

"Yah," said Gensemer, "I've been readin' your stories. Ya know, this iss a great town for newsmen 'cause there are so many blabbers—gossips. I'm one myself, a real *wonnernaus.*"

Wheel grinned. "Should I ask what that is?"

"Idt's simple," said the comic. "Idt's a vonder nose, an inquisitive person. The other day down at market, I listened in on two ladies talkin'. Vun sez, 'Hello, Mary, I ain't seen ya fer such a long time. How are ya?' N' Mary sez, 'Ach, Rachel, I ain't so goot. N' my daughter, Ethel, she ain't so goot neither. She's been laidt up in bedt vith arthuritis fer three weeks.' N' Rachel sez, 'Ach, *himmel,* arthuritis?' N' Mary sez, 'Yah, fer three weeks she's been laidt up vith arthuritis. Undt that can be badt.' N' Rachel sez, 'Ya know that can be badt. I know them Itis boys, n' that Arthur iss the vorst one of the whole bunch!'"

They all roared with laughter, and the other diners in the

restaurant turned to see what was going on. When they saw Doctor Fuszganger at the table, they laughed, too, even though they hadn't heard the joke. He had an infectious quality about him. While Gensemer had been telling the story, a waitress had placed a drink in front of him. No one had really ordered it; Gensemer's drinking habits, however, were well known to the staff.

"Ya know, Ernie," the comic went on, "I got a friendt who's a dentist. N' the other day a lady came in who hadt trupple vith a toothache. Oh, this vas hurtin' her somesing vunderful. Doc sez, 'Vhat's wrong?' N' she sez, 'Oh, I vant a tooth pulled, but I'm so nervous, so scared. Ya know,' she sez, 'I believe I'd chust as soon haff a baby.' 'Vell, make up your mindt,' sez Doc, 'so's I can adchust the chair.'"

Again, raucous laughter.

"Do you ever run out of material, Earle?" Wheel asked.

"Neffer! Somehow, the Pennsylvania Dutch provide a steady source of stories. N', of course, I can switch lots of chokes chust usin' the accent."

"Do you have any jokes about pow-wowing?"

"Nope."

"Why not?"

The comic was sober-faced for the first time. "Vell, *hexerei* chust ain't funny."

"What you're saying, then, is that it was murder."

Deputy Painter had just received a report from the Pennsylvania State Police arson squad about the fire at the home of Lizzie Zearfoss.

"That's about the size of it." State Police Sergeant Alvin Hummer leaned back in the chair in front of Barry's desk. "There's no doubt that the place was torched. Crudely, too. Gasoline was poured around the base of one side of the building—the north side, to be specific. That old place went up like tinder. It was just about burned out when the first fire company got there. There was nothing they could do."

"A professional job?"

"No way," Sergeant Hummer said confidently. "We found

an empty five-gallon can just about twenty yards from the building. Someone had discarded it there. There was no apparent effort to hide the arson. They just poured out the gasoline and lit a match, I'd guess. Very basic."

"Sounds to me," said Barry, "like the old lady didn't have a chance."

"Probably not. She might have been asleep when the fire started. The body was found well within the house, indicating that she made no effort to get to the door."

"Now what?" asked the deputy.

"I've sent the can to the lab," said Hummer, "and we might get lucky with some prints. If we don't, then there might be a chance that someone saw the arsonist in the area. A stranger out there would stand out."

"Yeah, maybe," Barry said, "but it's pretty remote."

"Let's hope the lab turns up something on the can. If they don't, well. . . ."

"May I ask a favor of you?"

"Certainly."

"Let's keep this murder probability to ourselves," the deputy requested, "until I have an opportunity to talk to the sheriff. I don't imagine it will hurt anything if we just keep quiet about it until tomorrow."

"No sweat," Hummer assured him. "We'll be in touch." He rose to leave. "Oh, by the way, one of the local firemen out there told me that the old lady was a pow-wow doctor. Could that mean anything?"

"That," said Barry firmly, "is just so much bullshit!"

"Just thought I'd mention it." The state policeman grinned. "That stuff seems to be in vogue around here."

Dottie Kissinger was uneasy as she rode the elevator to Joshua Oberdick's apartment. She hadn't been there for nearly a year, but she always turned to the old man when she was in trouble. Dottie felt guilty about that.

Dr. Oberdick had delivered her baby, fourteen years earlier. When she became pregnant, Noah Saylor wouldn't permit her to consult a physician. "My mother had me without a doctor," he told her, "and you don't need one either." It was only after the panic of the first labor pains that she picked Oberdick's name out of the phone book. That was her first crisis association with him, but not the last.

When Noah, his troubled mind unable to accept the responsibility of a family, deserted her and the baby, Oberdick again came to Dottie's aid with money and advice. When her second marriage to Sam Kissinger began to dissolve in a torrent of gin, she had turned once more to the old doctor. In her entire unhappy life, Josh Oberdick was the only one she could really call a friend. His strength became her strength; he seemed always to be there when she needed him. She needed him now.

The elevator stopped and the door slid open. Dottie stood there for a moment, undecided about whether she should step out. The doors, working on the automatic timing device, started to close and she hurried to push the "Door Open" button. She held her finger on the button, and in a few seconds the recollection of her last meeting with Dr. Oberdick was repeated again.

It had been Thanksgiving Day a year earlier. Dottie Kissinger, in yet another effort to create some home life for a drunken husband and a son about whom she worried constantly, had prepared a lavish holiday meal. Turkey, filling, vegetables, cranberry sauce, pumpkin pie. The recollection of that day was as much of a nightmare as the original had been.

She had tried to get the turkey done early in the day, in an effort to serve the meal before Sam was tempted to go to the bottle. As she took the bird from the oven, she had called to her husband and son: "Come on, now, get to the table! And, Larry, could you give me a hand with this turkey? It's heavy."

Larry came into the kitchen. It seemed to Dottie that the boy realized that this dinner was a last ditch effort to preserve their home. He was much more helpful than usual.

"Looks great, Mom!" he had said.

"Yeah, I think the whole thing came out real well."

Then, sotto voce, the boy added, "I sure hope *he's* going to like it."

"Of course Sam will like it," Dottie assured him. "He loves turkey."

"Don't know how he's going to taste it, though, with all that gin in him."

"Already?"

Larry realized he had said the wrong thing. "Oh, I guess not yet, Mom. Let's get it to the table."

As the mother and son moved to the dining room with the food, Dottie called out to her husband, who was seated before the television set watching the Macy's parade in New York, "Come on, Sam, the feast is on!"

Sam Kissinger sullenly joined his family at the table. As he sat down, Dottie suggested quietly, "Maybe, Sam, we ought to offer a little prayer."

The man was startled by the suggestion. But it was clear that his wife was serious, and he bowed his head. Dottie took a deep breath. "Dear God," she said, "on this special day, bless this food." There was a short pause. "And bless this family."

No one spoke. Larry could not remember ever having heard a prayer in this house. Sam appeared uneasy. Dottie broke the silence. "Now, Sam, what'll you have?"

"What's the boy want?"

Dottie smiled. Maybe this *was* going to be a good day. "Larry?"

"Oh, I'll have a leg. But there are two of them, and Sam can have the other one."

"Okay," said Dottie breezily, "it's a deal. You two take the drumsticks. I like the white meat better anyway." This was beginning to sound like a real family, yet all three knew the situation was strained, even artificial.

Dottie sliced off the legs and filled the plates with filling and vegetables. Not a word was spoken as she passed the plates. Sam took a big bite out of the juicy, dark leg. It seemed he chewed it forever. Finally, with an audible gulp he swallowed the mouthful. The sound of the swallow was almost deafening.

"Good?" Dottie asked.

Sam returned the turkey leg to the plate. "Yeah, but I guess I'm just not hungry."

Another silence. How can three seconds be so long?

"You really ought to eat something, Sam," the boy suggested, "rather than. . . ."

"Rather than what?"

Larry was unsure whether he should go on. But he did. "Well, rather than drink all the time. You know it's not healthy just to drink. You gotta eat, too."

Sam spoke directly to Dottie. "Do I really have to take advice from this boy?" There seemed to be no anger in the question; it was more an appeal for understanding.

"Sam, Larry is just trying to be helpful," Dottie said. "You know you ought to eat more." Now she was hurrying her words. "And if you have some good food in your stomach maybe you won't need as much to drink. You know, the doctors say that you ought to do everything in moderation—eating and drinking."

"Yeah," the boy added, "if you only drink, well. . . ."

"Dammit!" The attempt at quiet reason had failed. "Dammit! Dammit! You both talk to me like I was some kind of incurable drunk. Just because I *like* to drink is no reason to start the damned lectures!"

Even then Dottie still had hopes that the day might be salvaged and she remained quiet. Larry caught her mood. "Ah, Sam, this is a great meal. Why don't you just eat?"

"Because I'm not hungry! And don't forget, boy, you're only 13, and I'm your father!"

"You're my stepfather!"

"But I'm still your legal father!" The voices were loud now, with razor sharpness, and Dottie couldn't find the words to calm the argument.

"Legal, maybe," Larry said, "but no damn legal paper is going to make a drunk my legal father!"

In one sweeping motion, Sam picked up the turkey leg from his plate and smashed it across the boy's face. Blood started from his nose.

Dottie screamed. "Sam, stop it!"

Her husband looked at her for a moment, then rose and walked out of the house. The boy was seemingly unperturbed. He slowly wiped his face with a napkin, as blood stained the cloth.

"You know what, Mom?" His mother just shook her head, the tears starting down her cheeks. "Mom, I'm gonna kill that sonofabitch some day!"

His flat, hard tone frightened Dottie. "Larry, I don't want to hear you say anything like that again! Sam has his problems, and he needs help."

The boy rose slowly to his feet. "I'm sorry about the dinner, Mom, I really am. But if that bastard ever comes back to this house, I swear I'm gonna kill him!" He dabbed at his nose with the napkin.

It was then that Dottie went again to Dr. Oberdick for help. She had come up on this same elevator, but not with the same hesitancy. There was no reason to hesitate; the doctor was her friend and advisor. She remembered how she had knocked on his apartment door, and how she had fallen into his arms, sobbing wildly. She had poured out her story to the old man, and he had consoled her, had calmed her, had reassured her. Josh had taken her back to her home that night, talking for hours with young Larry, dissipating the heat of his anger. Later, when Dottie decided to divorce Sam Kissinger, it was Josh who directed her to a good lawyer and helped her with a loan for the legal costs.

Now, a year later, Dottie released the elevator button and stepped out into the hallway. She was an attractive woman. Twenty years earlier she had been stunning—a natural blonde, a heart-stopping figure, a sweet face. Angelic, some would have said. But she had a flaw; she was accident-prone when it came to men. That flaw ruined her life. Dottie pushed at her hair, took a quick look at herself in the mirror by the elevator and stepped up to Dr. Oberdick's door. Again. She rapped softly.

As she waited for her knock to be answered she heard the doctor talking to someone inside. The door swung open.

Josh was obviously surprised. "Dottie! Come in, come in!"

She could see there was another man in the apartment and she hesitated. "Oh, I'm sorry . . . you're busy. . . ."

"Nonsense," he said, taking her by the arm and guiding her inside. "This is a former patient of mine, as are you. Ira Lotz, this is Mrs. Kissinger . . . Dottie Kissinger."

The man, a round and bald little pixie, simply nodded an acknowledgment of the introduction.

"Pleased to meet you, Mr. Lotz," she said. "I'll go now and come back later. I didn't mean to interrupt anything."

Lotz raised his hand in protest as the doctor spoke. "No, no. We had concluded our conversation and Mr. Lotz was just leaving."

"That's right," the man said, taking Oberdick's cue. He shook hands with Josh and departed quickly.

Dottie tried again to apologize to the old man. "Sometimes I just don't think. I shouldn't have barged in like this."

"Okay," Josh said, smiling, "so you barged in. I'm glad to see you, very glad."

She looked at him for a long moment. "I told myself I'd never impose on you again. . . ." Tears began. "Josh, the sheriff thinks Larry had something to do with a murder! He's in jail!" She wept in earnest.

"I know, I know," he said kindly, "but it may not be as bad as you think. From what I know of this thing, I'm certain that Phil Stauffer doesn't think your son had anything to do with murder."

"But Larry's in a cell. And he's frightened, Josh!"

Oberdick tried to reassure her. He glanced at the clock on the mantel. "Look, Dottie, it's nearly eight o'clock on a Sunday evening. There's not much we can do tonight."

"I wanted to come to you yesterday," she sobbed, "but I couldn't bring myself to. . . ."

"Hush, hush. Larry is in no immediate danger. We can do something about this in the morning—first thing in the morning. Have you seen a lawyer?"

"No." She dabbed at her wet eyes.

"Well, then," he said as though the problem was already

solved, "first thing tomorrow I'll call my friend, Bob Hoffman. He's a crackerjack lawyer, and he'll go over there to the courthouse, find out what charges, if any, are being filed against Larry, and get him bailed out so that he can come home to you again."

"But I don't have any money for a lawyer. Or for bail."

"A detail, young lady," Josh said with a smile, "a tiny detail. We'll work it out." His face sobered and he took her hands in his. "Dottie, of this much I am certain. Larry Saylor didn't kill anyone! He had nothing to do with the Strickler murder. Just trust old Josh."

She was in his arms, sobbing. "Oh, Josh, you're so kind. . . ."

"One other thing is certain. You're not going back to your place tonight and be alone there."

"But. . . ."

"But, nothing! You'll be a basket case if you keep on carrying on like this. So, right now, you sit down over there on the sofa, we'll talk about nice things, and you start to relax. Those are doctor's orders!"

She followed his orders, leaning back into the soft depth of the sofa. Dr. Oberdick sat beside her, moved her head to his shoulder, and cradled her in his arms. She sobbed softly that way for a few moments, then the sobbing stopped. She was protected. Josh gently stroked her hair. Nothing was said. Time went by that way; five minutes, then ten.

"Feeling better?" he asked, finally.

"Yes."

"Good." The doctor rose. "I think a hot toddy might do you some good." There was no objection. As Josh prepared the drink at the bar he called out to her, "Just stretch out there on the sofa and relax. You've got a right to relax, don't you think?"

Dottie smiled and did as he told her.

When he returned to the sofa with the hot drink, he dropped to the floor by her side and offered her the mug. "Old Doctor Oberdick's guaranteed cure for all that ails you." He laughed.

She sipped the drink. The old man just stayed on the floor

beside the sofa, occasionally stroking her hair. When she had finished the toddy, he took the mug and set it on the floor.

"Thanks," she said.

"For what?"

"For being so kind."

"You know, there's a well-worn cliché that fits here," he said lightly. "What are friends for, etcetera."

"Thanks, anyway."

"You're welcome." He rose slightly and kissed her gently on the mouth. It seemed right, somehow, and she put her arms around his neck and kissed him back.

"Just as I suspected."

"What?"

"My diagnosis is correct."

"What diagnosis?"

"That what Dottie Kissinger needs," he said, "is some tender lovin' from a good man."

She smiled. "Well, I'll admit that there hasn't been too much of that in my life."

Josh returned the smile. He picked up the mug and took it to the bar. When he came back to the sofa he sat on the edge of it, and leaned over to whisper in her ear. "Relax now, dear." His hands cupped her face and he kissed her again, this time with some fervor.

For a fleeting moment she wanted to push him away. She didn't. In a sudden passionate move, she threw her arms around the doctor and answered the kiss. As they kissed, she could feel his hands on her body. She didn't resist, even when he led her from the sofa into the bedroom. He carefully undressed her. She responded to the old man with a fury not unlike her first wedding night.

The two of them had gone to sleep in the doctor's large bed. It was daybreak when she awoke. As she stirred, Josh reached for her.

"No, Josh," she said quietly.

He propped himself up on one elbow and looked at her. "Why not?"

"Well, for one thing," she answered, without looking at

him, "I was vulnerable last night and I was as much to blame as you were. For another, you're old enough to be my father."

"Grandfather, even." He laughed.

"And you think that's right?"

"I can't for the life of me imagine what age has to do with it. Old enough to be your grandfather, but young enough to be your lover." He smiled at her.

Her attitude softened. "That's true enough."

Josh leaned over and tenderly kissed her. "Tell you what, young lady, you get in the shower and I'll make us some breakfast." He leered at her. "We solved one problem last night, but we've got another one to tackle this morning."

He kissed her again. *"Hala, hala, hinkeldrek, bis morga fre gaet ollus weck,"* he said.

"What's that?"

"Oh, just an old Pennsylvania Dutch version of 'kiss it and make it well.'"

"You really are a sweet old man."

"Ain't I though!"

Their laughter filled the apartment.

5 MON., DEC. 1, 1969

PMS LEAD · HEX MURDERS
By Ernest Wheel

Missionville, Pa., Dec. 1 (CNS) — This conservative Pennsylvania Dutch community has been shocked for the second time in a week by a murder associated with pow-wowing, the regional equivalent of witchcraft.

Mrs. Lizzie Zearfoss, 98, an acknowledged pow-wow "doctor" of nearby Miller's Grove, was found burned to death in her remote rural home yesterday afternoon. Young County Sheriff Philip Stauffer announced this morning that a Pennsylvania State Police investigation of the fire has determined that it was the work of arsonists.

Mrs. Zearfoss's death came just four days after the killing of hexerei practitioner Charles Strickler, believed to have been bludgeoned to obtain a lock of his . . .

Wheel sat ramrod straight at his typewriter, turning out his story for the afternoon dailies subscribing to the Continental News Service. It was 11:35 a.m., and the reporter was only twenty-five minutes away from his deadline for the p.m. budget filings. As he wrote he could not shake the disturbing image of the drawn and strangely haunted face of Sheriff Stauffer. It was the most compelling thing he had carried away from the morning news conference in the sheriff's office, and it could not be made a part of the story. . . .

Phil awoke that morning squinting his eyes in the sunlight filtering through the venetian blinds. He turned to look at the bedside clock: 7:05. *Why hadn't the alarm gone off at 6:30?* He turned to look at Nancy lying beside him. She, too, was awake, watching him intently.

"Didn't you set the alarm?" he asked.

"No. I wanted you to sleep as long as possible."

"Well, I've certainly done that," he said resolutely. "I've got to get up and get going." He moved to get out of bed.

His wife grasped his arm. "Phil, wait. I'm worried about you."

"I'm fine! I had a rough week and it all kind of caught up with me yesterday. But, thanks to you, I've had a good sleep and. . . ."

Nancy interrupted him. "I've been thinking about this, and it seems to me that Pastor Fenstermacher's sermon upset you more than you're willing to admit. Phil, what *is* wrong?"

"I'm okay, I tell you." He smiled and kissed her on the mouth. "Everyone wants to be a detective, even my wife."

"Don't do this to me, Phil."

"Don't do what?"

"Don't shut me out. I've never seen you like you were yesterday morning. It frightened me, and I want to know what's wrong!"

Stauffer flopped back on the pillow in feigned exasperation. "Good gosh, woman," he said in a jesting manner, "your master and provider is just fine. And I promise you I'll never get tired again."

"You're going to drive me to an early grave, Philip Stauffer! I was awake most of the night worrying about you, and you joke about this thing."

"There isn't any *thing*," he insisted. "I'm fine. I'm rested. I'm raring to go. And I'm in love with you."

"At least the last part of that sounds real." She got out of the bed, brushing him on the nose with her lips. "I'll get some breakfast while you get dressed."

"That's a bargain."

"Some bargain," she mumbled. But she didn't leave the room. Momentarily, she debated with herself. Then, "Phil, Barry called late yesterday, after you had gone to sleep. I told him I didn't want to bother you."

"I appreciate that." Phil stretched, rising from the bed. "Anything startling from Mr. Painter?"

"That Zearfoss woman—she's dead."

"What?"

"Her house burned down. She was caught in the fire."

"Any other details?"

"No." She smiled faintly. "I guess I was a little sharp with Barry. I asked him whether he expected you to bring her back from the dead."

Phil laughed. "What'd he say to that?"

"Nothing. That stopped him."

The sheriff took Nancy in his arms. "You *are* a mother hen, aren't you?" A kiss was interrupted by the ringing of the phone. Phil sighed. "That's probably Barry now. I'll get it."

The phone rang twice more before he could get into the den to answer it.

"Hello," he said cheerily. If Nancy could hear him he wanted to be certain that she understood he was in a good mood.

"Sheriff Stauffer?" a male voice asked.

"Yes."

"Ya don't know me, sheriff, but I haff somesing important to tell ya." There was a distinct Pennsylvania Dutch accent.

"Who is this?"

"It don't matter none," the voice said coldly. "I chust wanna varn ya that you're in league viss the divel."

"What?"

"You n' that schmardt-ass Pastor Fenstermacher are messin' in somesing ya don't unnerstandt. Pow-wowin' iss the vork of the Lordt, undt it vas long before churches n' all that book-readin' schtuff."

"Damn it! Who is this?"

Nancy had come into the den to see who was calling, and when she heard his angry tones she clutched his arm. Phil tried to signal her with his eyes not to be alarmed. The signal failed.

"Only a schtupid man in league viss the ewils of the divel vould deny the true povers of Godt the Father, Godt the Son, and Godt the Holy. . . ."

"I'll not listen to this any longer," Phil snapped. "Unless you identify yourself, I'm going to hang up!"

There was a cruel laugh. "If ya hang up, you'll neffer know

aboudt Debra."

"Debra!" Phil gasped the name. There was a tiny scream from Nancy, her fingernails digging into his arm.

"Yah, Debra. She's your daughter, ain't? Vell, Mistah Schmart-Ass, the povers of hexerei haff placed a schpell on the girl. Chust ya vait undt see!"

The caller hung up. Stauffer held the instrument in his hand for a shocked moment before he placed it in its cradle. Nancy was weeping.

"What about Debbie, Phil?" she cried. "What about Debbie?"

"It was just a nut call, Nance, just some nut."

She screamed at him, anger and fear twisting her face. "Phil, not again! I want to know what this is all about! Right this minute!"

He placed his fingertips on her lips. "You'll wake the kids." Phil placed his arm around his distressed wife and guided her into the living room. "You're right," he said with resignation, "you ought to know."

Phil and Nancy sat on the sofa, both still in their nightclothes, and the sheriff quietly told his wife of the experience with Strickler's lock of hair and the still unexplained Mosser illness. And he told her what the telephone caller had said.

"And that's all there is," said Phil. "Fenstermacher's sermon upset me because of those doubts in my own mind. And the telephone call . . . well, we both know that it isn't the first nut call we've had. It goes with the territory."

There were no longer any tears from Nancy. She was, in her own way, as tough and as resilient as her husband.

"Phil, darling, I know that we can't allow our lives to be ruled by all the crazies out there," she said calmly. "But this one scares me. It *really* scares me."

An alarm clock sounded in another part of the house, then a second one.

"It's 7:30," said Phil, "the kids are going to be getting up. I think we ought to keep this to ourselves for the moment."

"But what about Debra?"

"You make some excuse to drive the kids to school this morning," he told her, "and I'll have some excuse for picking them up this afternoon. Nance, I really don't believe there's anything to this. But we'll be cautious and I'll see whether I can't get a lead on that phone caller."

"Oh, Phil . . . I'm *so* frightened!"

The sheriff didn't want to tell her that he was frightened, too.

By 8:30, Stauffer was in his office, where he was briefed by his deputy on the Lizzie Zearfoss developments. A half hour later, Phil called in the press to disseminate the bare details of what he knew.

"A preliminary analysis of the gasoline can," he told the reporters, "revealed no fingerprints. State police are now checking the can manufacturer to determine whether we can develop a lead along those lines. At the moment, that's it."

"Do you believe there's a pow-wow connection in Mrs. Zearfoss's death?" Ernie Wheel asked.

"No!" Phil looked straight at Wheel. "But I don't imagine my denial will stop you from that kind of speculation in the newspapers."

"Sheriff," asked a woman reporter from CBS News, "is there a connection between Mrs. Zearfoss's murder and the murder of Charles Strickler?"

"No." Phil noted to himself that the networks had picked up on the story; that didn't please him.

"Just 'no'?"

"Your question could have had two answers—yes or no." Stauffer didn't try to hide his annoyance. "My answer was *no!*" He left the reporters standing in the courthouse hallway.

Inside the office, Barry Painter said to him, "Phil, there just might be a connection between the two murders."

"Of course, but I don't know that there is. Do you?"

"No," Barry admitted, "but. . . ."

"But it seems that there ought to be." Stauffer sat down wearily behind his desk. "Barry, there's been too damned much speculation in this case. We've allowed ourselves to be mesmerized by all this pow-wow nonsense. I've been as guilty of that as anyone else. Starting right now, however, we're going to do some old-fashioned, nit-picking police leg work. And we're going to stop reacting to all that newspaper crap about pow-wow and witches." His fist pounded the desk. "Right now!"

The deputy understood Phil well enough not to contradict his boss.

"Without any further delays, then," Phil went on, "we're going to lay out what we know and what we don't know. And then, we're going to get some answers about those things we don't know. Okay?"

"Sure, Phil." Barry picked up a lined yellow note pad.

"First, there's Strickler himself." He had returned to calm and deliberate reason. "What do we really know about him? If Mosser, or Saylor, or young Burkholder didn't kill him—and we have good reason to believe they didn't—then who did? I want you to dig out everything you can on Strickler. Habits, friends, enemies, everything. We need a new lead."

"Right, Phil."

"At the same time," the sheriff continued, "I'm going to be doing the same thing on Lizzie Zearfoss. My gut tells me that there's some common denominator that we've overlooked." Stauffer paused. Should he tell Barry about the phone call? When he spoke again it was about another subject. "By the way, Barry, what do you know about Martha Lotz, the girl who Johnny Mosser married?"

"Not much," answered the deputy. "I know that she went away right after that beating by Johnny. Let's see . . . we looked for her, remember, Phil, when Johnny escaped from the nut house. She was supposed to have gone to Arizona, but the cops there never came up with anything. Why? Is that important?"

"Probably not," Phil admitted. "It's just that loose ends have a way of bugging me."

Stauffer's phone rang. He answered it, listened for a brief moment, and hung up. "The D.A.," he explained to Painter. "Stick close for a couple of minutes. I won't be long."

Fred Barringer was agitated when the sheriff walked into his office. "As anticipated," he said, "the shit has hit the fan. Both Saylor and Burkholder will be out on bail shortly. Their lawyers are going before the court in about fifteen minutes."

"To be bailed on what charge?"

"Aggravated assault. You know I can't go in with a murder charge. Aggravated assault is as far as I can go."

"I know," said Phil, "but I'd feel a lot better if those two were behind bars for a few more days."

"No chance. I'm going to ask for ten-thousand bail, but the court will probably cut it in half. Both of the kids will be able to make bail, I understand."

"I know about the Burkholder dough, but where in the hell is the Saylor boy getting that kind of money?"

"That's the odd part, Phil," the District Attorney said. "Bob Hoffman, who doesn't come cheap, is representing him, retained by one Dr. Joshua Oberdick, in behalf of Mrs. Kissinger. Bob tells me that the old man will put up the full cash—no bail bondsman. Surprise you?"

"Not really. It never surprises me when Oberdick is involved where there's a pretty woman."

"Do you think he's laying her?" Barringer asked lightly.

"Probably."

"I sure hope I'll be able to get it up at eighty."

"Don't count on it," grinned Phil. "Old Josh is one of a kind." They laughed. "But listen, what about Johnny Mosser? Is anybody doing anything for him?"

"I'll be asking the judge to appoint an attorney for him," the D.A. explained, "and will be recommending that he be held for a psychiatric examination."

"Justice!" The sheriff was bitter. "It may be blind, but it sure can hear the rustle of long green. I really feel sorry for Johnny."

The door was opened suddenly by Deputy Painter. "Sorry to interrupt," he said excitedly, "but Phil, they just called from the high school. Debbie's sick and they've taken her to the hospital!

Phil and Nancy sat disconsolately in the waiting room at the hospital. They held hands. Nancy, try as she might not to, wept. Phil kept lightly squeezing her hand as a signal of reassurance.

"It won't be long now," Phil said. "Appendectomies don't take very long."

"I know." She stared at the block pattern of the floor tiles, then brought her eyes up to his. "Phil, why did this happen?"

"These things happen," he answered with a shrug. "Appendicitis is a very common thing."

"But that phone call this morning...."

He grabbed her by the arms and held her firmly. "Now, listen to me, Nancy! That phone call had nothing to do with this. There is no such thing as a pow-wow nut conjuring up acute appendicitis!" Phil fought to control his emotions. "There is *no such thing!*"

She nestled in his arms, weeping harder. "I know, Phil, and I try to tell myself that the phone call had nothing to do with this, but...."

He stroked her hair. "Nance," he said gently, "it is just a coincidence. A frightening coincidence, perhaps, but a coincidence, nevertheless."

They sat silently that way for a long while and Nancy's sobbing ended. There was no need to say anything more. They had their mutual love and strength. Phil was still holding her when the surgeon came into the waiting room. Quickly, they both came to their feet.

"Relax," said Dr. Aaron Mabley. He was smiling. "Everything is fine. She came through the operation well, there were no complications. Just as soon as she's moved from surgery to her room you may go and be with her."

"Thank God," breathed Phil.

Nancy, tears coming again, asked, "What caused it, doctor?"

"What caused it? Well, it could have been any number of things. The appendix, as you know, is a rather useless narrow tube extended from the large intestine in the lower right-hand part of the abdomen. We doctors call it the vermiform appendix. What is known as appendicitis is simply an inflammation of that tube. There's no single cause for that inflammation. Indeed, it could come from any number of irritants: a piece of corn, for example; or a tiny fish bone, or even a tooth-brush bristle."

"But this came on so suddenly," Nancy persisted.

"It frequently does," Dr. Mabley explained. "You see, sometimes—and we're not sure why—the growing inflammation gives us no warning. No pain, no fever. It may produce no more than vague abdominal uneasiness. So vague, in fact, that we pay it no attention. Then, suddenly, the inflammation advances into a violent stage. There is extreme pain, often vomiting. Also, sudden high fever. And we have acute appendicitis. It must be relieved immediately through surgery. That's what we had here."

"And there was nothing else?"

"No, nothing." The doctor smiled. "I don't want to minimize the seriousness of any abdominal surgery, Mrs. Stauffer, but this kind of thing is really routine. We'll have your daughter walking a few steps tomorrow and, in three or four days, you'll be able to take her home. With normal postoperative care, that will be the end of it."

"Thank you, doctor," Phil said. He reached out and shook the physician's hand. "We appreciate what you've done."

Dr. Mabley acknowledged the thanks with a nod of the head. "The nurse will let you know when you can see . . . ah, what's the young lady's name?"

"Debra," said the sheriff.

"Of course, Debra. Well, the nurse will be coming for you in just a few minutes. Nice to have met you." He was gone.

"What'd I tell you?" Phil said with a grin. "All is well."

"I'd feel a lot more assured if he could have remembered her name." Phil laughed and his wife joined him, wiping away the last of her tears with her handkerchief.

As they sat down again the hospital intercom intoned: *Sheriff Philip Stauffer, Sheriff Philip Stauffer, you have a telephone call at the front desk.*

Nancy was startled. "Phil, what. . . . ?"

"Now, don't get excited again. That's probably Barry, checking about Debbie. You stay here and wait for the nurse and I'll get the call." He walked briskly down the hallway toward the front desk.

"Stauffer," he said when he took the phone.

"Vell, vot do ya sink now, sheriff?" It was the same voice of the earlier call. "Are you conwinced now uff the ancient powers uff hexerei?"

Phil was stunned. "How'd you know?"

"I know, Mistah Schmart-Ass," the voice said ominously. "Undt now ya know nodt to meddle in somesing vhere ya haff no business."

The sheriff looked around to see that he was not being overheard. "Listen, you sonofabitch. . . ." Phil heard a click. He put down the phone hurriedly and tried to compose himself.

On the way back down the hallway toward the waiting room, he could see Nancy chatting with a nurse. There was a water fountain on the wall and he stopped to get a drink. *Get yourself under control!* A couple of sips of water and Phil straightened up and joined his wife and the nurse.

"Just as I thought," he told Nancy. "It was Barry. I told him Debbie was just fine!"

6 TUES., DEC. 2, 1969

It was Dottie Kissinger who opened the door of Josh Oberdick's apartment to the knock of Deputy Sheriff Painter.

Barry, surprised to see her there, stammered, "Excuse me, Mrs. Kissinger, I'm looking for Dr. Oberdick."

"You've come to the right place," she said sweetly. "Please come in. Josh said you were coming."

Dottie held the door open for the police officer and Barry walked into the living room. He found himself staring at the woman he knew as the waitress at the Central Diner. It ran through his mind that she was a beautiful woman; he wondered why he had never realized it before.

"Josh, dear," she called into the interior of the apartment, "the deputy is here."

She led Barry to the sofa and motioned to him to be seated. Dottie was wearing a satin-type robe (Barry never was very good at identifying materials) and it clung to her ample body in a most enticing way.

Dr. Oberdick entered the room from one of the bedrooms. "How's Larry this morning?" he asked the woman.

"He seems to have had a good night's sleep."

"That's marvelous." He pecked her on the cheek. "A good morning, deputy. Please sit down, sit down."

Barry had come to his feet when the old man entered the room. It embarrassed him now that he stood there staring at the tableau of the handsome older man and the beautiful, much younger woman. He had a feeling of having intruded on something he didn't quite understand.

"Darling," Oberdick said to Dottie, "would you mind getting us a couple of cups of coffee?" Then, to Barry, "Lovely woman, lovely woman."

135

The deputy struggled for a way to start the conversation. "I'm glad to get this chance to come and see you here. I've always wanted to see these apartments. I've been thinking about moving here." He quickly added, "I'm single, you know."

"Then this is the place for you," Josh chuckled. "Lots of action here for a single man."

Dottie placed the two cups of coffee on the table in front of the sofa. "I'll leave you two alone." She bent and kissed Oberdick. *Passionately,* Barry thought. His eyes followed the retreating figure. When he turned his head to the doctor again, he found Josh grinning at him.

"I know Dottie from the diner," he tried to explain.

"Of course."

"Ah . . . doctor," Barry stammered, "what I want to talk to you about is that case you had a few years back involving Charlie Strickler. The one where you tried to get Strickler on a practicing-medicine-without-a-license charge. Since the case never really got to court, the records are incomplete. And I thought you could fill me in. We're looking for anything we can find about Strickler."

"Oh, the case isn't going well?"

"It's going okay," the deputy said defensively. "It's just that we have to be extra thorough when preparing a case for court these days."

"Is Johnny Mosser going to be indicted for the murder?"

"I don't know, doctor. That's not my department. The sheriff and the D.A. make those kinds of decisions." Painter tried to get control of the conversation. "Now, doctor, exactly what was that case about? What did you have on Strickler?"

"It involved a Missionville man named Nelson Yoder," Josh started slowly, "who was suffering from tuberculosis. Through a friend, he had been recommended to Charlie Strickler. Most pow-wow doctors thrive, as you probably know, on word-of-mouth advertising, so to speak."

Barry was rapidly taking notes.

"TB was known as consumption by the old timers, and when Yoder first went to Strickler that was his diagnosis—consumption. The pow-wow treatment, if that's the correct word, included only an incantation. Just a moment, I think I can find it for you."

Josh rose and went to his book shelves, pulled out a volume and returned to the sofa. He leafed through some pages.

"Ah, yes, here it is," he said. "The incantation Strickler must have used goes like this: *Consumption, I order thee out of the bones into the flesh, out of the flesh upon the skin, out of the skin into the wilds of the forest.* That was followed by three signs of the cross or invoking the Trinity—Father, Son, Holy Ghost, that kind of stuff.

"Our friend, Mr. Yoder, got no better," the doctor continued, "so he went back to Strickler. This time Charlie gave him a potion—a powder that included some sugar, borax, oil of cloves, an odd assortment of spices, some steel filings...."

"Steel filings?" Barry interrupted.

"Yep, steel filings. For a direct infusion of iron, as I understand it. And, just to give the stuff a kick, a few grains of opium."

"Where in the hell did he get the opium?"

"We never did find out. It was one of the things left undetermined when the case collapsed." Oberdick sighed. "Anyway, Yoder was supposed to take a pinch of that junk twice a day. His specific instructions were to take an amount that would fit on the tip of a knife. Well, he did that for three days and his tubercular cough got worse, as you might imagine. Mr. Yoder was not a true believer in the pow-wow arts, so he went to see a medical doctor because he had become genuinely worried about his condition. When he told the doctor what he had been taking, the physician reported it to the medical society and I, as president, got into the act."

Oberdick stopped to take a sip of the coffee.

"And then what?" Barry was pressing.

"Yoder agreed that he would cooperate in a case against Strickler. We went ahead in preparing the material needed for an indictment. But when we got Yoder in front of the Grand Jury, his memory suddenly failed him. He couldn't deny that someone had given him the powder, because he had turned it over to us for an analysis. But Yoder's sudden problem was that he couldn't remember where he got it. The whole damned case just fell apart on us. Yoder was threatened with all kinds of things—perjury, obstructing justice, and all that, but it didn't budge him."

"Why didn't he talk?"

"The man was honestly frightened," Josh went on. "Someone had gotten to him and scared the hell out of him. It was enough to keep him quiet even under the threat of going to jail. I'm sure it was Strickler's doing, but what method he used to frighten Yoder, I don't know."

"Was Charlie called to testify?"

"He had been subpoenaed," Oberdick explained, "but when Yoder went mute, there was no point in taking Strickler's testimony. Without Yoder saying where he got the powder we had no case at all. And . . . well, that's the sad story."

"Is Yoder still living?"

Josh pondered for a moment. "I believe he is. He did get proper treatment for the TB and it was arrested. I'm not certain, but I think he still lives here in Missionville. He was a stocking boarder, working at the Mertz Knitting Mill, as I remember it."

"Did you know Charlie Strickler well?"

"Too well for my tastes."

"Did he have any enemies?"

"Certainly!"

"For example?"

Josh smiled. "Well, *me*, for example. And his poor wife, I would imagine. Maybe Nelson Yoder. Charlie Strickler was a fourteen-carat sonofabitch. He probably had a ton of enemies."

The Lotz home was in Weiser Township, just outside the Missionville city limits. It was a small frame building with nothing to distinguish it from a hundred other houses in the suburban neighborhood. It was a house—period. There was a neat little yard around it, and no fences to mark the property lines. Simple, clean, unpretentious.

Phil Stauffer knew only a few facts about the Lotz family as he stopped his car in front of the house. Ira and Hanna Lotz were like so many other married couples in this area: hard-working, God-fearing, uncomplicated people who raised their children, paid their taxes, and got their entertainment on the weekend with a couple of glasses of beer at the bar in the basement of the local volunteer fire company, or at a bingo game at the American Legion hall. They were a proud people who put their flag out on national holidays, who voted the straight Democratic ticket every election, and who owned their small house free and clear. Welfare was something for other people, but not for them. They had their small prejudices, but rarely enunciated them. Their friends were carbon copies of themselves. They read the local newspaper every day, but were little concerned about the events in Biafra, or Lebanon, or Iraq, or Pakistan. Vietnam worried them some, primarily because a neighboring family had a grandson fighting there. But the newspaper was for obituary notices, for birth announcements, for supermarket advertisements with their weekly supply of discount coupons, and for details on the weather. "The paper wants rain," one would say to the other. They were not much involved in the organizations of the community—PTA, League of Women Voters, or the Taxpayers Association of Young County. For them it was enough to be affiliated with the volunteer fire company, a church, and perhaps a lodge like the Patriotic Order, Sons of America.

Ira Lotz, the sheriff knew, had worked for years at the Missionville Shoe Company as a janitor. His son, Ira Junior, also worked at the shoe company, as night watchman. Their daughter, Martha, had been the wife of Johnny Mosser. That was the link the sheriff wanted to know about. It bothered him that his files were so incomplete on the Mosser-Lotz relationship. Any further background on Mosser might, he felt, help him understand the baffling nature of Charlie Strickler's murder.

Phil was greeted warmly by the Lotzes. Hanna insisted that he come into the kitchen and sample her freshly made chocolate cake. She gave him a steaming cup of coffee and a large slice of the dark chocolate cake, heavy with icing.

"Sometimes this job has its compensations," Phil commented.

The Lotzes smiled. Phil couldn't help wondering whether either one of these simple people even knew the meaning of the word "compensation." He took a forkful of the delicious cake, and a swallow of the coffee, before he spoke. "I asked to come out here to talk about Johnny Mosser."

"Oh, poor Johnny," Mrs. Lotz said sympathetically.

"Poor Johnny, indeed," agreed the sheriff. "I'd like to fill in some material I don't seem to have in the files. Now, in 1959 he married your daughter. . . ."

"No," Ira interrupted, "that was in 1958, just at the end of November."

"Well, it was in 1960 that I first met Martha," Phil continued, "right after she had that trouble with Johnny."

"Yes, that was awful." Mrs. Lotz was pained at the recollection.

"Can you tell me about Johnny and Martha?"

The husband and wife looked at each other and finally Ira began to talk. The words came hesitantly at first. "Sheriff, Martha was a nice girl. We worried a lot about her when she was growing up. We wanted her to have a nice home, a good husband, and to be happy. But sometimes, we thought that maybe she shouldn't get a husband at all. Because, well, sometimes she was . . . not too good."

"You mean sick?"

"Yeah, sick. Oh, it wasn't so bad always, just a little bit sometimes. She'd get a little spell, or something. We took her to old Doc Oberdick and he said she had . . . what was that he called it, Mom?"

"Oh, now I don't remember," Hanna said. "It seems so long ago. It was spells, though. You know, fits."

"Epilepsy?" the sheriff volunteered.

"Yeah, that was it," the father agreed. "But not bad, you know, just little spells. Doc had a funny name for that, too."

Again Stauffer offered a suggestion. "*Petit mal?*"

"I just don't rightly know, sheriff," Ira said, shrugging his shoulders. "But the Doc said it wasn't really bad, and he gave her some medicine."

"Did it help?"

"Yeah, it did. But, we were worried, you know."

"I can imagine you were," the sheriff said kindly. "Please go on."

"Anyway, we thought maybe that this not feeling good would keep Martha from getting married, and all that, and we went to see a pow-wow doctor about it."

Stauffer resisted the temptation to interject the question *Why?*

"We went to see old Lizzie Zearfoss. . . ."

"Ain't that terrible about Lizzie?" Hanna cut in. "Dying in that fire and all?"

"Yes, it was terrible," Phil said.

"Anyway, we went to see Lizzie," Ira continued, seemingly anxious to keep the story going, "and she told us that Martha would get married okay, and the man who would marry her had a spell on her and that was what was keeping her not so good all the time. But Lizzie said that if Martha married that man, then everything would be okay again."

"Did she tell you who the man was?" Stauffer asked.

"Yeah, she said it was John Mosser."

"How did she know that?"

"Oh, I don't know," Ira said. "They know all kinds of strange things."

"And did you tell Dr. Oberdick about all this?"

"Yeah, we did," the father said gravely. "Old Doc Oberdick said too that Martha could get married, just like Lizzie said. Doc said Martha was supposed to keep taking her medicine and . . . well, that's what he said."

"What did you do then?"

"We found out where Johnny lived and. . . ."

"You mean you didn't know Johnny Mosser before this?"

"No. Not before Lizzie mentioned him. Anyway, we went over to see Johnny and his folks, and Johnny told us a voice kept telling him to marry Martha."

Stauffer was beginning to doubt his own senses. "Did Johnny know Martha before this visit?"

"No."

"You just went in there, and Johnny said voices told him to marry Martha, whom he didn't know, and you *believed* him?"

"Oh, sure. Since Lizzie had already told us that, too, how could Johnny know the same thing if it ain't true?"

The sheriff just nodded.

"Well, Johnny and Martha got married," Ira went on, "and it was just like Lizzie said. She didn't get sick no more."

Phil disliked interposing too many questions, but he was trying to keep some coherence in the strange recital. "Did Martha want to marry Johnny?"

Mrs. Lotz spoke up. "Not at first, sheriff. But she saw it was best when we explained it all to her. And she heard what Lizzie and Doc Oberdick said. So it all worked out."

"How old was Martha then?"

"Seventeen, but that's old enough to get married, you know, if the parents sign off."

"I know," said the sheriff. "Now, Johnny and Martha got married. What happened then?"

Ira picked up the story. "It worked fine at first, but then there was some hexing again. Johnny started to get sick and he came over here with Martha and we talked about it. I guess it was Hanna here who said we ought to go see Lizzie Zearfoss again and we did. Lizzie said Johnny was hexed, but that she didn't know who was doing it. She said Johnny might be told by a sign. About three nights later he came over here awful upset, and crying. He said he had a sign and that it was Martha making him sick by putting something in his food."

"Did you believe that?"

"Not at first," Mr. Lotz admitted. "I asked him what the sign was and he said voices spoke to him, just like the time when they told him to marry Martha. Well, we took Martha and Johnny back to Lizzie and she said that it was true. That Martha was putting stuff in Johnny's food to make him sick."

"What did Martha say about that?"

"Oh, she said she didn't do it," the father added, "but Lizzie said she probably didn't *know* she was doing it, that somebody had a spell over her and was *making* her do it."

"Another spell?" Phil hoped he wouldn't lose track of the story's continuity.

"Yeah. But anyway, Lizzie said that it would probably go away and she gave Martha some powders and told her to sprinkle them on the doorsill and that it would keep the spirits away . . . the spirits that were making her put the bad stuff in Johnny's food."

"But the powders didn't work?"

"They did for a while," Ira insisted. "Then, I guess the spirits got too strong for the powders. Anyway, Johnny got sick again, and the voices told him Martha was doing it, and he just got mad, I guess, and. . . ."

"And he nearly beat her to death!" The sheriff was aware that he was beginning to show his annoyance with this nonsense.

Hanna joined in. "Yeah, he whipped her bad. And you know what happened to Johnny. They put him in the insane hospital."

"I know that," Phil said, "but what happened to Martha after all this?"

"When she got out of the hospital," Mrs. Lotz continued, "she wanted to go away somewhere so we sent her out west to Arizona."

"You gave her the money to go?" Doubt was evident in Stauffer's voice.

"No," said the mother, "Doc Oberdick helped us. He had some people he knew in Arizona, and they got Martha a job in a restaurant out there."

"Just where was that?"

"Oh, I don't remember," answered Ira. "Doc told us once, but I don't know now." His brow furrowed.

Stauffer phrased his next comment carefully. He didn't want to cut off the flow of easy conversation. "And, I imagine, Martha is still there and happy."

Ira's face clouded. "We don't rightly know, but we think so. You see, when Johnny got out of the hospital he came here looking for Martha. We were scared. So we asked Doc Oberdick what to do and he said he thought we shouldn't tell Johnny where she was. Then Doc said he'd get Martha a new address and would keep it to himself so's no one could go and hurt Martha."

"Then you don't know where she is now?"

"No, but the Doc does. So I guess she's okay."

"Doesn't she write to you?"

"No."

Phil thought he saw a strange expression on Hanna's face when the question of Martha's current whereabouts was raised. But he dismissed the thought. He smiled. It was a deliberate act for the benefit of the Lotzes. "Well, I guess it's best that Martha's living her own life now," he said softly, "and I'm sure she's happy. That's fine country out there in Arizona." He rose. "Thanks for your help and for the coffee and cake. The cake was just great, Hanna."

She was pleased with the compliment. "I always like to see somebody eat good like you do, sheriff."

"Oh, by the way, Ira," Phil said, feigning a second thought, "did Dr. Oberdick loan you the money for Martha's trip to Arizona?"

"Gosh, no, sheriff!" Ira was very serious. "I don't make the kind of money to pay him back. I told him that and he said just to forget it. He said someday I could do him a favor."

Stauffer nodded and said his goodbyes. It had been a depressing experience.

Missionville, like hundreds of small towns across the nation, had many of its streets named for trees: Maple, Elm, Pine, Chestnut, Ash, Hickory, Willow, Mulberry, Birch, Walnut, Cedar, Poplar, and others. A favorite of Missionville planners was cherry; there was a Cherry Street, Cherry Drive, Cherry Court, even Little Cherry Street. It was the basis of several ribald jokes that a one-time house of ill repute had been located on Cherry Drive. Nelson Yoder lived on Little Cherry, at number 1132.

Little Cherry Street, like so many others in Missionville, had brick row houses on each side of the street. They were substantial homes, three stories high, all strung together in a solid row. Between every two residences was an arched alleyway (called by some a "side alley") that appeared to have been bored through. Each alleyway was shared by the residents of two homes, and provided an entry from the street to the tiny, rectangular back yards, with postage-stamp size plots of grass and peony bushes with their large, double flowers of red, pink or white. Peonies seemed to thrive in the restricted environment of those yards. The alleyways were narrow, just wide enough to accommodate one adult at a time, but they were marvelous places for children to play when it rained. Some of the alleyways had locked gates on the street end; others were open at the front and had the locked gates at the immediate entrance to the back yards. There was a time when locked gates were unnecessary, but, unhappily, that time was only remembered.

There were wide wooden porches in front of each home, about four feet above the sidewalk level, and reached by five or six steps up from the sidewalk. In the summertime, those porches—boasting gliders, rocking chairs, and even swings—were social centers. It was an ideal place to sit and watch the world flow by. It was a place, too, to wait on the summer evenings for the Good Humor truck to come by. The porches were always immaculate. Housewives would drain their weekly wash water into buckets after the family laundry had been done and slosh the warm, soapy suds over the porch floors, scrubbing hard with a broom. Such acts were part of the waste-not-want-not attitude of the people who lived in the row houses.

One imagines that, when the row houses were first built, the porches and the wooden trim on the doorways and windows were all painted the same color. But over the years, the individual owners had repainted to their own tastes, and each street became a riot of color, intermixed with the basic red brick hue, ranging from white to the darkest gray, and from a yellowish cream to bilious green. Those porches that had awnings also reflected the individualism of their owners. There were red-striped sailcloth awnings, and green-striped ones, some with dual-colored strips, and numerous solid shades. Some of the awnings were of permanently-installed aluminum, attesting to the success of the salesmen who periodically flooded these neighborhoods with aluminum storm windows, doors and awnings. Occasionally, a passerby could spot a row house on which aluminum siding covered the brick; truly a triumph of salesmanship. One or two of the owners in every block had drop shades on the porches, split bamboo strips that were woven together in some manner, and were easily rolled up when not in use by a simple pulley system. If a family with those drop shades didn't roll them up and down often enough in the Spring, small birds would frequently build nests inside the roll. On some of the porches, more adventurous owners had replaced the original wooden support posts with ones of fancy cast-iron scroll work. And, every once in a while, there could be seen two adjoining porches with a solid wall built between them — "spite fences" erected by feuding neighbors who were, day-in and day-out, separated from each other by only the thickness of the building's walls.

One thing remained constant in those homes, however; the nearly flat, sheet metal roofs (called "tin roofs" by all), every one painted with a bright red lead paint.

The row houses led to unique communities that were most often close and cooperative, conducting block parties to raise money for playgrounds, or summer camping trips, or for charitable work. But sometimes the enforced closeness of the residents led to friction, especially when the ethnic character of the neighborhood was changing. Little Cherry Street had resisted such change. Its home owners were nearly all of Pennsylvania Dutch origin, with names like Yoder and Mertz and Stoudt and Greenawald and Biehl and Hess and Rissmiller and Sassaman and Unger.

Deputy Painter had difficulty finding a parking space on the narrow street, and he had to walk more than a block before he got to Nelson Yoder's home at 1132. As he walked up on the porch, Yoder opened the door. "Been keepin' an eye out for you. Guess you had trouble parkin', huh?"

"Sure did."

"It's one of the reasons I got rid of my car," Yoder said. "There are no garages on these properties and the alleys in the back are too narrow to get in and out with a car anyway."

Barry, trying to maintain a businesslike attitude, resisted engaging in the small talk. He followed Yoder into the neat house.

"It ain't much of a home, anymore," the man said apologetically. "Not since the wife died."

"Mr. Yoder," Barry said, taking the chair offered to him, "you probably don't want to talk about this anymore, but I must ask you some questions about Charlie Strickler."

"Yeah, I expected to hear from you folks when I saw by the paper that he'd been killed."

"Dr. Oberdick has told us of the details of the case against Strickler when charges of practicing medicine without a license was filed against him in 1964. So there's no need to go into all that preliminary material."

"I'm sure Dr. Oberdick didn't tell you anything good about me." Yoder's face was sad.

Painter was noncommittal. "The doctor gave us the details. But what we need to know now is *why* you refused to testify against Strickler?"

Yoder sat dejectedly, his hands clasped, staring at the floor.

"We don't want to make it tough on you, Mr. Yoder, but with a case like this we have to follow up on every potential lead. We have to really know the victim, because that way we can establish the pattern of why he was killed. Hopefully, that will lead to who killed him."

"Well, I might as well tell you. The damage has been done now anyway."

"The damage?"

"Yeah. Charlie Strickler killed my wife!"

Barry was startled. "Killed your wife?"

"Not so you could convict him for it, but he killed her sure enough!" The slim little man was angered, his hands clasping and unclasping. "You see, I agreed with Dr. Oberdick that Strickler ought to be put in jail. The doctor explained to me how his treatments could kill some innocent people. He said I was lucky to be smart enough to go to a real doctor with my TB, but that not everybody is smart enough to do that. And the poor, ignorant ones, he said, could die because of what Strickler did. I agreed with him then. I know it sounds strange, but I still agree with him. But Oberdick wasn't here that night Charlie came here."

Painter said nothing. It was obvious that Yoder was going to tell the painful story without prodding.

"Flossie—that was my wife—had been sick for a long time. A weak heart. And when I started to get sick, I had to try everything I could to get well again. I *had* to work. Flossie needed all kinds of doctors, and they were expensive. Anyway, I got sick and nothing seemed to help. Then my neighbor next door told me about Strickler and I went to see him. I was ready to try anything, you understand."

Barry nodded sympathetically. "Sure."

"Well, Strickler didn't help me either. I went to another doctor—a real doctor—and told him what I was taking from Strickler. That's when it all started. So when Strickler learned I was going to testify against him, he came here one night and raised hell. He screamed and cursed, and Flossie had an attack. Somehow, I got him to leave. But Flossie, she was so afraid of what might happen that she got me to promise that I'd get out of that mess. I promised her. You should have seen how sick she was, deputy." Yoder ran his hand over his face. "Well, the day I had to go to the grand jury, Flossie had another attack and they had to take her to the hospital. When I got into that grand jury room, I couldn't say anything. I couldn't!"

"Of course, you couldn't," the deputy agreed.

"Then, after the charges were dismissed against Strickler, he came here again. Thank God, Flossie was still in the hospital. He pushed me around—he was a big man—and said if I ever changed my mind and talked, he'd come back and kill me. In about a week, Flossie came home from the hospital, and I was taking treatment for the TB. Luckily, it wasn't a real bad case and I was soon able to go back to work. One day I came home from work and Flossie was all upset again. Strickler had called on the phone and told her: 'Tell that stupid husband of yours to keep his damned mouth shut!'"

Barry interrupted. "Did he call more than once?"

"No, just that once. But that was enough. Flossie kept fretting and just about three weeks later she had another heart attack, and that one killed her." The voice dropped into a whisper. "That one killed her."

"I'm sorry to put you through this again," Barry said. "Did you ever explain this to Dr. Oberdick?"

"I tried to, but he didn't want to talk to me. I don't really blame him, but. . . ." Yoder looked up at the deputy. "Maybe now *you* can tell him."

"I will, Mr. Yoder." Barry wasn't sure how to proceed as he looked at the distraught man. "Mr. Yoder, did you hate Charlie Strickler?"

"I was always taught not to hate," he answered softly. "My mother taught me that since I was old enough to understand. But, yes, I hated him!"

"Enough to kill him?"

"Yes."

"Did you kill him?" There was nothing accusatory about the question.

"Never for real. But I did many times, in my mind. I never had the courage to do it." Yoder dropped his face into his hands, and wept.

Painter went to the man and put his hand on Yoder's shoulder. "Mr. Yoder, I'm very, very sorry that I had to do this."

"Don't apologize," Yoder said, still sobbing. "Every man has a job to do."

"Well, thanks, Mr. Yoder. I'll be going now."

Yoder didn't get up and Barry went to the door alone. As he turned the knob, Yoder called to him. "You'll be sure to tell Dr. Oberdick?"

"Sure."

It was midafternoon when the sheriff got to Sarah Strickler's home. He had not been able to inform her that he was coming, because she had no telephone. There was no immediate answer to his knock on the front door and he knocked again. A movement of the window shade in the living room caught his eye. Sarah was peeking out. He waved to her. She waved back and went to open the door.

"I got to see who it is," the woman explained, "before I open the door. You never know anymore these days."

"That's wise, Sarah," Stauffer assured her. "May I come in?"

She swung the door open for him. In the living room the furniture was old-fashioned, overstuffed and in somber colors, but the room was neat.

"Sarah, I don't like to bother you," Phil said apologetically as he sat down, "but, to be honest with you, we're not doing too well in trying to find out who killed Charlie."

"Johnny Mosser didn't do it?"

"We're pretty sure he didn't. There are several things that indicate that he didn't do it." The sheriff was not prepared to discuss those details with the widow. "I'd like to know, Sarah, whether you know of any enemies Charlie had."

She laughed bitterly. "You can't arrest all the people who hated Charlie."

Phil smiled faintly. "Maybe so, but can you give me some names?"

Sarah was deep in thought. "Well, let's see . . . there's Rufus Collins. He's another pow-wow doctor over by Westville. He's a nigger, you know."

"I don't know him at all," Phil admitted. "Tell me about him."

"Like Charlie, Rufus got his powers from Lizzie Zearfoss. . . ."

"Lizzie Zearfoss?" It was strange how the same names kept popping up. But, like a merry-go-round, the investigation always seemed to come back to the same point—with no brass ring.

"Yeah. You know that pow-wow powers can only come from man to woman, or woman to man. That's the only way they can hand them down. When Charlie was young, Lizzie passed on the powers to him. Then, years later, she also passed on the powers to Rufus. Charlie got mad about that."

"Why?"

Sarah was surprised by the question. "Why? Because he's a *nigger*, that's why! Anyway, Charlie had a helluva argument with Lizzie about it and she said she'd take the powers away from Rufus. That made Rufus mad. He said he'd kill Charlie."

"*Did* Lizzie take the powers away from Rufus?"

"She said she did, but Charlie never believed her. Rufus is still pow-wowing, I think."

"So Rufus Collins had reason to dislike Charlie," the sheriff recapped. "And so did Lizzie Zearfoss, it would seem to me."

"Oh, yeah," Sarah agreed. "She was always trying to put spells on Charlie, but Charlie said he was too strong for her."

"Okay. Anyone else?"

There was a pause. "Greg Miller in Missionville." Again, a pause. "You see, I used to live in Missionville in an apartment house and one night Charlie caught me and Greg and . . . well, Charlie beat him up."

"Did Miller threaten to get revenge on Charlie?"

She shrugged. "Gosh, I don't know. I never heard from him again."

Stauffer looked at her sympathetically. "Sarah, isn't it true that when you lived away from Charlie, in that Missionville apartment, there were several fights? Didn't Charlie beat up on a number of your . . . ah, friends?"

"Yeah."

"Miller was one of them. Who were the others?"

"I don't know all of them," she said sadly. "Some of them didn't have names."

Phil persisted. "What names *do* you remember?"

"It was a long time ago, sheriff," she sighed. "I try to forget it."

"You'd do me a big favor, Sarah, if you'd try to remember. I know it's difficult for you. Believe me, I do know."

"Well, let's see. . . ." There was a silence of perhaps ten seconds. "Hell, sheriff," she said in exasperation, "I don't know."

"That's all right, Sarah," he assured her softly. "Just a couple more questions, if you don't mind. How was it that you came to . . . ah, take up residence in Missionville?"

She sounded very tired when she answered. "Charlie put a spell on me and said I wouldn't have any kids. I didn't believe him. I went to a doctor and he said I was okay. I told him so and he beat me up."

"That's when you left?"

"Yeah. My doctor said I should."

"Who was that?"

"Why, Josh Oberdick." She seemed surprised that he

didn't know.

"Oberdick?" That damned merry-go-round was coming around again.

"Yeah, he said I had to get away from Charlie. That Charlie would kill me."

"And Oberdick told you to . . . ah, take up with other men?"

"Oh, no!" she said firmly. "That wasn't his doing. Josh didn't like that either. It made him mad, too, and he wouldn't come and see me anymore."

"Huh?"

"Yeah, Josh got the apartment for me and he'd come there every once in a while."

"Did Charlie know about Oberdick?"

"Sure."

"And nothing happened?"

"Happened?"

"Yes, didn't Charlie have a fight with Oberdick as he did with your other friends?"

"Not as far as I know," Sarah insisted. "I think Charlie was scared of Josh. Charlie raised hell with me about Oberdick, but he never got in a fight with him. I'm pretty sure of that."

"Why would Charlie Strickler be frightened of Josh Oberdick? My God, Charlie could have beaten him to a pulp! He was so much younger and stronger than Josh."

"Charlie thought that Josh could put him in jail. Josh kept telling me he'd put the bastard away some day. He told that to Charlie, too."

Stauffer took a deep breath. "Now let me get this clear, Sarah. It was Oberdick who recommended that you leave Charlie. And he got you an apartment. Did Oberdick pay the rent?"

"Sure," she said flatly. "I didn't have any money."

"What about the other men?"

She was suddenly angry. "It wasn't like that at all! I never took a dime!"

"I'm sorry," Phil apologized. "I'm just trying to understand how it was."

"Well, that's how it was," she said sharply, still angry. "I wasn't no whore! It was just that Charlie made me so. . . ." She began to cry.

"Sarah," the sheriff pleaded, "please don't. I'm really sorry that I've raked all of this up again."

She dabbed at her eyes.

"May I ask one more question?"

Sarah didn't reply. It really wasn't important to her any more what Phil asked her. The hurt she had buried for so many years was now alive again.

"Would you say that Josh Oberdick was an enemy of Charlie Strickler?"

"Not the way you mean it," she said defensively. "Josh would never have done anything like killing Charlie." The voice softened. "Josh was a kind, gentle man."

Stauffer looked at her steadily. "And you loved him?"

Tears started down her cheeks again. "Yeah, I loved him."

Detective Lieutenant Pat Rogers hung up the phone, glanced down at an open file on his desk, and turned to his office companion. "Pres, have you ever heard anything about a broad named Martha Lotz, or Martha Mosser?"

"Nope, doesn't ring a bell with me." The answer came from a thing young man named Harry Truman Mayfield. It was inevitable that he should be called "Pres." Mayfield didn't like it, particularly, but he had long since reconciled himself to the nickname.

The men—Rogers and Mayfield—had been together as members of the Phoenix, Arizona, police department for eight years now. They made an efficient team. Rogers was the boss; Mayfield, as Detective First Grade, was the underling. But they never worked that way. In their own minds they were equals.

Rogers sat looking down at the record. "Of course, you wouldn't have heard of her," he said finally. "That was before your time on the force. In 1960 it was. We got this query from the Young County sheriff's office in Pennsylvania, wanting to know about this girl named Martha Lotz, married name Mosser. We checked her out at the address they gave us—the Frontier Restaurant—and drew a blank. Never heard of the girl, they said, or anyone matching her description. They also asked us to keep a lookout for her husband, who escaped from a mental institution, name of John Mosser. Well, we never saw the girl and we never saw the husband. And that's about it."

"And now they're asking about her again, nine years later?"

"Yeah," Rogers answered, "and this time they're sending out a special investigator. We're asked to give our cooperation. He'll be here tomorrow. A guy named Barry Painter."

7 WED., DEC. 3, 1969

The pretty blonde smiled, showing a perfect set of teeth. "Goodbye, sir. Fly with us again!"

"So long," said Barry, ducking his head slightly to leave the airliner. The hot, dry air of the desert hit him as he walked down the ramp. At the bottom of the ramp stood a tall, thin man who was certainly from the Phoenix Police Department. He was the stereotype of a plain-clothes cop. There was no mistaking that.

"Deputy Painter?" the tall man asked as Barry reached the last step.

"Yes, sir." Barry extended his hand.

"I'm Harry Mayfield. Detective Mayfield. Welcome to Phoenix."

They exchanged comments about the 80-degree weather, picked up Barry's luggage, and were off to the hotel. On the way, the deputy outlined what he hoped to find in Phoenix. He gave Mayfield a detailed rundown about Martha Mosser, nee Lotz, and about the perplexing Charles Strickler murder investigation. Barry was thorough.

Mayfield finally spoke. "What's your speculation about this girl? Are you certain she even came to Phoenix? We checked out that Frontier Restaurant again late yesterday, after we heard you were coming, and had no luck. As a matter of fact, the place isn't even called the Frontier anymore, and it's had two ownership changes since 1960. I'm afraid that's a dead end."

Barry sighed. "We're reasonably certain she came to Phoenix. Or, to put it another way, we are reasonably certain that she had an airline ticket to Phoenix. Whether she just went through the airport here, or whether she stayed for a time, or whether she's still here, hell, we just don't know."

"It seems to me that you're grasping at straws."

"You might say that," agreed Barry. "But my boss has a hunch. And Sheriff Stauffer's hunches are usually pretty good. He thinks that she lived in Phoenix for a time, maybe not working at all. Or maybe she did work somewhere and didn't want anyone to know what she was doing."

"You mean something illegal?"

"It's possible," Barry said flatly. "She was a well-stacked broad and not too smart. Hell, she could have very easily become a whore."

Mayfield feigned shock. "In *Phoenix?*" Then he laughed.

Barry joined in the laughter, but he sobered quickly. "I've been giving this a lot of thought coming out on the plane. Now, myself, I believe that she never used her real name. After all, she was running away from a man who had beaten her very badly; a man who was a known mental case. So the best way to stay out of his way was to change her name totally. Now, let's suppose a couple of things. Suppose she got here and ran out of dough? And suppose she turned to making money the best way she could? In that case, she might have become a pro and you might have her in your files. Right?"

"We might," agreed Mayfield. "And that's where you want to start?"

"As soon as we can."

Mayfield nodded. "Okay. But a question is nagging at me, deputy. What does this girl have to do with your murder investigation?"

Barry grinned. "A damned good question. You know, we're just not *sure* what she has to do with the murder investigation. Maybe nothing. Right now, however, what has happened to Martha Lotz Mosser is an unanswered question and we feel we can't afford to leave those kinds of holes. We hope that something comes of this, but. . . ." He trailed off.

Mayfield pulled the car up in front of the hotel. "We booked you in here," he told the deputy, "because it's so convenient to headquarters. Just about 150 yards down the street. You get settled, Barry, and I'll start pulling some files on our ladies of the evening. Starting about 1960, did you say?"

"Yeah, from late Spring or early Summer."

"Fine. See you in a little while." Barry followed the doorman into the hotel lobby as Mayfield drove away.

Searching through arrest records is a tedious job. It's more tedious when you aren't sure you're even in the correct category. Detective Mayfield had provided the prostitute arrest records for 1960, starting with April, and the Young County deputy sheriff had been going through them with great care.

He had found no Mosser or Lotz; nothing even close, for that matter. And nothing in the photographs really looked like the single snapshot he had of Martha Lotz. Barry looked up from the files and glanced over at the adjoining desk where Mayfield was typing a report. "A nice file," said the visitor. "Very complete. Looks like you fellows here keep close tabs on the hookers."

Mayfield smiled. "Close enough. But it's kind of tough in a resort town. Too damned many amateurs."

Barry laughed.

"Any luck?" Mayfield asked.

"Not yet. I've been trying to make some guesses about what kind of an alias she might have used. She wasn't too bright, from what little we know of her, and I don't think she would have been too inventive with a name."

The detective furrowed his brows. "Ever thought about trying for a name that ties with something she really knew well? A town name, or the name of a school, or some friend's name?"

"The town name wouldn't work too well," Barry said. "Martha Missionville isn't much of an alias."

"True."

There was a silence and Mayfield used it to get back to his typing. Barry stared at the files in front of him, then rearranged the pile and started through it again. He looked carefully at each page, comparing each police mug shot with the snapshot of Martha. Then he saw it. "Hey!"

Mayfield looked up. "Find something?"

"Hell, yes," Barry said elatedly. "Don't know why I didn't

spot this before. Your suggestion about a town name did it. Look at this!" Barry rose and carried one of the arrest sheets to Mayfield's desk. "Look! Marty Young!"

"Young?"

"Sure. Young for Young County, Pennsylvania."

"Makes sense. Do the pictures match?"

Painter laid them side by side. The girl's face in the police photo was young, thin, her hair blonde. The girl's face in the snapshot was young, too. But it was heavily round; the hair was dark.

"The hair is easy to explain," said Mayfield. "Bleach. Also, a different hair style really changes a woman's appearance. It's also possible that she could have lost a lot of weight. There's a slight facial resemblance, although that snapshot isn't too clear." He took a closer look at the records. "Only one arrest. Now, that's not normal. Usually those broads are picked up again and again. But I think it's worth checking."

"Is the address familiar to you?" Barry asked.

"Yeah. It's in the right district for this kind of activity. Come on, I'll give you a hand." He clapped the deputy on the back. "Anyway, I want to stay close to you. Anyone as lucky as you are has to be worth working with. Do you have any idea what the odds were against making even a tentative match?"

Detective Mayfield pulled the squad car into a curved driveway in front of an attractive apartment house, the Aztec Arms. It boasted a pseudo-Spanish architecture.

"Nice headquarters," Barry commented.

Mayfield grinned. "Yeah, and it almost always is a hotbed of whores, if you'll pardon the pun." Barry groaned.

The two men left the car and pushed open the glass doors into the lobby. A cold blast from the air conditioning struck them like a blow from a fist.

"The superintendent's name is Mallory," Mayfield explained. "Jim Mallory. He won't know anything."

They walked into the superintendent's office. The detective introduced Painter to the gray-haired, portly man, showed him the picture of "Marty Young," and received a swift negative shake of the head.

"Come on, now, Mallory," Mayfield insisted, "you wouldn't recognize your own mother's picture the first time around. Take another look."

Mallory peered at the arrest-file photograph. "Hell, Pres, I don't know. What'd she do?"

"Arrested for prostitution. May 28, 1960. Gave this place as her address."

"That don't mean she lived here." Mallory was strongly defensive. "A smart broad would give any address."

"She lived here all right," Barry said.

"What makes you so sure?"

"Because she wasn't a smart broad. She was strictly a small-town product who hadn't been around here long enough to know the ropes."

Mallory took the picture again and stared at it. He turned it toward the light of the window and stared some more. He mumbled, "Marty Young?"

"What?"

The superintendent looked at Barry. "I just said 'Marty Young.' Well, maybe. She might have been the girl who lived with Kathy Samson. But not long, as I remember it." He shook his head. "I'm not sure."

"Kathy Samson? Still living here?"

"Yeah. Apartment 6-D."

"Thanks, Jim," Mayfield said sarcastically, "you've been your usual sweet self." He grabbed Painter's arm. "Come on, deputy, I'm going to introduce you to an old friend. You must have seen her picture in our exclusive collection."

The two police officers left the superintendent's office and moved toward the elevators. Mayfield leaned over to Barry and said confidentially, "Now, by the time we get to 6-D, our friend Mallory will have tipped her off on the house phone. Maybe, if we timed it right, some poor bastard on a matinee is pulling on his pants and beating it down the stairway."

Barry laughed. "It doesn't seem right, somehow."

Mayfield pushed the "up" button and the elevator door slid open. "No, it doesn't," he said, also laughing. "But by the time we get there, Kathy is going to be ready with her Whistler's Mother act. A real innocent, that broad."

Kathy Samson hung up the phone and said aloud, to no one at all, "Damn! Damn!" She moved to the closet, discarded her terry-cloth robe, revealing total nudity, and reached for a severe grey suit. She dressed hurriedly. By the time the door buzzer sounded she had only to push her feet into a pair of low, comfortable shoes. She moved deliberately to the door, opening it slowly.

"Hiya, Kathy," Mayfield said cheerfully, "may we come in?"

"Social call?"

"Like always, Kathy." Mayfield smiled crookedly. "I'd like you to meet a friend. Barry Painter. Deputy Sheriff Painter, to be exact, from back East."

Kathy looked intently at Barry, letting her eyes search him from head to toe. "Nice specimen," she said flippantly. "Come on in." As she led them into the tastefully furnished living room, she asked, "Care for a drink?"

"Not right now," Mayfield said. "We're looking for a girl and we believe you might know her." He handed her the Marty Young photograph.

"Well, sit down," she said, "while I look it over." She tossed herself into a deep, comfortable arm chair, carelessly exposing her attractive legs well past the knees. She was petite, her figure well proportioned. Auburn-haired. The two men sat on a sofa opposite her. Kathy gazed at the picture for about ten seconds. "Yeah, I knew her, but it's been a long time. Around sixty, maybe." She handed the photo back to Mayfield.

"Name?" the detective asked.

"Marty Young." She wasn't volunteering any information.

"Where'd she say she came from?"

"Oh, I don't know. From the East. New Jersey or Pennsylvania, or one of those places."

"How long was she here?"

"About three weeks. Maybe not even that long."

"What'd she do?"

Kathy looked up, startled. "What'd she *do?*"

"Yeah," said Mayfield.

"What the hell do you think she did?" the girl asked sarcastically. "She was a gawddamned grape picker. This is headquarters of the United Grapepickers of the World. Didn't you know that?"

Mayfield smiled. "Okay, so it was a dumb question. What ever happened to her?"

"I don't know." Kathy's face was sober, her voice calm. "She got busted and then after that she just up and left. I never heard from her again."

Barry joined in. "Did she ever mention the name Lotz?"

Just a brief pause. "Lotz? No."

"The name Mosser?"

No pause this time. "No."

"Anyone ever come to see her?"

Kathy's tinkly laugh filled the room. "You guys are in great form today! That's Dumb Question Number Two. You wanna try for three?"

Barry grinned. Somehow, he liked her style. "Okay, did anyone ever come to see her by the name of Mosser?"

"We don't ask for names or references."

"You never heard the name Mosser?"

"No."

"Or the name Lotz?"

"No. You're repeating yourself, deputy."

"Yeah, I guess I am," said Barry. "I have one other question—how did you come to meet Marty Young?"

Kathy pondered for a moment. "Well, I don't think it's any of your business . . . but, hell, she was introduced to me by a close friend. He asked me to take care of Marty, to take her in, so to speak . . . and I did."

"A close friend?"

"Yeah."

"Any name?"

"Yes," she said coldly, "he has a name, but I don't see that it'll mean anything to you." Kathy looked at Mayfield pleadingly. "You know how it is, Pres. . . ."

There was a pause. Mayfield didn't let it grow too long. "Well, thanks, Kathy. Gotta be going."

"Okay." She rose and the two men came to their feet. "Anytime I can help, just give me a call."

"Sure," said Mayfield. Kathy led them to the door.

As Barry and the Phoenix detective moved down the

hallway to the elevator, the deputy asked, "What the hell was all that about? The name of the guy who brought Marty Young here might be damned important! He might be our key to finding her now!"

Mayfield pushed the elevator button. "Look, Barry, there's a lot of muscle in this business. Kathy's a rarity—a whore without a pimp. But to stay that way, she has to do favors once in a while. So some procurer comes to her with this new girl, and Kathy has to put her up for a few weeks. I'm sure it has happened before. There was no way that Kathy was going to give you that name. She's afraid of what might happen to her if the police put the heat on that pimp."

Barry was adamant. "That doesn't make any damned sense! Martha was a total amateur. How in the hell would she get mixed up with a pimp?"

"How do you think a procurer get his new girls?"

"Yeah, well. . . ." Barry said sullenly. "But that guy might know where Martha is. Don't you see that?"

"I doubt it," said Mayfield. The elevator arrived at their floor, the doors slid open, and they entered. "Girls like Marty Young are a dime a dozen. In for a few weeks, then out again when it doesn't work out right. Who knows what the hell happens to most of them? They go home, or they go to another city, or they wind up marrying some bum and having three kids."

Painter shook his head. "I guess I'm dumb, but the name of that man seems critical to me."

The elevator reached the lobby floor.

"Look, deputy," Mayfield tried to explain as they crossed the lobby, "we might be able to follow up on Marty Young some other way. But you are never going to get that name out of Kathy Samson."

"You're that sure?"

Mayfield maintained his firmness. "I'm sure!"

Phil Stauffer had always told himself that he was a detail man, that he enjoyed the minutiae of his job, handling it with dispatch. Yet here it was almost noon and he was bogged down with detail that he was no longer relishing. His deputy had left for Phoenix only that morning and the sheriff was beginning to have a new appreciation of just how much of the minor detail he had been passing off on Barry Painter. Stauffer glanced at his watch and groaned aloud. "Crap!" he said to the emptiness of the office, opening the middle drawer of his desk. Into it he shoved the small mountain of paper work over which he had been laboring.

The sheriff had wanted to use the morning to follow up on Rufus Collins, the black pow-wow doctor who had reason to hate the late Charles Strickler, if the widow Strickler's evaluation was to be accepted. Now, however, the morning was at an end and he was still bound to the desk. Stauffer slammed the desk drawer closed, moving to the clothes rack to get his coat. As he was putting his arms into the sleeves, the door opened and District Attorney Barringer strolled in jauntily.

"I see I figured my time just about right," Fred said. "You're ready to leave for the luncheon."

"Luncheon?"

"Of course—the Chamber of Commerce 'Man of the Year' luncheon at the country club."

Stauffer winced. "Oh, God!" He glanced down at his calendar pad. There, under Wed., Dec. 3, he saw printed in bold letters: MAN OF YEAR LUNCH. "It completely slipped my mind."

The D.A. laughed. "And you a member of the selection committee."

Disgusted, Phil slumped back into his chair. "Fred, do you think there's any way I could pass it up? Barry's away, I'm swamped and I'm at least half a day behind in my schedule."

"Well, I don't give a damn whether you go or not," Barringer said lightly, "but since you were on the panel which selected Josh Oberdick 'Man of the Year' I don't see how you can bug out now."

"I guess you're right. You know, there are eight million other places I'd rather go right now than to that luncheon."

"Eight million?"

"Well, maybe two or three." The sheriff grinned. "But maybe I can get some business in anyway, since Doc Oberdick is certainly going to be there."

"He will if he hasn't forgotten it, too."

Dr. Joshua Oberdick's sheer effrontry amused Phil Stauffer. There sat the old man at the guest-of-honor table at a Chamber of Commerce luncheon (the most important such luncheon of the year), with Dottie Kissinger by his side. Everyone in the room, and that included the alleged pillars of the community, knew that Dottie was Oberdick's latest conquest. She was obviously ill at ease, but the elderly physician was the epitome of what the kids called "cool" these days. Josh joked with the chairman of the luncheon on his right and occasionally leaned over and whispered into Dottie's ear to his left, patting her hand or her knee.

As the waiters began to serve dessert, the chairman, banker Oscar Lord, stood, rapped a glass with his fork and began the ceremonies.

"For the past 29 years," said Lord, "the Young County Chamber of Commerce has been honoring a 'Man of the Year.' In each of those 29 years the honor could have gone to today's 'Man of the Year.' And, while he hasn't done anything of note recently . . ." Lord looked at Oberdick as he said those words and the doctor winked at him. For several moments the laughter rolled over the room, as Dottie blushed deeply and old Doc Oberdick just smiled broadly.

Order finally restored, the banker continued, "And, while he hasn't been active in the community in recent years . . ." Again, the rollicking laughter. Now the chairman was totally flustered, but Oberdick was enjoying the scene.

"Something tells me," Lord said as the laughter subsided again, "that I ought to forget that approach." He waited for the secondary laughter that came. "Dr. Joshua Oberdick is known to you all. He has served long years as the Young County Health Officer, he has been the very active president of the Young County Medical Society, he has never shirked his community responsibilities, he has always been there when service was called for . . ." Guffaws erupted.

"Oh, hell," Lord said, rapping the glass for order, "you people know what I want to say! We in this county owe Doc Oberdick a great deal and finally, though belatedly, we are getting around to acknowledging our debt. Dr. Joshua

Oberdick, I am proud to designate you as Young County Man of the Year for 1969!"

As one, the audience rose to its feet, applauding, whistling, cheering. The sheriff thought he had not heard such enthusiasm since the Missionville High School basketball team reached the state finals eleven years earlier. Josh bowed to the right, to the left, and raised his arms high in the air. Then, in a sudden move, he reached down, took Dottie's hand and pulled her to her feet. She was startled, but there wasn't much she could do except follow the lead of the old man. The applause and the cheers and the whistles grew even louder.

Oberdick let go of the embarrassed woman's hand, and she collapsed into her chair. Grinning broadly, the doctor also resumed his seat and, eventually, the applause trickled away. When it was quiet again, Josh rose, his visage sober, to face the microphone.

"You do an old man great honor," he said. "In my eighty years I have seen a lot here in Young County, Pennsylvania; a lot that has made me proud and a lot that has made me angry and frustrated. But pride or frustration, I have always tried to do my best. It's nice to know that one's best efforts are recognized occasionally. And I thank you."

There was applause again, but it ended quickly when Oberdick maintained his sober manner.

"What I am not sure of," he said, his face a grave mask, "is whether I am being honored today for community service, or whether—at eighty—it is just the ability *to service* that compelled you to give me this high award."

The impish grin returned to the handsome old face and, again, the audience rose to its feet. There was another loud demonstration as the head-table guests began to pump Oberdick's hand, and the hand of the flustered Dottie Kissinger.

As the luncheon crowd began to disperse, Stauffer made his way to the doctor's side. When he had his attention, the sheriff said, "You are an old fraud, Doc, and congratulations on the award."

"I understand you are one of those I have to thank for this."

"Oh, the selection wasn't so difficult. We couldn't think of anyone who'd done anything worthwhile, so we said, 'Hell, let's give it to old Josh. He's always good for a laugh.'"

Oberdick leaned over and whispered into the sheriff's ear, "I did make them swallow it, didn't I? I'm just sorry it was a bit rough on Dottie. But I couldn't resist doing it."

Stauffer laughed. "I hope Dottie survives this."

"She will, she will," Josh said with assurance. "She's of sturdy stock."

"Listen, Doc," the sheriff said, "in a couple of minutes, when the room clears out a bit, could you give me five minutes? I need your help."

"The Strickler case?"

"That's it, Doc."

"Just give me a minute or two." Oberdick turned to other luncheon guests, shaking their hands and accepting their congratulations. Dottie stood off to the side now, watching the old man operate. A smile spread across her pretty face. She was beginning to enjoy the situation. Oberdick knew his woman— *sturdy stock!*

By the time Josh was able to extricate himself from the well-wishers, Stauffer had seated himself at one of the tables already cleared by the waiters and the doctor joined him there.

"Now tell me what I can do to help you."

"Do you know Rufus Collins?"

"I certainly do, and he is not one of this county's most exemplary citizens."

"Tell me about him."

"As you know, I'm sure," the doctor began, "Collins is a black man, the only black pow-wow practitioner in this area that I know of. I've heard that Collins and Charlie Strickler were not the best of friends. Charlie was such a bigoted sonofabitch."

"I have one story," the sheriff interjected, "that says the rift between Charlie and Rufus came because Rufus's powers were passed on to him by Lizzie Zearfoss, who also performed the same for Charlie. Might that be true?"

"It is true," Oberdick said firmly. "Old Lizzie was very liberal in her proliferation of the pow-wow magic." He smiled. "She was positively evangelistic about John George Hohman and the legacy he left. You know, of course, about the theory that pow-wow powers must be passed from man to woman, and vice versa?"

"Yeah."

"Well, Lizzie was the well-spring of the woman-to-man onpassing, so to speak. She didn't give a damn at all about the fact that Rufus Collins was a Negro. Charlie, though, challenged Lizzie on it and she agreed, as I understand it, to withdraw the powers from Rufus. Rufus, on the other hand, didn't pay any attention to all of that and kept right on doing his thing."

"Uh huh. Well, that brings me to the key question," Stauffer said. "Was the dispute between Strickler and Collins severe enough to lead to murder?"

"Is Rufus Collins capable of murder?" the old man mused. "Yes, Rufus is capable of anything you can imagine. But somehow, I don't see him as the murderer of Charlie Strickler."

"Why not?"

"Rufus is a totally practical man. Unprincipled, but practical. Even though he probably hated Charlie's guts, he wouldn't have killed him unless he figured to gain something from it. For the life of me, I can't see how Charlie's death could be considered a gain for Rufus."

Stauffer looked purposefully at the old man. "If he had been paid to murder Charlie, wouldn't that have been a gain?"

"That's a point," Oberdick admitted. "It would also suggest some conspiratorial activity. Is your investigation moving in that direction?"

"No." The flat denial was because the sheriff had no intention of discussing the details of the investigation with Oberdick. He moved back to the point of his discussion with the doctor. "I'm going to see Collins this afternoon. Am I going to have trouble with him?"

"I wouldn't think you'd have any trouble at all. He's extroverted, arrogant, opinionated, confident that he can outwit any man. He's going to enjoy jousting with the sheriff of Young County."

At that juncture, Phil was tempted to ask Josh about what he knew of the whereabouts of Martha Lotz Mosser. Better wait, he told himself, until Barry reports from Phoenix. Right now, Rufus Collins was on his mind.

Westville was a Pennsylvania Dutch community not unlike several dozens of other small communities in the area. A crossroads town, with a long main thoroughfare, sprinkled with small businesses and neat homes. Dominating the town, in size, was the old feed mill hard by the railroad spur. It had once been the leading business in the community, but now it was in disrepair; lawn fertilizers, tulip bulbs, and tomato seed packets were its stock in trade. The more important milling part of the old building had long ago ceased to operate. The social center of the town was the volunteer fire company, where carefully polished engines and a rescue squad unit filled the garage, and where a well-stocked bar made the basement room an always-busy hangout. At the rear of the fire company building was a covered steel-and-concrete stage, where country music stars performed every Saturday night during the summer, providing the cash flow that enabled the small fire company to maintain some of the best fire-fighting equipment in the state.

It was on the main thoroughfare—called, appropriately, Westville Avenue—that Rufus Collins operated a small grocery store. It was in the front of what had been a two-family house; the two living rooms had been put together into a large store facility. But the original covered porch of the home remained, as did the green and white striped awning. There was no specific sign on the front of the building to indicate that this was a grocery store run by someone named Collins, but perhaps a dozen metal signs, bolted on to the brick veneer of the front of the house, told the story: Coca-Cola, Red Man Chewing Tobacco, Sunshine Bread, STP, TastyKake, Lucky Strikes, etc.

Sheriff Stauffer knew, from a query he had made at the fire company, that Collins lived in the rear of the building. As he walked up onto the porch, he wondered whether there was any Collins family. Nothing he knew of Rufus suggested that there was a wife and children. He tried the door, but it was locked. He looked around for a sign that would indicate the store hours, but found none. The Collins store apparently operated as did many small independent grocers in the area—open only when the supermarkets were not. Stauffer knocked on the door. There was no immediate answer, and he knocked again, this time more firmly.

"We're not open, for Christ sake!" The voice was angry and it came from deep within the building.

"This is Sheriff Stauffer," Phil shouted through the door. "I'd like to speak to you."

"Okay, okay." The sheriff could hear footsteps approaching the door, a lock was turned, and the door flung open. A bell on a spring above the door jingled madly.

"Sorry, sheriff," the black man said, "but these ain't store hours. Sometimes I think people want you to stay open twenty-four hours, just so's they can get a fuckin' quart of milk anytime they want. They just ain't got no feelin's for others."

"I understand," Stauffer said in his quiet way, "and I regret having to disturb you."

"No sweat. Come on in."

Collins slammed the door shut behind them, the bell jingling again. He snapped the lock. Collins was a big man—Phil thought of *giant*. Maybe six-five, weighing close to 275 pounds, massive hands, and his rolled-up sleeves showed heavy, muscular forearms. His head was shaved bald. His face had several scars that gave him a mean appearance. Moving easily on his long legs, the Negro led the way through the crowded little store and into a kitchen in the rear, where he directed Stauffer to take a seat at a round table covered with a flowered oilcloth. Somehow, the flowers were alien to the man.

Without asking whether Phil wanted any coffee, Collins took a pot off an electric stove (the pot looked tiny in his great hand), found two cups in a cupboard above the stove, and filled them with the hot, black liquid. He shoved one in front of Phil, keeping one himself. He made no mention of any cream or sugar.

Dropping into a chair opposite Phil, he said, "It's your move, sheriff."

Stauffer found himself amused by the brusque act played for him by Collins. "You know, of course," he began, "about the Charlie Strickler murder?"

"Yeah, I've been readin' that shit in the newspapers."

"You know, then, that there is speculation that pow-wow had something to do with it."

"Uh-huh."

"Well, Mr. Collins," the sheriff went on, "I have information that you and Strickler were not the best of friends, and that you might have had reason to want him dead."

"That's true enough!"

The candor of the answer didn't really surprise the sheriff. He waited for an elaboration, but it didn't come.

"I'm going to have to ask you," Phil said, breaking the awkward silence, "to give me your version of your relationship with Charles Strickler." The sheriff's request was in formal tones; there was an element of command in the words.

"You and I both know," said Collins, with a slight grin, "that I don't have to tell you anything. There are legal procedures set up for this kind of interrogation and I haven't seen any warrants or a subpoena."

Suddenly, Collins was a different man. The drawled speech, sprinkled with crude vernacular, was gone. It had been, Stauffer realized, a defensive sham. He knew, then, that Doc Oberdick was correct when he predicted that Collins would enjoy a "joust" with the sheriff. Phil decided quickly not to take obvious note of the change in Collins' verbal style.

"Mr. Collins," he said calmly, "I don't always stand on all the legal formalities. Most times they aren't necessary and, in all honesty, are sometimes cumbersome in an investigation. But if you insist, I can get an arrest warrant, and we will conduct this interrogation at the county lock-up."

Collins laughed a deep, rolling, happy laugh. "Just checking, sheriff, just checking. So you want to know about my association with the late Charlie Strickler?"

"That's the idea."

"Sheriff, I'm not a man given to hate. It's an emotion I don't care to harbor. It's stupid, debilitating. But, I *hated* Strickler—hated him passionately, you might say. He was ignorant, bigoted and belligerent. In the South he would have been called a 'red-neck.' I can imagine there might have been circumstances in which I might have killed him. But I didn't. Whoever did, though, performed a public service."

"For the moment," said Phil, "let's accept your denial. It would help me if you'd tell me what you knew of Strickler."

"I'd like to give you a little background first." Collins leaned back in the kitchen chair that seemed much too frail for his bulk. "It goes back almost twenty years. I was traveling with the Gitlin and Tilson carnival show as the resident strong man. It was a small show that played mostly still dates, sponsored by local Lions and Kiwanis and fire companies. There were two shows on the back end—the girl show and me. Strong man meant that I not only impressed the marks with feats of strength, but also took on whatever locals wanted to wrestle or box. Either one was okay. If I lost, the mark got fifty bucks. But believe me, I rarely lost."

"I can believe that."

"Every once in a while," Collins continued, "I'd run up against some wise guy who wore a big ring, or something like that, and the face shows it." He touched his scarred face with the tips of his fingers.

"You mean you boxed bare knuckle?"

"Oh, sure, it was quicker that way. Anyway, we were playing at a fire company not too far from here and I ran up against one of those local muscle boys who had been a boxer in college. He was good. He really cleaned me out, worked me over thoroughly. I hadn't had a loss in weeks, but when Izzy Gitlin had to lay out the fifty bucks, he wanted to deduct it from my pay, which was a lousy hundred and fifty a week. I told him what he could do with his job and left."

"Sounds like a wise choice," Phil said sympathetically.

"It was an easy decision," Rufus said. "I'd been through this area three or four times with the show and liked it. So it wasn't hard for me to decide to stay here. I got a furnished room in

Lebanon, got a laborer's job at Lebanon Steel, and was there about seven months when I read a story in the local paper about this old lady in Miller's Grove who was a pow-wow doctor."

"Lizzie Zearfoss?"

"That's the one," Collins answered jauntily, "and I decided to check out the pow-wow scam. I did a little reading in the public library and then went to see Lizzie. She was a kind old lady, really, and agreed to give me the powers. That's the way she put it. She had only one prohibition; I wasn't supposed to set up shop in her immediate territory. I agreed to that and she began to teach me. You know, she never once mentioned getting paid for it."

The sheriff interrupted. "You're aware that she's dead?"

"Yeah, I saw that in the paper." The big black man seemed genuinely sad. "Is it tied in with the Strickler murder?"

"Not that we know of," Phil told him. "But we do know that arson was involved."

"There are a lot of lousy people out there, Stauffer!" Collins opened and closed his powerful hands in anger.

"I agree." There was a pause. "Do you want to continue?"

"I was at Lizzie's place one day," Rufus said, "when this bastard Strickler came in. It turned out that he was also a pow-wow doctor (Lord, he really believed it!) and that Lizzie had been his patron. He took one look at me and it was instant dislike. He asked Lizzie right in front of me: 'Why are you helping this nigger?' Lizzie told him that anyone who wanted her help could have it. And it was strange, but I think the first time she was conscious of my color was when Strickler called me a nigger.

"Charlie screamed and carried on about me and Lizzie sent him away. But I learned later that he came back to put the squeeze on her, threatening to call in the authorities on her if she didn't dump me. When that didn't faze her, he turned to a little physical persuasion."

"You mean he struck her?" the sheriff broke in.

"*Struck* her?" Collins was infuriated by the recollection. "He beat the hell out of her! And, well, he forced her to rescind the powers she gave me. Now, that was really funny. I didn't *have* any powers; what she really taught me was the scam and how to handle the marks. I knew that, but Lizzie didn't and neither did Charlie. Lizzie, for God's sake, really had some kind of power—I never really understood what it was. But it was real. Charlie always thought he did, but he didn't have any more power than old Rufus here."

"So, your pow-wowing was all a sham?"

Collins looked at him inquisitively for a moment. "Sheriff, do you believe in pow-wowing?"

"I'm not sure," Stauffer said simply.

"And neither am I," Collins admitted. "I'm sure of one thing though—Rufus Collins is a fake. So was Charlie Strickler." He took a deep breath. "Anyway, Lizzie went through some ceremony that took my powers away and I left. I never saw her again. But I set up shop here in Westville, starting the store as a front, and to permit me to eat when the pow-wow thing didn't bring in enough money.

"Then, one day, Strickler walks into the store, screaming something about me defiling the ancient, magical powers of the Lord. When I tried to get him out of here, he hit me in the face. That man, was the biggest mistake he ever made. I wiped up the place with him, wrecked a lot of the store. I guess I would have killed him then if my next door neighbor hadn't called the police. The constable smoothed over the whole thing. Even got Charlie patched up somewhere without getting it on the record. Hell, I'm a local celebrity!" A hearty laugh rumbled up from his huge chest.

"Did you see Charlie again?"

"On and off in Missionville. We'd meet on the street, or something like that. But I always stayed away from him. And he wanted nothing to do with me. In addition to everything else he was, Charlie Strickler was a yellow coward!"

"You've never been to Strickler's farm?" Phil asked.

"Nope. Don't even know where it is exactly."

Stauffer sighed, scratching his chin absentmindedly with the end of his thumb nail. "Do you know any other people who might have wanted Charlie dead?"

"No."

"No ideas at all?"

"No. Look, sheriff, my connection with Strickler was brief and bitter. I have my own little thing here in this area and I don't pal around with people who call themselves pow-wow doctors. I'm just me, of Westville, Pa. I work a perfectly legitimate scam here that doesn't hurt anyone. End of story."

Phil grinned. "I've never before heard the words 'legitimate' and 'scam' used collectively in the same sentence."

"Well, believe it," Collins said defensively. "I sell a commodity some people want to buy. Faith, maybe, in a distorted kind of way."

"And you believe in what you sell?"

"Are you kidding?" Collins didn't ask the question sarcastically; perhaps *whimsically* would be more descriptive. "I have here in this black skull," he said, tapping his round, bald head, "more mumbo-jumbo junk than you can imagine. It has a real dollars-and-cents value, and not only for me. Did you ever hear the story of the start of the Missionville-to-Westville bus line?"

"No, I don't think I have."

"About eight years ago," Rufus began his explanation, "the Missionville Transit Company inaugurated a route to Westville, based on a petition from local citizens. For the first couple of days the business was fantastic. Full buses every run, sometimes with standees. Then, the business dropped off more than half. Well, the transit company got suspicious that the driver was skimming fares, so they put a checker on several of the trips. Sure enough, the fares were exactly what the driver said they were. But how to explain full buses in one period, and only half-full buses later?"

Collins's grin grew broader and broader as he warmed to the story. "The bus company executives called in the driver and asked him, 'How come?' The driver told them that there was a pow-wow doctor in Westville who works only during full moon, and that it was just a coincidence that the route was started during a full moon. And that's the way it's been ever since—full buses during full moon because of me! You'd think that the transit company would give me a cut." He laughed loudly. "Or, at the very least, an engraved plaque."

Stauffer joined in the laughter. "I never heard of that before, about pow-wow doctors only working during full moon."

"Well, sheriff," Rufus said proudly, "that's *my* gimmick! *I* started that. You might call it my contribution to the fine art of *hexerei!*"

Phil grinned. "You are a scoundrel, aren't you?"

"Oh, yeah, but one with a very retentive memory. For example, do you know the names of the angels of the twenty-eight houses of the moon?"

"Can't say that I do."

"Well, sir," Collins said with studied importance, "they are Asariel, Cabiel, Dirachiel, Scheliel, Amnodiel, Amixiel, Ardesiel, Neriel, Abdizriel, Jazariel, Cogediel, Ataliel, Azerniel, Adriel, Amutiel, Iciriel, Bethuael, Geliel, Requiel, Abrunael, Aziel, Tagried, Abheiel, and good old Amnixiel!"

"I'm impressed," Stauffer said lightly when Rufus had finished his rapid-fire delivery of the list. "And what does all that mean?"

"Mean? Sheriff, that impressive group of angelic names comes from what is known as the *Sixth and Seventh Books of Moses.* It's one of the tools of the pow-wow doctor. The content is supposed to have been translated from the ancient Hebrew, taken from the books of the Cabala and the Talmud for the so-called good of of mankind. It's old stuff; it's been around a long time—many centuries. It's the biggest bunch of verbal hash you ever saw. But the two books were supposed to have been revealed to Moses by God on Mount Sinai. They were handed down, it's said, to Aaron, Caleb, Joshua and to David, the father of Solomon. But David's high priest, a guy named Sadock, was supposed to have hidden the magical powers of the books from David. The story goes that they were rediscovered by the first Christian Emperor, Constantine the Great, and turned over to Pope Sylvester in Rome for translation. One source says these books were expunged from the Old Testament because of their *black magic* powers."

"Powers like what?" the sheriff wanted to know.

Collins grinned, his black face shining. He was enjoying himself. "Well, the Sixth Book of Moses involves the seven secret seals that enable you to conjure, which means to summon a spirit, or a devil, to do your bidding. Each of the seven seals has some special meaning. For instance, if you take the first seal and bury it in the earth where treasure is thought to exist, the treasure will come to the surface itself, without any digging. Or, as the book says, without any *presence in plane lunio,* whatever that means."

"Sounds like Latin."

"It probably is, but what I don't understand I just shove aside. There's plenty of stuff to use in the mumbo-jumbo." He sucked in a big breath of air, exhaling it slowly. "Just to give you the full import of these secret seals, the second brings its holder good fortune and blessings, the third causes you to be much loved and to defeat all your enemies, the fourth saves a person from misery and assures long life, the fifth protects you against illness, the sixth enables you to interpret dreams, and the seventh is back to treasure again—it reveals all of the precious minerals in a mine, a divining rod kind of thing."

"Handy stuff to have."

"You bet," agreed the black man. "Then, when you get into the Seventh Book of Moses, there are other goodies, called tables."

"Tables?"

"Yeah, it's more of the conjuring stuff. The first table, for example, is of the 'spirits of the air' and relieves the bearer of all necessity. I take that to mean that it provides all the needs of life. The second table conjures up fire, the third brings great fortune by water, the fourth gives you the treasures of the earth again, the fifth brings good luck in play, the sixth assists in overcoming law suits and disputes, the seventh lets you win all quarrels, the eighth . . ."

"Oh, there are more than seven this time," Stauffer commented.

"There are twelve tables," said Collins. "Anyway, the eighth will help you attain places of honor, the ninth will make you successful in all kinds of business, the tenth will give you wealth in chemistry, the eleventh gives you the treasures of the sea, and the twelfth—ah, the twelfth is my favorite!—will call forth all the spirits of magic and will serve you in all things."

"You can't ask for more than that."

"Exactly! The whole basis of all this nonsense is that it answers all questions and conquers all evils. Pow-wowing, or *hexerei*, promises the ultimate panacea. And, if you live a grubby little life, with little hope of real achievement; or, if you're ill, and the medical doctors can't seem to help you, *hexerei* might seem pretty good to you. It enables you to believe that there is some hope. And if you believe that, I guess there *is* hope." Rufus smiled wanly. "It's not all crap, you know."

"Do I detect," the sheriff said quietly, "some cracks in the armor of the cynic?"

"Not really," Collins answered soberly, "but, damn it, some people's lives are so desperate and if some of this mumbo-jumbo helps them believe that, for a minute or two, the desperation isn't quite so serious." He paused. "Then . . . hell . . . I give 'em mumbo-jumbo. And they give me some money. I'm happy and maybe they are, too. I don't really know." The black man threw up his hands. "But this is getting pretty far afield from Charlie Strickler's murder."

Stauffer rose from the table. "Yes, it is. And I've got a ton of work to do." He stuck out his hand to Collins.

Rufus was surprised by the abruptness of Stauffer's action. "You mean that's all you want to ask me?"

"You said you had nothing to do with Strickler's death, didn't you?"

"Yeah."

"For now," the sheriff said, "I'm taking that as the Gospel truth."

Collins also got to his feet and shook Phil's hand. "That's good to know." And he started into an incantation: *"I, your servant Rufus, conjure thee Spirit Ofel, by Alpha and Omega, Lezo and Yschirios, Ohin Ission Niva, by Tetragramaton, Zeno, by Peraclitus Ohel, by Orelenius, Lima, by Agla, that ye will obey and appear before me and fulfill my desire, thus in and through the name of Elion, which Moses named. Selah!"*

"What does that mean?"

"Who knows?" Rufus's voice was very tired. "Who knows?

But ain't it fuckin' impressive?"

Barry sipped the Drambuie and looked around the crowded hotel dining room. It had seemed a shame to him that he had to be here in Phoenix alone, that the delicious dinner he had just eaten had to be eaten alone. In idly glancing about, his eyes stopped on the attractive women in the restaurant, each with a male companion. Barry finished the liqueur and gestured to the waiter.

"Anything else, sir?"

"No. Just the check. A fine meal."

"Thank you, sir."

It had been a frustrating day. Finding "Marty Young" in the police files had appeared to be a big break. But Detective Mayfield's insistence that Kathy Samson would not reveal anything more about the Missionville girl had dampened Barry's spirits. The good meal had helped to revive him. *But, damn it, I hate to eat alone.* The waiter handed him the check, Barry gave him too large a tip, and the deputy was bowed out of the dining room.

As he walked through the lobby, a lighted sign caught his eye: *Telephones.* He paused, felt in his pocket for change, and walked to the rack holding the telephone directories. He found the number for the Aztec Arms and dialed it. The phone rang six times (Barry always counted the rings) before there was an answer.

"Aztec Arms." The voice was male and faggy.

"Miss Kathy Samson, please."

"I'm sorry, sir, she's not in right now. May I suggest you call back in fifteen minutes?"

Barry hung up. He shrugged his shoulders and walked through the lobby and out into the warm night. He looked at his watch. Only 9:30. Too early to go to bed. The deputy walked lazily down the street, carefully looking at the long-legged girls who passed him, gazing disinterestedly into shop windows. He walked almost ten blocks before he reached into his pocket and found he had no cigarettes. Up ahead was a drug store. Inside the store he killed some more time, glancing through the selection of magazines. As he started to open the pack of cigarettes, he saw a telephone sign again. This time he didn't have to look in the book for the number. That surprised him, because he usually had a poor memory for phone numbers. The phone rang only three times before it was answered.

That same faggy voice: "Aztec Arms."

"Kathy Samson."

"One moment, please."

Barry waited, lighting a cigarette as he did.

"Hello?"

"Kathy?"

"May I ask who's calling?" It was caution born of experience.

"This is Barry Painter. I was there earlier today with Harry Mayfield."

Caution held in the voice. "And?"

"And I thought I'd give you a call tonight."

There was no reply. Only silence.

"You know . . ." Barry said, now searching for the right words. He suddenly felt like a schoolboy. "A call to see if you were doing anything tonight."

Her loud laugh caused Barry to move the phone away from his ear. When he put it back she was still laughing.

"Well, that's Number Three! And, deputy, you win the prize. To see if I'm doing anything tonight. You *are* a winner, Mr. Painter!"

Only then did it occur to Barry how inane his remark had been. He joined in the laughter. "Maybe I'd better dial again and start all over."

"No need to spend the dime, Barry," she giggled. "What can I do for you?"

"Depends on how busy you are."

"Are you asking that as a cop or as a client?"

"A client." That sounded too commercial and Barry quickly added, "As a friend."

Kathy laughed. "Okay, friend, come on over. Are you nearby?"

"I haven't the slightest idea where I am. But I'll grab a cab right now."

The greeting at the door of Kathy's apartment was not unlike the first one he had gotten—a head-to-toe appraisal by those knowing eyes.

"I meant to ask you earlier," Barry said, now emboldened, "but it didn't seem to be the right time. Does the merchandise look good to you?"

"Not bad, not bad at all." She slipped her arms around his neck and the voice modulated. "Football player?"

She had struck the right nerve. Barry was pleased. "Used to be." He couldn't resist adding, "For the Philadelphia Eagles. Crapped up a knee and that was it."

She stood on her tiptoes and playfully stuck her tongue in his right ear. Barry flinched. She giggled, a little-girl giggle. "I'm not too much worried about knees, are you?"

"Not me," said Barry. "There are a helluva lot more important things."

"My sentiments exactly." She dropped her arms from around his shoulders, took his hand, and led him into the living room. "A drink this time?"

"This time, okay. Scotch, please."

Kathy went to a small bar in the corner of the room, brought out a bottle of Grant's 12 and held it up for him to see. "This okay?"

"Fine."

"On the rocks?"

"Fine."

She poured the drink over the ice cubes and brought it to him. "You're not too damned hard to please, are you?"

"Not when you're offering Grant's 12." He took the glass. "You not drinking?"

"I don't usually when I'm working."

"Are you working now?"

"Am I?" She bent down and brushed her lips over his ear.

Barry pulled her to him with his free hand and tried to kiss her, but she pulled away.

"Wait a damned minute," she said lightly, "the key question hasn't been answered yet. *Am* I working?"

Barry took a large swallow of the smoky Scotch, placed the

glass on the end table, and reached for her with both hands.

"Depends," he answered.

"On what?"

"On whether I have to buy or not."

She allowed his hands to catch hers and he pulled her into his arms, leaning back deep into the sofa. She looked into his face. "You're a cocky sonofabitch, aren't you?"

"I try to be."

"And a goddamned hick, too."

"Right again." He kissed her full on the mouth and, after an instant, she responded. Her left hand wandered around his neck and her fingers lightly ran back and forth over the short hairs. To Barry it seemed that little sparks were burning into his hair roots. Then she moved away from his lips.

"Only a hick," Kathy said, "would come into this apartment and try to get it for free."

"Right," he agreed with a grin, "only a hick."

He kissed her again. This time she relaxed completely, her hands wandering, setting off more little sparks. She drew away finally, looked inquisitively at him for a moment, then rose and walked to the telephone. She waited for the switchboard operator to answer and, in a rather prim voice, announced, "I'm out for the rest of the evening."

As she replaced the phone in the cradle she turned back to Barry, smiling. "Hicks are pricks."

"A well-turned phrase, ma'am," the deputy said. "And a well-turned broad, too. Shall we dance?"

8 THURS., DEC. 4, 1969

Barry came awake suddenly. For a moment he was disoriented, but then he remembered where he was. He blinked in the sunlight filtering through the flimsy curtains, and turned to look at the attractive girl sleeping beside him. He had always prided himself on his ability to satisfy women. This, he knew, had been another satisfying experience. He leaned over and kissed her on the cheek. She stirred, opening her eyes.

"Again?" she asked sleepily.

He smiled. "It's up to you."

"Hicks..."

"I know, I know!" They both laughed.

Kathy Samson propped herself up on one elbow. "You know, Barry, I have one failing."

"I hadn't noticed."

"No, it's true," she insisted, "I have one major failing. I *really* like it! Girls in my line of work aren't supposed to feel that way. And you, you hick, cost me about two hundred bucks last night, maybe three!"

Barry whistled appreciatively. "Prices are somewhat lower back in my town."

"I'll bet the quality is, too."

"You win the bet."

She dropped the sheet that had been covering her and moved lightly off the bed, heading for the bathroom. Barry's eyes followed her and the desire returned to him. When she came back, still naked, he reached for her and she came to him, covering his strong body with her smaller and whiter one. They lay together that way for several minutes, neither one moving. Barry kissed her lightly. "A question?"

"As a friend?" she asked.

"A friendly cop."

Kathy studied his face. "Okay, ask."

"Did you tell us the truth about Marty Young?"

There was a long pause as she continued to look into his face, searching for something, it seemed. She slid off his body, curled up alongside him and kept an arm tightly strung across his chest. Finally, she spoke. "First, may I ask *you* a question?"

"Sure."

"Did you come here last night with the intention of asking me whether I had lied to you?"

"Partly." He said it without hesitancy.

"Barry, honey, what the hell does that mean?" Kathy's voice wasn't calm anymore. He rolled over on his side and looked at her.

"That means," he explained, "that I came here wanting to get laid. And, I *also* came up here, as a second thought really, to ask you more questions about Marty Young. That's *partly*, right?" There was another silence. "Angry?"

"Nope. Just wanted to know where I stand." She sat up, pulling the sheet up to her shoulders. "So, ask your questions."

"How much did you really learn about Marty Young after she came here?"

"I learned her name—or what she said was her name—I learned she was from the East somewhere, and I learned that she was very unhappy. And that's it."

"Unhappy? Why?"

"Because she was scared out of her skull that some guy was going to come here and find her. She was so scared that I could never get her to open up about it." She thought for a moment. "I always thought that was the reason she left so soon."

"What were the circumstances of her leaving?"

"Well, it was sudden," Kathy said. "She got an envelope one day with some money, I think, and a plane ticket. She packed what few clothes she had and was gone."

Barry showed renewed enthusiasm for the questioning.

"An envelope—from whom?"

"I'd only be guessing."

"Guess a little."

"It was left at the desk downstairs one night. My guess is that my friend left it for her, because I know he was in town about that time."

"About that friend . . ." Barry started.

"No, Barry."

"Harry Mayfield said you'd never tell me because you're afraid of the muscle in this business."

There was a nervous laugh from Kathy. "I knew he'd think that, but that's *not* the reason."

"But, honey, the name of the guy who brought Marty here is critical to me!"

"Oh, Barry . . ." Kathy yawned and stretched, acting out boredom. As she stretched, the sheet fell to her waist. Barry was determined not to be distracted from his interrogation.

"Look," he said very deliberately, "I'm going to do something that might be dumb, but I'm going to lay out the whole thing for you. Then, if you don't want to tell me, well, okay."

Barry sat up in the bed and launched into the story of the Strickler murder, of the relationship between Johnny Mosser and Martha Lotz (a.k.a. Marty Young), and the arson death of Lizzie Zearfoss. He thought it valid to tie together the Strickler and Zearfoss deaths, even though the sheriff's office had no real connective links. Barry did not tell her he knew that Martha Lotz Mosser's airline ticket to Phoenix had been paid for by Dr. Joshua Oberdick.

"So, what we have," he concluded, "is a very, very strange case in which there have already been two murders. And maybe Martha Lotz, or Martha Mosser, or Marty Young, will be the third. I was going to say 'It's that simple,' but it's not simple at all."

She maintained her silence.

"Did you like Marty Young?" Barry asked.

"She was a nice kid."

"Then help her. Tell me who brought her here."

She reached over, put her arms around Barry's neck and

kissed him. "You big hick." She sighed. "Darling, in my whole lousy life there have been so few good people. You might—please notice the word 'might'—be one of them. But I'm sure the man who brought Marty Young to me *is* one of them." She held Barry close to her.

"Back about twelve years ago," she said quietly, "I was in San Franscisco. Just a kid, and in trouble. I was a junkie, main-lining heroin, and earning money for it any way I could. Some of those ways weren't pretty. Then I met this great man. He was sweet and kind and—not to be overdramatic—life-saving. He paid for me to go to a private clinic and kick the habit. It was terrible, but he saw me through it. Then, he gave me money to get back on my feet, and I came here."

She looked around the bedroom. "Maybe you'd say that all of this isn't much of a life, but if you could have seen the filth and despair that man brought me out of, well . . ."

"Don't you think he'd want you to help Marty Young if you could?"

Kathy went on with her narration as though Barry had not spoken. "He never asked me for anything . . . nothing . . . until he brought Marty Young here. I took her in, because I remembered—God, how I remembered!—how desperate I was once. I owed him, Barry. I still owe him—I owe him anonymity."

"This man," Barry asked. "Are you still in touch with him?"

"From time to time I hear from him, but not on a regular basis. I haven't really seen him in about two years."

"Where does he live?"

She released her hold on Barry, got out of the bed and walked to the window, still naked. "Barry, give it up! Please don't pressure me anymore." She was pleading. Then suddenly, she began to weep. He went to her and gathered her in his arms.

"I *need* to know, Kathy," he said gently. "Honest to God, I need to know. I really believe that girl's life is in danger." The words were spoken almost in a whisper, but the urgency was clear.

Kathy pushed him away at arm's length. "He lives in New York," she said with resignation.

"New York?" The information surprised him.

"You see," she said, "it's just a coincidence that he knows Marty Young. He had nothing to do with your damned Pennsylvania pow-wow."

Barry tried to reassure her. "He probably doesn't. But the key to this is finding Marty and protecting her. Your friend would probably want that, too."

Kathy came close to him again, putting her arms around his middle, and snuggling her head against his chest. "Deputy, are you for real?"

"Well, I . . ."

"Should I really trust you?"

He kissed her on the top of the head. "You're going to have to make that decision, Kathy."

Her head stayed cradled on his chest. "His name is John Richards." She tilted her head and looked into his face. "His telephone number in New York is 555-5658. That's all I know." She let go of him and walked to the night stand beside the bed to get a cigarette. As she exhaled the first puff, she turned again to the deputy. "For God's sake, Barry, I hope I did the right thing."

"You did, Kathy."

She shook her head in doubt. Then she changed, smiling as though throwing off the doubt. "Come here."

He went quickly to her and they embraced, kissing passionately. In a quick move, she shoved him away. "Get into the shower and get out of here," she ordered, "or do I have to call the cops?"

Barry laughed, please to see the slightly cynical, bantering Kathy again. "Nope, I'll go peaceable-like. But, I'll be back."

"As a cop?"

His face sobered. "Oh, yeah, well ma-am, I ain't *really* a peace officer, ya see. I just made up that there tale."

She giggled that little-girl giggle again. "Oh, hell, get out of here! I've got to make some money today."

The deputy padded toward the bathroom. "Shameless," he said with a chuckle, "just plain shameless." She threw a pillow at his retreating naked figure.

Barry sprawled across the hotel room bed, waiting for the telephone to ring. He had called Sheriff Stauffer with his information about John Richards, carefully editing out the manner in which he had gathered it. Now he was waiting for Phil to follow up on it and call him back.

It had been 10 a.m. when he placed the call to his superior, but he had forgotten that ten o'clock Phoenix time was only 7 a.m. in Missionville. He had reached Stauffer at his home, just as he was starting breakfast. As he waited now, Barry tried to read a newspaper, but his mind wandered. He kept seeing Kathy in that comfortable, big bed, and the sensations of being near her kept coming back to him. He sailed the newspaper halfway across the room. Rolling over on his back, he stared up at the ceiling, counting the tiny cracks in the plaster. He pulled himself from the bed and paced the small hotel room.

"Oh, Christ!" he said aloud in his boredom. Yet it was more than boredom that made him so restless. He returned again to Kathy's reluctance to reveal the name of John Richards, and he wondered whether he had done the right thing in wheedling it out of her. *That was a lousy thing to do!—No, hell, I was just doing my job!* As he paced, he found himself methodically counting the lines in the striped wallpaper, hearing her name between each mental count: *One, Kathy, two, Kathy, three, Kathy, four* . . . The telephone rang. Barry glanced at his watch as he moved to answer it. The time was 11:30 a.m., Phoenix time.

"I called the New York number," Stauffer told him, "and got an answering service. They said Mr. Richards won't be available for three or four days, and they don't have a number where he can be reached. For the moment, then, it's a blank."

"Shit!"

"Don't be discouraged," Phil told him. "This is a solid lead. And, Barry . . ."

"Yeah?"

"Good work."

"Thanks." There was a slight pause. "Listen, Phil, maybe I ought to go to New York and . . ."

"Not right now. We've got plenty to do right here. When can

you get back?"

"Not today—no plane," he answered quickly. Barry couldn't remember ever having lied to the sheriff before. "But I guess I can get a plane out tomorrow morning."

"Good. See you tomorrow." As an afterthought, "Oh, Barry, did you get a description of this Mr. Richards?"

The deputy stammered in embarrassment. "Ah . . . ah . . . no, I didn't, Phil. My informant . . . ah. . . ."

Stauffer laughed. "Don't let it shake you, Barry. But maybe, before you get back tomorrow, you'll be able to do that."

"I'm not sure, but I'll try."

"Fine. See you tomorrow."

Barry was angry with himself as he hung up the phone. He slammed a fist into his palm, picked up the phone again, dialed "9" to get an outside line, and dialed Kathy's number once more.

"Aztec Arms," a voice said, not the same one the deputy had heard before. This time there had been an answer on the first ring. Not much action at this hour of the day, Barry thought.

"Miss Samson, please."

"Just one moment."

"Sonofabitch," Barry muttered to himself, still angry at his lapse. Then he heard her voice and the anger fled.

"Hi! This is Barry."

"Hi, honey."

"Listen, baby, I'm going to have to leave tomorrow morning, and I was wondering whether you were serious about making money today."

"Got something better in mind?"

"Well, I thought maybe we could spend the day together—a picnic, or something."

Kathy giggled. "*You* are really something, Deputy Barry Painter. A picnic, yet!"

"Well, why not?"

"Why not, indeed?" she said enthusiastically. "Hey, get over here right now. We'll use my car."

"Stand fast, wench, I'm already on the way!"

Phil and Nancy Stauffer sat nervously in the bright, spacious closed-in sun porch that served as a patients' sitting room at the Missionville Hospital. They were waiting for a nurse to come and tell them that their daughter was ready to be discharged. It was Thursday and Nancy had not forgotten the terror she had felt on Monday when Debbie was stricken with acute appendicitis. She looked at Phil, debating momentarily with herself as to how she would phrase the question she wanted to ask. "I guess there's nothing new on that telephone call we got about Debbie, huh?"

"No, nothing." Phil was embarrassed that he had to admit that his investigation had turned up nothing on the 'nut' call. "We're still looking into it, honey, but there's not much progress."

"It's scary, Phil."

"Yeah, I know." He squeezed her hand. "But I really think it was just a one-time nut call. What made it seem so bad was the coincidence of Debbie getting sick right after it."

"You're convinced it was a coincidence?"

The sheriff's answer was given lightly and with a smile. "Oh, sure, Nance. You might say the guy lucked out with his phone call. I'm sure when he made it he never had any idea that Debbie would actually be sick. He was just trying to annoy us. He had no idea, I'm sure, just how *much* he would annoy us."

She looked out of the big windows of the one-time porch. "I wish I could feel the same way about it as you do. I'm still frightened."

Phil, guilty with the knowledge that there had been a second call of which Nancy had no knowledge, wished his wife would drop the subject. "Debbie is fine now," he said, "and we'll be taking her home in a few minutes."

"You're still checking into the phone call, aren't you?"

"Certainly." There was a hint of annoyance in his voice. "You don't think I'm going to ignore this whole thing, do you?"

Nancy reached over and kissed him on the cheek. "Of course not, darling. You'll have to forgive a worried mother."

Phil returned the kiss. He sighed. "We'll get the bastard, believe me!"

The nurse entered the room to tell them that Debbie was ready to be discharged. "She wants to know, Mrs. Stauffer, whether you could come and help her with her hair."

Nancy laughed. "She always was a vain little lady."

"You go help her," Phil said, "and I'll stroll down to the front desk and get all the paperwork squared away. I'll meet you both there."

"Fine, darling." Nancy and the nurse moved toward the elevators. Phil moved leisurely down the long hall toward the lobby. At an alcove he passed a line of vending machines, looking at the variety of candy bars available. He shook his head, remembering that he had to watch his weight, and moved on.

At the front desk, Stauffer said, "I'd like to square away the bill on Miss Debra Stauffer."

"Certainly," said the woman clerk. "Oh, by the way, Sheriff Stauffer, someone has left a message for you." She handed him a plain white envelope, business-size.

"Thank you." He ripped open the envelope. Inside was a piece of white paper, three-quarters of an 8½ by 11 sheet. Apparently a printed letterhead had been torn off. The message on the paper was typed. As Phil read it, anger grew on his handsome face.

To the Smart-Ass Sheriff,

Today you are going to take Debra home from the hospital and right now you think her appendicitis was a coincidence. But it wasn't. I told you a spell would be placed on your daughter and it was. It's still on her. It's not ended, Mr. Smart-Ass. There are powers greater than you can imagine. Powers of life and death!!!! We will not allow unbelievers like you and Rev. Fenstermacher to live in defiance of the truth. Amen! Selah!

The sheriff read the note twice. Then he carefully examined the envelope. His name had been typed on the front of the envelope, but there were no other markings on it. "Excuse me, miss," Phil said to the hospital clerk, "where did this note come from?"

"I don't know, sheriff. It was on the desk here when I came into work this morning. About 9:05." She smiled. "I was a couple of minutes late this morning."

Phil looked at his watch. It was just past noon. So the note had been there for three hours; perhaps it had been there much longer than that. "Do you replace anyone when you come in in the morning?" Phil asked. "I mean, does anyone else use that desk?"

"No, sir. After I leave at night, the nurses and doctors drop papers and reports, and sometimes notes, on my desk here. I go through them every morning. But I'm the only one who uses this desk."

"So anyone could have put this envelope on your desk?"

"That's right."

"At any time from the time you left yesterday . . ."

"About five-fifteen."

". . . until you arrived here this morning at 9:05?"

"Yes." She began to show concern. "Is anything wrong, sheriff?"

He forced a broad smile. "No, no. Just someone playing a little prank. I can guess who it is . . . he's always playing little jokes."

"Yes, sir." The clerk went back to her paper work.

Phil was reading the note again when the elevator door in the lobby opened and he saw Nancy emerge, followed by Debbie in a wheelchair pushed by the nurse. He hurriedly jammed the note and the envelope into his inside jacket pocket and moved toward the group. "My, don't you look pretty!" he said to his daughter.

"Oh, my hair!" said Debbie. "It's a mess!"

Phil smiled. "Some mess." He bent down and kissed her on the cheek. "I just have to sign another paper over there . . ." he pointed to the desk ". . . and we'll be ready to go home."

The sheriff hurried to the desk. "Is everything in order with the bill?"

"Yes, sir," said the clerk. "Just sign here." She slid a paper across the countertop. "We'll send everything to the insurance company."

"That's a help." Phil scrawled his name at the bottom of the statement, not even glancing at the total. "Thanks much."

Then, in a confidential tone: "Listen, miss, please don't mention the envelope to anyone. I want to handle my funny friend in my own way." He winked at her.

"Yes, sir," she laughed. "I understand."

Stauffer returned to the group by the elevator. "Isn't it nice," he said to Nancy, "to be taking our little girl home again?"

"Wonderful, darling, just wonderful!"

For Barry and Kathy it had been an idyllic day. They had had their picnic, driving far out into the desert to be alone. They had chattered away all day, about subjects ranging from desert lizards to impressionist paintings. They had laughed, they had been serious, they had been close. But without pre-arrangement, they had not talked about Barry's job, or Kathy's lifestyle. Now they were back in Kathy's apartment. Barry was sprawled on the sofa, holding a Scotch. Kathy lounged in a big easy chair opposite him, her shoes kicked off and her feet propped on a hassock.

She grinned at him. "Nice day, huh?"

"The best! Tired?"

"In a nice, warm way." There was a silence. "Do you really have to leave in the morning?"

"Uh huh."

"Damn!"

"I'll be back." He was firm with the assurance.

Kathy rose from her chair, moved to the sofa and sat down next to the sprawling Barry, pushing him a little bit to find room to sit. "You know, I haven't known you long enough to even find out your shirt size."

"Sixteen-and-a-half collar, two sleeve."

". . . And, yet, I find myself wanting to say that I love you. I'm not going to say it, though, because I think I ought to be prudent and cautious. But maybe, just maybe, that moment could be soon."

He took her face in his hands, pulled her toward him, and kissed her lightly on the lips. "A question?"

"Sure."

"Is saying 'I love you' important to you?"

"Yeah," she said soberly, "because if I find someone I can

honestly say it to—well, that's going to be a very important day in my life."

"When did you say 'I love you' last?"

Kathy surprised Barry with her frankness. "I said it several times to John Richards. Frequently, even. But it's not the kind of love I'd like to feel with you. I love John for the image he is—kind and considerate and, it seems to me, a totally unselfish man."

"Did you go to bed with him?" The question was asked in a flat tone, with no hint of accusation or jealousy.

"No."

"Didn't he attract you that way?"

"Oh, he did! But, he's much older than I am. Somehow, however, our relationship didn't develop along those lines." She smiled at the recollection. "He's a charming and handsome old devil, too." She shrugged. "It just never came down to going to bed. I suspect that he didn't need me that way."

Barry nodded. He had gotten some kind of a description of John Richards without pumping Kathy for it. And while the description was only fractional, he wanted to let it go at that. "Kathy, it's been a great day for me!"

"How many hours do we have?"

The deputy looked at his wristwatch. "Well, it's nine-fifteen now, and I have a plane at eight in the morning. So less than eleven hours."

Kathy rose to her feet. She reached down, took him by the hand and tugged at him. "Come with me, hick. I want you to hold me for as many of those eleven hours as possible."

Arms locked around each other, they slowly walked into the bedroom.

Reverend Nelson Fenstermacher, answering the ring of his parsonage bell, opened the door to find Sheriff Stauffer standing there. "Phil! How nice to see you!"

"I'm sorry to bother you, pastor, especially on a Thursday night, when I know you must be working on your sermon."

"No, no," the minister said quickly, "I'm finished with that already, and I was just trying to catch up on some reading. But

I'd much rather chat with you. Please, come in."

Stauffer, who had told Nancy that he had some paper work to complete at the office, entered the parsonage. Mrs. Fenstermacher greeted him warmly, then judiciously excused herself, as the minister led the sheriff into his study. Once seated there, Phil poured out the entire story of the buried lock of hair, of his reaction to the Fenstermacher sermon, of the cruel phone calls—the one at the house and the one at the hospital after Debbie's operation. And finally, the sheriff showed Reverend Fenstermacher the typed note he had received at the hospital earlier that day.

Fenstermacher held the note in front of him. "We are living in a very sick world, Phil, but I suppose you would know that better than I do. But let me tell you this: You must not allow this kind of sickness . . ." he tapped the note ". . . to destroy your basic faith. I'm aware that you will do everything possible to bring this . . . this sick mind to justice. But in the final analysis, your reaction to this kind of thing *must* be tempered by your own faith." He smiled. "Anyway, that's the way I always handle this kind of thing."

"*You* get this kind of stuff?" Phil was genuinely surprised.

"Of course," the pastor answered in a matter-of-fact manner. "I could not represent my God adequately if I did not espouse his cause strongly, sometimes strongly enough to draw criticism, even unbalanced criticism."

"In specific terms, did last Sunday's sermon draw that kind of reaction?"

Fenstermacher laughed heartily. "It certainly did! And I rejoiced in it, because it meant that I'm doing my job."

Stauffer's face was solemn. "I'd like to know about those reactions."

"Oh, Phil, those kinds of things I keep to myself. They're really not matters for the police." He waved his hand as though dismissing Phil's request.

"Pastor, I have a job to do, too."

"Of course you do." The old minister was apologetic. "One of my failings, Phil, is that I look upon my own job as the most important calling of all, and I forget that others have commitments to duty as well. I'm sorry about that." He sighed and leaned back in his chair. "Well, immediately after returning to the parsonage from church last Sunday morning, I got three telephone calls."

"*Three?*"

"I've had better ratings on other sermons." He laughed again. "Let's see . . . yes, there were three. Two of the voices I recognized. Repeat callers, you might say, who see fit to comment anonymously on a lot of my sermons. My own personal devil's advocates, I would say. But the third call . . . now that one was different. A male voice chastizing me for my failure to recognize the spiritual value of pow-wowing, and warning me of future harm to myself if I persisted in my ignorance."

"A Pennsylvania Dutch accent?"

"Yes, but there's nothing unusual about that."

"Maybe not," said Phil. "I asked that only because the man who called me had a Pennsylvania Dutch accent."

Reverend Fenstermacher grinned. "You know, Phil, this may be somewhat perverse, but I get some kind of pleasure out of jousting with these callers. I admit, however, that it gets a bit frustrating when they hang up just as I am about to make my most scholarly point."

The sheriff shook his head. "Pastor, you take these things too lightly."

"Perhaps." It was obvious that the old man was unconvinced about the seriousness of the situation.

"Did you get anything in writing?"

The pastor thought for a moment. "Oh, maybe six or seven."

"*What?*" Again, Stauffer was astounded.

"Yes, this one brought out a few more such complaints than I normally get."

"Do you keep them?"

"Gosh, no," said the minister. "I look them over briefly and toss them into the waste basket."

"They've been thrown out, then?"

"Perhaps not." Fenstermacher rose and went to his desk, bending down to pick up the waste basket. "They may still be here. My wife usually keeps this cleaned out, but I've impressed on her over the years not to empty it until *after* I finish my sermon. Often times I throw away a note I need to retrieve." He looked into the basket and then dumped the contents on the desk. "Let's see now. Well, here's one of them." He handed a wadded-up piece of paper to Phil, who had joined him at the desk.

Stauffer uncrumpled the paper and smoothed it out on the desk. It was a lined piece of paper, torn from a notebook, and it contained two words, block printed in pencil. It said simply: *YOU STINK!*

"To the point." Phil grinned—for the first time.

"They often are," Fenstermacher said. "They all seem to be here." He was smoothing out pieces of paper, which were of varied sizes. "Now here's an interesting anonymous letter." The paper he handed to the sheriff was pink, expensive writing paper, with a distinctive monogram in the upper right-hand corner.

Phil laughed out loud. "This is marvelous! An anonymous letter on a paper that even a high school boy could trace." He held the letter up and read it: *Dear Sir, I must object strongly to the subject of your sermon of this past Sunday. We come to church to be instructed in the words of of the Holy Scripture, not to be lectured on some hogwash in the public press. Yours truly.* There was no signature.

"Of course, I know who sent that." Fenstermacher smiled. "The dear old lady uses up a good deal of her fancy stationery in castigating me on my sermon subjects." He had now smoothed out the other letters and gave them to the sheriff. "Come, sit down." The men returned to their chairs.

Stauffer read the others.

Written in pencil on the blank reverse side of a local supermarket advertisement: *I always thought that ministers were supposed to talk about something they know about. What the hell do you know about pow-wow?*

Printed, with the lines on a slant, with an orange felt-tip pen: *Pow-wow saved my grandfather from the grave. He had cancer when he was 43, but he lived till he was 92. So don't make fun of something until you understand it. The Lord don't only work in churches, you know.* It was signed,

A True Christian.

Typed, obviously on one of the newer electric typewriters, on off-white bond paper: *Why do you talk about something you don't understand? Pow-wow is as much a part of our lives as your church. Keep that in mind.*

The sheriff shuffled to the next letter, and paused momentarily. "This was written by the same person," he said, "or at least on the same typewriter." The off-white bond paper, and the electric typewriter type-face, were identical.

"Yes," Fenstermacher laughed, "I think someone was trying to stuff the ballot box."

Don't forget that pow-wow has been around longer than you were. That's a fact. Keep that in mind. This one had a typed signature, however. *Anonymous.* "Not much originality," the sheriff commented.

The minister said nothing. He was watching Stauffer carefully as he got to the seventh letter. Phil read it to himself and then looked up at Fenstermacher.

"It's your man, isn't it?" the pastor asked.

"Absolutely! The same paper with the letterhead torn off, the same old type-face, and the same kind of message."

To Mr. Smart-Ass Pastor—You can defile the true work of God the Father, God the Son, and God the Holy Ghost all you want, but the time will come when you will learn of the real life and death powers of the Lord. The ancient powers remain with us who preserve them. There was no signature.

"Phil, I believe I can identify every one of those correspondents, except the last one. That's a new one to me." The minister paused briefly. "As a matter of fact, that's the only one that didn't come in the mail. It was dropped in our letter slot."

"Pastor, I must tell you that this man frightens me."

"Can we be certain it's a man?"

"Pretty much so," the sheriff said. "There's no question that my caller was male. And there are things about the notes that don't sound like a woman. The use of the phrase 'smart-ass,' for example. That has a strictly masculine ring about it."

"You're probably right."

Phil looked intently at the old man. "Doesn't this kind of thing frighten you?"

"Frighten? No. It fills me with despair sometimes, but it doesn't frighten me. I am a soldier in the army of the Lord."

"I always thought that I was, too, but now I'm not sure anymore. What happened to Debbie, and Nancy's reaction to what she knows of this, adds to my fright. I don't mind admitting that to you, pastor."

Fenstermacher rose and came to Phil's chair. He placed his hand on the sheriff's shoulder. "Faith is a very simple thing. It's believing, not only in God and His Son, Jesus Christ, but also in the basic tenent that good *will* triumph over evil. Once you have accepted that premise, fright goes."

"My faith is wanting, then?"

"No, I don't believe so." The minister's tone was reassuring. "What you think of as fright, I believe, is really concern ...concern for the safety of your loved ones. And don't forget, Phil, faith really isn't that fragile. Faith can be trampled and still survive. Your faith is always there." He smiled. "Emily Dickinson once wrote a revealing little thing that says:

> *Faith is a fine invention*
> *For gentlemen who see;*
> *But microscopes are prudent*
> *In an emergency!*

Perhaps this is the time for you to be prudent—to use that microscope. You'll find that your faith has been there all the while."

"Thanks, pastor. You've been a big help."

"I try."

Stauffer pointed to the anonymous letters. "May I take these with me?"

"Only the last one, please," the old minister said firmly. "The others can't help your investigation. They're *my* continuing problem, not yours."

The sheriff rose to his feet. "Well, I hope we both have some success in solving our problems."

"We will," Reverend Fenstermacher guaranteed him," with the Lord's help."

9 FRI., DEC. 5, 1969

Ernie Wheel was just about to enter the door of the *Missionville Star* when someone called his name. He turned to see a derby-hatted character climb out of a shining Model-T Ford and move toward him.

"Goot mornin', Ernie. I vas chust pullin' up in my flivver undt I seen ya there. Remember me? I'm Doctor Fuszganger."

Ernie smiled. "Of course. Earl Gensemer. How are you this morning, Doctor?"

"Chust fine," said the comic enthusiastically, "chust fine. I chust seen my oldt grandpappy down by the hardvare store. He's such a fine oldt chentleman. . . ."

"Is he now?" said Ernie, playing the straight man.

"Ach, yah. He luffs to rite buses, ya know. N' the udder day he got on a bus—vell, idt vas chust aroundt fife o'clock undt everysing vas full already, n' grandpappy got the last seat. N' right alongsite stoodt a beautiful blonde. Yeah, she vas one of them *decided* blondes—she hadt only decided that mornin'. Anyvay, grandpappy sez, 'Young lady, I'm an oldt man. You can sit on my lap. Idt's all right.' So, she didt—she sat down. Undt right avays the bus took off schpeedy-like. Round the corners, n' ower the gutters, n' ower the *blutzes,* n' up the hills, n' down the hills. Undt pretty soon grandpappy sez, 'Young lady, ya better gedt up. I ain't as oldt as I sought I vas.'"

Wheel roared with laughter. "Grandpappy seems to be a man of the world."

"Ach, he iss," said Gensemer. "Undt like me he's a *wonnemaus.*"

"Ah, yes, an inquisitive person."

"Yah. Undt I heardt somesing the udder day that you might

be interested in onct."

"What's that?"

The comic's face became a serious mask. "Vell, I heardt that the sheriff's daughter . . . you know, the vun what vent to the hospital?—vas under a schpell. Undt that the sheriff iss tryin' to find oudt who idt vas who called him n' toldt him that Debbie—I sink that's her name—vas gonna gedt sick."

"Do you mean that someone has been threatening the sheriff?"

"Idt zounds that vay, from vot I hear."

Wheel frowned. "I'm not going to ask you where you got this, but are you sure of your source?"

"Ach, yah!" Gensemer looked at Wheel very soberly. "Do ya sink idt has anysing to do viss the Strickler murder case?"

"It's certainly in the same pattern."

"Yah, vell." Gensemer shrugged. "I gotta go now, but if I hear anysing more, I'll let ya know."

"Good."

"Oh, by the way," Gensemer added, "do ya know Dan Hummel down the street, the undertaker? He's oudt estimatin' these days, ya know." He was back into his comic personality.

"He is, is he?" Wheel was already laughing.

"Yah, he iss. Ven his business iss slow, he goes oudt givin' estimates. Yesterday he vent oudt to see oldt Ruth Reich, the oldt maid. Undt she sez, 'Vot brings you here, Daniel?' He sez, 'I've come to estimate your funeral. I try to do this so ven the time comes ya haff somesing to say aboudt your own funeral, vissoudt all those udder nosey vuns pokin' into idt.' 'That zounds like a goot idea,' Ruth sez. 'Vot do ya vant to know?' So, they decided vot flovers Ruth vanted, n' vot kindt uff clothin' to be laidt oudt in, undt then Dan sez, 'Vot kinda coffin do ya vant?' N' she sez, 'Vot are they vearin' chust now?' 'Vell,' sez Dan, 'fer a lady vot's neffer been married, ve use a pure vhite coffin. N' then fer a lady vot's been married, ya know, ve haff a lavender coffin.' 'Vell,' Ruth sez, after sinkin' fer a minute or two, 'make mine vhite viss a couple of splashes of lavender.'"

"I loved that one," Ernie laughed. "It's one I want to

remember, although I'll never be able to tell it with the accent!"

"Ach, that von't make no neffer mind. I'm schure idt vasn't done in Dutch the first time anyhow. Goot mornin', my friend!" Doctor Fuszganger tipped his derby and walked off down the street.

Wheel watched him for a brief moment, and then entered the newspaper building, determined to seek out a private interview with Sheriff Phil Stauffer.

Barry stood in the small terminal at the Missionville Airport waiting for his suitcase to be unloaded from the commuter plane that had brought him from Philadelphia, after his jet flight from Phoenix. He had slept almost all the way from Arizona and felt refreshed. As he gazed out through the big plate-glass window of the terminal, he thought he caught a reflection of Kathy's face. He smiled at the illusion.

"You seem happy."

Barry turned. It was Sheriff Stauffer who had broken his reverie. "It's more like well-rested," said Barry.

"I'm glad of that. There's plenty of work here."

Barry retrieved his baggage and, as the two men walked to Stauffer's squad car, the small-talk conversation was predictable: the flying weather, the length of the layover in Philadelphia, the comfort of the small commuter plane. They were pulling away from the airport terminal when Phil asked the question that Barry knew was coming. "Were you able to get a description of John Richards?"

"In a sense. I've got a partial. That's the best I could do." When the sheriff didn't interject any comment, Barry went on. "All the way back on the plane, I've been thinking about this description. Who does this remind you of—old man, handsome, charming?"

Stauffer glanced at Barry quickly, then turned his attention back to the road. "Are you thinking Joshua Oberdick?"

"Exactly."

"Does that make any sense, Barry?"

"It does to me. Everything I've been able to learn about John Richards, and I admit it isn't a helluva lot, says Josh

Oberdick to me. While I wasn't able to get an exact physical description, I've come away with a sense of the man—and it reads Oberdick."

"Umm." Phil was silent for a moment or two. "It seems that Dr. Oberdick comes into this thing quite often—his connection with Strickler, his apparent friendship with Lizzie Zearfoss, his association with the Lotzes, his championing of young Larry Saylor. And now, your speculation. It *is* just speculation, isn't it?"

"Hell, yes." Painter's emphasis was strong. "A gut feeling, Phil."

"I've never been able to deprecate a valid gut feeling." He grinned. "I have too damned many of them myself to poo-poo them." Stauffer exhaled deeply. "The time has come, I believe, to have a long talk with Josh. To ask some pertinant questions."

"It appears that way, Phil."

The sheriff stood in the communications room of the Young County courthouse and watched the wire photo machine spinning a picture of Josh Oberdick. The steady beep, beep of the machine had a mesmerizing effect. Stauffer had called the New York City police and had asked them for their cooperation in checking out John Richards for him. He wanted them to check Richards against a recent photograph of Oberdick, and he was transmitting the picture to New York now. The phone rang and Phil reached over to answer it.

"Sheriff, this is Ernie Wheel," the voice said, "of the Continental News Service."

"Yes?" Stauffer's tone was one of caution.

"I'd like to have the opportunity to do a solid interview with you, sheriff. In depth, so to speak. I was wondering whether we might set an appointment?"

Phil frowned. "My policy, Mr. Wheel, is not to give interviews regarding any ongoing investigations, and I gather that you want to talk about the Strickler case."

"Yes, sir."

"I can't do that. I'm sorry."

Phil was about to hang up when the reporter spoke again. "I

have information, sheriff, that you have been receiving anonymous threats associated with the Strickler case."

"Every criminal investigation turns up those kinds of nuts."

Wheel played his trump card. "But my information is that your family is involved in the threats, perhaps your daughter."

Stauffer was stunned, but he tried to maintain his calm demeanor. "And this so-called information is going to be used by you, Mr. Wheel, as subtle blackmail to get you an exclusive interview on a very saleable murder story?"

"Sheriff, I had no such intention," Ernie protested. "I *do* have. . . ."

"Don't shadow-box with me, Mr. Wheel! You may think this is a small town and you can get away with your heavy-handed methods. Well, the bottom line is this: If you have information regarding a criminal investigation, you are duty bound, as a responsible citizen, to present it to the proper police authorities. If you intend to do that, Mr. Wheel, I will, of course, make time available to see you. Otherwise, I have no interest in you. Keep this in mind, however. If you engage in a conspiracy to hamper a criminal investigation, you can be arrested. And if I find that is the case, Mr. Wheel, you can be assured that I will do just that—arrest you, that is. Do I make myself clear, Mr. Wheel?"

"Perfectly."

"Very well, then, if you wish to see me, I'll be free at nine-thirty tomorrow morning. That's Saturday, December sixth."

"I'm aware of that, sheriff."

"I simply like to keep the record straight," Phil said. "Will you be here, Mr. Wheel?"

"Yes, sir."

"Very well." Stauffer slammed the phone down into its cradle. He was angry. He didn't like reporters and now this one had tried to pressure him. Phil really wanted to meet with Ernie Wheel immediately, because he wanted to know what the reporter had on Debbie's illness. But he also knew that he had to maintain the upper hand in his dealings with newsmen, especially this one. Stauffer returned to the wire photo machine just as it was completing its transmission of Oberdick's picture. *Josh, old man,* the sheriff thought, *you have just been whisked to New York with the speed of light. Well, maybe not that fast, but fast enough.* He stripped the black-and-white print from the machine and headed back to his office. Halfway there, the words of Ernie Wheel played back through his mind again. Phil cursed aloud. "You bastard, Wheel!"

Josh Oberdick was ill at ease and the feeling disgusted him. He was a man who usually set the pace of his own life. He made his own liberal rules of conduct, and he was unaccustomed to being put on the defensive. Yet that's what Phil Stauffer had done to him. The sheriff had called him earlier in the evening, had told him he wanted to talk to him on a matter of extreme importance. Stauffer had told the old doctor that he didn't want Dottie Kissinger or her son present at the discussion. So Oberdick, inventing a rather lame excuse, had dismissed the pair for the evening. Now he sat in his comfortable apartment and forced a smiling face as he looked across the coffee table at Sheriff Stauffer and his deputy, Barry Painter. Both men were stonily sober.

"I gather," Oberdick said, "that this is an official call, and it would be inappropriate for me to suggest that we have a drink."

"No drink for us, thank you," Stauffer said quietly, "but if you want to have one, please go ahead."

The doctor shrugged. "Well, perhaps later."

Phil shifted his weight in the easy chair, preparing his first question in his mind. He had told Painter that he wanted no comments from him unless he was asked to speak, and Barry knew his boss was deadly serious about that prohibition.

"Josh," the sheriff started, "we asked to come here tonight because we have some disturbing information. I hope you'll be able to fill in some blank spaces."

"Does this have to do with the Strickler case?"

"Probably." Stauffer was not going to be forced out of the pattern of questioning he had prepared.

Oberdick, knowing that he faced a stern opponent in the Young County sheriff, tried, nevertheless, to seize the initiative of the conversation. "I think I've told you and your deputy all I know about Strickler and indeed, about the murder itself, of which I really know nothing at all."

"And we thank you for that." Phil's voice was flat, unemotional. "Some things have come up that lead to some additional questions, however. For example, do you know a woman named Kathy Samson?"

"No."

Barry had to stifle a gasp. He had expected that the mention of Kathy's name would draw at least a flicker of recognition from the old man. It did not. *Christ, maybe he wasn't John Richards!*

"Would it help, perhaps," Phil went on, "if I suggested to you that Miss Samson lives in Phoenix, Arizona?"

"No." Again the flat denial.

"You are familiar with Phoenix?"

"Oh, yes, I used to vacation there frequently some years back." A flicker of a smile came across the doctor's face. "I love that area."

"Isn't it a fact that you gave Ira Lotz the money to send their daughter, Martha, to Phoenix?"

"Yes, that's a fact." Oberdick seemed very much in command of himself. "As you are aware, Phil, the girl was badly frightened by her experiences with Johnny Mosser, and the Lotz family was deeply disturbed. I thought it best for her to leave this area for a time. So I helped out."

"You gave the Lotzes money for her air fare?"

"Yes."

"Was that all?"

Oberdick smiled again. "No. I got the young lady a job in a Phoenix restaurant through a friend of mine, and I gave her two hundred dollars to tide her over until she got settled."

"An act of charity, then?"

"If you want to call it that," said Oberdick. "The Lotzes are fine people, and they had more than their share of trouble. I had the opportunity to help them, and I did."

"Why?"

The doctor was startled by the question. "Why?"

"Yeah, why?"

"Well . . . ah . . . hell, Phil, just because I wanted to."

"Uh huh." Stauffer paused momentarily. "Now, going back a few years, did you finance the apartment taken in Missionville by Sarah Strickler?"

"Yes, that's true," admitted Oberdick.

"Why?"

A tiny little bit of anger began to show in the doctor's face. "Why? Again? Sarah needed help. I gave it to her. It's as simple as that."

"Another charitable act?"

Oberdick, obviously annoyed, rose and went to the bar to pour himself a drink. "Look, Phil, if you're going to accuse me of something, let's get to it!"

Switching again, and ignoring the doctor's comment, Stauffer pressed on. "Would it surprise you if I told you that, for a time in Phoenix, Martha Lotz Mosser lived with a girl named Kathy Samson?"

"Surprise me? No, I guess not." The old man returned to his chair with the drink. "I had no way of knowing what Martha did, or did not do, in Phoenix. I tried to get her settled there, and that's about it. I didn't keep constant check on her."

"Then you don't know that she moved in with Miss Samson?"

"No."

"And you don't know that Miss Samson is a prostitute?"

"No."

"And you don't know that Miss Samson trained, shall we say, Martha Lotz Mosser in the fine arts of that profession?"

"No, damn it!" Oberdick set the drink glass down on the end table with a firm move of exasperation, splashing some of the liquid out of the glass. "What the hell are you getting at, Phil?"

"Okay," said the sheriff, brushing aside the doctor's question. "Now . . . how would you characterize your current association with Dorothy Kissinger?"

"Ah . . . well. . . ." Again, Phil's sudden shift in direction had shaken Oberdick.

"A charitable act also?"

"No. The woman was in trouble and she needed a friend. And, well. . . ."

"Did the fact that Mrs. Kissinger's son was involved in the Strickler case motivate your charity?"

"Phil, this line of questioning is ridiculous!"

Stauffer was unrelenting. "Did you take in the Kissingers—mother and son—to gain control over an impressionable boy, perhaps to take the opportunity to hone, shall we say, his story about what happened at the Strickler house?"

Oberdick threw up his hands. "How in the hell do I answer something like that?"

Phil's face was an icy blank. "Where is Martha Lotz Mosser?"

"What? I don't know!"

"Is she in Phoenix?"

"I don't know!"

"You have no idea where she is?"

"None! Absolutely none!"

Stauffer exhaled a deep breath. "All right, now, Josh, who sent Johnny Mosser to Lizzie Zearfoss? Who suggested to him that Lizzie might be able to help him when he was ill?"

"How would I know that?"

"You knew Johnny Mosser at that time?"

"Of course." Oberdick's answers were beginning to show more and more annoyance.

"Did you tell Lizzie Zearfoss to suggest to Johnny Mosser that it was Charlie Strickler who had a spell on him?"

"No!"

"In other words, Josh, did you set up Johnny Mosser to be blamed for the murder of Charlie Strickler?"

The old doctor came to his feet. "That's it, Phil! I'm not going to sit here in my own home and be party to this kind of insanity! If you have something sensible to ask me, then get to it! If not, I suggest that you and your deputy there leave now!"

Stauffer fixed his gaze on Oberdick's face. "Please sit down, Josh." He said it so quietly that Barry barely heard it.

"No, sir! You come to the point, or leave!"

The sheriff sighed. "I had hoped that we could get this questioning out of the way in an intelligent, reasonable...."

Oberdick broke in. "*Intelligent? Reasonable?* What kind of crap is that? You come in here with the most disjointed—

and, yes, insulting—series of questions, and *dare* to speak of intelligence and reason?"

"You're right," Phil said apologetically. "You're right. Please, sit down." After the doctor returned to his chair, the sheriff continued. "I guess I have been going around the barn, Josh, so I'll get to the point. Do you know a man named John Richards?"

Oberdick was stunned. He tried to pick up his glass, but the hand quivered so much that he abandoned the idea. It was obvious to both Stauffer and Painter that he had been struck a telling blow. They watched as the old man struggled to get control of himself. Finally, he spoke. "Perhaps I had better have some legal advice."

"Then you do know John Richards?"

The doctor looked at the floor. "Yes."

"And John Richards knows Kathy Samson?"

"Yes."

"And John Richards brought Martha Lotz Mosser to Miss Samson in Phoenix?"

"Yes."

"And John Richards knew that Miss Samson was a. . . ."

"Let's stop the charade, sheriff," Oberdick said, raising his gaze and looking Phil squarely in the eyes. "You know that I'm John Richards, don't you?"

"That's right," Stauffer admitted.

Josh sighed deeply. "Well, then *I* know I need some legal advice, although I've done nothing wrong, Phil." The voice had a defeated quality.

Phil spoke slowly. "I always thought that aiding and abetting prostitution was against the law."

"Phil, it wasn't really like that at all! I never . . . ah . . . well. . . ." He trailed off.

"Maybe you'd better call your lawyer." Stauffer seemed genuinely concerned about the well-being of the old doctor. "But I would like to ask one more question."

The fight had gone out of Oberdick. "Go ahead."

"Where is Martha?"

"In New York."

"Is she okay?"

"Sure." He sighed again. "I'll give you the address."

The sheriff rose. "Josh, I'm sorry I had to do this. Frankly, it got to be a contest between friendship and duty."

"And duty won."

"That's about it."

Oberdick sat dejectedly in his chair, nodding his head. His advanced age was now evident. "You know, there's something terribly ironic about all this. That bastard Charlie Strickler has beaten me again. If he hadn't been killed, you never would have started this investigation and you never would have learned of John Richards." He looked up at Phil. "You know that I didn't have a damned thing to do with Strickler's death, don't you?"

"Yeah," said Sheriff Stauffer, "I know."

"I thought I knew you pretty well, Phil, but now I'm not so sure."

Barry's comment brought a smile to Sheriff Stauffer's face. The two men were in Phil's squad car, heading for the Young County courthouse following the strange interrogation of Dr. Oberdick.

"Never knew the old sheriff had so many tricks up his sleeve, eh?"

"No, it's not that," Barry said seriously. "I never knew you had a killer instinct. You clobbered the old man."

"Aren't you over-reacting?"

"No, I don't think so. And there's another thing."

"What's that?"

Barry showed some annoyance. "Well, it was painfully obvious that you haven't filled me in on everything. I know you well enough to know that you wouldn't have brought up 'John Richards' at all if you weren't sure of it. What made you so sure?"

Stauffer grinned again. "Barry, I do owe you an apology. I wasn't really holding out on you; it's just that I didn't want anything to get screwed up." He glanced over at his deputy. "You've got to admit, Barry, that sometimes you don't know when to shut up."

"Yeah, maybe. But I'm getting a little tired of hearing about that, too."

Phil chose to ignore Barry's comment. "Just before we left for Oberdick's I got an answer on my query to the New York City police. I had sent them a wire photo of Oberdick and asked them to check him out. It didn't take long to discover that Oberdick was John Richards. It was damned simple, as a matter of fact. They got an exact address, using that phone number the Samson girl gave you, went there with the Oberdick wire photo, and got it identified as John Richards. They learned, too, that there was a second person living at that address—a girl named Marty Young. Okay?"

"So you went into Oberdick's apartment," Barry said, "with both barrels loaded."

Again, the grin from the sheriff. "You might put it that way."

"With your deputy going along as the damned spear carrier," Barry said sullenly.

"Okay, I'm sorry. I apologize. But, sometimes I like to do things my own way."

The deputy was still sober-faced. "Why all that twisting and turning during the interrogation?"

"Doc Oberdick is no fool," Stauffer answered. "I had to get him off balance, because I wasn't sure where all of this was taking us. Josh's name kept coming up every time we moved, but Josh Oberdick as the murderer of Charlie Strickler, or even a conspirator in the case, just didn't make sense to me. But why, I asked myself, are we always stumbling over Oberdick? Then it came to me. We found Oberdick only when a woman was involved—with Sarah Strickler; with Martha Mosser, alias Marty Young; with Dottie Kissinger; and with that girl in Phoenix. Old Josh's one big failing is women—especially young women. He's got to get laid."

"Not Kathy Samson," Barry said defensively.

"Huh?"

Barry began to back off. "Oh, I just meant that I don't think he was sleeping with Samson. That was a different thing entirely, I believe."

The sheriff glanced over at him again, a question written in the glance. "Well, if he wasn't laying that Phoenix woman, he sure was breaking the pattern."

Barry decided not to pursue the point. "Just a thought."

"Anyway," Stauffer said, as he swung the squad car into the courthouse parking lot, "once I convinced myself about just what Oberdick's involvement in this whole thing was—namely women—all the pieces began to fall together." He pulled the car into his parking space, and the two men got out.

"There's another thing I don't understand," Barry admitted. "Why the alias John Richards?"

"We'll get to that when we can talk to him again, after he consults with his lawyer. But I would bet money that the alias is just a part of the old man's romantic notions—an adventure, perhaps, outside of the realm of Young County where he was just Josh Oberdick. A juvenile lark, even though he's eighty."

"I'm curious about another thing. You seem pretty sure that Josh isn't a suspect in the Strickler murder."

"I don't believe he is."

Barry shook his head. "I wish I could be so sure about that."

"Aren't you?"

"I'm just taking a leaf from the book of my mentor, a guy named Phil Stauffer. Never, never count out a suspect until you have absolute proof."

"You have just made a telling point on your mentor, Deputy Painter."

Phil and Barry entered the building and walked in silence to their office. Once there, the sheriff said, "Barry, you mentioned that I haven't filled you in on everything."

The deputy raised his hand in protest. "Oh, that's understandable, Phil."

"No, it's not! There is something I've been keeping under my hat, and I want you to know it." He reached into his desk drawer and brought out the two typed notes—the one he had received at the hospital, and the one dropped into Pastor Fenstermacher's letter slot. "Take a look at these."

As Barry studied the notes, Stauffer gave him all the details of the threats against Debbie. He didn't hold back anything, including his own fears. And then, he completely dumbfounded his deputy with the story of having reburied Charlie

Strickler's lock of hair.

"Jesus, Phil," Barry said when his boss had finished, "this is getting crazier and crazier!"

The sheriff was sincerely apologetic. "I'm sorry, Barry, I should have told you this before. But. . . ."

"No sweat, Phil. You had your own reasons." He grimaced. "But we still have the real problem—who in the hell killed Charlie Strickler?"

"And Lizzie Zearfoss."

"Yeah," said Barry, "and Lizzie Zearfoss!"

Will Burkholder held the phone tight to his ear, cupping his hand around the mouthpiece, and whispering. "Listen, I'm in real trouble with this damned thing. It was me who was in that cell, and it's me who has his old man on his ass!"

"Don't get so agitated," the male voice on the other end of the line told him. "All you have to do is ride it out. How in God's name can they pin anything on you? Just be calm and tight-lipped."

"Maybe so," said young Burkholder, "but I wish I had never listened to you. If I hadn't told you about Mosser tying up old Strickler, this thing wouldn't have happened."

"Just stick to your story, Will. You didn't do anything," the voice insisted.

"Yeah, but *you* did. And I'm mixed up in it. My old man will skin me alive if he finds out."

"Your father will be the least of your worries if you don't shut up! That's all you have to do. Stick with your story, and shut up."

"And another thing," said Will. "When am I going to get my money?"

"You've already gotten a large part of it."

"But not all of it!"

"You are stupid," the voice said. "We can't be seen together at this time. And what the devil do you need with more money? You can't spend the three thousand you already have."

"The deal was five."

"And you'll get it! But not right now."

"Okay." Young Burkholder was downcast.

"And, Will, don't call me again. And don't ad lib anything. Your story is perfect; it'll stand up. Do you understand that?"

"Sure." The party on the other end of the line had broken the connection. Will placed the instrument in its cradle. He wiped his hand across his brow; he was sweating profusely.

10   SAT., DEC. 6, 1969

Attorney Robert Hoffman shook his head in disbelief as Josh talked. The lawyer had been summoned to the old man's apartment by a telephone call that had awakened him at 6 a.m. All night long Oberdick had discussed his predicament with Dottie Kissinger and, as Saturday morning dawned, he dialed Hoffman's number. There was sufficient urgency in the call to bring the attorney to the Yountz Apartments.

The two men made a study in contrasts. Oberdick's tall, lean, elderly dignity was almost the exact opposite of Hoffman's pudgy, disheveled, youthful appearance. Bob Hoffman was only 32, but he had already built a local reputation as a highly competent defense attorney. It was that reputation that caused Oberdick to retain Hoffman to represent the interests of young Larry Saylor in the mess over Charlie Strickler's murder. And now it seemed clear that Oberdick needed the attorney's expertise more than did Larry.

Dottie came out of the kitchen with a pot of freshly brewed coffee as the doctor continued his litany of the bizarre Dr. Joshua Oberdick-John Richards relationship. Her dark green robe fell open slightly as she leaned over to put a cup of coffee in front of the lawyer. He nodded an automatic "thanks" almost without noticing the attractive woman; Josh's story was much more compelling than her sumptuous body.

"So Dottie insisted," Josh said, looking up at her with a half-smile, "that I ought to call you immediately. It was not a new thought, of course, but I did wrestle with the idea of just telling the sheriff everything he wants to know and, to use a cliché, letting the chips fall where they might. But Dottie convinced me that I shouldn't let my natural ego blind myself to the trouble I'm in. And I guess I *am* in trouble."

"That's a fair evaluation," Hoffman said soberly.

Dottie, after serving the coffee, sat next to Oberdick and took his hand in hers.

"Just how much trouble," the lawyer went on, "depends a lot on how hot the sheriff wants to make it for you. There's the whole question of the movements of Martha Mosser, financed by you. Can that be interpreted as aiding and abetting prostitution? Well, it seems that such a charge might be brought in Arizona, if nowhere else."

"Isn't that too strong an evaluation of what went on?"

Hoffman thought for a moment. "Maybe not. Prostitution, by one definition, is the offering of the body of a woman to indiscriminate sexual intercourse for hire."

"But I didn't take any money!"

"Maybe not, but you certainly put Martha Mosser in the position to enter prostitution, and that might lead to an abetting charge. I wouldn't think that Arizona authorities would initiate such prosecution, but if Sheriff Stauffer gave them the ammunition, well. . . ."

Oberdick sighed. "I've been a damned fool!"

"True." The reply was without emotion. "Then, Josh, I don't know what Stauffer will make of the alias."

"Is there something criminal about using two names?"

"It depends."

"On what?"

"On whether you use an alias to conceal a crime. Or fraud of some kind. I would hope that the federal government isn't interested in your two selves—for tax purposes, that is."

The doctor raised his hand in protest. "No, no! There's nothing like that. I never had two bank accounts, or tried to file two tax returns, or anything like that. No, I guess I just used the name John Richards to conceal Josh Oberdick from . . . ah . . . from some embarrassments, or potential embarrassments."

"Hmm." Hoffman scratched his head. "If you admitted that to Stauffer, or any other authorities, the next question would be: 'Were those potential embarrassments of a criminal nature?' After all, an indictment on a prostitution charge could be embarrassing, right?"

"Yeah, I see what you mean." Oberdick groaned. "It's a mess, all right, but don't my motives count at all? Doesn't the fact that I was just trying to help a frightened girl count in my favor? There was never any plan for Martha to enter prostitution. I simply took her to an old friend whom I could trust; I took her there for her protection. That's all."

"That motive might help," said Hoffman, "but your association with the girl later on, the live-in arrangements in New York, don't seem to fall in the category of protection. Others may look upon that as exploitation." Hoffman looked at Dottie. "As a matter of fact, Josh, your current association with Mrs. Kissinger might fall into the same category."

"That's cruel," Dottie said sharply. "We love each other."

"Love?" Hoffman said cynically. "There are those who will say that Dr. Oberdick spreads his love pretty widely."

Dottie was about to speak again, but Josh silenced her with a squeeze of the hand. "Okay, Bob," he said, "what do I do now?"

"I believe your initial thought to tell Stauffer everything you know was a correct one. It's *how* you tell him that's important." Hoffman sat up erect, stretching himself. He picked up his empty coffee cup and held it out to Dottie for a refill. "What we have to do, Josh, is put together a complete statement; an affidavit, to which you will swear, and submit it to the sheriff's office. We want to make it crystal clear that we are cooperating one hundred percent. But we want to do it in a statement. We don't want to have Stauffer pull it out of you in another question-and-answer session. I want to avoid any more of the sheriff's cute interrogations."

"Gawd, me too!" said Oberdick, remembering his most recent encounter with Stauffer. "But, Bob, how complete is complete in this context?"

"Complete! Dates, times, exact associations with Kathy Samson and Martha Mosser. And, to back up your statements, a full disclosure of finances. . . ."

"Finances?"

"Sure. How much money did you give to Samson? When,

where, etcetera. The same with Mrs. Mosser. We must clearly establish that your interest in the two ladies was, indeed, charitably motivated. This is complicated a bit by your obvious personal interest in both women, but. . . ."

Dottie spoke. "You mean to strip Josh of all dignity." The statement had a bitter edge.

"No, Hoffman assured her, "I want Sheriff Stauffer to know, through this voluntary disclosure, that Josh had nothing to do with the Strickler case. That his association with Samson and Mrs. Mosser—and even you, Mrs. Kissinger—was coincidental."

Oberdick raised his voice in protest. "Wait a minute! Stauffer knows I didn't have anything to do with Charlie Strickler's murder!"

"Does he, indeed?" the lawyer asked.

"That's what he said!'"

"Hmm. Well, sir, I'll bet my fee on this thing that Philip Stauffer has not eliminated you from the list of potential suspects. To be honest with you, Josh, I don't know why he should at this stage of the game. You had motive, maybe opportunity, and you have engaged in some questionable dealings with at least two people—and maybe more—whose names figure prominently in the case."

"Maybe more? Who?"

"Well," Hoffman said, sipping his coffee, "you were intimately associated with Kathy Samson and Martha Mosser." He looked again at Dottie. "And with Mrs. Kissinger, whose son is involved. You knew, and hated, Charlie Strickler. You had a liaison with Strickler's wife. You know Johnny Mosser, the Lotzes, the deceased Lizzie Zearfoss, and, to put the icing on the cake, you are an acknowledged authority on *hexerei*, around which the murder investigation revolves."

"But. . . ."

"So what we have," the lawyer pressed on, "is that your name has been coming up at every turn in Stauffer's investigation. Without knowing more about where that investigation has taken him, I would say that Phil Stauffer cannot eliminate you as a suspect at this time."

Oberdick was stunned. "You don't pull any punches, do

you?"

"You didn't call me here to salve your conscience."

Dottie spoke again. Her words surprised the lawyer. "Mr. Hoffman makes sense, Josh. If it helps at all, you have my vote of confidence."

"It helps, darling, it helps." The old man smiled. "Well, counselor, let's start writing that statement."

Ernie Wheel was beginning to understand what it was that fascinated his editor about the Pennsylvania Dutch. Actually, he was learning rapidly that the term "Pennsylvania Dutch" was a misnomer. True, those people with German surnames dominated the population in this area of Southeastern Pennsylvania, and almost everywhere the broad "Dutch" accent was heard. Yet there was a strong amalgam of English, Irish, Polish, Greek and Latin blood in the community; it assimilated the diverse cultures with only an occasional errant nod to the prejudices that seriously afflicted other areas of the nation. Here Lutherans, Roman Catholics, Baptists, Methodists, Jews, Seventh Day Adventists, Quakers, Orthodox Greeks, et al—even the standoffish and doggedly fundamentalist Amish—shared a single community, taking care not to divide into militant factions. Wheel had found that it was not unusual for a Jew, whose family roots traced back to Russia, to identify himself as a "Pennsylvania Dutchman." Indeed, he had heard that boast from an Irish bartender, from a Greek chef in one of the local restaurants, and from a black man pumping gas into his Jaguar. Being Pennsylvania Dutch, then, was not an ethnic thing, but a deep, lasting pride in region. These people had devised a real, workable social melting pot. Such a claim had been made for New York City for generations, but it wasn't true. Why did it work here in Missionville, and in the other communities in the "Dutch" area?

The newsman pondered that question as he strolled through the big town square from his hotel to the sheriff's office in the courthouse. Had some sociologist ever studied the Pennsylvania Dutch phenomenon? Perhaps it had been done, Wheel mused, and it probably had gotten as little attention as do most of those studies. Ernie was going through his mental gymnastics because he was apprehensive about his meeting with Phil Stauffer. Keeping his mind busy with other matters helped to quiet his apprehensions. He was aware his meeting with the sheriff would be in the nature of a confrontation, and he had real doubts about his ability to compete one-on-one with the police officer. He admired Stauffer and his toughness, and Wheel knew that he approached the meeting from a position of weakness.

His conversation with Earle Gensemer had given him only a sketchy intimation that the sheriff, or rather his daughter, had been threatened by someone, and that those threats might have had something to do with the girl's hospitalization. He had very carefully rehearsed in his mind his opening question and now, as he walked into the sheriff's office, he wasn't sure he could carry it off. Stauffer's face was set hard. There was not even the slightest hint of a smile; nothing to indicate that he meant to be cooperative.

"I know you're very busy," Wheel said, "and I'll take just a minute or two." He pulled a cassette tape recorder out of his pocket and pushed the "on" button.

Stauffer pointed to the instrument. "What's that for?"

"I frequently use a tape recorder," explained Wheel. "It assures accurate quotes."

"You're making an assumption that there are going to be quotes. Turn it off!"

Wheel obeyed without hesitation. "I was hoping. . . ."

"Don't hope," said Phil. "Please sit down." As Wheel settled into the chair in front of the sheriff's desk, Stauffer snapped, "What is it you have?" He had taken control of the interview.

The reporter had planned to use kid gloves with the sheriff, to be soft and easy in his approach. Now, he changed his mind, adopting Stauffer's hard tones. "I have, sheriff, the knowledge that you have been receiving threats, and that they involve your daughter, Debbie. I have, too, the knowledge that those threats tie in with the Strickler case." That last was designed to force an admission from the sheriff.

Stauffer looked at him steadily. "Go on."

"Go on?"

"Yes, what else do you have?"

Wheel stammered in surprise. "What else? That's it."

Stauffer nodded. "I see." He rose and extended his hand to the reporter. "Thank you for coming."

"Do you have any comments on the threats?" Ernie was seeking survival now.

"No."

"Can you confirm that such threats have been received?"

"I was under the impression," Stauffer said quietly and coldly, "that you *knew* I had received such threats. Now, it seems, you're merely fishing. I don't get involved in fishing questions, Mr. Wheel." He looked away, turning his attention to papers on his desk. "Now, you'll have to excuse me. I'm busy."

Wheel stared at the police officer and was about to leave, then decided to give it one more try. "Are you denying, sheriff, by your silence on this matter, that you have received threats, either verbally or in writing?" He knew it was a weak, scatter-shot effort, not an effective salvo.

"I'm not doing anything," Stauffer said, looking up again. "You said you have some information for me. Instead, you show up with speculation. Well, you can't fish here. I thought I made that clear."

Ernie was pleading now. "But I have this information on good authority."

"And who is that authority?"

"I can't tell you."

Stauffer smiled wanly. "That's what I thought. This kind of thing always comes down to I-have-a-right-to-protect-my-source. Well, Mr. Wheel, I don't have time for that kind of nonsense."

"You believe the First Amendment is nonsense?"

"Of course not," Phil answered firmly. "But I'm not going to engage in a debate on the First Amendment. It gives you, sir, no special rights in questioning me about a murder investigation. None at all. As I told you on the phone, if you believe you have information that might help the police in their investigation, you have a duty as a citizen to reveal that information. However, I also know that it's a useless argument to make with a reporter, so I've learned never to make it. I just don't have the time for that kind of frustration." He walked to the file cabinets in the corner of the room, pulled open a drawer, and looked into one of the file folders.

"That's it?" It was Ernie who was frustrated.

Stauffer sighed, speaking without turning around. "I'll try to explain it to you again. If you have information relating to the Strickler case, I'll listen to it. If you don't, you're wasting your time—and mine."

"Listen, sheriff, I came here for an interview. . . ."

Phil wheeled around. "Ah, *now* we get to it—an interview! Mr. Wheel, I don't give interviews during an investigation. It's a rule of this office, as your friend, Nick Willson, could have told you." He looked at his watch. "I think I've spent enough time on this matter." Stauffer walked to the door and opened it. "Good day, Mr. Wheel."

Ernie walked disconsolately to the door. He was halfway out of the office before he spoke. "Could we go off the record, sheriff?"

"That would be difficult," Phil said, "because we've never been *on* the record."

"Then I'll just have to write what I have!"

"You do that, Mr. Wheel." Stauffer reached out and touched his arm. "But one word of this conversation today and I'll have you arrested for obstructing a murder investigation."

"I believe that's the second time you've threatened me with arrest."

"It's not a threat, Mr. Wheel, it's a promise." Phil closed the door. He walked to his desk, rested both hands on it, and stared off into nothingness. "Damn," he said aloud. "Who told him? *Who told him?*"

It was late afternoon before Deputy Painter had tracked down and interviewed the five men who had had physical encounters with the late Charlie Strickler because of the intimate attentions they had paid to Sarah Strickler. Barry was surprised that after the passage of the years, he was able to find all five. The names themselves were easy enough to dig out of the police records of Strickler's violent forays into Missionville while Sarah maintained her apartment in town. But there was every chance that all five had moved to other addresses.

"You know, Phil," the deputy said to Stauffer, "maybe we're starting to get lucky with this case. What do you think the odds were on finding all five of these guys in one day?"

"About a thousand-to-one, I guess." Phil smiled. "Did you find anything substantial?"

"Well, I have their alibis for Thanksgiving eve, and they all seem to have been at places where there were witnesses. Of course, I haven't had the time to check out the alibis yet. I'm not *that* swift. I just feel lucky that I was able to talk to them all."

Barry, reading from his notebook, ticked off the details for his superior.

Greg Miller, the one name that Stauffer had been given by Sarah, was a bartender at the VFW club in Missionville. He was on duty at the club on the evening of Wednesday, November 26, and there were at least two dozen VFW members in the bar that evening. The deputy had a list of nine drinkers who could be contacted to verify Miller's story.

Barney Hinnershotz, interviewed at his Texaco station at Front and Barnes streets, claimed to be at home with his family on the night in question. He could prove it if he had to, but he hoped the sheriff's department could check him out without talking to his wife. The escapade with Sarah and Charlie was still a touchy subject with Mrs. Hinnershotz.

Elmer Grumbauer, a farmer out in the country, had been to a special Thanksgiving service at his church on the evening of Strickler's murder. His pastor was his alibi. "Reverend Potter will remember," Grumbauer had told the deputy, "because I passed the collection plate that night."

John Klawitter, who ran an auto body shop in nearby Fritztown, said he was working late on that Wednesday evening, and his helper was with him most of the time. Also, there were the names of several customers who came in during the evening. Barry pointed out to Stauffer that Klawitter had been particularly badly beaten by Strickler, even though his only apparent contact with Sarah was to buy her a drink in a Missionville bar.

Painter smiled as he came to the next name on the list. "And you know who else I talked to?"

"Who?"

"Earle Gensemer."

"Doctor Fuszganger?"

"Yep, the same. He said that Charlie had worked him over pretty good when he found him in Sarah's apartment, but that he didn't press charges after Sarah asked him not to. I also got a couple of other stories. He's a funny guy, Phil."

The sheriff grinned. "Yes, he is. I'd forgotten that he was mixed up with Charlie. Anyway, where was Gensemer when Charlie was killed?"

"He says he was booked in Frackville, for a volunteer fire company smoker."

"So he'd have maybe a hundred witnesses to verify his alibi." Stauffer shook his head. "There doesn't appear to be much in those fellows."

"I wouldn't think so, Phil." Barry closed his notebook. "Of course, I can go through the motions of checking out the alibis, but I think it would be a waste of time."

Stauffer disagreed. "No, no, check them out. I'd start with that Klawitter fellow. From what you tell me, he got the worst of it from Strickler."

"Yeah, he had to spend a couple of days in the hospital."

"Why didn't he press charges?"

"He said he thought it would hurt his business if he got any publicity of that kind."

The sheriff shrugged in disgust. "Just think, if just one of those guys had pressed charges against Charlie, the whole chain of circumstances might have been altered."

"Yeah," said Barry. "For want of a nail, the battle was lost."

Stauffer laughed. "You surprise me, deputy. I didn't realize you were so literary."

Painter was embarrassed. "I'm not. I heard that on *Hollywood Squares* the other week."

"Who said that television isn't education?" Phil tapped a pencil in idle thought. "Crap, Barry, we still seem to be getting nothing but dead ends. A lot of detail, but just dead ends!"

Barry sat in silence. The phone rang and Phil answered it. He listened for a moment, then clapped a hand over the instrument. "Barry, try for a trace on this!"

"Now, listen sheriff," the familiar voice said, "I ain't foolin'. Ya schtop messin' aroundt viss this *hexerei*, or vot happened to Debbie vill be chust the beginnin'!"

"Who is this?" Stauffer demanded.

The caller chortled. "Vouldn't ya like to know?"

"Damn you!"

"There ain't no point in svearin', sheriff. I'm tellin' ya to forgedt *hexerei*, because idt's somesing ya don't unnerstandt. Undt that schtupid newspaper reporter vill gedt his, too."

"What does that mean?"

"Ach, I see." The man laughed again. "Ya ain't see the *Star* this afternoon yet."

"The *Star?*"

"Yah. That dumbass Vheel iss runnin' off at the mouse again. You undt Vheel make a goot pair!" He hung up.

Stauffer, angry beyond his own comprehension, slammed down the receiver. He stalked into the outer office where he found a copy of the afternoon edition of *The Missionville Star* on the clerk's counter. Wheel's latest story was given prominent play on page one:

Missionville, Pa., Dec. 6 (CNS) — Young County's beleaguered sheriff, Philip Stauffer, frustrated in his efforts to find a solution to the bizarre murder of pow-wow doctor Charles Strickler, has himself become the target of several anonymous threats on his life. It is understood, also, that Stauffer's teen-age daughter, Debra, is involved in the threats.

Sheriff Stauffer would neither confirm nor deny the receipt of threats, but at least one source in Young County reveals that Debra Stauffer's recent hospitalization for an emergency appendectomy may have been connected with a hexerei "spell" placed on the girl. It was an alleged hexerei (witchcraft) "spell" that apparently led to the murder of Strickler. It is known that the lock of hair cut from Strickler's head after his death was used to remove a "spell" supposedly induced by the pow-wow doctor.

Today's revelation of threats against Sheriff Stauffer and a member of his family is just the latest in a series of strange. . . ."

Phil crumpled the newspaper into a ball, muttering epithets. Barry reentered the room just as the sheriff hurled the newspaper against the wall. "Phil, what the hell . . . ?"

"That sonofabitch Wheel!" Stauffer's face was livid.

"Phil, calm down," Barry pleaded. "It can't be that bad."

"It is! It is! Don't you see?!" Phil sank into a chair and placed his head in his hands. "Debbie doesn't know anything about the threats, and now she's going to read that shit! And, Nancy . . . my God what's this going to do to Nancy?"

Barry just stared at the sheriff, unable to offer any help. After a moment he said quietly, "I tried to trace the call through the courthouse switchboard, but he wasn't on long enough."

"I know." Stauffer continued to sit with his head in his hands. Barry, unsure of what to do, retrieved the newspaper from the floor and tried to smooth it out so that he could read the offending article. It didn't take him long to understand the reason for Phil's anger.

"Phil, you can't let this get to you."

Stauffer looked up. "You're right, Barry," he said firmly. He stood up, forced back his shoulders in an exaggerated move, and walked over to his deputy. "I'm sorry I've been such an ass. Forgive me, please."

"Sure, sure." Barry was relieved that the sheriff's temper was subsiding.

"Listen, Deputy Painter," Phil said, trying for a light tone, "I think we're both beginning to come unglued over this case." He smiled. "Tomorrow's a day off, for both of us." The smile faded again. "I think it's probably best for me to spend a day with Nancy and the kids."

"Yeah, sure, Phil. That's best."

Stauffer walked back into his office. "We start now. See you Monday, deputy." Barry waved his hand and left. The sheriff quickly spun through his Rolodex file of phone numbers and found the one he wanted. He dialed the number; his face was grim.

"George?" he said when he got an answer. "Listen, could you give me a couple of days?" A pause. "Fine. I'll put the pay vouchers in on Monday. Now, this is what I want you to do. . . ."

11 SUN., DEC. 7, 1969

Phil was deeply immersed in reading the fat Sunday edition of *The Missionville Star*. He was making a major project of it, seemingly interested in every little item, concentrating on it with great intensity. As he read, Nancy moved through his consciousness, puttering in the kitchen, arranging and rearranging items on the mantel, shifting books on the shelves, dusting the coffee table in front of the sofa where the sheriff sat. Phil studiously avoided reacting to her activities. From the family room in the basement came the distant beat-beat-beat of the children's stereo, sending through the house the faint reverberations of Jimi Hendrix's "Smash Hits" album.

"I wish I understood that music," said Nancy.

"Hmm."

"Wonder what ever happened to melodies?"

"Gone, I guess." Phil did not look up from his newspaper.

For the third time, Nancy repositioned the Hummel figures on the what-not shelf. She sighed loudly, staring at the newspaper that was hiding her husband. "Are we ever going to have an end to that Vietnam mess?"

"Guess not."

"The Ladies Aid Society of the hospital is planning a Broadway show excursion after the first of the year."

"That's nice."

"They're going to see *Hello Dolly, Mame,* and *Fiddler on the Roof.*"

"Hmm."

She sighed again. "Wanna go?"

"Whatever you want."

The sheriff's wife dropped down on the sofa next to him. He

turned a page of the newspaper without looking at her. She said, "You're not going to talk about it, are you?"

"What?"

"Those damned threats you've been getting!" Her voice rose, commanding his attention.

Phil lowered his newspaper. "Look, honey, I've told you—I'm just not going to let my life be controlled by some nut." He said it firmly, but without anger.

"But I'm worried."

"I know."

"And so is Debbie. It's just not fair to. . . ."

"Nance, we had all this out last night." He put his arm around her. "I've gone over this with the kids, and they understand. You know that. The nuts we really have to worry about are those who don't say anything, who act without warning. The ones who send you letters, and who make phone calls, are just getting their jollies."

Nancy dropped her head on his chest. "Philip Stauffer, you're exasperating!" She looked up at his face and smiled weakly. "The kids are just like you. They can hide their feelings about something like this, but I can't."

He kissed her. "Darling, there's really no need to worry."

"You don't care about the threats?"

"Of course I care! And I'm going to find the bastard and put him away. But, you must understand. . . ."

"I understand that Debbie was in the hospital."

Phil showed anger for the first time. "Damn it, Nancy, stop it! Think about it. Do you *really* believe that this nut caused Debbie to become ill? Do you?"

The answer came hesitantly. "No . . . I guess not."

"Well, then. . . ." The ringing of the phone interrupted him.

"Oh, Phil!" Nancy was startled.

"It's only the phone." The sheriff rose and walked to the telephone as the ringing continued. "Hello." A pause. "Sure, Bob, I understand. . . . Let's make it first thing in the morning. Would 8:30 be too early? . . . Fine, I'll see you then." As he turned from the phone, he explained, "It was just Bob Hoffman setting up an appointment."

Nancy was curled up in a frightened ball, weeping. He went

to her and cradled his wife in his arms. "I can't even hear the phone ring," she sobbed, "without becoming terrified."

"It's okay," he said gently.

"When will it end?"

"Soon. I promise you. Soon!"

"What are you doing in Missionville," Kathy Samson wanted to know, "when you ought to be out here?"

Barry had called her in Phoenix, remembering the telephone number of the Aztec Arms as though it had been his own. It had been only two days since he had left her, but in every hour of those two days he had thought of her.

"Don't think I don't want to be there," Barry said. "Last night I thought about coming out on this morning's flight, but it just didn't make any sense. I'd have to come right back tonight and we'd only have four or five hours together."

"That's right," she giggled, "what could we possibly do in four or five hours?"

"I could tell you, but I don't think you're supposed to say those things on a telephone line."

They talked for more than an hour, with Barry telling her of all of the developments on the Strickler case since he left Phoenix. His biggest revelation, of course, was the identity of "John Richards." The deputy had thought that the news would astound her, but seemingly she received it calmly.

"It's funny," she said, "but I had a deep-down feeling that he would be somehow involved in that thing back there. I didn't know how that would be possible, but I felt that anyway."

"It's just another strange development in a very strange case," Barry said.

"Is he in real trouble?"

"My boss doesn't think so. Oh, he was damned embarrassed when we confronted him with the 'John Richards' identity, but Sheriff Stauffer says he doesn't think Josh has anything to do with the Strickler murder." Barry didn't tell her of his own misgivings.

"Is he angry with me?" Kathy asked.

"No, he can't be. We were discreet with the old man, and we didn't have to tell him where our initial tip came from."

"He probably guessed."

"Maybe," said Barry, "but we didn't tell him."

They went on to talk of other things; intimate things. The memory of her flooded over him.

"Listen, honey," he said finally, "I thing we'd better hang up now."

"Yeah, I guess. I wish you were here, hick."

"And I wish *you* were *here*." Barry stopped. "Hey, why not? You can get away. Why don't you fly in to Missionville? I'll make the reservations for you, and prepay the ticket, and. . . ."

"No," she interrupted, "I couldn't do that."

"Why not?"

"I might run into John . . . ah, Dr. Oberdick. It's a small town."

"Maybe that would be good," he said. "Maybe the best thing for you—and him—would be to meet him face-to-face and explain. . . ."

"Explain how I sold him out?"

"You didn't sell him out," Barry insisted. "You did what you thought was right. You said it yourself, honey, he's a kind man. He'll understand. And you won't have to carry all that guilt around forever."

"Oh, I don't know. . . ."

"Think about it."

"Okay," she said, "I'll think about it. But right now, I'd like to have you here with me."

"Sounds great!"

"Yeah, doesn't it. Goodbye, hick." The sudden end of the long conversation startled Barry. He held the dead phone in his hand for a long moment. Somehow, even that made her seem closer to him.

It was almost eight o'clock that evening when Ernie Wheel and Nick Willson met at the Missionville Inn for dinner. The two newsmen had agreed to meet to compare notes on the Strickler murder case, because Wheel faced an a.m. deadline for the Continental News Service and the flow of information about the investigation had slowed to a trickle. They sipped martinis as they studied the all-too-familiar menu of the hotel restaurant.

"I'm afraid my piece of yesterday," Wheel said, "has probably cut off Stauffer as any kind of a source from now on."

Willson agreed. "I ran into Barry Painter earlier today and he told me that Stauffer was really pissed off. As a matter of fact, Barry told me never to darken the door of the sheriff's office again, or something similar to that."

Wheel grinned. "The path of truth never runs smooth."

"Smoothly," Nick corrected.

"Okay—the path of truth never runs smoothly."

"Did you just coin that cliché?"

"Right here, on the spur of the moment, if you'll pardon yet another cliché."

They both laughed. The waitress came to their table and they gave their orders. Ernie grimaced when he ordered the pot roast. "I know this is going to come as a great shock to you," he said to Willson, "but I really miss those New York restaurants."

"No kidding? I can't imagine why." Willson glanced around the half-filled restaurant as he drained his martini glass. "Hey, look who's coming in."

Ernie turned to see Earle Gensemer, a.k.a. Doctor Fuszganger, entering the dining room. On the comic's arm was an attractive, dark-haired girl. She was perhaps five feet seven, with a trim figure, and was tastefully dressed. Wheel guessed that she was in her early thirties. "Who's the girl?"

"I have no idea," answered Nick, "but she doesn't look like local talent." He waved to Gensemer and the pair crossed the room to the reporters' table.

"Vhy fellas, ain't this nice now? I vant you shouldt meet my niece, Martha Lotz."

They exchanged greetings with the comic and his niece, who said nothing, but smiled sweetly.

"Martha Lotz?" said Nick as they sat down. "Martha Lotz? Johnny Mosser's wife?"

"*Former* vife," Gensemer said before the girl could answer. "*Former*. She's my sister's girl, chust in town onct fer a wisit."

"Isn't that nice." Wheel was entranced. "In town from. . . ."

"New York," the girl said soberly. "I live there now."

"I'm from New York. Perhaps we can get together some time."

"Perhaps."

Gensemer seemed to have a need to explain his niece. "Marty models, ya know? Does schtuff for this clothin' catalogue, n' all."

"My, isn't that marvelous," Ernie said, "we *will* have to get together."

Willson, smiling at Wheel's reaction to the woman, said, "You'll have to excuse my friend, Miss Lotz, he's been away on a desert island and. . . ."

Gensemer cut in. "Ach, everybody calls her Marty. Marty Young iss the name she goes by now."

"Well, Marty," Willson went on, "Mr. Wheel here has a thing for beautiful women. You may find this strange, but he actively seeks their companionship."

A half-smile came to her face.

"That's true," agreed Ernie, "completely true." There was an awkward silence. "Excuse me, Marty. We've made you uncomfortable. I know that this terrible thing with Johnny and the Strickler murder can't be too pleasant for you."

"Johnny was a long time ago." Her voice was flat.

"Yah, a long time ago," Gensemer echoed. "Marty ain't hadt no contact viss Chonny for a few years now, undt she don't know nossing aboudt Strickler's n' all that drek."

Wheel nodded. "Of course. Will you join us for dinner?"

"No, no," said the comic. "Ve chust dropt in fer a drink n' then ve gotta go. But vhen I seen ya here I vanted to say hello."

"Join us for a drink, then," Wheel persisted.

"I guess that vouldt be okay." Gensemer looked at his niece and she nodded an assent. "She'll haf a Scotch sour n' I'll chust haf a beer, thanks."

As the drinks were being ordered, Marty excused herself and headed toward the ladies' room.

"She's chust gone to powder her nose," Gensemer said, "n' that reminds me of a choke. My friend, Chon Auchenbach, vas goin' to York vun day n' his neighbor, Laura Spicher, asks him, 'Vhen ya gedt to York, vill ya look up my son, Donald—Don Spicher? I ain't heardt from him fer fife years.' Undt Chon he sez, 'Vhy schure! How can I findt him?' N' she sez, 'I don't rightly know, but I know he liffs in a liddle vhite house.' Now, Chon he knew that vasn't gonna be easy, but he sought he'd giff it a try. So vhen he gedts to York he schtops at a gas station n' he sez to the fella there, 'Do ya know vhere there iss a liddle vhite house aroundt here?' Undt the fella sez, 'Vhy schure, there's vun aroundt the back.' So, Chon Auchenbach goes aroundt the back n' schure enuf, there's a liddle vhite house n' a man iss comin' oudt of the door, puttin' on his coat. Chon sez to him, 'Say, are you Don?' N' the man sez "Yes.' N' Chon sez, 'Vell, vhy don't ya write your poor oldt mother?'"

The waitress, who had come in on the punch line, joined in the laughter at the old joke.

"There's nothing like an ancient one," Wheel commented.

"Triedt n' true," agreed Gensemer. "But listen, before Marty gedts back, I wanna tell ya how goot that story vas in the paper yesterday."

"Thank you."

"N' listen, Ernie, I sink I haf somesing else fer ya." The comic leaned close to the reporter and dropped his voice almost to a whisper. "I hear tell that Chonny Mosser's sickness, in the hospital ya know, vas because the sheriff dug up the lock of hair from vhere Chonny buried idt. I unnerstand that Chonny vas almost deadt vhen the sheriff put the hair back in the hole, n' then Chonny vas goot again."

"That's wild, Earle," Wheel said.

"Maybe, but I know idt's so."

Marty returned to the table and the conversation turned to small talk, with Doctor Fuszganger tossing in one-liners. The woman smiled a bit, but she never laughed. When uncle and niece had finished their drinks, they offered their thanks, and departed.

Wheel watched them intently as they walked across the restaurant. "My God, Nick, look at those legs!"

"Yeah, and you must have noticed the eyes."

Ernie leaned back in his chair. "Lord, yes . . .
*'Two of the fairest stars in all the heaven,
Having some business, do intreat her eyes
To twinkle in their spheres till they return.'"*

Nick laughed. "Well, I really wasn't thinking of her eyes in the terms of the Bard, but. . . ."

Wheel continued:
*"'What if her eyes were there, they in her head?
The brightness of her cheek would shame those stars,
As daylight doth a lamp; her eyes in heaven
Would through the airy region stream so bright
That birds would sing and think it were not night.'*
There, I knew that Shakespeare course in college would come in handy sometime!"

"I'm overwhelmed by culture," said Willson, "but the point I wanted to make is that her eyes were so sad."

Ernie sobered. "Yeah, there was something awfully sad about that young woman, except the beauty. She, Mr. Willson, is a stunner!"

"So was the news that old Fuszganger gave us."

"Dare we use it, Nick?"

"We certainly can't go to Phil Stauffer to verify it."

Wheel pondered for a moment. "I guess I have a new lead for the a.m. papers." He grinned. "Was it Sir Walter Scott who had that thing about 'eyes of hazel hue'?"

Willson threw the menu at him.

12

MON., DEC. 8, 1969

Dr. Joshua Oberdick and Attorney Robert Hoffman were early. It was about 8:20 when they walked into the sheriff's outer office. Only twenty minutes before that, Stauffer and Painter had sat down to try to bring together the pieces of the baffling Strickler case to begin a new week. The early arrival of the doctor and his lawyer interrupted their work. The sheriff felt a twinge of annoyance, but he quickly dispelled it.

"Push the state police lab on those reports," Stauffer said to his deputy, "and we'll get back to this stuff later."

As Barry left, Hoffman and Oberdick were ushered in, seated, and the amenities of greeting were dealt with. The young attorney dropped a fat file folder on Stauffer's desk.

"This is Dr. Oberdick's notarized statement," Hoffman explained. "We have tried, by working all this weekend and through most of this past night, to bring together all of the facts of what my client knows of the Strickler affair, or about those people who might have some connection with the case."

Stauffer picked up the folder and hefted it. He smiled. "Impressively weighty, I might say."

Hoffman returned the smile. "You might, and I'll forgive the pun." The smile faded. "I advised Dr. Oberdick to give you *everything* he knows, even though a lot of it might be extraneous. The idea, quite frankly, is to demonstrate our total cooperation in this investigation."

"I appreciate that."

The lawyer grinned again. "If appreciation is in order, you might give some to my secretary. I routed her out of bed at 3:30 this morning to type this thing, and she's not too happy with me right now."

"I'll bet she isn't."

"I realize that with this volume of material," the lawyer continued, "you probably won't want to deal with it right now. But when you have a chance to look it over, we stand ready to answer any specific questions on it, or to give you addenda if you need them. And if it's available, of course."

"Thank you."

Hoffman drew a deep breath. "Ah—Phil, there's one other thing I need to know to properly advise my client."

"And that is . . . ?"

"And that is the extent of his involvement in the Strickler investigation as it relates to his being a suspect."

"Uh huh." Stauffer rubbed his hand over his chin. "Well, I've already told Josh that I don't believe he's a suspect . . ."

"That's what I told Bob," Oberdick interjected.

". . . but, as you must realize, counselor, we have not completed our investigation. This . . ." he tapped the file folder " . . . will be a big help, I'm sure. But I haven't read it yet. If, to protect your client's interests, you want to withdraw it before I do read it, you have that prerogative. Then, of course, I'd have to take other measures to interrogate the good doctor."

"Naturally," said Hoffman, "I could advise Dr. Oberdick not to answer any of your questions."

"You could." Phil shrugged. "And I'd understand why you might want to. But a completely cooperative attitude in this investigation might, I believe, be in the best interests of your client."

Oberdick laughed lightly. "If you two guys are done sparring over me, maybe I'd better leave." He rose to his feet. "I *do* want to be totally cooperative, Phil, although I'm really not sure I want you to know everything that's in that statement. It kind of peels my hide back and exposes the innards."

The sheriff also rose and stuck out his hand. "Thanks, Doc. I'll make certain the exposure of the innards is kept in confidence."

At the same hour, Ernie Wheel strolled into the editorial

room of *The Missionville Star*. It was the busiest time of day for the afternoon daily. Deadline was noon, only three hours away, and nearly every desk was occupied, the noise of a dozen typewriters setting up a cacophony that was as familiar to Wheel as the beat of his own pulse. He greeted several staffers as he made his way to Nick Willson's city desk.

"It's a good story," said Nick. "Wanna see the p.m.'s lead in type?" He handed the reporter a galley proof and Wheel's eyes skimmed the article he had written about the buried and reburied lock of Charlie Strickler's hair, and Johnny Mosser's correspondingly strange illness.

"You know," Wheel said, "in rereading this in type, it sounds a great deal like fiction."

Nick grinned. "For you and me both, buddy, I sure hope it isn't."

"No, I have confidence in our Doctor Fuszganger." Wheel was deadly serious. "I really can't tell you why, but he knows what he's talking about. I regret that I had to fudge so many things in this piece, not being able to verify them with other sources, but I have no fear that the basic premise is factual."

"I know this," said Willson, "we are really going to be in Sheriff Stauffer's brick outhouse when this hits the streets."

Ernie nodded solemnly. "Nick, I know you're busy right now, but could you spare me about a minute . . . ah, privately?"

"Sure." Willson left the city desk and led his friend into a vacant office cubicle. "What gives?"

"I think I'm being followed."

"Huh?"

"Yeah, I became conscious of it yesterday afternoon," Wheel explained, "as I was driving out to that Pennsylvania Dutch place you suggested for lunch. Then last night when we were having dinner at the Inn, I spotted the guy again. I really didn't think much of it at the time, because this is a small town and I keep running into the same faces from time to time. But this morning, I saw him again, and . . ."

"Can you describe this fellow?"

"I think I can do better than that. If my suspicions are correct, I can show him to you. He's waiting for me out in front, on the square. As I was coming in I spotted him in the doorway of that shoe store—Fastner's—across the street. We can see that, can't we, from the window over there?"

They went to the window and peered out into the town square through the tilted venetian blinds. "Damn, I don't see him now," Wheel said. "No . . . no . . . wait! There he is! He moved up one storefront, to the drug store. The guy with the wool hat."

Willson's eyes followed Wheel's directions. "Yeah, I see him. Hey, that's George Sprenkel!"

"What's a George Sprenkel?"

"He's a special deputy for the sheriff's department. Stauffer has about five or six guys who work for him on a part-time basis—usually on accident cases, and serving subpoenas, and that kind of stuff. They get paid on an hourly or daily basis, depending on the assignment. Sprenkel is one of them. That's George, all right."

Wheel frowned. "Well, Mr. Willson, that special deputy has me under surveillance."

Nick waved away the thought. "Oh, I don't believe that. Stauffer's a tough nut and all, but why would he have you followed?"

"Maybe because he'd like to know my source on that threats story." Ernie clapped his hand to his forehead. "If Sprenkel really is following me, he saw us with Earle Gensemer last night. And when the paper comes out this afternoon, Stauffer is going to be able to put two and two together."

"How? One chance meeting with Gensemer is all he could have seen. He'd have no way of knowing that you had another meeting. You could have gotten that story about the buried hair from a lot of people. Gensemer was only one of the people he must have seen you with." Again, Willson waved away the idea. "But I don't believe he's following you."

"Well, let's find out."

"How?"

"I'll go out into the square and stroll down the street, trying to keep within the view of this window. You watch this Sprenkel fellow. If he follows me, you'll be able to see it."

"Sounds feasible."

Willson stood at the window, watching Sprenkel who was lounging disinterestedly in the doorway of the pharmacy. Ernie Wheel came into Nick's line of sight as he exited the newspaper building and began a leisurely move down the street. Nick saw Wheel stop to look into a jewelry store window and then move on. Sprenkel didn't move. Wheel continued his easy pace down the street. Suddenly, the special deputy left the doorway and crossed the wide square, dodging in between cars as he moved. His was an unhurried pace that brought him on the same side of the street with Wheel. Willson surmised that Ernie had also seen Sprenkel move, because Wheel crossed the square with the green light, and was slowly walking up the other side toward the drug store entrance Sprenkel had left just a few moments before. Sprenkel stopped, apparently reading an advertising poster wired to a metal light post. From that vantage point, Sprenkel could see Wheel all the while he was walking up the street. At the corner of Sixth Street, Wheel turned and went south on Sixth, taking him out of Nick's view and out of the view of anyone on the square. Sprenkel sprinted across the wide thoroughfare again and, once he was on the other side, walked hurriedly to Sixth and also turned south.

As Willson walked back to his desk the phone rang. A copyboy called to him, "Nick, a call on two!"

"I'm calling from a phone booth one block south on Sixth," Ernie said when Nick answered the call. "He *is* following me, isn't he?"

"Yep, he went south on Sixth just a moment or two after you did."

"I don't see him right now, but I'm sure he's in one of the doorways between here and the square. I'm going to double back now and go into the drug store for a cup of coffee."

"If you do that he'll tumble to the fact that you know he's following you."

"Screw him," said Ernie. "Maybe that way he'll get off my back!"

A state police squad car had delivered two lab reports to

Sheriff Stauffer's office and Phil and Barry were studying them. One report dealt with the empty gasoline can found at Lizzie Zearfoss's home. As had previously been determined, the report stated that there were no fingerprints on the can. It had been wiped clean. The can was a common type, sold through Sears stores throughout the area. An inventory check with Sears had revealed that several thousand cans had been sold at four area stores over the past year. However, the same can had been in the Sears catalogue for five years and there was no way to determine whether the can had been bought five days before the fire, or five years before the Zearfoss home was torched.

There was, however, one small development in a close examination of the can. Wedged in the wire handle, at the point where it was connected to the can, was a tiny thread—a gray-blue thread. It had been pulled, the report said, from a plaid garment, probably a topcoat. Comparison with various textiles indicated it was from a common type of material, but if such a garment could be found, it could be matched with the specific thread found on the can.

Stauffer said, "Well, it's something anyway."

The second report, on the typed notes, was more specific. Both notes, as had been suspected, were typed on the same machine. It was a rather old instrument, of American manufacture in the late Twenties or early Thirties by the Royal Typewriter Co. Inc., New York. The typewriter would carry a serial number which started with "14-9," followed by five other digits. Accompanying the report was a photograph of the variety of typewriter used. It showed a rather heavy machine of the type called an "office model," with a high, squarish front above the keys, and little glass windows on the sides, revealing the inner workings.

As for the type letters, the analysis pointed out that the "s" was out of alignment, striking well below the other letters on a line. The "o" was also distinctive; a portion of it on the right-hand side was worn off so that it looked somewhat like a "c." Several other letters were distinctive enough to be able to clearly identify the typewriter as the one used for the notes, if the machine could be found. Chemical tests on the ink in the type indicated that it was comparatively new, largely used on all-nylon ribbons, probably on an all-black ribbon, as opposed to one that was both black and red.

"Another needle in a haystack," commented Barry.

"But when we find this guy," Phil said with satisfaction, "this report will nail him!"

"I hope so. Oh, listen! I just remembered. As I was coming back to the office a few minutes ago, the switchboard operator handed me an envelope that had been left for you." He gave a large manila envelope to Stauffer. The sheriff tore it open, scanned the contents and, with a disgusted grunt, turned it over to his deputy.

There were two pieces of paper inside. One was a handwritten note: *Here's a galley proof of a story that will run in this afternoon's edition. I thought you'd like to see it.* The note was unsigned.

The second piece of paper was the galley proof of an article written by Ernie Wheel.

Missionville, Pa., Dec. 8 (CNS) — A hexerei, or witchcraft, ritual engaged in by Young County Sheriff Philip Stauffer has become part of the Charles Strickler "lock of hair" murder case in this colorful Pennsylvania Dutch community.

It has been learned that Strickler's lock of hair, apparently cut from his head during the murder, has played a role in the sudden mysterious illness of suspect John Mosser, and in the subsequent recovery of Mosser from that still unexplained illness.

Details are sketchy, but the chain of events is believed to have included: (1) Recovery of Strickler's lock of hair from beneath a tree where Mosser buried it; (2) The critical illness of Mosser; (3) The just-revealed reburying of the hair by Sheriff Stauffer; and (4) the recovery of Mosser from his illness. Mosser, incidentally, is still a patient at the Missionville Hospital, where he is believed to be undergoing psychiatric tests.

Mosser had originally buried the hair in order to end a spell he believed had been put on him by Strickler. Authorities on hexerei point out that believers in the witchcraft art would not, under any circumstances, dig up a charm (the hair) once it had been buried. Such an act, these authorities say, would tend to bring back the spell. It is not known whether Mosser had knowledge of the sheriff's department's act in recovering the lock of hair from its burying place, nor is it known. . . .

"Damn!" Barry tossed the papers on Stauffer's desk.

The sheriff was obviously trying to control his temper. When he spoke his voice was low, but the tone was bitter. "Three people knew about the reburying of the hair—me, Dr. Myers and you. Now, *I* didn't tell Wheel anything about this, and. . . ."

Painter interrupted him. "Christ, Phil, *I* didn't tell him! Honest to God, I didn't tell him!"

"You think Ed Myers told him?"

"No, no, I don't. But you *can't* believe that I told him, Phil!" There was panic in the deputy's voice.

Stauffer was not convinced. "God dammit, Barry. . . ."

"But I *didn't* tell him!"

The sheriff angrily picked up the papers and stuffed them back into the envelope. He was stony-faced and silent in his anger.

"Now, wait a minute," Barry pleaded, "there *was* one other person who knew the hair had been reburied—Johnny Mosser!"

"And I suppose Mosser went and told Wheel?"

Barry slumped dejectedly in his chair, knowing it was useless to argue with his boss when anger had him in its grip. The two men sat in silence for several moments, Stauffer seething and Painter in distress. The impasse was broken when Special Deputy George Sprenkel entered the office. The sheriff dismissed Barry and motioned Sprenkel to a chair.

"What's with Barry?" asked Sprenkel, looking after the retreating figure of the deputy.

Stauffer waved away the question. "What do you have on Wheel?"

"Well, he made me just about fifteen minutes ago."

"What?"

"Yeah, somehow he spotted me and ran me a goose chase back and forth across the square and then down South Sixth Street. He doubled back and went right past me. I'm certain that he knows I've been following him."

Phil groaned. "A smart bastard, our Mr. Wheel. Well, tell me what you have."

"Not much," the special deputy admitted. "After I got on him Saturday night, he had dinner alone at the Missionville Inn, and the only one he spoke to was the waitress. That was Lillie Greenawalt. At 10:15 p.m., he bought a couple of magazines at the Inn newsstand and went up on the elevator to his room. I hung around the lobby until 1 a.m. and then cut out."

"Go on."

Then, on Sunday, I was back at the hotel at 6 a.m. He came down on the elevator at 7:30, had breakfast alone at the Inn, then got his car out of the parking garage and went sightseeing."

"Huh?"

"Yeah, he drove all over the damned place. Went to the farmers' market at Bird-In-Hand over in Lancaster County, strolled around a bit there, and bought some candy. Then he drove back into Young County and went to that family Dutch restaurant near Shoemakersville. The *Distlefink*, you know?"

"I know the place."

"He had lunch there," Sprenkel continued, "and then just drove around the country, kind of looking at farms and stuff. He stopped only once, at 3:45, to look at some quilts at Mrs. Oberholtzer's place near Leesport. But he didn't buy anything. Then he came back to the hotel and went up to his room. At about eight o'clock he met Nick Willson in the Inn dining room and they had dinner. Aside from the waitress again, they spoke to only one other person; well, two actually. One was Earle Gensemer—you know, the fellow who calls himself Doctor Fuszganger. There was a girl with Gensemer. I don't know who she was."

"What'd she look like?"

Sprenkel consulted his notebook. "Dark-haired, about mid-30's maybe, well-dressed, about five-eight or five-nine. A real good looking girl she was."

"Did they talk long?"

"Nope. They had a drink with Wheel and Willson and left. They were together no more than ten minutes, and most of that time it seemed that Gensemer was telling jokes. Then the two guys ate dinner, talked a little while, and Willson left the Inn and Wheel went up to his room. That was about ten or five after ten. I waited again until one and picked him up this morning. He had breakfast at 7:30 again, then walked to the newspaper office and went in. About ten minutes later he came out again and we went through that back-and-forth-across-the-square routine. Then I came back here."

"Anything else?"

"No, except that I could have stopped him for speeding a couple of times. He really moves around in that Jaguar of his."

"And that's all?"

"Yep."

"He didn't meet Barry Painter at any time?"

"Barry?" Sprenkel was surprised by the question. "No, never. Why?"

"Oh," said Stauffer in an off-hand manner, "just curious." He stroked his chin for a moment. "So Earle Gensemer and that unknown woman were the only ones he met out of the ordinary?"

"That's about it."

"Ever see the girl before around town?"

"Nope."

The sheriff sighed. "Okay, sign this voucher and I'll get your money for you." He shoved a piece of paper at the special deputy.

As Sprenkel scrawled his name, he said, "I'm sorry that he spotted me, Phil, but there just weren't a lot of people around to screen me, and. . . ."

"Forget it." Phil raised his hand. "It happens. Oh, on your way out, ask Barry to come in again, will you? I think I might owe him an apology."

The sheriff felt like a voyeur. It was nearly nine o'clock and, seated alone at his desk in a circle of light made by a single desk lamp, he was reading the affidavit of Dr. Joshua Oberdick. Unique! That would have been a valid one-word description of the old doctor's lifestyle. My God, thought Phil, I could turn this over to a writer and he'd have a best seller. Or, at the very least, a couple of years of episodes for a soap opera.

There were sixty-three typed pages in the folder, detailing Oberdick's associations with Sarah Strickler, Kathy Samson, Martha Mosser (nee Lotz), Lizzie Zearfoss, and Dottie Kissinger. Much of the material was laced with attorney Bob Hoffman's legalisms, but the utter frankness of Oberdick's revelations overwhelmed the stiff language Hoffman had contributed to the document. Only the Lizzie Zearfoss narrative did not have sexual connotations. And the mention of Dottie Kissinger encompassed only three sentences. That affair, after all, was current and had not developed any substantial documentation. Oberdick did say that he believed very strongly that Mrs. Kissinger's son, Larry, played no significant role in Strickler's death; that the boy was merely an innocent pawn in the episode.

Phil was surprised at the depth of the Sarah Strickler liaison. He knew, of course, that old Oberdick and Sarah had been lovers. Sarah had told him that. But he had not known that the doctor had moved into the apartment he had rented for Mrs. Strickler and had lived there for more than a month. Josh admitted in the affidavit that he had moved out because of his annoyance with Sarah's determination to disseminate her sexual favors. Oberdick was a roué, but there was also a strong jealous streak in him. It occurred to Phil that the doctor, although he had never been married, approached each affair as though it was to have a permanence; a *marriage,* in a sense. Oberdick had had several violent arguments with the late Charlie Strickler about Sarah's conduct, but Josh made no mention of any actual physical encounters. This, too, paralleled what Sarah had told the sheriff.

Kathy Samson, the Oberdick affidavit said, had been met in San Francisco, where Josh had gone on a medical convention. It was during that escapade that the John

Richards pseudonym had been invented. It was done, he claimed, because he was at the convention with a large Pennsylvania delegation and he wanted to protect what the doctor called his professional integrity. There was a revealing statement in the document: *I felt that I could best help the girl by assuming an identity that did not hurt her and yet enabled me to maintain a certain anonymity. It was, in looking back on it, a lark.* Josh, after several trips to San Francisco to help her through her drug rehabilitation, suggested to the girl that he move her to Phoenix, because that city was where he spent his vacations. She had agreed and Oberdick had financed her move and had set her up in a comfortable apartment in the Aztec Arms. In complete candor, the doctor said he was well aware of Kathy's profession, and that he felt he had no right to demand that she change it.

The Samson girl's availability (that was Josh's word: "availability") in Phoenix was what led Oberdick to suggest that a distressed Martha Lotz Mosser go there to get away from her real and imagined fears of John Mosser. Josh detailed the terrible beating Martha had received at the hands of Mosser and admitted that he had totally financed the girl's move to Arizona. His initial association with Martha Mosser had not been intimate; that had developed on one of his trips to Phoenix when he and Kathy Samson had had a "small disagreement." After it did develop, however, Martha had expressed a desire to be closer to Josh. They felt it would not be possible to maintain such a relationship in Missionville, so he moved her to New York, where he already had a hotel apartment in the name of John Richards. There was that marriage syndrome once more. Martha had, on her own, developed contacts that led to small modeling assignments, but in reality, Oberdick still supported her. He had given her an American Express card and an addendum to the typed affidavit included several sheets of computer readouts of the credit company's billing.

In the context of Martha Mosser, there was an interesting aside. Her pseudonym, Marty Young, was invented by Josh, at first to foil Johnny Mosser if he came to Phoenix looking for his wife. Then later, it seemed the discreet thing to do when the New York-based relationship developed.

As he read, Sheriff Stauffer wondered about something. Why so much volunteered detail? The credit card readouts, for example? He surmised that it must have been Bob Hoffman's insistence for total revelation; overkill to establish for the sheriff that Joshua Oberdick was clean on the Strickler murder.

The credit card records showed that Martha was a frugal spender. There were no really major items on the bills; an occasional dress, a pair of shoes, a couple of restaurant tabs—and then it hit Stauffer. *Airline charges* for commuter flights between New York and Missionville. Six of them were listed, each about two months apart. But what really startled the sheriff was one flight on the most recent November billing. An airline charge dated November 25, just two days before Thanksgiving. Phil's eyes scanned the typed statement for any mention of Martha visiting Missionville since she had moved to New York. There was no such record. He recalled the conversation with Ira and Hanna Lotz just six days earlier in which they denied that they knew about the whereabouts of their daughter. Stauffer strained to remember the exact details of that interview. Ira Lotz had told him that they did not know where Martha was and that she didn't write to them. It was a complete denial of knowledge of the whereabouts of their daughter. Indeed, Phil had come away from the talk with the impression that they had not seen their daughter since she had left for Arizona.

The sheriff picked up the phone and dialed Oberdick's number. *Calmly now,* he told himself.

"Josh," he said when the old man answered the phone, "I've been reading your affidavit." Phil forced a jovial tone into his voice; a totally friendly approach.

Oberdick laughed. "Are you thinking of selling it to *True Confessions?*"

"The thought has crossed my mind." Phil joined in the laughter. "There's one question, though. I notice on the credit card readouts that Martha came to Missionville five or six times on the commuter flight from New York. I don't see anything in your statement about those trips."

"Oh, yeah. Well, she asked me if she could visit her folks every once in a while, and I told her she could." There was a slight pause. "Is that what you wanted to know, Phil?"

"Yeah, sure." Stauffer was still maintaining the good-old-boy attitude. "Just my nit-picking way of tying up all the loose ends. I certainly appreciate all of the cooperation you're giving us, Josh. It's rare in an investigation like this."

"It's the least I could do. Murder is an ugly business."

"Yes, it is. Well, thanks, Josh." Another pause. "Listen, there's just one other thing. Ira and Hanna Lotz know of your association with Martha, don't they?"

"Oh, certainly," answered Josh. "I'm not going to tell you that they were thrilled about it at first, but Marty convinced them that she's happy and, well . . . they've accepted it."

"And they know where she's living in New York?"

"Absolutely. They've been up there once that I know of. Spent a weekend with Martha and she showed them the city—the Statue of Liberty, Empire State Building, Radio City Music Hall, the whole tourist bit."

Stauffer laughed lightly. "Well, that satisfies my curiosity about that angle. Again, Josh, I want to tell you how much I appreciate your help."

"I hope it really *is* a help. I'd hate to think that I've bared my soul like this and then it didn't help."

"It's a help, Josh, believe me. Have a nice evening."

"It's almost over."

Phil laughed again. "Not for you, I'll bet."

"Probably not," the old man said with a leer coloring his words, "probably not."

When Phil finished the conversation with Oberdick he immediately dialed the number of Melvin Shriner, the commuter airline manager in Missionville. The two of them were members of the Exchange Club and Mel and his wife, Doris, were frequently at dinners and other social events with the sheriff and his wife. Stauffer apologized for bothering Shriner at home, and then asked him to get some information on a passenger who had flown from New York to Missionville on Tuesday, November 25.

"I want to know the arrival time in Missionville, Mel, and then the time of the return trip to New York."

"Okay," said Shriner. "And the name is Young—Martha Young?"

"I'm pretty sure it'll be listed that way," said Stauffer. "The first name might be Marty . . . M-a-r-t-y. And if you can't find a Young, try Mosser . . . M-o-s-s-e-r, or Lotz . . . L-o-t-z."

"You need this tonight?"

Stauffer wanted to say "yes," but he also didn't want to take advantage of his old friendship with Shriner. "No, no. Tomorrow will be fine."

"Will do, Phil."

"Give my love to Doris."

"You bet. Good night, Phil."

Stauffer hung up the phone and leaned back in his chair. He stared at the papers lying on his desk. Why had the Lotzes lied to him? Was it because they thought they were protecting their daughter? Were they embarrassed by her live-in association with Josh Oberdick? He shook his head and reached for the phone once more.

"Nance," he said when his call went through, "I'm wrapped up here. Be home in a couple of minutes."

"Finally," she said. "Have a tough day?"

"Uh huh, but damned interesting. Got any martinis made?"

She laughed. "Oh, *that* kind of day! No, but I'll stir up a batch."

"Gently," said the sheriff, "gently. Don't bruise the gin. I'm in no mood for any more bruising today."

13 TUES., DEC. 9, 1969

"There are times when I hate this job!"

District Attorney Fred Barringer dropped into the chair at Sheriff Stauffer's desk, slumping in dejection. He had come to report on an early morning meeting he had had in the chambers of President Judge August Schmehl, who earlier had ordered a psychiatric test for Johnny Mosser.

"The psychiatrist says that Mosser can't distinguish between right and wrong," Barringer said, "and, boiling down the gobbledygook, Johnny is therefore legally insane. Judge Schmehl says he has no choice but to commit him to the state mental institution." He dropped a large manila envelope in front of Stauffer. "This copy of the psychiatrist's report is for you. If I'm going to have to be depressed over this, you might as well join me."

"Gee, thanks."

"Think nothing of it." Barringer paused and sat erect. "Phil, do you get the same feeling that I have—that poor Johnny Mosser is the real victim in this case?"

"It has occurred to me," admitted Stauffer. "What happens to him now?"

"Well, Schmehl is going to have a hearing in two days. I'm to represent the state, of course, in asking for the commitment of Mosser. A public defender will go through the motions on his behalf. But to all intents and purposes, Schmehl will sign the commitment order on Thursday. Then, as soon as the doctors say it's okay, he'll be moved from the Missionville Hospital to the state mental hospital, probably before the end of the week."

Phil shrugged his shoulders. "Well, maybe it's better for him."

"Have you ever been in that place?"

"No, I can't say I have."

"Then don't say it's better for him!" Anger showed in his voice. "It's a hell-hole, a disgrace!"

Stauffer stared at the D.A. It wasn't often that he saw Barringer this moved, showing real compassion. Usually, he was all business, vehemently insisting that the system of justice was without fault. But not this morning.

Barringer smiled weakly. "I'm sorry, Phil. It's just that every time I get into one of these commitment things, I get bloody depressed. We have nothing better for these poor devils—and we ought to. We ought to!"

Phil had no comment.

"Well, enough of that," said the D.A. "Are we ready to go before the grand jury for aggravated assault indictments against Larry Saylor and Will Burkholder?"

"Frankly, Fred, I don't think so." Stauffer leaned his elbows on his desk. "The problem, my friend, is that we'd have to rely totally on the two boys. We have no other witnesses and, from what you've just told me, Mosser can't testify. Honestly, though, I've never thought of him as a witness. What I'm telling you, Mr. D.A., is that the fabric of this case to date is pretty ragged. I think we ought to wait."

"Well, I'm in no hurry. It's been less than two weeks since the murder."

"Seems like two years."

"Hmm. You got anything new?"

Stauffer brightened a bit. "I know where Martha Mosser is." He detailed the Oberdick information as it related to Josh and Martha, but he didn't tell the D.A. that he had an affidavit on the matter, nor did he mention any of the other details on the document. Phil had no real motive for keeping it from Barringer; it just seemed the right thing to do at the time.

"Is finding Martha Mosser important to the case?" Barringer asked.

"I'm not sure yet. It does close one loophole in the investigation and that's a plus any time."

Barringer rose. "Okay, keep me informed." He turned to leave and then stopped. "Say, Phil, I don't usually pay any attention to this crap, but I read Wheel's story in the *Star* yesterday. Is there anything to it?"

"It's essentially factual."

"You mean you actually reburied Strickler's hair?"

Phil smiled. "Yep. I'll try anything once."

Barringer looked sharply at the sheriff. "You don't want to talk about it."

"That's a fair statement."

"Okay, Phil." The district attorney headed for the door. "You can count on me for help when you need it." He was gone.

Deputy Painter was getting out of his squad car in the courthouse parking lot when someone shouted at him. As he turned he saw Ernie Wheel approaching. *Shit!* he said to himself.

"Got a minute, Barry?"

"Not really."

Wheel was at the deputy's side. "Look, I know your boss must be pissed off at me . . ."

"No kidding?"

Ernie ignored the sarcasm. ". . . but he's so damned inflexible. I went in the other day to talk to him about a tip I had—the one on the threats—and he practically threw me out of the office."

"That doesn't surprise me."

"I'd like you to tell the sheriff that I want to cooperate, but that I think cooperation ought to be a two-way street."

"*You* tell him." Barry was firm.

"Do you know that he's had me under surveillance?"

The deputy stood mute.

"Well, he has and it's damned disconcerting. What does he want from me?"

"Nothing, I guess." Barry permitted a little smile to show on his face. "I think the sheriff believes he can do his job without you."

Wheel laughed. "I'm sure he does." He took the deputy by the arm and lowered his voice into a confidential tone. "Barry, I know where Martha Mosser is."

"Huh?"

"Martha Mosser—Johnny Mosser's wife."

"Yeah, I know who the hell she is!" Barry was annoyed. "Okay, where is she?"

"Right here in town. I was introduced to her Sunday night."

"Is that right?" The deputy was trying not to show too much interest.

Ernie groaned. "Oh, what's the use? You're just like Stauffer."

"That's one fine compliment."

"Yeah, I guess you would think it is." The reporter started away. "Anyway, tell your boss that I told you about Martha Mosser. Maybe it'll help our relationship."

"I'll tell him. But, Wheel . . ."

"What?"

"Don't hold your breath."

Mel Shriner's information about Martha Lotz Mosser's travel was just what Sheriff Stauffer had hoped it would be. Commuter airline computers showed that Martha, traveling under the name of Marty Young, had indeed flown from New York City to Missionville on Tuesday, November 25. Specifically, she had arrived in Missionville at 4:45 p.m. on that day, on Flight 987. Shriner had been thorough. He had checked with his baggage agent and had gotten a description of the only woman who had arrived on that flight: Dark haired, five-eight, early thirties, well-dressed, a beauty. She had purchased a round-trip ticket in New York, using a valid credit card issued to a John Richards. She had departed Missionville on Flight 989 at 7:30 p.m. on Sunday, November 30.

"So she was in Missionville for almost six days," Stauffer commented.

"Yeah," Shriner said, "but that wasn't her original plan."

"Oh?"

"When she made the original reservation, she was booked to return on the 5:30 flight on Thursday, November 27—that was Thanksgiving Day. Shortly before that flight, she called in to cancel, saying she'd get back to the reservations clerk for another flight when her plans were firm. Then on Sunday, she called for a reservation on that same flight. But that one doesn't fly on Sundays and so she took the 7:30 flight instead."

"Uh huh. What's the number of the 5:30 flight?"

"Number 988, Monday through Saturday."

Stauffer checked over his notes. "I guess that's as much detail as you have."

"On that particular trip," Shriner said. "But when I was checking the computer, I noticed the same name again incoming on Flight 987. That one goes seven days a week. She arrived last Sunday—that was December 7—at five o'clock. The flight was about fifteen minutes behind schedule."

"Is she still in Missionville?"

"No, she left yesterday on the 5:30 flight."

Stauffer noted the new information. "Same details? I mean, did she use the John Richards credit card again?"

"Yes."

"Well, thanks, Mel, that's a big help. See you soon."

"Fine. Call me any time."

Barry had come into the office as the phone call was being terminated, and reported to Stauffer on the conversation he had just had with Ernie Wheel.

"So he met Martha Mosser on Sunday night?" the sheriff asked.

"That's what he said."

Stauffer stroked his chin. "Did he say where?"

"No."

"Well, let me tell you where. It was at the Missionville Inn dining room, and that girl—and we must assume that she was really Martha Mosser—was with Earle Gensemer. They had a drink with Ernie Wheel and Nick Willson."

The deputy was surprised. "Then you *did* have Wheel under surveillance?"

"Of course," Stauffer answered with feeling. "It's important that we know who's feeding him his information. Now the question is, what was Martha Mosser doing there with Earle Gensemer?"

"Oh, that's easy," Barry said jauntily, "Earle is her uncle."

"Uncle?"

"Yeah, Doctor Fuszganger is a brother of Hanna Lotz."

"When did you learn this?"

"Hell, I don't know, Phil. I've always known it, I guess."

Stauffer stared at the wall for a moment. Suddenly, he slammed an open palm down on his desk. "Bingo!"

"I don't under—"

"The key! Gensemer is the key to this mess. Don't you see it, Barry?"

There was confusion on the deputy's face. "No, not really."

Phil was grinning now. "The common denominator, deputy, the common denominator! One: Earle Gensemer was one of the men badly beaten by Charlie Strickler. Two: Earle Gensemer is the uncle of Martha Mosser. Three: Martha is the wife of the number one suspect in the case, Johnny Mosser; she had been badly beaten by him. Four: Earle Gensemer was the one person out of the ordinary to have been seen with Ernie Wheel. Do you see it now?"

"No, I. . . ."

"Earle Gensemer is our common denominator, right?"

"Yeah, I guess."

"And because he is," Stauffer went on enthusiastically, "an honest-to-God pattern and motive come to the surface. Charlie Strickler is killed because of what he did to Gensemer. Johnny Mosser is framed for Strickler's killing because of what he did to Martha, who just happens to be Gensemer's niece. The pieces fit, deputy!"

"What about Lizzie Zearfoss?"

Phil pondered the question briefly. "Well, try this on for size—Lizzie is recruited by Gensemer and Mrs. Mosser as part of the set-up against Johnny. She steers him to Strickler with that story that Strickler has a spell on him. Then, when things seemed to be getting hot, the old lady panics, threatens to talk, and they knock her off."

"Sounds possible. Can we prove it?"

Stauffer smiled broadly again. "As the poet said, Barry, there's the rub. But things are beginning to click. For example, I now know that Martha Lotz Mosser was in Missionville on both the night before Thanksgiving, when

Strickler was killed, and on the Sunday Lizzie's house was torched." The sheriff explained to Painter about the flight information he had secured from the commuter airline. "Okay, so much for Mrs. Mosser. Now, where was her uncle on the night before Thanksgiving? Did you check out that Frackville alibi?"

"Not yet," Barry admitted. "It didn't seem to have a very high priority."

"It does now. Make the check right now. Use the phone here."

As Stauffer waited impatiently, Barry made the call to the volunteer fire company in Frackville, located in the hard coal region. The conversation was brief. The deputy scrawled a few notes and hung up.

"That tears it, Phil. Gensemer was *not* there on the evening before Thanksgiving. The guy I talked to, by the name of Ignatius Kolakowski, is the social chairman of the fire company. Doctor Fuszganger was booked for their smoker, but he was a no-show. If I quote Mr. Kolakowski correctly, 'It's the last time we book that bastard.'"

"So both uncle and niece were in Missionville on the evening in question . . ."

Barry cut in. "I don't want to rain on the parade, Phil, but we *don't* know that Gensemer was in Missionville. What we know is that he wasn't in Frackville."

"Ah, Mr. Deputy, do you want to bet that our Doctor Fuszganger wasn't in Missionville?"

"Nope."

"And do you want to bet that Gensemer owns an old Royal typewriter?" Phil was elated.

"You mean you think that Gensemer sent the threats?"

"It makes sense, doesn't it?"

"It does," Barry conceded. "What now?"

"We move with all deliberate speed to get those two in custody," the sheriff said. "But first, I want to take a run out to see Ira and Hanna Lotz. I think that they might be able to supply some missing pieces to our puzzle."

Phil Stauffer's approach with Ira and Hanna was different

this time. He hadn't called them to tell them he was on the way; there wasn't going to be any low-key chat over coffee and cake. As he walked to the door of the Lotz home he had one small twinge of conscience—he liked the old couple—but he quickly dismissed it.

Ira opened the door to him. "Sheriff, your radar must be working." He laughed.

"What?"

"Hanna just took three apple pies out of the oven," Ira said cheerfully. "Come on in and have some with warm milk and cinnamon."

"I won't be able to today, Ira. This is just business."

The old man led him into the bright kitchen, where the tempting smell of warm apple pie was strong. Hanna was delighted to see him.

"I ain't baked apple pie in a long time," she told him. "I used to all the time, but now that I'm working at the hospital. . . ."

"You work at the Missionville hospital?" Phil chastized himself for not knowing that.

"Yeah," Hanna said, smiling broadly, "and I enjoy it so much. I'm a nurse's aide and I get to meet so many people. It makes me feel good to help people, you know?"

"Sit down, sit down," Ira insisted. He had already put a huge slice of apple pie in a bowl, and was pouring warm milk over it. He handed Phil a cinnamon shaker. "Put on yourself what you want. Some people don't like too much cinnamon."

Phil was trapped by the kind enthusiasm of the Lotzes. He ate the apple pie with obvious enjoyment. When the bowl was empty, he was served a steaming cup of coffee.

"The pie is so marvelous," Stauffer said candidly, "that I almost forgot what I came for." Both of the Lotzes sat at the big kitchen table with him and waited for him to continue. Their faces were sober, but unworried. "Remember the last time I was here, you told me that you didn't hear from Martha and didn't know where she was?"

"Yeah," Ira answered.

"That was a lie, wasn't it?" The question was very soft, more of a statement than an accusation.

Ira and Hanna stared at him without answering.

"Wasn't it?" Phil persisted.

"Yeah," Ira said finally. "We wanted to protect her, to make sure that Johnny didn't bother her again."

"I understand that. But you do know that she lives in New York, don't you?"

"Yeah."

"And she comes to visit you from time to time?"

Tears began to well up in Hanna's eyes. "Oh, sheriff, we only wanted to protect our little girl."

"I know," the sheriff said kindly, "but I have a job to do and you're making it very difficult."

"We're sorry about that, Phil," Ira said. His apology was genuine.

"That's okay. But no more lies?"

Both of them nodded agreement.

"Fine. Now . . . was Martha here for Thanksgiving?"

Hanna brightened. "Yes, and we had such a nice dinner!"

"What I need to know now," the sheriff continued, "is, was she here the night *before* Thanksgiving?"

"Sure, she came in for Thanksgiving," Hanna said. "Tuesday it was, ain't, Ira?"

"Yeah, Tuesday," her husband agreed.

"And she stayed here with you?"

"Yeah."

"She was with you all the time she was in Missionville?"

Hanna pondered the question. "I think so . . . no, wait, I think my brother came in on Wednesday night and they went out for a movie. Martha and her uncle were always so close."

"Your brother?"

"Earle Gensemer, you know. He's Doctor Fuszganger."

"Oh, certainly." Phil was trying to draw the story out of the Lotzes without alarming them. "So Martha and her uncle went out to the movies on Wednesday night, the night before Thanksgiving. That would have been Thanksgiving eve."

"Yeah."

"Were they gone long?"

"No, no," Hanna answered in a matter-of-fact manner. "When the movie was over, they came back. Martha said she had such a good time."

The sheriff moved slowly. "Then she had Thanksgiving dinner here and went back to New York?"

"Well, she was going to." The mother smiled at the recollection. "But then she said she was enjoying herself so much that she wanted to stay a couple of more days. She didn't leave until late Sunday." Again, Ira confirmed his wife's account with a nod.

"Now, what did Martha do between Thanksgiving Day and Sunday, when she went back to New York?"

"Do?"

"Yeah, did she stay here, or did she visit friends, or what?"

"She just stayed here mostly," Hanna said. "On Sunday, as I recollect, she went for a drive."

"A drive? Does she own a car?"

"No, she borrowed one from her uncle. He has that old flivver he drives, and a new car. She had the new car."

"Did her uncle go with her?"

"I don't think so," Hanna answered. "I think he was out of town working."

"So she just went for a drive alone. In the morning or afternoon?"

"In the morning, I think." The persistent questions began to worry Hanna Lotz. "Is something wrong, sheriff?"

"No, I just want to get all my facts straight." Then he took another tack. "What does Martha do in New York?"

"She models," Ira said proudly. "She's a pretty girl, you know?"

"I know," Phil said, smiling. "And I bet she has a lot of boyfriends."

The question brought an embarrassed silence. Finally, Hanna answered coldly, "She don't say."

The sheriff decided not to press the point. It was obvious that their daughter's association with Doc Oberdick was something they didn't want to talk about. Phil pushed himself back from the table. "Well, thanks for your help, and I ought to be going now. I sure did enjoy that apple pie, Hanna."

"Want another piece, sheriff?"

Stauffer grinned. "No, no." Then, as an afterthought, which he had carefully planned, "Say, Hanna, did you have anything to do with my daughter when she was in the hospital recently?"

"No, but I knew she was there. She was in another wing from where I work."

"I see."

"But I did see you there once."

"Me?"

"Yeah. I think it was the day you came to take her home."

"Why didn't you speak to me?"

"Oh, I didn't want to intrude," Hanna said. "But I felt so sorry for the little girl, with that hex stuff and all...."

"Hex stuff?"

"Yeah, I heard somebody put a spell on her."

"Heard it where?" The calm, reasonable attitude was slipping away from Stauffer.

"Oh, I don't know. I just heard it. You hear a lot of things at the hospital."

Phil fought the urge to grab the woman and shake an answer out of her. "Try to remember, please, Hanna ... *where did you hear it?*"

Hanna put her hand to her mouth nervously and knitted her brows in thought. "I can't remember, sheriff, honest. I just can't remember."

Stauffer sighed. "Well, tell me this—did you see Johnny Mosser in the hospital?"

"Yeah, he's on my wing. I talked to him a couple of times." Her face became sad. "Once he didn't know me. Oh, poor Johnny!"

"What did you talk about?"

"Oh, just things. He was so sick, you know." Hanna's face brightened. "He told me how you saved him by burying that hair and...."

Phil was startled. "Johnny told you that?"

"Sure. He was so pleased with what you done for him."

"Did you tell anyone else about this?"

"Ira, maybe...."

"And your brother?"

"Yeah, I guess I did." She giggled. "Ira keeps telling me I talk too much."

Darkness had fallen by the time the sheriff and his deputy arrived at the home of Earle Gensemer. It had taken most of the late afternoon before a search warrant had been issued. That wasn't because of any difficulties with the courts, but rather because of Stauffer's deliberateness in setting in motion his move against the comic. Phil was certain he was nearing a break in the Strickler case and he didn't want poor planning to scuttle the progress he was making. He had spent more than an hour in D.A. Barringer's office, going over the details. For the first time, he had revealed to Barringer the existence of the long affidavit from Josh Oberdick. Then the two men had gone to President Judge Schmehl's chambers to get his signature on the search warrant, and to brief the judge on the salient facts implicating Gensemer. Schmehl and Gensemer, it turned out, were both members of the Missionville Lion's Club; the judge was initially shocked by Stauffer's allegations. But as the sheriff piled coincidence on coincidence, and told of the collapse of the Frackville alibi, it was apparent to Judge Schmehl that the request for a warrant was a valid one.

"There are times," Schmehl said, "when this job is most unpleasant. I've always thought of Earle Gensemer as one of my friends. But then, when I think of it, I've never known him outside of the context of his Fuszganger role. What's that phrase? He's always 'on.'"

As Stauffer walked to the door of Gensemer's modest, story-and-a-half frame home on Elm Street, he wondered whether the comic would still be "on" when he learned what the sheriff wanted. Light coming through the windows of the house illuminated the porch as Barry punched the door bell button. The television could be heard through the door as the police officers waited for an answer to their ring. Phil thought he recognized the distinctive voice of newsman David Brinkley.

Gensemer was surprised when he saw who was at his door. "Sheriff! Vot can I do fer ya?"

Stauffer held up the legal paper. "We have a warrant to search these premises."

"A varrant! Iss diss a choke?"

"No joke, Gensemer," Phil said coldly. "May we come in?"

"Schure, schure." Gensemer held the door open for them. "But vot . . . ?"

Phil and Barry stepped into the small living room. The sheriff had been correct; Gensemer had been watching the evening news on NBC. The comic walked to the set and switched it off.

"Now, sheriff," Gensemer said, "vot the hell iss diss aboudt?"

"It's about a typewriter, for one thing. Do you own a typewriter?"

"Yah."

"May I see it, please?"

Gensemer, still puzzled, led Stauffer into the next room and pointed to a typewriter on his desk. It fit perfectly the description given to him by the state police lab: A Royal, old, high front, little windows on the side.

"Take it out to the car," Phil ordered Painter, "while I give Mr. Gensemer a receipt." Barry picked up the heavy machine.

"Now, chust a damned minute!" Gensemer protested.

Stauffer brushed aside the protest. "Is that your bedroom?" he asked, pointing to the door across the narrow hallway.

"Yah, but. . . ."

Phil moved purposefully into the bedroom, opened the clothes closet and quickly went through the clothes hanging there. No gray-blue plaid topcoat. He turned to Gensemer. "Do you own a gray-blue plaid coat?"

"No . . . no . . . but. . . ."

Phil walked back into the living room, the comic following him, exasperated.

"Can I see that varrant?" Gensemer asked.

"Certainly." Phil handed it over.

Gensemer studied the document. "It don't tell me much."

Stauffer knew he was in command of the situation. "We have reason to believe that you typed on that machine two threatening notes—one to me and one to Reverend Fenstermacher. Would you care to comment on that?"

"I don't know vot the hell you're talkin' aboudt!"

"Then you didn't type the notes?"

Gensemer stared defiantly at the sheriff. "I know my rights. I don't haf to answer who-struck-Chon questions. I'm gonna call my lawyer."

Phil reached out and caught his arm. "Just a moment, Mr. Gensemer. I also have a warrant here for your arrest." He handed him a second document.

"Arrest! Now, I *am* gonna call my lawyer!"

"You can do that after you've been booked." Quickly, Stauffer handcuffed the startled comic to his right wrist.

"Vait! Booked for vot?"

"Any number of things," said Stauffer firmly, "including conspiracy to murder one Charles Strickler."

Fright flooded Gensemer's face. "My Godt, my Godt!" He said nothing more.

Stauffer, leading Gensemer to the door, couldn't resist using the crusher. "We know, Mr. Gensemer, that you were *not* playing that smoker in Frackville on Wednesday, November 26, the night Charlie Strickler was murdered."

Gensemer just stared at him.

"Come with me, please," the sheriff ordered gently.

"I guess I ain't godt no choice."

"That's a good guess, Mr. Gensemer."

14 WED., DEC. 10, 1969

Barry Painter, in plainclothes, lounged easily in the terminal at the Missionville Airport. Lounging, when related to those molded plastic chairs, may have seemed an impossibility, but Barry carried it off. He glanced occasionally at a copy of a newspaper he carried, but his attention was on an attractive, dark-haired woman who waited at the luggage claim area for her bags to be unloaded from the 8 a.m. commuter flight from New York City. She glanced around, not nervously, but as though she was expecting someone to meet her. Barry was part of what Sheriff Stauffer called a "multi-pronged attack" on the Strickler murder case. Earle Gensemer had been arrested on the previous evening and, as part of that attack, had been jailed not at the Young County courthouse, but instead, at the small lock-up in Weiser Township. Gensemer had raged at Stauffer, but the sheriff had calmly informed him that formal charges were not yet processed and, until they were, he could not call his lawyer.

Also last evening, District Attorney Barringer had played his role in the attack, going to Josh Oberdick and his attorney, Bob Hoffman, and enlisting their cooperation. It was that cooperation, given reluctantly by Oberdick, that brought Deputy Painter to the airport at this hour.

As the dark-haired girl picked up her baggage—a briefcase and a larger traveling bag—Barry nonchalantly got to his feet, dropped the newspaper on the plastic chair, and strolled to the girl. "Miss Lotz? Martha Lotz?"

She wasn't startled by his approach. "Yes. Did Josh send you for me?"

"No ma'am." Stauffer had impressed on him the need to be polite. "My name is Barry Painter, deputy sheriff of Young

269

County." He showed her his badge.

"And?" Her attitude was more of curiosity than of concern.

He pulled a paper from his inside coat pocket. "I have a warrant here for your arrest."

She laughed. "Sometimes Josh goes too far!"

"It's not Dr. Oberdick's little joke, ma'am," he assured her. "The warrant is real enough."

Martha placed the two bags on the floor and took the paper from Barry. As she read, the deputy could see the concern growing in her eyes. She looked up from the warrant, distressed. "You *do* want to arrest me? On what charge?"

"It's there on the warrant, Miss Lotz."

"This says murder!" Her voice rose and several of the other people in the terminal turned to look at her.

"Yes, ma'am." Barry was enjoying being in the middle of the drama.

"I'm going to call Josh!" She was angry now.

"No, Miss Lotz," Barry said firmly, "you're coming with me. There will be plenty of time for phone calls." He took her by the arm.

In a sudden move she struck him hard in the face with an open hand. She screamed, "Help me! Oh, God, help me!"

In that instant, Barry lost control of the situation. Two of the men in the terminal rushed to the couple. One grabbed Barry's arms and pinioned them behind him. The other tried to calm the distraught woman, but she ran to the terminal door, pushed it open and headed for a taxicab. Barry struggled, but the man holding him was too strong. "Let me go, you bastard," Painter shouted, "I'm a deputy sheriff!"

"Show me!" the man demanded.

"My ident is in my inside coat pocket!"

The second man reached in the pocket and came out with Barry's wallet and the badge. "Yeah, he is," the man said sheepishly.

Barry's arms were released and he sprinted to the door. As he reached it, he could see a cab pulling away from the curb. He wanted to go back and pop the muscular Good Samaritan on the nose, but his duty got the better of him. His squad car was parked in the taxi zone and he was quickly in pursuit of the cab. He came abreast of it before the cabbie could leave the airport area. As he started his siren, the taxi pulled over and stopped.

The deputy vaulted out of his car, running to the cab. "Christ, officer," the cabbie was saying, "I didn't know she...."

"Shut up!" Barry reached down and opened the door. In the back seat, Martha Lotz was curled into a frightened ball, weeping. "Miss Lotz, believe me, you *are* under arrest!" He reached in and took her arm again. The fight was out of her. She meekly allowed him to guide her to the squad car, and he placed her in the back seat. For a moment, he toyed with the idea of putting her in the front seat, but quickly dropped it. The rear seat was barred.

"That was stupid!" Barry said as he slid in behind the wheel.

She was weeping so much now that she could hardly speak. "May I call Josh, please?"

The deputy looked back at her and suddenly felt sorry for the woman. It seemed to him that he had a lovely fawn penned up in that enclosed back seat. "Soon, Martha, soon." The fun had gone out of the drama for Deputy Sheriff Painter.

Austin Lester was an imposing figure. He, even more than others, was conscious of the impression he made on his fellows. It wasn't just because he was handsome, nor that he dressed in the best clothes cut to the latest fashion, nor that his voice had the trained intonations of a starring Shakespearean actor. Those attributes made up the veneer of the man. Lester was imposing because he projected a supreme confidence in himself. It seemed he moved in a perpetual spotlight, center stage at all times, accepting the plaudits of the masses because he deserved it. Yet his obvious ego brought no resentment. People from all walks of life genuinely liked him.

The lawyer, most often referred to as *the distinguished defense attorney,* strode into the district attorney's office. "I assume," he said to Barringer, "that I shall be able to bail my client before this day is out." There was no hint of a question in the words—it was a statement.

"I'm sure you're going to try," Barringer answered.

Lester grinned. He accepted Barringer's statement as a compliment. "Earle Gensemer is not a criminal, you know. His personal record is impeccable. The gentleman hasn't even had a traffic citation before. An exemplary citizen."

"If he's that clean, I can't see why he needs the expensive services of a powerhouse attorney like Austin Lester."

"Even a Pennsylvania Dutch comedian deserves the best." He laughed. "Are we going to play games, or are you going to tell me what you have?" He dropped into a chair.

"It's a bit early for disclosure," said Barringer, "but the charges—plural—are explicit. Gensemer, a.k.a. Doctor Fuszganger, wrote letters, or notes, to Sheriff Stauffer and to Pastor Fenstermacher in which he threatened their lives. He also engaged in a conspiracy to murder another human being. Is that enough for you?"

"One charge at a time. I must assume that you believe you have my client cold on the death threat charges, because the typewriter seized at his home has been matched to the typed notes."

"A valid assumption."

"Uh huh." Lester was not ruffled. "That's purely circumstantial, at best. Someone else could have used his typewriter to type those notes."

"Someone else could have," Barringer admitted, "but I don't believe it. And, Austin, neither do you."

Lester grinned again, ignoring the district attorney's comment. "Now, as to this other charge—conspiracy to murder. My Lord, Barringer, that's as thin as tissue paper! Do you have him on the scene of the murder of this . . . this . . . Charles Strickler?" His tone dismissed the name of the murdered man as something repulsive. "What conspiracy, old man? Do you have a corroborating witness, even one? Do you have the slightest hint of a valid motive?"

Barringer said nothing.

"Just as I surmised," the attorney said, taking the D.A.'s silence as confirmation of his own contentions that the case against his client was a weak one. "Now, let's talk bail!"

"Counselor, I am prepared to ask the court to set bail at one hundred thousand dollars."

Lester feigned shock. "You jest!"

"That's something I rarely do, Austin," Barringer said, "and certainly not about charges as serious as these. Threatening death to two of our most prominent citizens, one of them an officer of the law, is not something even you can take lightly. Nor is murder."

"Indeed, I am not taking any of this lightly. But, old man, one hundred thousand dollars! What judge would approve such an exorbitant bail?"

"President Judge Schmehl might."

"Is that old curmudgeon presiding at the bail hearing?"

Barringer laughed. "I'm pleased to see that the mention of Schmehl's name has even forced you into a redundancy."

"Eh?"

"Well, I've always thought that the use of 'old' with 'curmudgeon' was redundant, in that a curmudgeon is defined as a crusty, ill-tempered and usually old man."

"Usually, my dear fellow, usually, but not always. Therefore, the use of the phrase 'old curmudgeon' is not necessarily redundant." Lester drew himself up to his full and impressive height. "Nevertheless, I shall have to be at my best to convince that curmudgeon of a judge, old or otherwise, to reduce that ridiculous bail amount. One hundred thousand. Really!"

The D.A. laughed again. "You're marvelous, Austin Lester, counselor at law."

"Yes, aren't I?" He consulted his watch. "I shall have to fly." He snapped his fingers. "Oh, by the way, Mr. District Attorney, I am led to believe that you also have a Miss Martha Lotz in custody."

"Are you representing her, too?"

It was Lester's turn to chortle. "Would it bother you if Miss Lotz is also a client?"

"No, of course not."

"Well, at the moment, she is not. But Miss Lotz, as you well know, is a niece of Mr. Gensemer and I suspect that the conspiracy you allege may involve Miss Lotz."

Barringer remained silent.

"So! As the poet wrote, *After the last bulletins the windows darken.* I had better prepare myself for some surprises, eh?"

"I'm sure I don't have to tell the eminent Attorney Lester how to prepare a defense."

Lester looked at his watch again, "My, my, where *does* the time go? I would like to make one other point, Barringer. Have you seen the afternoon edition of the *Star?*"

"No."

"It contains what I believe is a very inflammatory article regarding my client." He reached into his brief case and extracted a clipping, handing it to Barringer. "This kind of thing can only be classified as being prejudicial to Mr. Gensemer. I would hope that your office is not responsible for the contents of this article."

The D.A. took the clipping and read it. It carried Nick Willson's by-line.

Pennsylvania Dutch comedian Earle Gensemer, known professionally throughout the state as "Doctor Fuszganger," was arrested last night by the Young County Sheriff's Department on an open charge.

Gensemer was jailed overnight in the nearby Weiser Township lock-up, instead of being held in the Young County Courthouse cellblock. The unusual circumstances of his arrest have led to speculation that Gensemer might be charged in connection with the recent "lock of hair" murder of reputed pow-wow doctor Charles Strickler. Weiser Township police would not comment on the arrest, except to say that Gensemer had been brought in by Young County Sheriff Philip. . . .

Barringer returned the clipping to Lester. "That's a pretty straightforward report."

"You don't find that inflammatory?"

"Certainly not."

"Well, I do," said the attorney, "especially in the light of the volume of other material published on the Strickler case in the past couple of weeks." He drew in a deep breath and then exhaled it slowly. "I am prepared, Barringer, to ask the court to close the bail hearing to the press and to. . . ."

"Oh, for Christ sake!"

"No," intoned Lester, "for my client's sake."

"Well, I can see that I'm in for a workout tomorrow," Barringer said. "The hearing is at ten, courtroom two."

"Ten it is! *En garde!*" He left the district attorney's office as he had entered, in grand style.

Barringer shook his head in disbelief, but he was no longer smiling.

Sheriff Stauffer stood in the jail cell and looked down at the distraught figure of Martha Lotz Mosser. She was curled up, in a fetal position, on a bare cot, weeping. Her beauty seemed clouded over with despair; she was a sad and lonely woman. Phil felt desperately sorry for her. He didn't welcome that feeling because it subverted his determination to get to the truth in the Strickler case. The matron had told Stauffer that Martha had turned aside all efforts at conversation, would accept no food or drink.

"Martha," Phil said quietly, "we have to talk."

She shrank away from him. It was as though the sheriff's voice made her smaller somehow, the cocoon of her unhappiness drawing tighter around her.

"Martha, please."

She turned slowly on the cot, looking up at him.

"Martha, it would be better if you talked to me."

"Who are you?" she asked.

"Phil Stauffer. I'm the sheriff."

"Why should I talk to you?" The question could barely be heard.

"Because you're in serious trouble."

"And talking to you is going to help that?" She sat up without putting her legs over the side of the cot, assuming a kind of lotus position.

"I believe it will," he said kindly.

The tears stopped. She looked around the little cell, then the eyes—the stunning eyes—came back to the sheriff. "Okay." The voice was still barely audible.

"Do you know why you're here?"

"Your deputy said something about murder."

"The words of a warrant," he said, "are sometimes unnecessarily harsh. But this is about Charlie Strickler's death. Did you know Strickler?"

"Yes."

"Do you know that someone killed him?"

"Yes."

Phil was carefully watching her face for any sign of emotion. It was sad. Just sad. "Were you ever in. . . ."

She interrupted him. "May I ask a question?"

"Certainly."

"Did Josh know that I was going to be arrested when he called me last night?"

"Yes, he did." Stauffer saw no point in fencing with the young woman.

"And his asking me to come down here was just so you could arrest me?"

Phil sighed. "That's so."

The muscles in her face twitched. She put her hands over her eyes and the flood of tears came through her fingers and dropped down on the cot. Her weeping seemed uncontrollable. The sheriff was moved. He dropped to his knees at the side of the cot and tried to console her. He wanted to take her in his arms, but he didn't. Three or four minutes went by before the crying subsided and she dropped her hands.

"He told me he loved me," she sobbed.

Phil said nothing. He gave her a handkerchief and she scrubbed at her face, trying to wipe away every tear, like a little girl. She gave the handkerchief back to him, even smiled a "thank you."

"Does Josh know I'm here now?" she asked.

"Yes."

"Has he tried to see me?" She sounded hopeful.

"No."

She simply shrugged; the tears were ended now. Her beautiful face took on a new strength.

Stauffer tried to comfort her. "Look, Martha, you must understand that Josh only did what he thought was right."

"*Right!*" she screamed. "Right! To put me *here?*" The

tears and depression were suddenly replaced by anger. Phil was astonished at how quickly she went from one emotion to another.

"Martha, you know, of course, that you don't have to answer my questions. But I would like to ask them anyway."

"Go ahead." Her voice was firm, defiant.

"Were you ever in Charles Strickler's home?"

"Yes."

The quick, certain answer, surprised Stauffer. He realized he would have to be more specific; it was conceivable that she had been at Strickler's home at one time or another. "Were you at Strickler's home on the evening of last Wednesday, November 26—the night before Thanksgiving?"

"Yes."

That admission did shock the sheriff. "Were you there alone?"

"No." She was volunteering no information.

"Was you uncle, Earle Gensemer, with you?"

"No!" The emphasis was strong.

"Who was with you, then?"

"Dr. Oberdick."

Phil was caught off guard. He took a brief moment to compose the next question before he spoke again. "Could you tell me what you did there?"

"Josh killed Charlie." It was a composed statement, impassive, with no emotion at all.

"*Josh Oberdick?*"

"Yes."

Stauffer, stunned, was still on his knees by the cot. He reached over and took her hands. "Are you telling me the truth, Martha?"

"Yes."

"Do you want to tell me how it happened?"

She easily shook loose of his hands, got to her feet and walked to the barred window, her back to the sheriff. "Josh beat him with the leg of a chair." Again, there was that passivity, that unemotional recitation.

The sheriff found it difficult to believe her. Yet she knew about the chair leg; she must have been there. How should he proceed? He walked over and stood next to her. Touching her arm lightly, he said, "The truth, Martha, the truth."

She turned to him, sudden hate twisting her beautiful face. "Yes! The truth! Do you think your precious doctor isn't capable of murder? Well, let me tell you, sheriff, he is! He is!"

"Martha," he said softly, "I only want to be sure. . . ."

"You sonofabitch," she snarled, "you don't give a damn about what really happened! Josh killed him! I saw him do it!" She was screaming. "Now, get away from me! Get the hell out of here!" Martha reached out and raked his cheek with her fingernails, drawing blood.

Phil recoiled from the attack, bringing his hand to his bleeding cheek. He stared at her briefly, then turned to call the matron to let him out of the cell. The mercurial behavior of the woman frightened him. When the matron unlocked the cell door, the sheriff whispered to her, "Keep an eye on her. She's very upset."

Had her resentment against Josh motivated the accusation against him? Or was it really the truth? Phil shook his head, trying to clear it of doubt. As he disconsolately walked down the corridor of the cellblock, Martha screamed after him, "That bastard Josh Oberdick is going to rot in hell!"

An eerie red glow, coming from the whirlybird lights of the rescue squad ambulance, danced on the emergency entrance of the Missionville Hospital. As the vehicle backed into position, a white-coated attendant leaped from the front seat, rushing to open the back doors. When he did, a frightened Dottie Kissinger came out, turning to look back at the still figure of Josh Oberdick lying on a stretcher, a blanket up to his chin, his slim body secured by two wide safety straps. The ambulance attendant and a hospital orderly quickly removed the stretcher, snapped down its wheeled undercarriage, and trundled it into the building. They pushed it down a wide corridor into the emergency room, with Dottie half-trotting behind them.

There was little that Dottie could tell the young intern on duty. She had been sitting with Josh in his apartment, drinking Scotch and chatting (they had been discussing

Martha Lotz), when he had suddenly collapsed. There had been no dramatic movements, no words; Josh simply fell against her. Dottie told the intern, in answer to his question, that Dr. Oberdick was eighty years old; that he would be eighty-one on the second of February. Any history of heart problems? Not that she knew. Was he a diabetic? Dottie wasn't certain, but she thought not. The intern's efforts to get a medical history from her were fruitless. She just didn't know. As the young doctor made his hurried examination he ticked off items which a student nurse recorded for him—pulse, blood pressure, temperature. He studied Josh's eyes. Was the patient on drugs of any kind? Dottie was emphatic with her "no." On any special medication? Again, she didn't know. The intern shook his head, puzzled. Oberdick, he said, would be admitted for observation and tests. He tried to assure Dottie that Josh was in no immediate danger, but he lacked practice in convincing assurances.

"Of course," the intern added, "he *is* a very old man."

Dottie nodded, and followed his directions to the waiting room. As she moved slowly along the hospital hallway, a man came up to her.

"Excuse me, are you Mrs. Kissinger?"

"Yes."

"I'm Ernest Wheel of the Continental News Service."

She was surprised to see him there. "How did . . . ?"

"The *Star* had a call from a tipster," Ernie explained, "who works with the rescue squad."

The woman made no comment.

"How is Dr. Oberdick?" Wheel asked.

"I don't know. He's unconscious. They're going to admit him. That's all I know."

"Would you mind telling me what happened?"

Dottie briefly repeated what she had told the intern.

"Was he upset about anything?"

"He was quite distressed," Dottie said, "about the arrest of Martha Lotz."

"Do you think he had a heart attack? Or a stroke?"

"How would I know?" Dottie snapped. "Please, I've told you everything I know." She started to walk away.

Ernie followed. "Do you think that *hexerei* had anything to do with this?"

She stopped and looked at him coldly. "Mr. Wheel, you remind me of a vulture!"

15   THURS., DEC. 11, 1969

"Well, friends, take it from ole Baxter Turner, the first snow of the season is on the way. Maybe as much as six inches. And that reminds me, because it's written down right here, that Hoffenstein's Hardware is having a pre-snow sale of . . ." Barry grinned as he drove to work in his squad car. Baxter was a former high-school buddy who had become a fixture on Radio WQQX's morning drive time. His pleasant, folksy style had built a large and loyal listening audience in the Missionville area. The deputy sheriff of Young County was one of those. Baxter Turner was a very successful big fish in a small pond. It ran through Barry's mind on this cold, white-clouded morning that a lot of the kids in his high-school class had done pretty well in life. Baxter, for example; and Clarence "Rube" Walters, now a lawyer; and Elsie Steuer, who ran that big wholesale flower nursery over on Maple Street; and "Skids" Cammarota, who had the largest beer distributorship in the county; and Mabel Persky, with her dance studio—and Barry himself, of course.

Baxter introduced Jackie De Shannon's *Put a Little Love in Your Heart*, and that seemed particularly appropriate to Deputy Painter. It reminded him of Kathy Samson. In truth, Kathy was foremost in his mind this morning. She had called him last night with the news that she was coming to Missionville. She was arriving at 3:30; Barry hoped the anticipated snow didn't delay the flight.

Barry whistled along now as *Put a Little Love in Your Heart* came to a conclusion. *"For all those good friends just rollin' out of bed,"* Baxter was saying, *"it is now 7:30 on Thursday, December 11th, and snow is headed our way. . . ."*

281

The deputy was pulling into the courthouse parking lot, and he reached over to turn off the radio. Just then Baxter started the local news headlines and Barry waited to hear them. After elaborating once more on the weather forecast, the radio announcer said, *"Eighty-year-old Dr. Joshua Oberdick, one-time head of the Young County Medical Society and winner of the recent county Man-of-the-Year award, was admitted last night to the Missionville Hospital. Details are sketchy, but hospital authorities say this morning that Dr. Oberdick's condition is critical. . . . Pennsylvania Dutch comedian Earle Gensemer and his niece, Mrs. Martha Lotz Mosser, are in police custody today, following arrests that are believed associated with the Thanksgiving-eve murder of. . . ."* Painter switched off the radio. *Oberdick!* Did the sheriff know about this?

He hurried into Stauffer's office with the news, but he was too late. Coroner Ed Myers was already slouched in a chair, reporting on Oberdick's condition.

"The reason the hospital called me," he was saying, "is that Obedick's symptoms are similar to those we had with Johnny Mosser—massive internal bleeding for no apparent reason. They thought there might be a connection."

Stauffer cut him off. "Ed, let's not get started with that kind of crap again. Josh Oberdick is eighty years old. He could have a dozen things wrong with him."

"Sure, sure, but you've got to admit the coincidence is a bit strange." Dr. Myers grinned impishly. "Now, if we only had another lock of hair to bury. . . ." He realized immediately that he had said the wrong thing.

The sheriff slammed his fist on the desk. "I don't want to hear of that incident again! Not even in what you may think is jest!" There was a strained silence. Stauffer finally broke it. "I'm sorry, Ed, but I've had enough of this pow-wow talk. It interferes with logical police work and it hasn't helped this investigation at all. What's Josh's condition?"

"Critical."

"Well, I'm really sorry to hear that. Especially now. It may mess up the investigation." He was thinking of the story he had heard from Martha Lotz. "Oh, well . . . keep me filled in, will you, Ed?"

"Sure." Dr. Myers got up to leave.

Barry watched him go. "Isn't there any chance, Phil, that the Mosser and Oberdick illnesses are related?"

"None!" Stauffer was adamant. "And listen, Barry, those reporters are going to be asking about this pretty soon. The sheriff's department's official position is that Dr. Oberdick's hospitalization has nothing *at all* to do with the investigation of the murder of Charlie Strickler. Period. Are you clear on that?"

"Yes, sir."

"Now, sit down. I've got something to tell you about Martha Lotz." Involuntarily, his fingers touched the ugly red scratches on his cheek. The deputy hadn't dared to ask about them.

State Trooper Mel Shriner flipped the switch on his siren and pulled abreast of the speeding Corvette. A young man at the wheel of the sports car looked over at the police officer, who signaled him to pull over onto the shoulder of the road. Shriner had been patrolling westward on the Pennsylvania Turnpike when the Corvette had sped by him. In a two-mile chase in the lightly-falling snow, the Corvette had ignored the whirlybird signal lights on the police car; Shriner had seen his speedometer hit eighty-five miles an hour. Now, however, the Corvette was stopping. Shriner pulled his police cruiser behind the stopped vehicle and got out cautiously. He noted that the license was a dealer's plate and he radioed the number to his headquarters. Carefully loosening the flap on his gun holster, Shriner walked to the car. The driver, only a boy, said nothing.

"May I see your driver's license and registration?"

A driver's license was promptly handed to the officer. "I don't have my own registration card yet," the young man said hurriedly. "I just got this car this morning and the dealer let me use his plates because I had this emergency trip. But he gave me a bill of sale just in case I was stopped or anything." He handed another piece of paper to the state trooper.

"Are you Willard Burkholder?" Shriner asked, reading the driver's license.

"Yes, sir."

The trooper studied the bill of sale. "And you say you bought this car this morning?"

"Yes, sir."

Shriner looked at his wrist watch; it was 8:15. "This dealer gets an early start."

"Well, he's a friend of mine," young Burkholder said with a slight smile.

"Do you know that your friend violated the law in letting you use the dealer's plate?"

"No. Mr. Almond said it would be okay."

"Well, it's not! Were you aware how fast you were going?"

"No."

"Would you be surprised if I told you I clocked you at eighty-five?"

"No." The answer was sullen.

Trooper Shriner put the driver's license and bill of sale into his summons book. "Would you step out of the car, please?"

The young man obeyed without a word. Shriner ordered him to spread-eagle himself against the '64 Corvette and frisked him for a weapon. He found nothing. *Willard Burkholder?* the trooper thought. *Why is that name familiar to me?*

He gave another order. "Come with me, please." He took the youth by the arm and led him to the squad car, opened the rear door and gently propelled him into the back seat. He pushed the lock button on the door before he closed it. It took Shriner only a few moments on the police radio to verify that the Corvette was indeed the property of the Missionville dealer from whom Burkholder had a bill of sale. There were no warrants against the car or the driver. Shriner sat quietly, studying the license and the bill of sale, idly tapping them on the steering wheel. *Missionville! Missionville! Burkholder! Why can't I remember?*

The state trooper turned to look at Burkholder through the security screen separating the front and back seats. "What was this emergency trip you had?"

"My grandmother's dying in . . . ah . . . Columbus. Yeah, Columbus, Ohio."

"Are your mother and your father living?"

"Yes."

"Aren't they also concerned about your grandmother?"

"Sure, but the old man is tied up with his business and my mother's not feeling well right now. That's why I'm going out there." Young Burkholder fished in his pockets for a pack of cigarettes. He lighted one, slowly blowing the smoke out of his nose.

The obvious lie caused Shriner to shake his head in disbelief. He turned forward again, looking once more at the license and the bill of sale. *Willard Burkholder? Missionville? Damn it, why can't I make a connection?* He turned the ignition key.

"Hey, where are you going?" the voice from the back seat asked.

"I'm going to take you into the Breezeway State Police station and give your father a call."

"No, don't do that!" Burkholder pleaded.

"Why not?"

"Well. . . ." The young man fell silent.

Suddenly it came to Shriner. *Missionville! Burkholder! Of course, that hex murder thing in Young County! The sheriff there might want to know about this kid.* He eased the squad car into the flow of traffic on the turnpike.

"What about my car?"

"We'll take care of that," the trooper assured him.

At promptly 10 a.m. President Judge Schmehl came to the bench in Courtroom Two of the Young County courthouse. "This is a preliminary hearing in the matter of the Commonwealth versus Earle Gensemer on charges—rather serious charges, I must say—of maliciously threatening the lives of two citizens and of conspiracy to murder. The record will show that Mr. Frederick Barringer, the district attorney of Young County, represents the state, and that Mr. Austin Lester is the attorney for Mr. Gensemer." He looked up. "I'm pleased to see you in my court again, Mr. Lester."

"Thank you, your honor."

"Now, gentlemen," Judge Schmehl went on, "this is a

preliminary hearing designed only to determine the amount of bail, if any, for Mr. Gensemer. I don't want, and won't permit, a tiresome parade of witnesses. Nor do I want any long harangues, but just the argument that applies to the question of bail. First, are there any motions?"

Attorney Lester came to his feet. "Your honor, the defense moves for a postponement of this hearing." Both the judge and the district attorney were caught by surprise.

"A postponement, Mr. Lester," Schmehl said, "would effectively deny bail to your client at this time, and keep him in jail. May I ask the reason for the motion?"

Lester gestured toward the judge. "Your honor, may we approach the bench?"

"Certainly."

At the bench, Lester said, *sotto voce,* "Just moments before we came into court, your honor, my client informed me that he wished to make a statement to Sheriff Stauffer. It must be obvious that I haven't had the opportunity to learn what he wants to say to the sheriff. In light of that basic ignorance, I need time to talk to my client in order to give him my best advice, and indeed, to dissuade him if I feel that making a statement to the sheriff at this time would be detrimental to him."

The judge looked at Barringer. "Mr. District Attorney?"

"I have no objection. A statement at this time might expedite matters."

"Very well."

The attorneys returned to their chairs.

"The court," said Schmehl, "grants a postponement of this hearing pending new developments. The district attorney's office will keep the court apprised of the situation. Clerk, call the next case."

"How do I put this delicately?" Phil asked his deputy. "It seems that the fecal matter has struck the rotary machinery." He had just hung up the phone.

Barry waited for the sheriff to continue.

"That was the state police out at Breezewood," Stauffer explained. "They've just picked up Willard Burkholder.

Stopped him for speeding. He was driving a 1964 Corvette and he says he was heading for Columbus, Ohio, to see a dying grandmother."

"What?"

"Yeah. And the Corvette he was driving was purchased just this morning at Almond's used car dealership on 11th Street. Apparently that's legit. He had a bill of sale on him."

"What do you make of that?"

"I have no idea," said Phil, "except it's pretty clear he was in a hurry to get out of Missionville."

"It's nutty!"

"Yeah, isn't it? Well, I've got to meet with the D.A. Earle Gensemer wants to make a statement, I understand, and we have to work out the ground rules with the eminent Austin Lester. You take a run out to Almond's used car lot and check out that Corvette deal, and then get back here so you're on deck when the state cops deliver young Mr. Burkholder."

Barry frowned. "Do you think we'll be clear by 3:30?"

"Why? You have something planned?"

"I'm supposed to meet someone at the airport."

"Business?"

"No, no, it's personal."

Stauffer looked at his watch. "Hell, it's almost noon now. The way things are going, Barry, I'd make alternate plans for any 3:30 trip to the airport."

Painter showed his disappointment. "Okay. I'll run out to Almond's right now." He started for the door.

"Hey, Barry," the sheriff called to him, "is this 3:30 someone a female?"

"Yeah."

"And you're not going to tell the old sheriff who she is?"

Barry let a moment of silence go by. "It's Kathy Samson."

"The Phoenix Kathy Samson?"

"Yeah."

"Good Lord!" Phil leaned back in his chair and contemplated his deputy. "I hope you know what you're doing, Barry."

"I do," Painter said sheepishly.

The sheriff smiled. "Oh, what the hell . . . get to work!"

"I find myself at a distinct disadvantage," Austin Lester told Barringer and Stauffer. "My client insists on making a statement to the sheriff, but will not confide in me. I've told him how dangerous that is, but he insists. Frankly, I'm soliciting your help in this matter."

Barringer spoke. "I would rather not take a statement from him without his having the advantage of the advice of his attorney."

"It must be obvious," said Lester, "that I feel the same way, but. . . ."

"Is Earle insisting that I be the only one present?" Phil asked.

"He hasn't put it that way. He simply doesn't want to inform me as to the content of his statement beforehand. And I don't know why."

"Then," the sheriff said, "maybe I have a solution."

"Please, my good fellow," Lester urged, "present it."

"Well, suppose we let Earle tell his story with the three of us present," Stauffer suggested, "but not on the record. After we hear the story, it can then be decided whether he wants to make the statement officially, and we can call in a stenographer."

"That has merit," said Lester. "It does have a drawback, however. Once he has told you something, you won't be able to erase it from your mind, whether or not it is on the record."

"But he won't have sworn to it," Phil insisted.

"True, but it is still fraught with danger for him."

"I, for one," said Barringer, "think it might be workable."

Attorney Lester frowned. "Very well, we'll do it that way. I can only hope that you two gentlemen will keep my client's civil rights in mind at all times."

"Agreed," said Phil.

"Agreed," added the district attorney.

The three men walked from Barringer's office and went down a flight of stairs to the cellblock in the basement. When they were let into Gensemer's cell, his attorney carefully explained the agreement they had reached.

"Do you understand that clearly?" Lester asked him.

"Yah."

"Very well, you may begin."

Gensemer sat on his cot in the cell; Barringer and Stauffer sat on a cot opposite him. Lester declined to sit, saying he preferred to remain standing. "Much more alert on my feet, you know."

"Vell," Gensemer started, "idt goes back aboudt three months. I vas at Doc Oberdick's place—Marty vas there undt me undt the Doc—n' ve godt to talkin' aboudt dot ole divel Charlie Strickler. Doc sez vouldn't idt be somesing wunnerful if ve couldt pay Charlie back fer all uff the misery he's caused, undt. . . ."

Gensemer, confident in his story-telling ability honed by the years he spent as "Doctor Fuszganger," calmly and with deliberateness spelled out the plot that had been hatched in Oberdick's apartment. It had been decided, largely under the guidance of the old doctor, to involve the slow-witted Johnny Mosser in the scheme, as almost a sub-plot, to gain a sort of revenge for his earlier treatment of Martha. It had seemed so simple at the outset: Johnny would have to be convinced that he was ill, and that his illness was the result of a spell placed on him by Strickler. It was inevitable, the doctor had said, that Johnny would confront Strickler and that the confrontation would favor the younger and stronger Mosser.

"Nobody saidt nothin' aboudt killin' Charlie," Gensemer insisted. "Neffer! Ve sought Chonny wouldt vork Charlie ower a liddle bit, dot's all."

Oberdick had suggested, the comic went on, that the three plotters stay in the background. It would not do for any of them to approach Johnny with the suggestion that Strickler had put a spell on him. That required an intermediary. The doctor told them he had someone in mind and would try to secure his services. Later, Oberdick reported to them that Willard Burkholder was to be the intermediary, that he would be instructed to gain the confidence of Mosser (the two of them frequented the bowling alley), and that through that confidence would plant the seed of doubt about Johnny's health. "The Burkholder kid can carry it off," Oberdick had assured Gensemer and his niece. "He's a bright young man."

Once Johnny became convinced that he was ill, he would be guided by Burkholder's suggestions to Lizzie Zearfoss, who would identify Charlie Strickler as the source of Johnny's troubles.

"Oldt Doc toldt uss," Gensemer related, "dot Lizzie owedt him a fawor or two n' she'd do idt okay. Ve laughed a lot aboudt it. Idt vas kinda fun plannin' the whole sing. So the Burkholder kidt schtarts on Chonny n' idt vent chust like Oberdick saidt idt vould."

There were almost daily bulletins about Burkholder's progress passed on by Oberdick to Gensemer and Martha; there were many phone calls to New York when Martha was there. Oberdick drove out to see Lizzie Zearfoss and the final stage of the plot was set. But then, doubts began to set in.

"I guess idt vas me first," the comic told the trio in the cell, "vot schtarted to gedt vorried aboudt vot might happen. But they chust laughed like, undt the sing vent on. Ven ve heardt dot Chonny vas finally gonna go to see Strickler Doc saidt maybe ve'd all bedder be in town ven it vas happenin' so's ve'd haf an alibi in case anysing vent vrong. Dot vorried me somesing awful. I hadt a bookin' in Frackville, but I decided nodt to go because I sought I ought to be here viss Marty. Chust in case, you know."

Burkholder's report on the first evening of activity at the Strickler household—that was Tuesday, November 25—brought relief to Gensemer. He urged Oberdick to call the whole thing off at that point. Go to Mosser, he had urged the doctor, and tell him it was all a joke. However, Oberdick persisted. Marty, Gensemer realized, was enjoying the intrigue. On Thanksgiving eve, the comic decided to stay close to his niece and he went to the Lotz home to invite the girl to go to the movies with him. That way, he thought, if anything "went wrong" at Strickler's they'd be an alibi for each other.

Sheriff Stauffer interrupted the flow of the story for the first time. "I want to get something clear, Earle. What time did you go to the movie?"

"Vell, ve vent to the early show, aboudt six-thirty. The movie lasted aboudt two hours, so ve vere back to Marty's house about eight-thirty. Yeah, dot's aboudt right."

"Then, what did you do?"

"I vent home n' left Marty viss her parents."

"Thank you. I simply wanted to establish the time element."

Later that evening, Oberdick called the comic and told him that Mosser and Strickler had indeed had a confrontation and that Mosser had knocked him down and bound him with ropes. The doctor laughed about it, Gensemer said, and commented that "the old bastard must have shit in his pants when Johnny jumped him." Strickler, he said, was all right and would be able to free himself from his bonds in time. The details of the incident had been relayed to Oberdick by young Burkholder.

"It vas the next mornin'," Gensemer continued, "ven I heardt dot Strickler vas deadt. It scared the hell oudt uff me. I called Oberdick undt he vas a liddle scared, too. But he saidt to chust keep my mouse shut n' ewerysing vouldt be okay. He saidt ve veren't the vuns vot killed him so ve hadt nossing to vorry aboudt."

The murder, however, continued to deeply concern Gensemer. The concern grew when the newspaper started to play up the *hexerei* angles of the case, which he knew would keep it alive. He was afraid that the plot would eventually come to light. Then, on the following Sunday, Lizzie Zearfoss was killed.

"I done somesing dumb then, real dumb," he said. "I decided to try to mess up the sheriff viss the phone calls n' all. Nodt to scare him, chust mess up the case. Undt ven I heardt aboudt Pastor Fenstermacher's sermon, dot seemed to be a goot take-off point."

The sheriff interrupted again. "Then it *was* you who sent those typed notes and who made the phone calls?"

"Yah."

"Just a moment," Attorney Lester interjected, "I'm afraid this is compromising my client. He's said too much already."

"No, Mister Lester," said Gensemer, "I'm gonna tell idt all! I chust godt to!"

Lester shrugged.

"One more thing about the letters and phone calls,"

Stauffer added. "How did you know about Debbie's hospitalization and all?"

There was a slight smile. "Ain't dot strange though? I saidt somesing aboudt Debbie to you undt then she gedts sick. My sister, Hanna, vorks at the hospital n' she toldt me sings then dot I chust used. She didn't even know she vas doin' it."

"It was you, wasn't it," asked Phil, "who gave those tips to Ernie Wheel?"

"Yah."

There was a protracted silence. Gensemer looked around at the three men. Finally, he said, "Undt dot's aboudt idt."

"Incredible!" commented his attorney.

"Are you willing to put all of that into a formal statement?" Barringer asked the comic.

"Wait now," interrupted Lester, "I believe I should have the opportunity to meet privately with my client to advise him properly before he makes a sworn statement."

"Fair enough," said Barringer.

"I have a few more questions to clarify several points," Stauffer suggested. "For example, Earle, were you ever in Strickler's home?"

"Neffer!"

"What about Martha?"

"No, neffer!"

"Do you know whether Doctor Oberdick was in Strickler's home during this period?"

"I don't know, but I don't sink so."

"Uh huh." Phil paused for a moment. "Earle, what do you know about Lizzie Zearfoss's death?"

"Nossing! Dot's a strange vun to me."

"To me, too," admitted Stauffer.

Austin Lester clapped his hands together, putting a period to the conversation. "Well, gentlemen, that seems to be the conclusion of this adventure. May I respectfully suggest that I be given some time alone with my client?"

"Of course," Barringer agreed.

The district attorney and the sheriff were let out of Gensemer's cell. As they walked down the corridor, Phil introduced another subject. "Oh, by the way, Fred, there's something I've been meaning to tell you. Willard Burkholder has been picked up by the state police near Breezewood. He was, you might say, on the lam."

"Are you Miss Samson?" the cabbie asked the attractive redhead.

Kathy had just arrived at the Missionville airport and her eyes had been searching for Barry. Now, the question from another man startled her a bit. "Yes, I am."

"Deputy Painter is tied up at the courthouse, Miss. He asked me to meet you and to give you this." He handed her an envelope.

Showing some disappointment, Kathy tore open the envelope. *Darling,* the handwritten note inside said, *all hell has broken loose and I'm tied up. The cabbie will take you to the apartment. The key's in here. Just go in and make yourself at home. I'll be there no later than six. Love you— Barry. P.S. Josh Oberdick is in the hospital. Condition is critical. P.P.S. Really love you. Welcome to Missionville.* She fished inside the envelope and found the key.

The cabbie had been watching her intently as she read the note. "You ready to go, Miss Samson?"

"Yes. Those two bags over there." She pointed to her luggage and the driver picked them up. He guided her through the terminal door and to his cab.

As they moved along the city streets to Barry's apartment, Kathy read the note again. Her eyes kept coming back to *Josh Oberdick is in the hospital. Condition is critical.* She looked at her wristwatch. It was 3:55 p.m., at least two hours before she would see Barry. "Listen, cabbie," she said, "how long before we get to Spruce Street?"

"We're almost there now."

"And how far is it from there to the hospital—is there more than one?"

"Nope, just one. It's about five minutes from the Spruce Street address."

"Fine," said Kathy. "I'd like to drop my bags at the apartment and then go right to the hospital. Would that be possible?"

"Sure, anything you say."

At 234 Spruce, Kathy quickly made her way to Barry's apartment, had the cabbie carry the luggage into the living room, and left immediately. She didn't even stop to look around the comfortable little bachelor pad. Suddenly, seeing Josh—or John Richards—seemed vitally important to her.

The cabbie had not exaggerated; it was just a few minutes before they pulled into the curving driveway in front of the Missionville Hospital.

"Could you wait for me?" Kathy asked.

"Sure."

"Thanks, you're sweet."

The cabbie grinned.

On the drive to the hospital, Kathy had made up her mind that she was not going to be put off from seeing Josh by any hospital regulations. She asked for his room number at the front desk now, and the clerk told her that Dr. Oberdick was not allowed to have visitors.

"But I'm his niece," she lied. "I've just come in from Phoenix. He asked for me."

The clerk, in doubt about what she should do, directed Kathy to the third floor nurses' station. "Ask them," she said. "They might let you see him."

The slow-moving hospital elevator irritated her; she wished she had used the stairs. At the nurses' station on the third floor, she told a nurse her fabricated story.

"Gosh, I don't know," said the girl. "Dr. Oberdick is critically ill. I have my orders."

"I didn't come all this way," Kathy said quietly but forcefully, "not to see him. He asked for me."

"Well, all right. He's in 304. But please don't stay very long. May I have your name, please?"

"Kathy Samson—S-a-m-s-o-n."

The nurse wrote it down. "Okay. Room 304."

Kathy hurried down the corridor, looking for the number. When she found it, she stopped momentarily to compose herself, then pushed open the door. The old man was motionless on the bed in the half-dark room, an intravenous tube in his arm. She took a step inside the room before she realized someone else was there. A pretty blonde woman sat by Josh, holding his hand. Dottie Kissinger rose from her chair and came to meet Kathy.

"Are you in the right room?" she whispered.

"Yes," the visitor said, also whispering, "I'm Kathy Samson."

"From Phoenix?"

"Yes."

"How'd you know . . . ?"

"Barry Painter informed me," Kathy said. "How is he?"

"Not good."

"Is he conscious?"

"Sometimes."

Kathy looked over at the bed. "Dare I go over there?"

"He might like to know that you're here," Dottie answered.

Very tentatively, Kathy approached the bed and looked down at the old man. "John?" Dottie, who had not moved, could not make out what Kathy was saying. "John, it's Kathy."

The eyelids fluttered and opened. The voice, when he spoke, was from somewhere far away. "Hi, Red."

Kathy fell to her knees by the bed and took his hand, squeezing it gently. She fought against her tears. "John, I'm so sorry!"

"About what?"

"I told them about John Richards." Now she wept.

There was a weak pressure from his hand. "Kathy, darling, it's all right. They would have found out sooner or later anyway."

Kathy, choking back her sobs, found it difficult to speak. "I love you, John."

"I know." He closed his eyes again.

Kathy came to her feet, carefully released the hand, and bent to kiss him. She returned to where Dottie Kissinger was standing. "He looks so weak," Kathy said.

"He is. The doctors say it's massive internal bleeding."

There was an embarrassing silence. In that silence you could almost hear each woman rehearsing the proper next phrase in her head. It was Dottie who broke the silence. "Are you going to be in town long?"

"For a time. I don't know how long. Do you think I might come back tomorrow?"

"Of course," Dottie said emphatically. "You're very special to Josh."

That brought on a full flood of tears and Dottie gathered the woman from Phoenix into her arms, patting her, consoling her and, at the same time, consoling herself in a sense. In a moment or two, Kathy regained control, wiped the tears from her cheek with her hand, and left the room without another word.

The sheriff's small office was filled for Willard Burkholder's return to Missionville—Phil, D.A. Barringer, Deputy Painter, and a very disturbed Paul Reisinger, the Burkholder attorney.

"Damn it, Fred," Reisinger complained to Barringer, "you've known all afternoon that Will was being brought back by the state police. Why did you have to wait until the last minute to notify me?"

"Paul, I'm really sorry," the district attorney apologized, "but this has been a most hectic day. Other things have been happening. I called you just as soon as I. . . ."

The door opened and a uniformed state police sergeant half-pushed young Burkholder into the room. "Here he is, sheriff. Please sign this release?" He shoved a paper at Stauffer. He seemed annoyed.

"He give you trouble?" asked Phil.

"The jerk offered me five hundred dollars to drop him off along the road. Can you imagine that?"

"Do you want to file charges?"

"Well, I'm certainly going to file a report. I'll see what my superiors say about it."

"Fine." Phil signed the release. "Thanks, sergeant."

As the state trooper left, Stauffer shoved a chair toward Burkholder. "Sit down." The voice was cold. "Aside from trying to bribe a police officer, what else did you do today?"

"Oh, for God's sake, Phil," attorney Reisinger protested, "common sense should tell you that I have to talk to the boy before you start an interrogation."

"Paul, I love you and all that," the sheriff said sarcastically, "but the only reason you're here at all right now is because the district attorney insisted on it. Now, I want to know what this young punk has been up to, and I mean to find out." He turned to the youth to find him still standing. "I said sit down!"

Will obeyed sullenly.

"Now, where in the hell were you going in that Corvette?"

"Sheriff, I protest!" Reisinger turned to the district attorney. "Fred, you know that this is highly irregular!"

"It's the sheriff's ballgame," Barringer answered.

Stauffer wished he could smile at Barringer's retort, but he restrained himself. "Will, how about an answer?"

"I was going west."

"To where?"

"Just west. I'm sick of this God-damned town!"

"No more sick of it than it is of you!" Phil walked to the Burkholder boy and stood over him. "Where'd you get the car?"

"I bought it."

"Bought it? With what?"

"With money." Will grinned crookedly. "What the hell do you think? They don't give 'em away."

"Where'd you get the money?"

Burkholder didn't answer.

"Do you have a hearing problem? I said where did you get the money?"

Still no answer.

The sheriff walked away from him in disgust. "Tell him, Barry," he instructed the deputy.

Painter took something from a file folder he was holding. He held up a rectangular piece of paper. "He bought it early this morning at Bill Almond's used car lot with this check for three thousand dollars—a check written by Dr. Joshua Oberdick!"

"What?" Paul Reisinger was astounded.

"That's right," said Stauffer, "from Josh Oberdick." He gestured toward young Burkholder. "This no-good punk, Paul, is up to his fat head in a conspiracy to murder Charles Strickler. I think you ought to know that when you consider whether or not you want to remain as his attorney. And if you do, I strongly suggest that you advise your client to try to remember what the word *truth* means. This young bastard has been lying ever since this damned thing started. I, for one, have had a bellyful of him!" He turned to Barry. "Take him to a cell."

"Just a moment," said Reisinger, now angry himself. "I have a right to talk to my client."

"And you may do that—in the cell!"

Reisinger looked pleadingly at the district attorney. "Am I going to be able to bail him tonight?"

Barringer appeared to be giving the question some thought. "I don't see how that will be possible."

The Burkholder attorney sputtered. "But . . . Otis is never going to understand this."

"I'm afraid," Barringer commented, "that it's about time that Otis Burkholder begins to understand this young man. Maybe long past that time, Paul."

Barry led Will from the room, followed by the disconsolate attorney.

Phil dropped into his chair, heaving a deep sigh. "Thanks, Fred."

"My pleasure, Phil. Believe me, my pleasure."

"Something tells me," the sheriff said, "that I'm supposed to feel elated. We're just this far away from ending this mess." He indicated a very narrow gap between two fingers. "But I'm sad, Fred, just sad."

Barry pounded on his own apartment door. "Hey, in there, open up! You have the only key!"

Instantly the door flew open, and Kathy fell into his arms. She kissed him savagely. Barry picked her up and carried her inside, using his foot to close the door behind them. They embraced again. She began to cry.

"Whoa," he said, "what's all this?"

"I saw John Richards today." She still couldn't bring herself to call him Josh Oberdick.

"Oh." Barry led her to the sofa, pulling her on to his lap. "Okay, tell me about it."

"He's dying, Barry! He looks so helpless."

"Yeah, I know." He kissed her lightly on the forehead.

Kathy waited for a moment before she spoke again. "I knew when I walked into that room that I loved him very much."

"Still?"

"Yes."

He drew a heavy breath. "Do we have a problem?"

"No, not really. I love him, but it's different, Barry. It's . . . I can't explain it."

"You don't have to explain it for me," he said gently.

Her arms went around his neck and she held him tightly. "I'm a very fortunate woman. I've had two men in my life who love me. Not too many women even come up with one." She kissed him; she didn't want to stop kissing him.

"Hey," he said, holding her face in his hands, "I surrender."

"Would you be angry with me if we talked some more?"

"Nope."

"I confessed to him today. About what I told you about John Richards."

"What'd he say?"

"He said it was all right. But he's *dying,* Barry!" Tears started again. "She said I could come back tomorrow. Is that okay with you?"

"She?"

"A blonde woman in his room. Very pretty." She shook her head. "I never did ask her her name."

"Oh, that must be Dottie Kissinger," Barry explained.

"Who's she?"

"She lives with him now—kind of."

"She was very sweet to me."

Barry kissed her. They held each other, saying no words. After a time, Barry spoke. "Practical time. Wanna go out somewhere for dinner?"

"Depends."

"On what?"

"Depends on what you're hungry for."

"Do you have to ask?" He leered at her.

"Nope," she said. And she smiled for the first time since she had come to Missionville.

16 FRI., DEC. 12, 1969

It was just after 6 a.m. Nancy Stauffer shook her sleeping husband violently. "Phil, get up! There's someone in our driveway! A strange man!"

The sheriff was not a jump-out-of-bed-feet-on-the-floor type; his waking-ups were normally leisurely matters, stretching and yawning. But not this day. Nancy's urgency was real. Phil hurried to the bedroom window and looked out through the slats of the venetian blind. Parked in the driveway was a car (an old Ford sedan, he thought) and a man was sitting behind the wheel. In the half-light of the beginning day, he could not make out the features.

"I don't recognize him," he told Nancy. "It's too dark."

"Oh, Phil, what's he doing there?"

"Now, calm down, Nance! It's probably nothing. A drunk, maybe, who pulled into a driveway—any driveway—to sleep it off. Stay here and I'll check it out."

Stauffer pulled on a robe he had picked up from the back of a chair and went to the front door. He slipped the safety bolt and opened the door cautiously. No point in taking any chances. Through the partially opened door he could get a closer look at the car and its occupant. It was Rufus Collins! Phil stepped outside.

As soon as the black man saw the sheriff he opened the car door and came up the driveway to him. "Gosh, sheriff, I'm really sorry to bother you at this hour." He grinned sheepishly. "I've been sitting out here about an hour and a half debating with myself on whether I wanted to ring the bell."

"It must be important," said Phil.

"I don't really know, but I thought I ought to come to you."

"Well, come on in." Phil led the way inside. "We'll get some coffee and talk."

Nancy stood rather tentatively half in and half out of the living room, clutching her robe about her, as the two men entered. Phil introduced her to Rufus Collins, without identifying him as a pow-wow doctor from Westville. He asked whether she could get some coffee for them, as he directed the black man to a chair. Nancy padded into the kitchen; she was clearly annoyed.

"What's all this about?" the sheriff asked.

"You're going to think I'm crazy, sheriff, but it's about a dream—a recurring dream that I just can't shake."

"Hmm."

"Last night it was so damned real that I decided I'd better tell you about it. Right now, I feel like a damned fool!"

Phil yawned involuntarily. "It's about the Strickler case, isn't it?"

"Yeah." Collins didn't seem surprised that the sheriff would make that deduction. "And what makes it so real is that Charlie Strickler is in it all the time. There's no doubt about it being Strickler. It's always the same. Charlie on the floor of a room, tied hand and foot, and some woman standing over him beating him with a piece of wood."

"A woman?"

"Yeah, but I don't see her too clearly. She's screaming at Charlie and beating him. She kills him, I think."

"Old woman? Young? What?"

"She's very vague, sheriff. But certainly a woman."

Phil remained sober-faced; he was not making light of Collins's dream. "Is anyone else in this room you see in the dream?"

"In the background," Rufus said with assurance. "I don't quite make him out. Thin. A man. Or maybe a boy. Young, anyway."

Nancy came into the room with the coffee and the conversation stopped. She said nothing as she set a tray on the coffee table. Collins watched her as she departed again into the kitchen. Phil offered a cup of coffee to his visitor.

"What is this woman using to beat Strickler?" Phil asked.

"A kind of round piece of wood. Something broken. Like

the thin end of a busted baseball bat." He concentrated on it for a moment. "Maybe a chair leg. Yeah, like a chair leg."

Stauffer took a sip of the hot coffee. "How long have you been having this dream?"

"Three, maybe four nights. I dream and it wakes me up. Then I dream again. I've had the damned thing maybe a dozen times." He shrugged his massive shoulders. "Hell, sheriff, you know how I feel about all this mumbo-jumbo crap, but this has gotten to me." He shook his head. "Oh, hell, I'm sorry I bothered you about this."

"No, no," said Phil. "I've learned a long time ago not to automatically dismiss anything in an investigation."

"Do you think there's anything to this?"

"Yes."

The sheriff's answer shocked Rufus. "You do?"

"Yes, and I'll tell you *why* I do," Stauffer said firmly. "The murder weapon used to kill Charlie Strickler *was* a broken chair leg. But we never revealed that publicly. So it wasn't mere subconscious knowledge that put that broken chair leg in your dream."

Collins knitted his brows in concern. "Sheriff, it occurs to me that my knowledge of that chair leg might be interpreted as putting me on the actual scene. Dreaming of the act might be a guilty conscience coming to the fore."

"It might," Phil agreed.

"But you're not thinking that way at all."

"Nope. I think your dream is genuine."

Rufus smiled. "Well, you have more faith in this stuff than I do."

"Always the cynic, eh?"

"Yeah."

"Then why did you come here?"

"I don't know, sheriff. I just don't know."

The alarm rang at 6:45 a.m. Barry took a swipe at the offending clock, knocking it off the nightstand and onto the floor, but it continued to ring. "Damn!" He struggled out of bed, retrieved the clock, and silenced the alarm. When he turned to get back into bed, Kathy was grinning at him.

"Good morning, darling."

"Hey," he said in mock surprise, "where'd you come from?"

"Just flew in from Phoenix and my arms are tired."

"Good God, woman, vintage jokes at this hour of the morning?"

He sprawled across the bed and kissed her. She responded readily.

"Deputy," she said, "it's much, much cozier under the covers." She lifted the blankets, inviting him to join her. They cuddled together.

"Glad you came?" he asked.

"Yes."

There was that special silence again as they just basked in each other's presence.

"Wanna stay?"

"Want me to?" she countered.

"Uh huh."

"How long?"

"Oh . . . maybe a day or two."

"Thanks a lot!" She slapped him playfully.

"I don't know whether I could survive more than a day or two."

"Mr. Painter," Kathy said resolutely, "I have no doubts at all about your staying powers. None!"

"Flattery," he laughed. "I deserve it."

His hand roamed lightly down her slim leg, then slowly back up again, over her flat abdomen, stopping finally on one breast. "Want to?"

"Want to what?" she asked teasingly.

They made love.

Turnkey Harry Meltzer brought breakfast to prisoner Earle Gensemer at exactly 7 a.m. "Did you sleep well?" he asked as he unlocked the cell door.

"Vell enuf, I guess," Gensemer answered. He pointed to an unshaded light bulb glowing from the corridor ceiling just outside his barred cubicle. "I might haf schlept bedder if ya hadt bedder lightin' aroundt here."

"Yeah," Meltzer admitted, "that's pretty glaring."

"Idt remindts me uff an oldt schtory." It seemed a strange place for "Doctor Fuszganger" to surface; perhaps Gensemer thought of it as a momentary release from his considerable problems. "Chake Swoyer vas elected fer the first time to the church consistory—ya know, them fellas vot run the church. Undt right avays ven he vent to his first meetin', the minister sez, "Fellas, ya remember ven ve met the last time, ve talked aboudt gettin' a chandelier fer the church. Vell, I looked into idt n' idt'll cost fife hundred dollars.' So Chake sez, 'Now, chust a minute, pastor. I don't sink ve oughta buy a chandelier.' Undt the minister sez, 'Vell, vhy nodt?' N' Chake sez, 'Vell, if ve haf fife hundred dollars to schpend, I sink first ve oughta do somesing aboudt the terrible lightin' in the church.'"

The turnkey laughed loudly.

From the far end of the cellblock corridor there came a shout, "Hey, you old farts! When you get done fucking around up there, I'd like some breakfast!"

"Willard Burkholder," Meltzer said disgustedly, pointing his thumb down the corridor.

"Yah, I know. A sveet childt!"

Sarah Strickler stood in front of the old, smoky mirror and put on lipstick. It was something she had not done in nearly a decade. The night before she had shampooed her hair and had carefully put it up in rollers. She was out of bed at 5 a.m., fixing her hair, trying on several dresses (the selection was painful), taking shoes from boxes covered with a thick layer of dust. Sarah was getting ready to visit Josh Oberdick.

The night before, Dottie Kissinger had come to see her, carrying a message. "Josh is dying. He wants to say goodbye."

Sarah had wept. It was a deep, cleansing weeping, a catharsis. Dottie had consoled her, as she had consoled another woman earlier in the day.

"I loved him once," Sarah had told her visitor.

"I know," said Dottie, "he is a man much loved." She added, after a pause, "And who has loved."

Now, on this morning, Sarah was going to see him again. She realized, as she fussed with the lipstick, that she could not roll back the years from her face. But, at least, she'd try.

She had asked her neighbor, David Mitzel, to drive her into Missionville. He went to the farmer's market there every Friday. The old Westminster clock on the mantel chimed the quarter hour—7:15 a.m. Outside, farmer Mitzel honked the horn of his pick-up truck.

Johnny Mosser was in a wheelchair, being pushed toward the ambulance entrance of the Missionville Hospital. He was dressed in light blue pajamas, with a dark blue terry-cloth robe, and dark-blue terry-cloth slippers. There was no lettering stenciled on the clothes, but they said "institution" nevertheless.

He had lost weight from that bulky body during his hospital stay. It showed most in his face. His dull eyes were lost in deep hollows. The skin was sallow. He seemed only mildly interested in what was going on.

Two white-coated attendants flanked him as a hospital nurse pushed the wheelchair. Johnny looked up at one of them. "Are you guys from Wernersville?"

"Yeah."

Johnny smiled. "I walked out of that place once."

"I hope you're not going to do that again."

"No." The smile faded. "There ain't no point no more."

One of the attendants hurried ahead and pushed open the big double doors, revealing the Wernersville State Mental Hospital ambulance waiting there. When the wheelchair came abreast of the ambulance, the two attendants reached down to lift Johnny from the chair. He waved them off. "I can walk okay. I'm strong again."

They permitted him to get into the back of the ambulance by himself. He moved slowly, weakly. Once inside, they helped him onto a stretcher cot, securing him with broad leather straps.

"You don't need to do that," he said.

"It's just that we don't want you to roll out on the curves," one of the attendants said.

Johnny Mosser laughed heartily. He was still laughing when they closed the ambulance doors on him.

It was at the same hour—7:30 a.m. by attorney Paul Reisinger's watch—that the lawyer arrived for a breakfast appointment with Otis Burkholder. He had agreed to this early meeting on the night before, when he and the elder Burkholder had had a traumatic exchange concerning the failure to have Willard released on bail. At least it was traumatic for Reisinger; he could still feel the wounds. He wasn't so sure that tough old Otis was damaged at all.

Reisinger was directed to the den by the family butler, to be greeted effusively by Otis.

"I'm sorry about my temper boiling over last night," the Burkholder patriarch told him. "It's just that I'm concerned about Will."

"Of course you are," said the lawyer. "So am I."

"Right." Burkholder clapped him on the back. "Now, what'll you have for breakfast? I'm having kippers."

"Kippers?" Reisinger grinned. "Not exactly a Pennsylvania Dutch delicacy."

Otis lowered his voice into a confidential tone. "I'll tell you something—I'm not crazy about most of the Pennsylvania Dutch foods. But I *love* kippers. Try some."

"No, thanks. Too salty for me. Could I just have some bacon and eggs?"

"Of course." Burkholder turned to the waiting butler. "Mr. Reisinger will have bacon and eggs."

"Over light, please."

"Certainly, sir." The butler left the room.

Burkholder led the way to a table in the corner of the den, already set with linen and silver. A large, ornate silver coffee urn, kept hot with a canned-heat burner, dominated the center of the table. A cup of coffee was poured for the attorney and he added cream from a silver pitcher. Real cream.

"Now, let's talk about our mutual problem," Burkholder said. The two men sat at the table. "How bad is it?"

"On a scale of one to ten, it's about nine and three-quarters.

To be brutally honest, Otis, Will is in serious trouble this time. Very serious."

"Specifics, please." Burkholder was all business.

"For starters, the sworn statement he has already given to the authorities is riddled with lies. It seems clear to me now that he was an active participant in a plot to harm Charles Strickler. It was, it appears, a conspiracy in which Willard was paid by Dr. Oberdick to play a role."

"Damn." The word was just breathed.

"The authorities will say," Reisinger went on, "that it was a conspiracy to murder. I think not. And it will be my job to contain the conspiratorial angle; to keep it divorced from Strickler's eventual death. But. . . ."

"Willard will have to go to jail." It was a statement by the elder Burkholder, not a query.

"It's likely."

The butler entered with Reisinger's bacon and eggs. There was no talk until he left the room again.

"Okay," said Burkholder, "what must we do?"

The lawyer tasted the eggs, then added a touch of pepper. "Will must tell the total truth about what happened." He paused for emphasis. "The *total truth!* Otis, that's our basic problem right now. I'm not sure that Will knows what telling the truth means. I'm going to ask the sheriff to permit you to sit in on today's interrogation. It has been my observation that Willard respects only one authority, and that's you."

"You mean he's frightened of me. That's a hell of a difference from respect."

The attorney didn't disagree with Burkholder. "If it gets the truth. . . ."

"All right." Burkholder calmly poured himself a second cup of coffee. "Now, Paul, what's the bottom line?"

"Willard is a minor. The court will take that into consideration. Then, it might be well to consider petitioning the court for an independent psychiatric examination of the boy. . . ."

"And do what—substitute a mental institution for a jail cell?"

Reisinger didn't reply. Otis Burkholder had answered his own question.

"Just what is Dr. Oberdick's condition today?" Coroner Ed Myers asked the question of a young intern at the Missionville Hospital.

"Somewhat improved from yesterday," the intern replied. He consulted a medical chart. "We've been able to stabilize him a bit. The hemorrhaging continues, but not as severely as before, and we've been able to continue the transfusions without losing ground. In a nutshell, though, he's still critical."

"Would you say he's stronger this morning?"

"I wouldn't use that word, necessarily. Somewhat improved is more accurate."

"Have the tests given you any handle on the causative factors?"

The young doctor frowned. "Not at all."

"Sheriff Stauffer would like to interrogate him sometime later today. Will that be possible?"

"Perhaps. He has asked to see some people, two to be exact, and I've given my approval."

"Who?"

"A Mrs. Strickler and a Miss Samson."

Dr. Myers smiled slightly. "Then he must be stronger."

"Well, he is certainly strong-willed. That's a positive factor. With consideration for Dr. Oberdick's condition, some questions by the sheriff might be possible."

"Fine. We'll be in touch." Ed Myers walked off down the corridor. He wondered whether he had time for breakfast before reporting to Stauffer. A clock at the nurses' station showed 7:55 a.m. The coroner decided that breakfast would be limited to coffee. Well, maybe an orange juice, too.

"Thanks for coming in at this hour to meet with me," attorney Bob Hoffman said to the district attorney. It was just 8 a.m. They sat in Fred Barringer's office.

"Hours don't seem to mean anything anymore," Barringer commented.

"I asked to see you before your day gets hectic," Hoffman said, "because I have a quandary of sorts. Josh has asked me, through Mrs. Kissinger, to represent Martha Lotz. I don't think

I can do it. I see a conflict of interest coming up."

"What are you asking me?"

"I'm already uncomfortable representing both Josh and young Larry Saylor," the attorney said. "And I guess what I want to know is whether the legal interests of Dr. Oberdick and Miss Lotz are on a collision course. Could I safely represent both of them?"

Barringer leaned his elbows on his desk. "Bob, if I were you I would *not* undertake to defend both of them at the same time."

"Why not?"

The D.A. smiled. "I knew that was going to be the next question. Let me say this: I plan to ask the court, as soon as it is in session this morning, to appoint a public defender for Martha Lotz."

"That's exactly what Josh doesn't want to happen," Hoffman interrupted.

"It's imperative that she have legal counsel, however. In light of what we know of her story, she needs that counsel immediately. I've instructed Sheriff Stauffer not to interrogate her again without the presence of an attorney."

"So he has interrogated her already?"

Barringer's answer was hesitant. "Ah . . . he's talked to her."

"What does that mean?"

The district attorney rose from his desk and walked to the office window, looking down on the town square. "There are times when I wish I could be the district attorney of some big city, where I didn't have such close ties to every other lawyer who comes into my office." He turned to Hoffman. "Where I didn't have so many friends."

"Then what would you do?"

"I'd tell you to get the hell out of my office."

"Well," said Hoffman, "this isn't a big city. And the fact that it's a small town is really good, I think. Maybe our justice—if that's the right word—is a bit more personal, a bit more realistic."

Barringer, still standing, idly scratched his head. "Don't take the Lotz girl's defense, Bob."

"But why not?"

"Because, damn it, she's told Stauffer that it was Josh Oberdick who beat Strickler to death! And she was a witness to it!"

"*What?*"

"That's right. And that's all you're going to get out of me for the moment."

Hoffman groaned. "That's enough. What the hell am I going to tell Josh?"

Barringer return to his desk and slumped into his chair. "I can tell you this—you're not going to tell him about Martha's accusation. What I've told you is in confidence. I did it only to enable you to make an intelligent decision on whether or not to represent the girl. The matter is *entre nous,* friend." He put a strong emphasis on the last word.

"Now I'm sorry I asked you to come in."

"How's that?"

"Because it's a lousy way to start a day!"

Dottie Kissinger worked disinterestedly in the kitchen of Josh's apartment, making breakfast for her son. Larry sat in the tiny breakfast booth and watched her. She scrambled eggs and kept an eye on the toaster, waiting for it to pop up. "If you want some juice get it out of the refrigerator," she said.

"Nah, I don't want juice. Do you?"

"No, thanks."

She took a plate from the cupboard, waited for the toaster to cough up two slices of browned bread, and then slid the eggs on to the plate. She carried the modest breakfast to the booth and placed it in front of the boy.

"Ain't you gonna eat?" he asked her.

"Later maybe. I'm not hungry now." She slipped into the booth opposite her son. "You know, we have to make an appointment with the school pretty soon to get you back into class. You're probably going to need some tutoring to catch up."

"I've had it with school." He took a forkful of egg.

"But you're only fourteen. The law says you have to go to school."

He made no comment, not wanting to argue with his mother. They sat silently as he ate. When he had finished the eggs and toast, he pushed the plate away from him. "Mom, I've been thinking," Larry said. "Josh is gonna die, ain't he?"

"Of course not," she said with false bravado. "He's very sick, but the doctor told me last night he was improved."

"I know he's gonna die," the boy said with conviction. "That's the way it always is with us. First, it was my old man running away, than that drunken sonofabitch Sam Kissinger, and now Josh. Josh was good to us, for a change. But now he's gonna die and we get the shitty end of the stick again."

"Larry," she said with annoyance, "where do you get that kind of language?"

He ignored his mother's question. "It's true, Mom, we always get shafted, one way or another."

Dottie wanted the subject ended. She half twisted around in her seat to look at the kitchen clock. "Oh, God, 8:10! I've got to rush if I want to be at the hospital when visiting hours start at 8:30." She turned back to Larry and took his hand. Her voice was gentle. "If anything does happen to Josh, we'll still have each other."

"Yeah, and a lot of damned good that's gonna do!"

Ernie Wheel and Nick Willson sat at the counter of the Missionville Inn coffee shop and compared notes. It was 8:15 a.m.

"Gensemer in jail, Martha Lotz in jail, the Burkholder kid back in custody, Johnny Mosser on the way to the nut house, Josh Oberdick in the hospital, dying for all we know, and where in the devil are we?" Wheel summed up the frustrating situation facing the newsmen.

"We've got a lot of action," Willson agreed, "but damned little solid information out of the sheriff's office."

"In all my born days," said Ernie with a weak smile, "I've never seen so many closed-mouth people. Late last night I tried to talk to Paul Reisinger about Will Burkholder and I'm still trying to thaw out from the icy looks he gave me."

Nick laughed uneasily. "I've come to the startling conclusion that *no one* killed Charlie Strickler. Are we even sure

Strickler is dead, for God's sake?"

"Something has got to break today. There's just too much going on not to produce some major development."

A waitress came to where they were sitting and they both ordered coffee. Wheel flipped through his notebook. "I don't even know who to try to talk to anymore. It's getting so that I think my deodorant's failing me."

Willson poked him in the ribs. "Have you tried that guy?" He jerked his thumb in the direction of one of the coffee shop booths. "That's the great Lester Austin, the attorney for Earle Gensemer."

"Will he talk?" Ernie asked.

"You usually can't shut him up."

"That's my guy." Wheel left the stool and headed for the booth. Willson followed. "Excuse me, counselor," Ernie said, "I'm Ernest Wheel of the Continental News Service. This is Nick Willson, whom you know, I believe. May we speak to you?"

"My, my," said the attorney, "this is a distinct pleasure, gentlemen. Please sit down."

The reporters slid into the booth.

Ernie didn't want to let this opportunity get away from him. "Mr. Lester, what does your client have to do with the Strickler case?"

"Ah, a man who has never heard of preliminary sparring."

"I don't have the time," Wheel said. "Is Earle in this thing deeply?"

"That depends on who you talk to."

"I think I'm talking to you."

"In that case," the lawyer said with a smile, "the answer is no. I think it is safe to characterize the sheriff's case against Mr. Gensemer as flimsy. There's a lot of innuendo, you understand, but very little concrete evidence."

Ernie sighed. "Crap, counselor, I don't even know all the innuendo."

The waitress, having spotted the move of Wheel and Willson from the counter to the booth, brought their coffees to them. To Lester she said, "Your breakfast will be out in a moment." She left them.

"You know," Lester said, "your arrival at my table this morning might be fortuitous." He leaned forward. "I might need some help. You obviously need some help. Perhaps we can help each other."

Nick spoke. "How, counselor?"

"You know my client, of course?"

"Sure," said Wheel. "He's a very funny man."

"And a very popular one, too, in this area. Now, sirs, how would you like to have an exclusive interview with Mr. Gensemer? One in which my client would bare his soul, so to speak."

Wheel was cautious. "Sounds good, but why do I have the feeling that there's a catch to it?"

"No catch," Lester assured him. "You would, through my aegis, be able to interview Mr. Gensemer to the fullest. I would have only one prohibition. . . ."

"Ah, now comes the kicker."

"No, no 'kicker,' as you say. You would have to print the interview verbatim, in the question and answer form, with no personal interpretations. And no rebuttal article from the police authorities for twenty-four hours."

"Why?"

"I want Mr. Gensemer's story to get the fullest exposure without having it watered down with . . . well, with intrusions from other sources."

"Okay," said Wheel. "And why do you want that?"

Lester brushed a hand across his mouth. "I feel I'm going to need this exposure for the well-being of my client when the other developments in the Strickler case are made public."

"Do you know what those 'other developments' are?"

Lester was candid. "If I did, old fellow, I wouldn't need you to tell my client's story. And I dare say, you wouldn't need me."

Ernie thought for a moment, then he looked at Nick. "Speaking only for myself, I'll buy it. But I need the interview as soon as possible today."

"Of course." Lester looked at Nick. "Mr. Willson?"

"I'm letting Ernie carry the ball on this one."

"Fine." Lester looked up as the waitress approached with

his breakfast. "I'll be in touch. I know that you'll excuse me. I have a ... ah ... peculiar habit. I always prefer to eat breakfast alone."

Martha Lotz had eaten her breakfast in a cell in the women's section of the county lock-up in the basement of the old courthouse. There were only four cells in that section, which was one corridor removed from where Earle Gensemer and Willard Burkholder were confined. Martha was the only occupant in the women's section.

When the matron came to take away the dishes, she was pleased to see that the prisoner had eaten everything. "Now, that's better," she said. "I'm glad to see that you have your appetite back."

Martha smiled wanly. The matron was pleased to see that, too. The woman seemed to be coming around, after the initial depression following her arrest. "Is there anything else I can get for you?" the matron asked.

"I'd love to have a bath. Would that be possible? I feel so . . . grungy."

"We don't have very good facilities here," the matron admitted. "This lock-up wasn't made for what you might call permanent guests." She laughed at her little joke and Martha joined her. "There's a shower for the men prisoners, but we could use that, if I stand guard at the door while you're in there."

"Oh, would you?" Martha asked sweetly.

"Sure, honey, be glad to. Just let me go and check whether it's free right now."

When the matron returned she carried with her a towel, a washcloth and a big piece of yellow soap. She unlocked the cell door and Martha came out. The two of them walked down the corridor, made a left turn, and the matron pointed to a door. "Right in there, dear. I'll stay right here. Just knock on the door when you're finished."

Martha surprised the matron by kissing her on the cheek. "Thank you, you're very kind."

Inside she found a high-ceiling, tiled room, with two large shower stalls, a couple of toilets and four washstands.

Narrow, rectangular windows let in the outside light; they were flush against the ceiling and covered with a heavy security screen.

She undressed slowly, kicking off her shoes first, then removing her blouse, the dark skirt she wore, her brassiere, then her pantyhose. Very deliberately, she tore the blouse into strips; she tried to same thing with the heavier skirt, but she couldn't tear it. She tied the strips of the blouse together into a rope. Having accomplished that she took the pantyhose and, with one big tearing tug, she separated the two legs. Those she intertwined with the blouse-rope, weaving the whole thing until it had strength. It was perhaps four feet long.

Martha walked into one of the shower stalls and turned on the water, manipulating the hot and cold faucets until she had the right temperature. She lathered herself with the bar of soap, not using the washcloth, and luxuriated under the stinging jets of water. She rinsed the soap off her slim body and, without turning off the water, she walked to the large mirror spanned above the washstands. Using the soap as a crayon, she lettered something on the mirror—only seven large letters—and walked back into the shower stall. She discarded the soap, picked up the hand-woven rope and soaked it thoroughly.

With surprising agility she climbed up on the top of the partition that separated the two shower stalls. Leaning over, she tied one end of her rope to the plumbing that held the shower head. The other end she looped around her neck, tightly tying two knots under her chin. She tugged at the rope to make certain it was securely fastened to the pipe.

She jumped.

The clock on the courthouse steeple chimed the half hour. It was 8:30 a.m.

A day had begun, as distinctive as a fingerprint, as unique as the "night eyes" on a thoroughbred's legs. A day unlike any other.

Phil Stauffer stared at the draped body on the wet floor of the lock-up shower room. He tried to comprehend the despondency that would have driven the stunningly beautiful girl to take her own life. It sickened him. It was strange, but at this moment Reverend Fenstermacher's words ran through his mind: *"Love of God and belief in pow-wow . . . are as different as the day is from the night. One is bright and clean; the other is dark and foreboding. One speaks of life and happiness; the other tells of death and despair."*

He turned to look at the mirror where Martha Lotz Mosser had printed two words with the bar of soap—ASK JOSH.

But would he be able to ask Josh? Would this whole senseless episode that started with the death of Charlie Strickler ever be explained? *". . . death and despair."* Phil shook his head sadly.

The sheriff had been in his office, talking on the telephone to the New York City police, when turnkey Harry Meltzer had rushed in, panic-stricken. "She hung herself! She hung herself!" he kept shouting. Stauffer had followed him on the dead run to the basement cellblock and into the shower room. There he found the matron hysterically trying to get the body down. Water was still pouring out of the shower-head. Phil turned off the water and, with the help of Meltzer, was finally able to loosen the soaking hand-woven rope. They gently laid Martha's nude body on the floor. On orders from the sheriff, Meltzer rushed to get a sheet to cover the body. With great difficulty, Phil was able to extract from the matron the story of what had happened.

"It's all my fault," she sobbed, "it's all my fault!"

Stauffer tried to console the woman, but she could not stop weeping. Now she stood in the corner of the tiled room, her clothes dripping wet, and kept repeating, "It's all my fault!"

Coroner Ed Myers came into the shower room in the wake of turnkey Meltzer. He pulled back the sheet, revealing again the horror of the swollen tongue and the protruding, staring eyes. Meltzer hurried to one of the toilets to vomit. Dr. Myers made a cursory examination, then covered the face again with the sheet.

"She did a thorough job," Myers said to the sheriff. "The neck is broken. My best guess is, without an autopsy, that she fractured one or all of the first three cervical vertebrae, damaging the vital centers of the spinal cord. Death was pretty quick, I would say, although not instantaneous. But certainly within thirty or forty seconds."

"Let's get an ambulance over here for the body," the sheriff ordered, "but no sirens, for God's sake. I want to keep a lid on this as much as possible." He spoke to the turnkey. "Harry, I want you to take the rest of the day off. I'll get a special deputy to fill in for you. And make sure the matron gets home okay."

Meltzer didn't object.

"And Harry," Stauffer reiterated, "keep your mouth shut about this for now."

"Sure, Phil." Harry guided the weeping matron out of the room.

"This is an ugly business," Dr. Myers commented. Then he spotted the soaped message on the mirror—ASK JOSH. "What the hell does that mean?"

Phil stared at the mirror for a moment. "Ed, I wish I knew."

Barry Painter had been late in arriving at the office, but the sheriff brushed aside his apologies to tell him of the suicide of Martha Lotz.

"One rule for now, Barry—no comment on this thing. If there are any queries at all, just plain no comment."

"You bet, Phil."

Stauffer walked over to Fred Barringer's office to break the news to the district attorney. They agreed, after Barringer related his earlier conversation with Bob Hoffman, that the young attorney would be told of the death, but in strict confidence. When the sheriff returned to his office fifteen minutes later, attorney Austin Lester was waiting for him.

"I'll not take much of your time," the lawyer said. "I have but a simple request."

"Name it."

"A deputy down in the cellblock tells me that I need your permission to have someone come in to talk to Earle Gensemer."

"Other than yourself, you mean?"

"Yes."

"You have an associate counsel?" Phil asked.

"No, nothing like that." Lester was hesitant. "Actually,

there's a journalist. . . ."

Phil cut him off. "Absolutely not!"

"That seems a most unreasonable attitude."

"Maybe so," said the sheriff, "but as long as Earle Gensemer—or anyone else, for that matter—remains in a cell, he's off-limits to reporters. You, of course, can come and go as you please. But no reporters! That's an unbreakable rule of this office."

The lawyer was angry. "You forget, sheriff, that I gave my fullest cooperation in the . . . ah, unprecedented interrogation, and sworn statement, of Mr. Gensemer and. . . ."

"I appreciate that cooperation, but my answer must be 'no.'"

"Perhaps a judge would think otherwise."

Phil smiled. "If you want to make an ass of yourself by petitioning the court on a matter like this, well, be my guest."

The phone rang and Barry answered it in the outer office. A moment later, the deputy stuck his head in. "Phil, it's for you. New York."

"You'll have to excuse me, counselor," Stauffer said to Lester, "I'm very busy right now." The attorney drew himself up majestically and stalked out of the office.

"Stauffer here," Phil said as he answered the phone.

"Sheriff, this is Lieutenant Hymie Weinstein, Fourteenth Precinct, New York."

"Yes, lieutenant, what have you learned?"

"We got that search warrant for the John Richards apartment, and we think we found what you wanted."

"A blue-gray plaid topcoat?"

"Right," said Weinstein. "A woman's coat. At least, the style would indicate that. Size, too."

"That's marvelous." Phil was enthusiastic. "How soon can you get it here?"

"I'll get it into parcel post right now."

"No, listen, if it's not too much trouble, how about taking it out to LaGuardia? There's a commuter airline flight to Missionville this afternoon. Have the pilot hand-carry it. I'm sure they'll do that for us."

"Okay, you got it."

"I can't thank you enough."

Weinstein laughed. "Just a part of the Big Apple service."

Phil hung up the phone and leaned back wearily in his chair. A woman's coat. Martha's coat. If the thread on the gasoline can found at Lizzie Zearfoss's house matched the coat, another piece of the puzzle would fall into place. But... had Martha been there alone? Indeed, would that prove that Martha had been there at all? There was a certain satisfaction in having found the topcoat in Dr. Oberdick's New York apartment. But Sheriff Stauffer hated circumstantial cases. One thing was certain; Martha would never be able to tell him. He closed his eyes, trying to shut out the recurring image of the tortured, dead face of that beautiful girl. It didn't help.

It was two o'clock before all arrangements could be made for the re-interrogation of Willard Burkholder. Attorney Paul Reisinger had convinced Barringer and Stauffer that it might be advantageous to have the boy's father involved. Thus, there were six people in the district attorney's office— Barringer, Stauffer, Reisinger, Otis Burkholder, Will, and stenographer Mollie Sameth.

After the D.A. had put the time and the date and the circumstances of the interrogation on the record, the sheriff took over the questioning.

"Will, we already know that you went to Charles Strickler's home on the evenings of Tuesday, November 25, and Wednesday, November 26, in the company of John Mosser and Lawrence Saylor. What we don't know is why."

The boy was slumped sullenly in his chair. "What the hell do you mean, why?"

"Young man," Stauffer said sternly, "I've had just about my fill of your smart-alec attitude. The next time you answer a question with another question, we're just going to end this interrogation and this whole mess will dump on you. Is that clear?"

"Yeah."

"Now, then, why did you go to Strickler's home on those two evenings?"

"Because Johnny Mosser wanted to."

"And why did Johnny Mosser want to?"

"Because he thought that Charlie had a spell on him and he wanted to get a lock of his hair to break the spell."

"Did Johnny get that idea himself?"

Will shrugged. "I guess so."

"Isn't it true," the sheriff pressed on, "that it was under your prodding, your suggestions, that Mosser decided it was Strickler who had put a spell on him?"

"Maybe."

"No maybes. Isn't that true?" Phil's voice rose.

Young Burkholder inhaled and exhaled loudly, blowing the breath out through puckered lips. "Yeah."

"Now, why did you make those suggestions to Mosser?"

Will looked around the room, studying every solemn face. "Because Josh Oberdick asked me to."

"Did he pay you to do that?"

"Yeah."

"How much?"

"He promised me five thousand," Will said firmly, "but he only paid me three. He still owes me the other two."

The sheriff wanted to have the record clear on this matter. "So Josh Oberdick paid you to implant in Johnny Mosser's mind that he was ill, and that it was Charlie Strickler who, through a pow-wow spell, was making him sick. Do I have that right?"

Willard sat up straight in his chair. There was an element of pride in his answer. "Yeah, you have it right, kind of. They got old Lizzie Zearfoss to tell Johnny that it was really Charlie. But aside from that, I did a good job on that dumb bastard."

Stauffer again led the teenager through a step-by-step explanation of the two visits to Strickler's home; what Johnny did, what young Saylor did, what the Burkholder boy himself did. It astounded Phil that Will still insisted he didn't take any money from the Strickler home, but he saw no need to press that point. The sheriff was thorough. He consulted a copy of the transcript of the earlier interrogation.

"Now," Phil said, "Johnny Mosser has attacked Strickler, has knocked him down, and the two of you—Saylor and yourself—help Mosser to bind Strickler with the ropes. What happened then?"

"We left."

"In this earlier sworn statement you said that Mosser hit Strickler, just once, with a chair leg. That wasn't true, was it?"

"No."

"What really happened?"

Will chuckled. "Nothing. We left. That's all. But it sounds better the way I told it the first time."

Otis Burkholder gasped, appalled by his son's attitude.

Stauffer ignored it. "In the first interrogation you also said that you and Saylor left Mosser alone for a few minutes with Strickler. That's not true either, is it?"

"No, we all left together, I think."

The sheriff got to his feet and went to the boy's side, placing his hand lightly on his shoulder. "Now, Willard, tell us what happened when you went back to Strickler's later that evening."

Will was startled. His head snapped around to look up at Stauffer. "That's a God damned lie! I never went back there again!"

"Oh, but you did!" Phil kept his hand on young Burkholder's shoulder, applying a little pressure to emphasize his point. "And let me tell you how I know you did. No one other than the people closely associated with this investigation knew that the chair leg was the murder weapon. But you did. When you mentioned it in the first interrogation, I just let it ride. Now, however, we are faced with this point—if Johnny Mosser didn't use the chair leg to strike Strickler, and you say he didn't, then you had to be there at another time when someone else did. That's the only way you could have known that the chair leg was used to beat Strickler to death. The only way, Willard!"

Stauffer's revelation brought gasps from several in the room. Will was on his feet, shaking loose from the sheriff's grasp. "No! No! I read about that damned chair leg in the newspaper!"

"No you didn't," Phil said calmly. "It was never mentioned in the newspaper."

"I read a lot of newspapers, not just that crap from Missionville!"

"It was never in *any* newspaper, Will."

Young Burkholder looked around wildly, a trapped animal seeking an avenue of escape.

Otis, trying to help his son, said to him, "Tell him, Willard. It'll be best for you."

Will walked over to his father, hate written on his face. "What the hell do you know about what's best for me?" He was screaming. "You don't care about me! It's always Clay this and Clay that! That sonofabitch brother of mine is all you care about!"

Otis struck the boy hard across the face, knocking him backwards.

"Otis," attorney Reisinger shouted, "stop it!"

Stauffer and Barringer watched the scene as fascinated spectators, while Mollie Sameth's fingers sped over the keys of the stenograph machine, recording every word. But her eyes were bugged wide; this was high drama.

Will, glaring menacingly at his father, raised a hand to his stinging cheek. "You bastard!"

Phil stepped in and took the boy's arm, guiding him back to the chair. "Sit down, Willard."

He obeyed.

"Now, tell us what happened," the sheriff said, "when you went back to Strickler's for the second time on the evening of Wednesday, November 26."

Will sat bent over in the chair, his head nearly on his knees. He mumbled when he spoke. "Well, after we got back to Missionville the first time, I called old. . . ."

"Mr. Barringer," the stenographer interrupted, "I can't hear him."

"Please speak up," the D.A. requested.

The Burkholder boy raised his head. "When we got back to Missionville the first time, I called Oberdick and told him what happened. He said 'okay' and that was it. But after about an hour, Martha Lotz called me." Now the story poured out.

"She said that she had heard from old man Oberdick and that she wanted to go back to Strickler's. She said something about unfinished business. I said I couldn't get the car again, but she kept after me. She told me I was getting paid and I had to do it. So I snuck out of the house and went down to the lumber yard and took the pick-up truck. The keys are always under the floor mat."

"What time was that?" Phil asked.

"Oh, I don't know. . . ."

"Later than 8:30?" the sheriff suggested, remembering the time Earle Gensemer had said he and his niece had returned from the movies.

"Oh, yeah, later than that. About ten, maybe."

"Okay, go on."

"I got the pick-up," Will continued, "and drove out to her house and picked her up. Then we drove out to Strickler's. We went in the house and he was still tied up there. When he saw us he started swearing again, and she swore back at him. She said all kinds of crazy things. Then—well, she just went nuts! She picked up the chair leg off the floor and started hitting him on the head. Real hard, too. He jumped around a lot at first, screaming and swearing, but then he got quiet. But she kept hitting him. I finally made her stop."

Will Burkholder had described the scene from Rufus Collins's dream. The realization shook Stauffer. "Ah . . . Will . . . you say Martha hit him many times?"

"Christ yes," Will answered emphatically, "maybe a couple of dozen times. I was scared, because I knew she'd killed him. Then she asked me to help her get some of the stuffing out of the old sofa there, and she spread it all over him. She got a coal-oil lamp and poured some coal-oil over him, but there wasn't a lot of it. Then, for God's sake, she set the stuff on fire!"

"And you left?"

"You're damned right! I wanted to get out of there!"

"One point, Will," Stauffer said. "Did she wipe off the chair leg with anything, a rag, or something like that?"

"I don't think so. It was all bloody. She just let it drop."

"Was she wearing gloves?"

Will closed his eyes in thought. "I'm not sure. Maybe she was. Ah . . . yeah. Those little ladies' kind of gloves. You know, the ones that don't come up . . . ah, over the wrists. I don't know what you call 'em."

"Okay, what happened after that?"

"I took her home and I never saw her again."

Phil waited for a moment before he asked his next question. "Didn't you see Martha Lotz when you went to Lizzie Zearfoss's place with her?"

"Huh?" The boy was startled.

"Didn't you go to Miller's Grove with Martha Lotz on the following Sunday?"

"No. I don't know anything about that."

The sheriff returned to his chair and sat down. "One other thing, Will. Where were you going when the state police picked you up yesterday morning?"

"Just away. I heard that Martha Lotz got arrested, and then I heard on the radio that old Oberdick was in the hospital, dying, and I just split, that's all."

Stauffer looked around the room. "Any other questions?" There were no answers. "Okay, that'll do it. I'll get Barry to take Will back to his cell." There was dead silence in the room while Phil made the phone call to his office down the hall. Nothing more was said until after Willard Burkholder was escorted from the room.

"It's my fault, my fault," Otis said, trying to fight back tears.

His lawyer tried to console him, but he was not successful. The elder Burkholder wept unashamedly. Sheriff Stauffer left the office. This unhappy day was not yet ended.

A copy boy flipped the afternoon edition of *The Missionville Star* onto Ernie Wheel's desk. The reporter glanced down at his page one by-line story.

Missionville, Pa., Dec. 12 (CNS)—Sources close to the Charles Strickler "lock of hair" murder case, an investigation that has centered around practices associated with the Pennsylvania Dutch witchcraft known as "hexerei," indicate that a solution may be close at hand.

Police authorities, however, will neither confirm nor deny. . . .

In disgust, Wheel shoved the newspaper away from him. He looked over at Nick Willson, who was checking the just-printed edition for errors. "I'm certainly not going to win a

Pulitzer with that crap."

Nick grinned. "Some days are better than others."

"My friend," Ernie said, "this has not been one of the better ones. I sure wish I knew what the hell is going on."

What was going on, of course, was that Phil Stauffer was moving swiftly to make Ernie Wheel's vague news lead a reality.

The blue-gray plaid topcoat, neatly packed in a Gimbel's box, had arrived on the afternoon commuter flight from New York. Barry had been dispatched to rush it to the state police lab for comparison tests with the tiny thread found on the can of gasoline at Lizzie Zearfoss's torched home. The sheriff had no doubt at all that the match would be made. His doubts now centered on motives.

"It's frustrating," he told the district attorney, "to know that Martha Lotz killed Charlie Strickler, and to know that she probably killed Lizzie Zearfoss as well, and not to know why."

"The 'why,'" Barringer suggested, "might simply be an unbalanced mind."

"Oh, that's part of it, I guess." Phil's hand went to the still visible scratches on his face from Martha's attack. "But my gut tells me there's more. Maybe I ought to do what Martha asked me to."

"What's that?"

"Ask Josh." As soon as he said it the scene in the shower room flooded back into his mind.

Barringer shook his head in doubt. "The old man's dying, Phil. I don't think you're going to be able to get anything out of him."

"Ed Myers tells me that Josh spent some time today with Sarah Strickler and that girl from Phoenix, not to mention Dottie Kissinger, who's at the hospital almost all the time. If he's strong enough for that, he ought to be able to talk to me."

"The girl from Phoenix? What's she doing in town?"

Phil laughed. "She's the guest, if that's the word, of my adventurous deputy."

Barringer joined in the laughter. "Not everything in this case is a total loss!"

Stauffer knew that Dr. Josh Oberdick was gravely ill, but he was not prepared for what he found in Room 304 of the Missionville Hospital. The once-vital man lay on his back like a slim corpse, his arms at his sides (they seemed to have been placed there by an over-tidy housekeeper), one of his arms connected with the life-sustaining plastic tube from the suspended bottle of plasma. His face was the color of chalk. One had to look closely to see the movement of breath; he breathed regularly enough, but shallowly. What struck the sheriff was that the man was so *old*. Old even beyond his eighty years—mummy-like, Phil thought.

Permission to interrogate Oberdick had been given by the hospital doctors, but Stauffer was cautioned not to excite the patient. A nurse was stationed just outside the door in the event that she would be needed.

Josh's eyes were closed as Phil quietly approached the bed. "Doc?" he said softly.

The eyes came open and the old doctor smiled. "Good to see you, Phil." The voice was weak, hollow. Oberdick looked past the sheriff. "No troops with you?"

"You sure sound like your old self."

Josh chuckled. "*Old* is the operative word around here. Pull up a chair and be comfortable." Stauffer did.

"Doc, I know this is hardly the time for a lot of questions," Phil started apologetically, "but I find I must ask them."

"That's okay."

"In the interest of not prolonging this thing, let me say that we know of the . . . ah, plot regarding Charlie Strickler. Gensemer and young Burkholder have told me of that. What I need from you is confirmation."

Oberdick sighed. "I was a fool, Phil. I permitted Strickler to become an obsession with me. But you must know by now that we didn't kill him. That's as much a mystery to me as it is to you."

There was no need for comment on the statement. "What do you know about Lizzie Zearfoss?"

"Oh, that dear old woman."

"Do you know anything of the circumstances of her death?"

"Nothing." He closed his eyes again.

"Is this tiring you, Josh?" Stauffer was concerned.

"No." The old man breathed deeply. "I have great reservoirs of strength." He opened his eyes and grinned. "A tough old bird, is Joshua Oberdick." He tried to make a gesture with his hand, but he didn't have the strength. "Do you think you could crank up the bed a bit? It'll make it easier for me to see you."

"Dare I?"

"Sure, I'm the doctor here." There was another chuckle.

The sheriff went to the foot of the bed and cranked. He raised the head of the bed about six inches.

"Much better," said Josh.

Phil returned to his chair. "My main problem, Doc, is the role Martha played in this. Gensemer has told us some of it, but the story seems incomplete and Martha has been . . . ah, uncooperative."

"How is Martha?"

"Missing you, I think."

"I've done terrible things to that girl," Oberdick said slowly, turning his head to look at Phil, "and all in the guise of trying to help her."

"You *have* helped her," Phil tried to assure him.

"Well, maybe." He paused. Phil permitted the silence to run its course. "Martha's role in our sad conspiracy," Josh went on, "was minimal. It was my crazy idea for revenge on Strickler and she, in her loyalty—or maybe love—simply went along."

"Umm."

"Will she be charged in this mess?"

"No. I'm sure of that."

That brought another smile to Oberdick's tired face. "I'm glad of that. She's had such a tragic life."

"Yes, she has," Phil agreed. He was beginning to dislike his task there in the hospital room. It had become more difficult than he had anticipated. But, as always, duty prevailed. "When I wondered about her past association with Strickler, she said 'ask Josh.'" He hated the lie.

There was a deep sigh, almost a moan, from the inert

figure in the bed. Josh began a slow, deliberate recital. "You don't know this, Phil, but perhaps you ought to. Martha had been a pow-wow practitioner, a student, God help us, of Charlie Strickler. That started, I believe, sometime after the beginning of her unhappy marriage to Johnny Mosser. Somehow she got the idea that knowing pow-wow would help the marriage." He stopped, drawing on that reservoir of strength he had mentioned. "In the course of their association, Strickler raped her. Her hate of him was very real and it was for that reason that she went along with my stupid plan."

Oberdick stopped. The only sound in the room was his breathing. Stauffer became alarmed and had decided to go for the nurse, when the old doctor spoke again.

"In truth," he said, "Martha played no role in this thing. She was a spectator, Phil, nothing more."

"Did you ever discuss it with Martha after Strickler's death was revealed?"

"No, she couldn't talk about it. I worried about her. She was so . . . so . . . mercurial."

It was the very same word Phil had used earlier to describe the woman. He searched his mind for another germaine question, but it didn't come. He had got his motive; a basic one—*hate*. There was still the question of the motive for burning down Lizzie Zearfoss's home, but Stauffer felt he could deduce that one; fear that the old woman would reveal the conspiracy. If that wasn't it, it would have to do.

"Well, Doc," Phil said, "thank you for your help."

An old hand reached out weakly. "No, don't go yet. We can talk some more."

"I'm afraid I'm tiring you badly."

"Nonsense. Call it therapy. The women were in and out of here today and I enjoyed that. But there were always tears. I don't need tears anymore."

Phil was silent; he would just listen now.

"You know, it's about this time that an old man should say that it's been a good life." He smiled. "Well, in my case, maybe *good* isn't the right word; I think interesting might be better. Even fascinating. Certainly never dull. I can say, with some assurance, that my life has been full."

The voice was getting weaker and Phil had to lean closer to the bed to hear him.

"With all that's been written and spoken about *hexerei* in the past couple of weeks," Josh continued, "a lot of people have missed the point, including your Pastor Fenstermacher. Even I, in my cynicism and my utter disgust with the likes of Charlie Strickler, have often set that point aside. In Hohman's *Long Lost Friend* there is an incantation against death: *I know that my Redeemer liveth, and that he will call me from the grave. . . .*"

Oberdick's voice trailed off. His eyes had closed again and the breathing was so subdued that Phil feared for an instant that it had stopped altogether.

"Josh," Phil said quietly, "I really ought to go."

"The point missed most often is the faith . . . the faith . . . inherent in what we call a superstition. I told that young reporter from New York . . . what's his name?"

"Wheel. Ernie Wheel."

"Wheel. Of course. I told him that I wasn't arrogant enough to try to find an explanation for all of the things about life that we don't quite understand. And that's still true, Phil. I know I'm dying. . . ."

"Doc, don't talk like that."

"No, it's true. I *am* dying. And the doctors here don't know why. Hell, I'm a pretty good doctor and *I* don't know why. No, the good young doctors here don't know why they can't stop my hemorraghing, anymore than they knew why Mosser's bleeding stopped when you reburied that lock of hair. There are so many things we don't know . . . so many things. Yet, when a simple man like John George Hohman comes along with some possible answers, we learned fellows scoff. I'm dying, Phil, and I want you to tell. . . ."

The words turned to mumbling. Stauffer, genuinely alarmed, went to the door and summoned the nurse. She came to the bed and took his pulse as the mumbling continued.

"I'll call the doctor," she whispered, and hurried out.

The sheriff stood there helplessly, trying to make some sense out of the mumbled syllables. Then the sounds stopped. Phil bent over the old man to see whether he was still breathing, only to have Josh open his eyes and pick up the conversation where it had trailed off into unintelligibility.

". . . to tell those stupid people out there not to be so damned smug in this last half of the twentieth century. What the hell do they know? Nothing."

"Josh, please. . . ."

"Phil, will you tell me the truth about something?"

"Certainly."

"Martha's dead, isn't she?"

Stauffer was stunned; he had nothing left but the truth. "Yes, she is."

"Well, Martha, the hurt is ended," the old man said.

Dr. Joshua Oberdick smiled and closed his eyes. For the last time.

SISTER SATAN

Dana Reed

SHE WAS
THE DEVIL'S SPAWN

Lauren had been blessed – or cursed – with mysterious powers since birth. As a shy, lonely teenager, she longed for a sister to share the joy and pain of growing up, and began hesitantly experimenting with the strange forces within her. And she succeeded only too well, for she found to her horror that she had called into being an exact duplicate of herself who was the personification of pure evil. As Rachel grew stronger and more malevolent with each passing day, Lauren was driven to the brink of insanity. How long would it be before she herself became the victim of her hellish alter ego? Was there any way to destroy the evil creature she had summoned? Would even her own death put an end to its fiendish power?

0-8439-2152-8   Price: $3.75 US/$4.50 CAN

THE FELLOWSHIP

Mary C. Romine
Aden F. Romine

BEWARE
THE BROTHERHOOD
OF BLOOD!

The marriage of Ken DeVane and Karen Scribner begins happily enough – until Ken discovers that Karen has fallen under the spell of Anton Marek, the master of The Fellowship, a worldwide cult of vampires. At first unable to believe in Marek's supernatural powers, Ken is soon totally convinced, his skepticism replaced by the horrified realization that his adversary is indeed immortal. Desperate to save Karen and Marek's other victims, he is forced to pit his puny human strength against an ageless force for evil, a being whose power seems invincible...

0-8439-2142-0   Price: $3.75 US/$4.50 CAN

EERIE NOVELS OF HORROR AND THE OCCULT BY J. N. WILLIAMSON, THE MASTER OF DARK FANTASY

1168-9	**THE RITUAL**	$3.25
2074-2	**GHOST**	$2.95
2133-1	**THE OFFSPRING**	$3.25
2176-5	**PROFITS**	$3.25
2228-1	**THE TULPA**	$2.95

MORE BLOOD-CHILLERS FROM LEISURE BOOKS

2039-4	**LOVE'S UNEARTHLY POWER** Blair Foster	$3.50
2112-9	**SPAWN OF HELL** William Schoell	$3.75 US, $4.50 Can.
2121-8	**UNDERTOW** Drake Douglas	$3.75 US, $4.50 Can.
2152-8	**SISTER SATAN** Dana Reed	$3.75 US, $4.50 Can.
2185-4	**BLOOD OFFERINGS** Robert San Souci	$3.75 US, $4.50 Can.
2195-1	**BRAIN WATCH** Robert W. Walker	$3.50 US, $4.25 Can.
2215-x	**MADONNA** Ed Kelleher and Harriette Vidal	$3.75 US, $4.50 Can.
2220-6	**THE RIVARD HOUSE** Edwin Lambirth	$3.25
2225-7	**UNTO THE ALTAR** John Tigges	$3.75 US, $4.50 Can.
2235-4	**SHIVERS** William Schoell	$3.75 US, $4.50 Can.
2246-X	**DEATHBRINGER** Dana Reed	$3.75 US, $4.50 Can.
2256-7	**CREATURE** Drake Douglas	$3.75 US, $4.50 Can.

Make the Most of Your Leisure Time with
LEISURE BOOKS

Please send me the following titles:

Quantity	Book Number	Price

If out of stock on any of the above titles, please send me the alternate title(s) listed below:

Postage & Handling _____

Total Enclosed $_____

☐ Please send me a free catalog.

NAME _____
(please print)

ADDRESS _____

CITY _____ STATE _____ ZIP _____

Please include $1.00 shipping and handling for the first book ordered and 25¢ for each book thereafter in the same order. All orders are shipped within approximately 4 weeks via postal service book rate. PAYMENT MUST ACCOMPANY ALL ORDERS.*

*Canadian orders must be paid in US dollars payable through a New York banking facility.

Mail coupon to: **Dorchester Publishing Co., Inc.
6 East 39 Street, Suite 900
New York, NY 10016
Att: ORDER DEPT.**